TRACKING A KILLER

"All this is just a precaution, Cathy," Markham said. "In case he tries to make contact with you, to leave you another note—that is, if the notes you received five years ago are related to Tommy Campbell's murder to begin with."

"They are, Sam. You *know* they are."

"I can't be sure—might be just a strange coincidence. However, since it's all we have to go on right now, we'll see how far that road leads us. But the last thing you want right now is for the press to know the extent to which you're involved in this. In fact, if my gut is right, I think that's just what the killer wants to happen."

"What do you mean?"

"It's obvious that whoever murdered Tommy Campbell and that boy had been planning this crime for a long time—perhaps even years. And until the autopsy results come back, until we get an idea of exactly how this person murdered and preserved his victims—how he actually created that sick sculpture of his—the only window into his motives right now is *you*. You and your book."

"So you're saying you think this maniac is using me?"

"I'll have a better idea once I read your book. But judging from the great lengths to which the killer went to put his sculpture on display in Dodd's garden—a display that the killer obviously intended as some kind of historical _____ dedicated to *you*—well, it's clear _____ thought you of all peop _____ tives . . ."

THE SCULPTOR

Gregory Funaro

PINNACLE BOOKS
KENSINGTON PUBLISHING CORP.
www.kensingtonbooks.com

PINNACLE BOOKS are published by

Kensington Publishing Corp.
119 West 40th Street
New York, NY 10018

All Kensington titles, imprints, and distributed lines are available at special quantity discounts for bulk purchases for sales promotions, premiums, fund-raising, educational, or institutional use. Special book excerpts or customized printings can also be created to fit specific needs. For details, write or phone the office of the Kensington special sales manager: Kensington Publishing Corp., 119 West 40th Street, New York, NY 10018, attn: Special Sales Department; phone 1-800-221-2647.

ISBN-13: 978-0-7860-2212-0
ISBN-10: 0-7860-2212-4

First printing: January 2010

10 9 8 7 6 5 4 3 2 1

Printed in the United States of America

The best artist has that thought alone which is contained within the marble shell; only the sculptor's hand can break the spell to free the figures slumbering in the stone.
—Michelangelo Buonarroti

Prologue

"Shake off your slumber, O son of Jupiter."

Tommy Campbell, lightning fast wide receiver for the Boston Rebels, opened his eyes expecting to see the end-zone. He could hear the cheers of the crowd—that familiar drone of *"Sooooup!"* coming from the stands—and his heart was pounding, could feel it pumping in his thighs as he ran. Yes, he was sure that he had caught the ball—his fingertips, the palms of his hands electrified with that familiar sting of *"Touchdown!"*

But as the cries of his fans quickly faded, as his vision cleared into a bright ball of light, amidst a milky haze Tommy Campbell understood all at once that he had been dreaming. Yes, he was lying down—could feel something cold, something steel-hard on his back and buttocks. He felt groggy, doped up on something, but at the same time alive with energy. And he thought he recognized the light hovering above him.

From a movie? Or from that time in the hospital. When they operated on my—

"That's it," said a deep voice to his right. "Come forth from the stone."

"Not my knee again, Doc," said Tommy. His throat was dry, and his words came out in spurts of cracked whispers. "Tell me it's not my knee . . ."

No reply, but instead a dull prick, a tug at the skin on his forearm. His heart was racing now—even more so than before his first start as a freshman at Boston College; even more so than before his first game as a second round draft pick with the Rebels. But this was different. Indeed, Tommy felt as if there was a war raging inside him: one side trying to drag him back down to his dream, to his winning thirty-seven yard touchdown versus the Dolphins; the other, trying desperately to pull him awake, to bring him back to reality—to *wherever he was now.*

"Where am I?" Tommy whispered. The light above him solidified into a white rectangle—like a floating movie screen only a few feet from his face, its edges sharp against the surrounding darkness. Yes, his senses were returning quickly now—the blood pumping fast through his veins—and with every beat of his heart the memories came flooding back.

He had been drinking a beer on the porch, looking out over the water—had made only a brief appearance at the victory celebration that afternoon in Boston; had wanted to spend time with his parents down at Watch Hill in Rhode Island before the big game, before flying off to Tampa to prepare for the Super Bowl versus the Giants. He had been alone—*Yes, Vicky is gone now, and Mom and Pop had gone to bed.* And it had been cold, the January moon dancing playfully on the frigid waters of Foster Cove—those very same waters in which Rhode Island's favorite son used to swim with his father as a boy.

"Pop?" Tommy croaked. "You there, Pop?"

Then he remembered the wasp—*Wasps in January?*—the hiss, the sharp pain as if something had bitten him on the neck, right on the jugular. Tommy Campbell had shot up instantly, sure that the top of his six-foot-six frame would crash into the low ceiling of the wraparound porch. But he did not remember coming down, did not remember landing on the wooden planks the way he still remembered landing on the five yard line last season versus the Texans— the now *infamous* landing that the networks played over and over again; the landing that dislocated his knee and caused him to fumble; the landing that—as those asshole Monday morning quarterbacks put it—cost his team the AFC championship.

But this was a new season, and the tough-as-nails twenty-six-year-old had healed up quickly. And since his career threatening injury less than a year earlier Tommy "Soup" Campbell had broken the record for most pass receiving yards in a single season. Never mind his personal problems, the split with his fiancée—*Hell, in a way I have Vicky to thank for it!* No, the beloved wide receiver had defied the odds, had returned to the NFL with a vengeance, and most of all had led his team to the Big One—*what those same asshole Monday morning quarterbacks were already calling "The Souper Bowl."*

But now something was wrong. He could feel it in his chest, in his fingers and his toes—pumping hard, pumping *painfully*. Tommy tried to get his bearings, tried to turn away from the glowing white rectangle hovering above him, but his head was locked in place—something pinning him down at his forehead, something preventing him from moving side to side. Instinctively, Tommy made to reach for it, but realized at once that his wrists were locked down also; and although he could not see his chest, his thighs or his ankles, he suddenly became aware of pressure in those places, too.

"Pop, you there?" Tommy called out again. "Did I fall on the porch? They got me in traction or something?" His voice was clear now, shaky, and his senses razor sharp, when suddenly the screen above him flickered into life.

The image was of a statue—dirty white marble against black, so that the figure appeared to be standing, *floating* in the darkness just inches from his face. The statue was that of a naked man—*a Greek god or something,* Tommy thought—but he could not be sure, could not remember ever having seen the figure before. At the same time, however, he felt as if he recognized it from some place. It was not the pose itself that struck Tommy as familiar—the awkward way in which the god was standing, the bowl raised in his right hand as if in a toast. And it certainly wasn't the curly hair—*or are they little grapes?*—surrounding the god's face that sparked a memory in Tommy's feverish brain. No, there was something about the face itself, something about the *body . . .*

As his mind scrambled to remember, to understand, the statue began to rotate as if it were on a turntable. Tommy saw that behind the statue was another figure—*a child, perhaps*—that came up to the god's waist. The child—*Is it a child? What's wrong with his feet? His legs?*—was smiling impishly with a handful of grapes. It appeared to be hiding behind the god, almost supporting him.

Yes! Tommy thought. *The guy with the bowl looks like a staggering drunk, like he's having a hard time standing up!*

Incredibly, amidst his confusion, amidst the pounding of his heart, flashed fragmented memories of parties at Boston College; of nights out in Vegas with his teammates; of the time he met Vicky at that posh party in Manhattan . . .

Pop didn't like her from the start. Fucking models. He was right. I must have been out of my mind proposing to that—

"That's it," said the voice again. "Shake off your slumber, O son of Jupiter."

Tommy tried in vain to turn his head, to search the darkness out of the corner of his eye, but he could see nothing but the strange image before him. It had morphed into a close-up of the statue's head. Yes, those had to be grapes, had to be leaves surrounding the god's face—a face with rolling eyes, a face lolling forward with a half-open mouth.

"Who are you?" Tommy cried. "What am I doing here?" He began to panic, began to strain against the straps as the image before him moved again. Tommy watched as it slowly panned down over the statue's chest, over its somewhat bloated belly, and finally to its hairless groin—to the place where its penis *should have been.*

Yes, the god before him, whoever he was, *was missing his crank*—had only a pair of swollen testicles between his legs.

"What the hell is going on?" Tommy screamed.

He was sweating profusely now—his heart pounding loudly in his ears, the straps boring into his wrists like string on an Easter ham. Then suddenly the image flickered, and Tommy Campbell saw himself, saw *his face* on the screen before him—as he was now, lying down, his head strapped to a table. Only Tommy could not see the strap. No, surrounding his head were clusters of grapes and leaves like the face of the nameless god to whom he had just been introduced.

"What the fuck is—"

Then Tommy froze—watched in horror as the image on the screen began to pan down over his own body. The camera had to be someplace above him—*beyond the screen, to the right a bit from where that voice had come*—but Tommy could see no sign of it or the cameraman—just the image of his own muscular physique on the screen before him. Tommy began to tremble violently, thought he could feel his brain squirming behind his eyes, and in a frenzied burst of adrenaline tried desperately to free himself—the body above him writhing as he writhed, jerking as he jerked. Yet as strong as Tommy Campbell was, he could no more break his bonds than if he had been sealed inside a block of marble. Worst of all, Tommy Campbell could not take his eyes off himself, and amidst his panic the young man watched as his tanned, hairless chest—*there was the strap!*—passed slowly across the screen to his belly.

Only *then* did Tommy Campbell understand.

"This can't be happening," he whimpered—the merciless, deafening war drum in his chest a brutal herald of what lay over the horizon, of what he knew he was about to see. "I must be dreaming!"

"No, my Bacchus," said the voice in the darkness. "You are finally awake."

And as Tommy Campbell began to convulse, upon the terror of his confirmation, the young man's heart all at once stopped beating forever.

EXHIBIT ONE
Bacchus

Chapter I

Furious, Dr. Catherine Hildebrant threw the student's cell phone out the window—watched it explode in a puff of smoke on the lawn outside the List Art Center.

"Another cell phone goes off in my class and you'll be taken out back and shot!"

Then Cathy stopped.

There's no lawn outside my window, she said to herself. No window in my classroom either.

The cell phone kept ringing—Beethoven, Für Elise.

"Miss Hildebrant?"

Cathy turned to face her art history class, who behind her back had changed to her classmates from the third grade at Eden Park Elementary School. Mrs. Miller was staring at her impatiently—show and tell, Cathy's turn, anger at once replaced by panic. Cathy's classmates began to snicker at her with whispers of "Ching-chong, ching-chong!" She could feel the fear tightening in her chest as the room brightened, as she stared down at the smooth white blob in her hands.

What is this? What did I bring for show and tell today?

Amidst the laughter and the cat-calls, the white blob suddenly burst outward into snow as Cathy's classroom dissolved into the morning sun of her bedroom—her cell phone *Für Elise*-ing on the nightstand beside her.

She opened it.

"Hello?"

"Hildy?" It was her boss, Dr. Janet Polk, Chair of the Department of History of Art and Architecture at Brown University—the only person in Providence who dared call Catherine Hildebrant "Hildy" to her face.

"Hey, Jan," Cathy yawned. "Christ, what time is it?"

"Almost eleven."

"My God, that wine must have been roofied. Was up late last night grading those final—"

"Sorry to bother you on a Sunday, Hil, but did that FBI guy call you yet?"

"Who?"

"I think he said his name was Markham, or maybe it was Peckham. I'm not sure. Was kind of flustered by the whole thing."

"What are you talking about?"

"He just left here not five minutes ago—caught me and Dan turning the flower beds out back. He said that he was looking for information in connection with the disappearance of that football player."

"Tommy Campbell?" Cathy asked, sitting up.

Although she was an attractive woman, Cathy could not deny that she had been a nerd all her life—never had a taste for sports; would much rather have listened to a lecture on Donatello than be caught dead at a football game in college. However, even she had become smitten with Rhode Island's favorite son— that dashing, blond-haired, blue-eyed lightning bolt that nobody in the NFL could seem to catch. And more and more last season Cathy found herself doing something she had never dreamed of: sitting in front of a television watching football on a Sunday.

"Yes," Janet said. "That's him. Tommy Campbell—the one who disappeared back in January."

"Why did the FBI want to talk to you?"

"He actually wanted to talk to you, Hildy. Said he needed to talk to an expert on Renaissance art—Italian Renaissance, to be exact."

"Let me guess. They found him on a beach somewhere with a stolen Botticelli?"

Since Tommy Campbell had vanished without a trace nearly four months earlier, since the Boston Rebels had lost the Super Bowl to the New York Giants in early February, theories about what had happened to the wide receiver were as numerous as the Rebel fans themselves—from his drowning in the waters of Foster Cove to his having been kidnapped by the coach of a rival team to his simply disappearing into anonymity à la Elvis Presley. Cathy had always suspected the latter, for she saw something of herself in the modest, soft-spoken "Mama's boy" who the tabloids claimed still visited his parents whenever he got the chance—that desire not for fame and fortune, but just to live his life with those he loved, in obscurity, doing what made him happy.

"The FBI agent wouldn't say anything more about it," Janet sighed. "When I told him that it wasn't my area, that you were our go-to-gal for the Italian thing, he said he knew that. He asked me where he could find you. Said he'd been by your office and your house already but you weren't home. Then I realized he meant your *old* house."

Steve must have spent the night at the slut's, Cathy thought. *Still won't bang her in our old bed. Fucking actor. Fucking spineless pussy.*

Cathy gazed around the bedroom of her new digs—new to *her*, but built around the turn of the twentieth century; its architecture, a seamless blend of Victorian elegance and modern practicality characteristic of many of the three-story houses that line the Upper East Side of Providence. Cathy lived on the first floor; had moved in on the very same day the news broke about Tommy Campbell—less than a week after she discovered the e-mails and Steve confessed to her about the affair. And now, three months later, boxes of her former self still littered every room of her two-bedroom, overpriced condominium. She had needed to break it fast and clean from Steven Rogers, and got lucky with a spur of the moment rent-to-own on East George Street—the life she built with her husband down the drain because the childish theatre professor could not keep his dick in his pants, could not keep his hands off the only semi-good-looking graduate student to grace his presence in nearly ten years of marriage. That was the hardest part. Even at thirty-eight Catherine Hildebrant knew she was smarter and better looking than her husband's mistress, but the little slut had one thing that Dr. Hildy didn't: *youth.*

"Hildy, you there?"

"Sorry, Jan. Did you tell the FBI guy where I am now?"

"I did. I couldn't remember the exact address, but I gave him your cell number. I'm sorry, Hildy, but I didn't know what else to do. You're not mad at me, are you?"

"Of course not. Let me get a shower and I'll give

you a ring after he calls. And thanks for the heads up, Jan. Love ya."

"Love you, too," Janet said, and Cathy closed her phone. She smiled. Cathy really did love Janet Polk, had thought of her as a second mother ever since she was her teaching assistant at Harvard. Indeed, it was Janet who, only days after she defected to Brown, literally stole Cathy from a junior lecturer position at her alma mater. It was Janet who, for better or worse, introduced Cathy to Steven Rogers; Janet who kept Cathy on track to see that her tenure went through; and, most of all, it was Janet who had been there for Cathy when her real mother died five and a half years ago.

"I don't know what I'd do without ya, kid," Cathy whispered to the boxes in the corner.

And with that she hopped in the shower.

Chapter 2

Pulling her wet, jet-black hair into a ponytail, Cathy Hildebrant despised what she saw in the bathroom mirror that morning. Her skin looked pasty, and her normally bright, brown eyes were puffy—the half-Asian, half-German smile lines in their corners deeper and more pronounced. *The wine?* she wondered. *Or am I just getting old?* She did not remember her dream about the third grade, about her botched show and tell assignment, but felt a gnawing anxiety that she had been laughed at nonetheless. Then she thought of Steve, of their first date and the dumb joke he made: *"Oh you're half-Korean? I just thought I was putting you to sleep!"*

I should have asked for the check right then. Thanks a lot, Janet.

The doorbell rang, startling her, and instinctively Cathy reached for her cell phone on the bathroom sink.

"Dummy," she muttered, and donning her black-rimmed glasses, she slipped into her sweatpants and a two-sizes-too-big Harvard T-shirt and made for the front door.

"May I help you?" Cathy called through the peephole.

The man on her front porch looked like he just stepped out of a J. Crew catalog—the khakis, the windbreaker, the lightweight sweater underneath—*a nice change from all the artsy-fartsies on the east side,* Cathy thought. He appeared to be in his thirties, good-looking, with close cropped brown hair and a square jaw. Cathy understood that the man had purposefully stepped back from the door so she could get a good look at him. And just as he was reaching underneath his jacket, Cathy realized that FBI-guy Markham or Peckham or whatever-his-name-was had decided to drop by unannounced.

"I'm Special Agent Sam Markham," he said, raising his ID to the peephole.

So it is *Markham,* Cathy thought. *You ain't ready for retirement yet, Janet old girl.*

"I'm with the FBI, Behavioral Analysis Unit. I'd like to ask you a few questions, Dr. Hildebrant."

Behavioral Analysis. This is serious.

Cathy had seen *The Silence of the Lambs* six times; had seen enough of those police dramas on television to know that the Behavioral Analysis Unit was the division of the FBI that handled murders—especially *serial* murders.

She opened the door.

"I'm sorry. Janet told me you were going to call."

"Dr. Polk gave me your phone number, ma'am. But we traced your new address before we needed to call it. The Bureau likes to handle this kind of thing in person."

The agent smiled thinly.

"I see," Cathy said, embarrassed. "Please, come in."

Shutting the door behind him, Cathy stood awkwardly for a moment in the tiny entryway. She recognized Markham's cologne—Nautica Voyage. She had bought a bottle for her husband last fall after smelling it on one of her graduate students—had all but begged Steve to wear it—but the selfish prick never even took the plastic off the box.

"You'll have to forgive me," Cathy said. "I'm still unpacking and I don't have much furniture yet. Why don't we go into the kitchen—unless you don't mind sitting on boxes in the living room."

"The kitchen's fine, ma'am."

Cathy led him down the narrow hallway to the back of the house. Special Agent Markham took his seat at the table.

"I was up late last night grading papers. Coffee isn't on yet, but it'll only take a couple of minutes."

"No thank you, Dr. Hildebrant. I don't drink coffee."

"Some orange juice then? Some water?"

"No, ma'am. I don't plan on us being here very long." Cathy detected a hint of Yankee in his voice—a disarming but relaxed formality that made her like him.

"Well, then," Cathy said, sitting down across from him. "What can I do for you, Agent Markham?"

"I assume Dr. Polk told you why I was looking for you?"

"Yes. Something about the Italian Renaissance and the disappearance of Tommy Campbell?"

"Yes, ma'am, that's correct." Markham produced a thin stack of Polaroids from his jacket pocket. "What

I'm about to show you is confidential, though probably not for long. The Westerly Police were called to the scene first—early this morning, before the state police arrived and our Field Office in Boston was notified. Even though Campbell disappeared down at Watch Hill, given his public profile, his celebrity, the case has been ours from the beginning. We've been able to keep things quiet thus far, but now with the locals involved, there's always more of a chance of details leaking out to the media before we give the go ahead. Most likely the story will break this afternoon, but can I have your word that, until then, you'll keep what I'm about to show you between us? Meaning, you won't repeat our discussion to anyone, including your boss, Dr. Polk?"

"Yes, you have my word."

Agent Markham peeled off a Polaroid and slid it across the table.

"Do you recognize the figure in this photograph?"

"Of course," Cathy said immediately. "It's Michelangelo's *Bacchus*."

"Are you sure? Please look closer, Dr. Hildebrant."

Cathy obliged, although she did not have to look a second time; for even though the photograph was a full body shot—taken somewhat at a distance and from the side—Dr. Catherine Hildebrant, perhaps *the* foremost American scholar on the works of Michelangelo, could have described the details of *Bacchus* with her eyes closed. There before her once again was Michelangelo's controversial but ground-breaking sculpture of the Roman god of wine—drunk, unsteady, almost staggering off his rocky base. There was the bowl of wine raised in his right hand, and the tiger skin, the cluster of grapes by his side. Cathy could also see the goat-legged satyr behind him, smiling as he munches on the fruit which slips from the god's left hand. Cathy knew the sculpture of *Bacchus* as intimately as her own body—had taught a whole unit on it at Brown; had traveled to Italy to study it for part of her dissertation on Michelangelo at Harvard. Yes, if Special Agent Markham wanted to know anything about good ol' boy Bacchus, he had certainly come to the right place, for Dr. Catherine Hildebrant had written the book on *Bacchus*—*literally.*

"I can tell you that this is a reproduction, however," Cathy said finally. "The background, the bushes behind the statue—this picture was taken outside. The original now lives in the Bargello National Museum in Florence. It's a fantastic copy, I'll give you that—right down to the coloring. But I don't see what this has to do with the disappearance of Tommy Campbell."

Special Agent Markham was silent for a moment, then slid another Polaroid across the table. This one was of a close-up of the statue's head—the crown of grapes, the mouth ajar, the eyes rolling backward as the head slumps forward. However, unlike the first photograph, Cathy noticed immediately that something was *off.*

Then like a slap on her heart it hit her.

"Oh my God," she gasped. "It's *him!* It's Tommy Campbell!"

"Yes. He was found this morning down at Watch Hill, in the garden of an investment CEO not half a mile from his parents' house. They've already given a positive ID. It appears that whoever killed Campbell somehow preserved his body and articulated it into the pose you see now—right down to the coloring, as you said."

Cathy felt the shock washing over her, the words

sticking in her throat, but knew she had to push through it.

"Who? I mean, who would do something like this?"

"That's what we're hoping you'll help us find out, Dr. Hildebrant. We've got a forensic team down there now doing a preliminary investigation, but we need you to take a look at the crime scene before we move the bodies."

"*Bodies?* You mean the satyr? It's a real person, too?"

"A young boy, yes," Markham said weakly. "The top half, that is. The bottom appears to be the hindquarters of a goat."

"Dear God," Cathy groaned. And despite a subtle wave of nausea in her throat, despite the tears welling in her eyes, she managed to ask, "Who is it?"

"We can't be sure—got an agent working with missing persons as we speak, but it might take some time before we get a positive ID. You see, unlike Campbell, the child's face seems to have been signif-icantly . . . *altered*—contorted to duplicate the expres-sion of Michelangelo's satyr."

Cathy felt her stomach drop, felt herself go numb.

"Would you like to change before we leave?" Markham asked. "It's a bit cold for April, a bit cooler down by the water."

"Why me?" Cathy said suddenly. She was in a daze, her voice not her own. "You obviously have your own experts on the subject—people who recognized the statue, who knew it to be a Michelangelo. I mean, what could I possibly tell you that one of your agents couldn't find on the goddamn Internet?"

Without a word, Special Agent Markham slid the

last of his Polaroids across the table. Cathy gazed down in horror at a close-up of neatly chiseled letters—an inscription at the base of the outcropping on which the mummified body of Tommy Campbell was standing. It read simply:

FOR DR. HILDEBRANT

Chapter 3

The outer shell of the carriage house was still the original brick—built in the 1880s by a wealthy textile family in what was then a more rural part of East Greenwich, Rhode Island. It sat back about thirty yards off of the main house and could be accessed either by a flagstone path leading from the back porch, or by a dirt driveway that veered off its paved sister and cut through the trees at the western edge of the heavily wooded property.

The house itself was a rambling, three-story affair graced by a long, circular driveway with a waterless fountain at its center. The "front door" was actually located around the side of the house, facing a line of trees to the east. Hence, most visitors (although there were very few nowadays) climbed the steps leading up to the mud room, which was located just past the library windows that overlooked the driveway.

The Sculptor, however, almost always used the *back* door; for The Sculptor almost always had business to attend to in the carriage house before joining his father in the home of his youth. The Sculptor's family had lived there since 1975—moved there just after The Sculptor was born. By that time, the carriage house had long since been converted to a two-car garage with a room above it in which the previous owner's caretaker had lived. And as a boy, The Sculptor would often play alone in the empty loft for hours. Most of the time, however, he would just hide out there when his parents fought, or when his mother got drunk and hit him.

The Sculptor's mother hit him quite a lot as a boy—when his father was away on business or playing golf at the country club. And when he was *super naughty*, sometimes his mother would fill the bathtub with ice water and hold him under until he started choking. Sometimes she would lock The Sculptor in the bathroom and pour bleach on the floor and make him breathe the fumes. Most of the time, however, she just hit him—always on the back of the head, so the bruises and lumps beneath his curly mane of dark brown hair would not show. The Sculptor's mother told him that if he ever squealed to anyone she would die and his father would kill himself. And for a long time The Sculptor believed her— after all, The Sculptor loved his mother and his father very much and would do anything to protect them. The Sculptor's father called him Christian back then—had no trouble remembering his name. But that was a *long, long time ago,* and now Christian's father *never* called him Christian.

Christian almost never called himself Christian now either; hardly ever thought of himself as having been anything other than The Sculptor—only when it could not be avoided, in public, when he signed for his father's prescriptions or when he had to purchase medical supplies over the Internet. The Sculptor hated the Internet, but had long ago resigned himself to accepting it as a necessary tool to accomplish his work. And as long as it stayed out back in the carriage house he could tolerate it—for out back in the carriage house was where the technology lived; out back in the carriage house was where *all the work was done.*

The Sculptor's father did not know about his son's work in the carriage house—did not know much of anything anymore. He spent most of his time in his bedroom—on the second floor, directly above the kitchen—looking out the window at the bird feeders his son had installed many years ago in one of the large oak trees. Sometimes The Sculptor would play music for his father on the old record player—mostly crackly 33-1/3s of classical music, the kind of stuff his father had been fond of before the accident. The Sculptor also installed a CD player inside the shell of an old Philco, jury-rigging it to play recordings of vintage radio shows from the 1930s and '40s. This seemed to please his father greatly, who in turn would sit smiling at the radio for hours.

Mostly, however, The Sculptor's father just sat motionless in his wheelchair by the window. He still could turn his head, still had use of his right hand, but he rarely spoke except now and then to ask for someone named "Albert." For the first few years after the accident, The Sculptor had no idea who Albert was. But after digging into his family's history, The Sculptor discovered that his father had an older brother named Albert who had committed suicide when his father was just a boy.

As Cathy Hildebrant and Agent Markham turned onto Route 95 on their way to Watch Hill, miles away,

The Sculptor was removing an intravenous line from his father's wrist. He usually fed his father by hand—a mixture of oatmeal and other ingredients that he had researched for optimum nutrition—but found over the years that after a night of barbiturates, this method was more effective to stabilize his father's system. He had been out for nearly sixteen hours—had been intravenously fed a steady dose of mild sedatives while his son had been away—and now all his father needed was just a little extra TLC to bring him back around.

"That's it," said The Sculptor, wiping off the spittle from his father's chin. He threw the rag into a white bin marked LINENS and with one arm lifted his father from his bed to his wheelchair. He turned the steamer beside the bed on to low, for sometimes his father's nostrils dried out and his nose bled. Indeed, almost everything The Sculptor needed to care for his father was at hand in his father's bedroom: boxes upon boxes of medical supplies; an adjoining bathroom that had been outfitted with a sit-down shower; a small refrigerator in the corner for his father's medicines; and three intravenous units—each holding different bags of different liquids for different purposes. And were it not for the red wallpaper, the richly stained woodwork, and the four-poster bed, his father's bedroom would have looked no different than a hospital ward.

"Time to watch the birdies," The Sculptor said, parking his father before the large bay window. The Sculptor dropped a record on the turntable—Domenico Scarlatti's *Sonata in D Minor*—and as the first strains of Baroque guitar washed over the room, The Sculptor headed down the servants' stairs to the kitchen. There he rinsed his hands and fixed himself a protein drink, gulping it down with a handful of vitamins and supplements. He was hungry, *ravenous* from his work the night before, but resisted the temptation to eat more and stepped out onto the back porch. Yes, he must stick to his diet, must be in tip-top condition for all the hard work ahead of him.

Even back when he was known as Christian, The Sculptor always kept himself in good shape. Six-foot-five since the age of seventeen, before the accident he had lettered in both football and lacrosse for Phillips Exeter Academy. Since the accident, however, he had focused only on building up his body—what he saw from the beginning as a necessary component of caring for his father. The accident had been his mother's fault. Christian would never know the exact details—had been away at boarding school when it all happened. But from what he could gather, there had been an incident at the country club. His father's lawyer told Christian a week after the funeral—the same week he turned eighteen and became legal custodian of his family's fortune—that his mother had been cheating on his father with a young tennis pro not much older than Christian himself. There had been a scene, a fist fight at the country club—Christian's father laying out the tennis pro and dragging his wife out by the hair. They had just turned onto Route 95 when the semi broadsided them. His mother died instantly, but his father survived—paralyzed from the waist down, his left arm useless, his brain a vegetable soup.

Christian had been granted early acceptance to Brown—had planned on majoring in history like his mother—but after finishing out his final year at Phillips, opted to enroll in nursing school in order to best take care of his father. There had been a lawsuit filed against the trucking company on Christian's behalf. The driver of the semi had been drinking when he slammed into Christian's parents, and a settlement was reached out of court awarding Christian both compensation for his mother's death and enough money to care for his father for the rest of his life. The judgment gave Christian little consolation, as the young man would not have needed the money anyway. No, Christian's father had earned enough money in his lifetime to care for a dozen invalids a dozen lifetimes over. And at first Christian kept his father in an adult care facility, but after graduating from nursing school, Christian took the burden of caring for his father solely upon himself.

Besides, Christian knew he would never ever have to work for money.

No, Christian's work would be of a different kind— would serve a different purpose. That purpose had only become clear to him in the last few years, when he fully began to understand why his mother had beaten him and cheated on his father and, consequently, caused him to become the vegetable upstairs. Yes, his own life, his own personal tragedy was only a symptom of a much larger disease. And now that he had become The Sculptor, now that he understood his purpose, the man who once called himself Christian also understood that the disease could be cured; that he could use his insight to help others; and that he was put on this planet to save mankind from its own spiritual destruction. And so, just as he himself had awakened from a lifetime of slumber, The Sculptor would see to it that others would awaken as well.

The Sculptor stepped off the back porch and headed down the flagstone path to the carriage house. He began to giggle, for even though The Sculptor hated the

Internet, he could not help feeling excited about what was waiting for him.

Yes, The Sculptor had the utmost faith that his plan would succeed.

And Dr. Catherine Hildebrant would be the one to help him.

Chapter 4

"Are you feeling better now?" asked Special Agent Markham.

"Yes, thank you," Cathy lied, shaken. She had been staring out the window at nothing in particular as row upon row of nameless buildings whizzed past her. Then all at once Cathy realized that, despite the morning's events, she had been unconsciously searching for the big blue bug on the roof of the New England Pest Control building. Cathy hated that big blue bug—a monstrous, tacky sculpture that appeared to have been built by a four year-old—but always found herself staring up at it, actually looking for it when she headed into Providence from points southward.

"And thank you for the coffee," she added after a moment.

"Don't mention it." The FBI agent had fixed it just the way she liked it—*grande,* nonfat milk, two Sweet'N Lows—and had not even blinked at double parking his black Chevy Trailblazer right outside of Starbucks, right where the GPS navigation system said it would be in the middle of congested Thayer Street. *A job with "perks,"* Cathy thought, then quickly felt ashamed of her private joke at a time like this.

"Do you mind if we ask you a couple of questions, Dr. Hildebrant?" It was the FBI agent in the backseat, a woman by the name of Sullivan—blond, early thirties, with chiseled features that Cathy envied. She was with the Field Office in Boston, Markham told her— had been waiting in the Trailblazer while he was meeting with Cathy.

"Go right ahead," Cathy said.

Agent Sullivan produced a small, digital recording device from her jacket pocket and held it to her mouth.

"This is Special Agent Rachel Sullivan en route with Markham and Dr. Catherine Hildebrant. The date is Sunday, April 26. The time is 12:20 P.M."

Sullivan placed the recorder between Markham and Cathy—its red light making Cathy self-conscious.

"Dr. Hildebrant," Sullivan began, "you're the author of the book on Michelangelo titled *Slumbering in the Stone,* is that correct?"

"Yes."

"Is that your only published work?"

"No, but the only one dedicated solely to Michelangelo's sculptures—and the only one to cross over from the academic market to reach a more popular audience."

"It's sold a lot of copies then?"

"Not a *New York Times* bestseller by any means, no. But, as far as these things go in academia, yes, you could say it's sold a lot."

"And what else have you published?"

"I coauthored an introduction to art history textbook with a former colleague of mine from Harvard, as well as publishing the obligatory articles now and then in various academic journals."

"I see," said Sullivan.

Cathy did not like her tone. She had none of Markham's charm, none of his informal directness. No, Special Agent Rachel Sullivan spoke like an attorney on one of those bad spin-offs of a spin-off courtroom drama with which Cathy had become so engrossed as of late—another bit of "mindless entertainment" she once thought she'd never be caught dead watching in a million years.

"But *Slumbering in the Stone* is by far your most important work," Sullivan continued. "The one that really put you on the map, wouldn't you say?"

"Relatively speaking, yes."

"And you require *Slumbering in the Stone* for your classes?"

"Only one—a graduate seminar. Yes." Cathy suddenly felt defensive—like Sullivan was setting her up for something. She looked around the cabin uncomfortably, her eyes falling on the speedometer. Markham was doing eighty, but held the wheel as if he were coasting through a school zone.

"And when was this book published?"

"About six years ago."

"Was this before or after your tenure?"

"Just before."

"And you have been requiring your book for your class for how long now?"

"It'll be five years next fall."

"I'd like you to take a moment," Agent Sullivan said with a calculated change of tone. "Take a moment and ask yourself if you've ever had a student during that time—or at any time, for that matter—

that struck you as particularly odd. One that said or did or perhaps even wrote something out of the ordinary—something that went beyond a creative extreme into the realm of—well, something *else*. Perhaps a drawing or an essay or even an e-mail that you found particularly disturbing."

Cathy's brain began to spin with a kaleidoscope of faces—nameless, dark, and blurry—and the art history professor felt a wave of panic upon realizing she could not recollect even what her current students looked like.

"I can't think of anyone," she said finally, her voice tight. "I'm sorry."

"What about a colleague? Someone in the department? Anybody ever mention to you that they had a student by whom they felt threatened?"

"Not that I can recall."

"Have you ever felt threatened by one of your colleagues in your time at Brown or at Harvard? Anyone with whom you didn't get along? Perhaps someone who was fired? Someone who may have had a grudge against you?"

"No, not at all."

"Any of your students ever make a play for you?" asked Agent Markham. Despite the gist of his question, Cathy found his sudden presence in the conversation a welcome relief from the prosecuting attorney behind her. "Any of them ever go beyond what could be termed as innocent flirting? Something that was perhaps a little more aggressive?"

Cathy had always been a bit shy, but never a bit stupid; and even though before her husband she had dated only a handful of men, had only one semi-serious relationship while at Harvard, she was not ignorant to the "vibe" she got from some of her male students.

However, in her twelve years at Brown, only two of them ever got up enough nerve to ask her out for a cup of coffee—and both times Steven Rogers's dutiful wife politely declined.

But then there were the notes.

"Yes," Cathy began. "About five and a half years ago. At the beginning of the fall semester—just after my mother died—I started receiving some anonymous notes."

Cathy saw Markham catch his partner's eye in the rearview mirror.

"Love notes?" Sullivan asked.

"Not really. They were little quotes at first, one-liners that I took to be, well, gestures of encouragement and support in the wake of my mother's death. Then later on I received the sonnet."

"A sonnet?" asked Markham. "You mean like a love sonnet? A Shakespearean sonnet?"

"Not a Shakespearean sonnet, no, but one written by Michelangelo." Markham looked confused. "In addition to being a painter and a sculptor, Michelangelo was an accomplished, albeit second-rate poet. He wrote hundreds of poems on subject matter across the board. However, the most famous of his poems are the sonnets he wrote to a young man with whom he was in love—a young man by the name of Tommaso Cavalieri. The sonnet that I received was originally written for Cavalieri around 1535 I think, during the first couple years of their friendship when Michelangelo was about sixty years old and Cavalieri in his early twenties."

"So how many notes would you say you received?" asked Sullivan.

"Four—one sonnet and the three little quotes, which were also written by Michelangelo. I got one every other week or so for about a month and a half—at different times, in an envelope under my office door when I was out. Then they just stopped appearing. And I haven't received another note since."

"You said the notes were anonymous. Did you ever find out who sent them?"

"No, I did not."

"Any ideas?"

"The handwriting was feminine. And as Michelangelo's sonnets to Cavalieri were of a homosexual nature, I assumed that my admirer was a female."

"A homosexual nature?" asked Markham.

"Yes. It has been well established for some time now that Michelangelo was a homosexual. The only argument thrown around academic circles nowadays is whether or not he was *exclusively* a homosexual."

"I see," said Markham. "And, if I may ask—the content of the sonnet you received, did it deal with unrequited love?"

"Sort of. There's every indication that Cavalieri actually returned Michelangelo's affection, but the evidence also supports that the two never consummated the relationship. The sonnet therefore dealt with more of an unattainable spiritual love than any sort of carnal desire—the kind of love that could not be pursued or even named in Michelangelo's time. And even though the two remained the closest of friends, the relationship with Cavalieri caused Michelangelo great anguish until the artist's death."

"Do you still have these notes?" asked Markham.

"I kept them for a while," Cathy said, embarrassed. "But when I showed them to my husband, he asked that I get rid of them. I did. That was foolish of me, I know. I shouldn't have listened to him."

If only you didn't listen to him the night he proposed . . .

"Do you remember the title of the poem this person sent you? Was it numbered or something like Shakespeare's sonnets?"

"Scholars have numbered some of them, I think, but not with the kind of agreed upon consistency as Shakespeare's sonnets. I could be wrong, as it is not really my area of expertise. But I can tell you for sure that there was no number or title on the poem I received. I remember that. If you'd like, I can give you the gist of it and the quotes—"

"But you'd recognize both the poem and the quotes if you saw them?"

"Yes."

Agent Markham switched off the recorder.

"Sullivan, call your tech-guy down at the crime scene. Make sure he has a laptop online and ready for us so Dr. Hildebrant can conduct a search on the Internet. And see if you can get someone to dig up a hardcopy of Michelangelo's poetry, too."

"Yes, sir."

"I'm also going to need class rosters for Dr. Hildebrant and all her colleagues in the History of Art and Architecture Department going back over the last ten years. Hell, get me a roster for every class with art or history in the title. It's Sunday, but get someone on the go ahead today—so we can be there when the offices open tomorrow."

"Yes, sir," said Sullivan, and began dialing her cell phone.

"Agent Markham," Cathy said, the discussion about Michelangelo had grounded her, made her feel more like herself. "I realize that, because my name was on the base of that wicked thing, you think I might be somehow connected to this psychopath. But do you really think the person who sent me those notes could be the same person who murdered Tommy Campbell and that little boy? Couldn't it have been just some nut job who read my book? I mean, do you really think that this person could have been one of my students?"

"I don't know," said Markham. "But Tommaso is Italian for Thomas. And I'll tell you that, at the very least, I think it's a bizarre coincidence that you were given a poem originally intended for a young man named Tommy, and that you now have a statue of a young man named Tommy dedicated to you as well."

Cathy suddenly felt afraid; but more so she felt stupid—felt her cheeks go hot for not making the connection between the two names when she first mentioned Cavalieri.

But mostly Cathy felt stupid because Special Agent Sam Markham *had*.

Chapter 5

The carriage house loft was covered in soundproof foam that ran up the walls to the peak of the low-pitched ceiling. The windows had long ago been blocked out, and even when all the fluorescent lights were on, the black of the foam bathed the room in an overwhelming and seemingly infinite darkness. During his renovations, The Sculptor had purposely exposed the building's trusses to give the space a little more height. These, too, were painted black, and at the far end of the loft, where the original carriage hoist had hung, The Sculptor outfitted the beams with an automatic winch system. This allowed the old mortician's table to be raised and lowered through a trap à la *Frankenstein*; and sometimes, when he was feeling a bit silly, The Sculptor would allow himself a ride between floors.

On the other side of the room, where the door was located, in one corner lived The Sculptor's technology: an L-shaped desk with two computers, three flat-screen monitors, and a printer; a flat-screen television with cable; digital and video cameras; and various other gadgets that The Sculptor needed from time to time to accomplish his work. In the other corner The Sculptor stored some of his medical equipment—equipment not at all like the type in his father's bedroom, equipment for an entirely different purpose altogether.

The Sculptor turned on the monitor that displayed the video feed from his father's bedroom. There was his father as he left him, sitting by the window, staring out at the birds. The Sculptor turned on the sound feed as well, and the loft was at once filled with the sweet sound of Scarlatti.

The Sculptor booted up his two computers and hit the remote for the television—Fox News, no sound, just as he left it. There was nothing yet about his first showing—what he knew was going to be a *spectacular entrance* into the public eye—but that was all right. Nothing to dampen his mood. No, The Sculptor was confident that news of his creation would dominate all the media outlets very soon. He smiled at the thought of it, wishing that the details would trickle out slowly as they often did in cases like this. That would pique the public's curiosity; that would whet the public's appetite for more.

Above all else, however, The Sculptor was excited for Dr. Hildy to see his work—for Dr. Hildy was really the only person who could *truly* understand his *Bacchus.* And once the news got out about the inscription, once the public learned of the connection to Dr. Hildy, well, that certainly would make them want to know more about her. Perhaps all those big-shot journalists might even want to interview her—*now wouldn't that be something!* At the very least, the public would want to read her book on Michelangelo. Then they would all begin to understand; then they would all begin to finally *wake up.*

With both of his computers logged onto the Internet—Drudge Report and CNN—The Sculptor removed from the desk drawer the only book he allowed in the carriage house: his copy of *Slumbering in the Stone*. He flipped through it—the cover tattered, the pages dog-eared, underlined, with notes in the margins—until he reached the back jacket flap. There was the picture of Dr. Catherine Hildebrant. She wore her hair shorter six years ago. *Looked a little heavier,* The Sculptor thought. Perhaps it was the black and white of the photo; perhaps her glasses—*yes, the black frames she wears now look much better on her than those old wire-rims.* Objectively, The Sculptor thought Catherine Hildebrant to be attractive material, but in the long run such superficialities in women did not matter to him. No, The Sculptor knew that, like the material he used for his sculptures, Dr. Catherine Hildebrant's real beauty lay within, *slumbering in the stone.*

Smiling, feeling a little silly, The Sculptor returned his book to the desk drawer and rode the mortician's table down to the first floor. The gears were a bit noisier than usual. "Need a little oil," The Sculptor said to himself as he sent the table back upstairs. He would get to that next, after he finished tidying up his studio.

The first floor was drastically different from the loft above it. Here, too, the windows had been blocked out, but the walls were the original exposed brick. On one wall was a tool rack, while on another was a sheet of corkboard on which the plans for The Sculptor's *Bacchus* still hung. A large white van, which could be driven in and out through one of the two overhanging doors, took up nearly half the space; while the other half was reserved solely for The Sculptor's studio. There was a narrow stand-up shower and slop sink, as well as a small floor drain which his father told him had been used in the 1800s to catch the blood from deer carcasses. On this side, too, was all the necessary equipment for The Sculptor's work, including a drafting table and chair, an arc-welder and power supply, a small anvil, a vat of "special paint" and a pump sprayer, ultraviolet lamps, rolls of plastic sheeting, and, at the rear of the carriage house, a large stainless steel hospital tub. The tub was the most complex piece of The Sculptor's equipment, for he had outfitted it not only with an airtight cover, but with a refrigeration unit and a vacuum pump as well. In a small lean-to behind the carriage house were stored the barrels of chemicals The Sculptor brought up from the cellar when he was ready to prepare his material.

The Sculptor clicked on the video monitor that sat atop the drafting table—his father by the window, the Baroque guitar now filling the entire carriage house—and proceeded to pull down his plans from the corkboard. He twisted them into a tight log—the sinews of his powerful forearms rippling through his skin. He would light a fire in the parlor this evening; would bring up a bottle of Brunello di Montalcino from the cellar and watch the plans burn. *Why not? I've behaved myself. I can have a little reward for all my hard work.* Yes, surely the news about his first showing will have broken by that time. If not, he could always tip off the media himself—after, of course, he was sure Dr. Hildy had seen his work; after he was sure she got his "thank you" note.

Perhaps she's on her way down there right now, he thought, smiling.

And as The Sculptor began to straighten up his studio, he concluded that it was too risky to check for himself, to follow Dr. Hildy around like he had in the

past. No, surely the FBI would be expecting something like that; surely it was smarter to find out
through the media like everybody else.

"Besides," The Sculptor said out loud, "I won't
have time to spy on Dr. Hildy. For tomorrow is Monday. And Monday is the day I begin my next project."

Chapter 6

Special Agent in Charge William "Bulldog" Burrell had mixed feelings about the hand that fate had dealt him. As the newly appointed SAC of the FBI's Boston Field Office, the Tommy Campbell case had been his baby from the beginning—one that he had seen to personally. A twenty-two-year veteran of the FBI, Bill Burrell knew his way around an investigation. He had served in the Washington, Chicago, and Dallas Field Offices, as well as held a number other of high-profile SAC positions, including section chief of the Strategic Information and Operations Center at FBI Headquarters, before landing the gig in Boston. The six-foot-three former Marine with the buzz cut had been called "Bulldog" since his football days at the University of New Hampshire—not only because of his hulking frame, his heavy jowls, his menacing stare, and his hot temper, but also because of the way he always tore into his opponents: straight ahead for the red until he ripped his man to shreds.

However, in the three months since Tommy Campbell's disappearance, Bulldog had not a shred of evidence to show for himself. He had long ago exhausted his leads, had long ago begun to feel desperate, and had since lost countless hours of sleep over what had been sizing up to be his first big failure since he took over the Boston Office the previous November—*the first big failure of his career.* What a mixed bag it was then that the kid's body should have turned up on the very same weekend Supervisory Special Agent Sam Markham had arrived in preparation for a three-day seminar on the latest forensic and profiling procedures at Quantico; what a mixed bag that Markham had gotten to the crime scene before he had; and what a mixed bag that Markham should be the one to jump on their very first lead now that the disappearance of Tommy Campbell had been deemed a homicide.

Yes, now that they had *two* bodies and a serial killer on their hands; now that it was clear that they were dealing with something much, much bigger than just a murder or a suicide, Burrell, whether he liked it or not, would need Sam Markham. And although it had not yet been six hours since the horrific white sculpture had been discovered down at Watch Hill, already Special Agent in Charge William "Bulldog" Burrell was not happy about the way the investigation was moving ahead.

It was not that Bulldog had anything personal against Markham. On the contrary, Bulldog actually admired the legendary "profiler," the man who had brought down Jackson Briggs, aka "The Sarasota Strangler"—that son of a bitch who killed all those old ladies in Florida. And then, of course, there was that nasty little business in Raleigh, North Carolina. Yeah, no one would ever forget what happened there.

Indeed, word on the street said that it was only a

matter of time before Markham took over as chief for the Behavioral Analysis Unit-2 at the National Center for the Analysis of Violent Crime. However, Bill Burrell knew such a position was not one the forty-year-old Markham was gunning for. No, Markham was like him—happier with his boots on the ground, slugging it out in the trenches *himself*. And now that the Tommy Campbell disappearance had been deemed a homicide, if Burrell had to work with somebody from Quantico, he was glad that it was Sam Markham.

Nonetheless, the fifty-year-old lifer could not help but feel cheated that the first and only break in the biggest case of his career had fallen into Markham's lap, for no matter how much he admired Markham, Bill Burrell was instinctively territorial. Like a bulldog. And this was *his* junkyard.

It was for this reason that the phone call from Special Agent Rachel Sullivan, Burrell's NCAVC coordinator, went right up his ass. His technician had briefed him on their conversation as soon as Burrell arrived at the crime scene—a scene that had pulled him away from a visit with his sick mother in New Hampshire; a scene that demanded the hardnosed SAC show up at Watch Hill *in person*. And although Bulldog was pleased with the way his forensic team had secured the site, that Markham should have given orders to his men was simply unacceptable.

Burrell stood at the bottom of the gravel driveway, frowning over a Marlboro. He dared to smoke only on a case—when he knew he would not be home for a while and his wife would not be able to smell it on him.

But how the hell did he get them in here? Burrell asked himself, gazing out over the impeccably landscaped property.

The mansion belonged to a wealthy investment CEO by the name of Dodd, who had been sleeping soundly with his wife when his caretaker discovered the statue in the southeastern corner of the topiary garden. A row of high hedges separated almost the entirety of Dodd's estate from his neighbors on either side—except for the eastern stretch, which sloped down toward the beach. It was in this area that, upon their initial sweep of the crime scene, Burrell's team discovered a set of fresh footprints running back and forth in the sand from the property next door. The neighbors on this side were summer folk—not "year rounders" like Dodd and his wife—and consequently the house remained unoccupied in the off-season. The man who made the footprints in the sand had known this. However, the man who made the footprints in the sand had also known to wear something—*probably plastic bags*—over his shoes; for in all the prints not a single tread could be found.

"Yes," Burrell whispered in a plume of smoke. "He had to have parked next door. But then that means he also had to *carry* Campbell and that boy around the back, across that narrow span of beach and up the grassy slope. Now that's one strong, one determined son of a bitch."

Burrell heeled his cigarette into the gravel and crossed the large expanse of lawn to the entrance of the topiary garden. He looked at his watch: 12:58 P.M.

Where the hell is Markham? he thought, scanning the sea of blue FBI jackets.

The topiary garden was roughly a thirty-by-thirty-meter courtyard divided into quarters by a brick path with a marble fountain at its center. And save for the wall of twelve-foot high hedges that separated Dodd's property from his neighbors, a series of arched "windows" and "doors" had been cut into the remaining three sides, giving people inside the garden a lovely view of Dodd's property—including the beach and the Atlantic Ocean beyond it—while at the same time enclosing them in a separate space altogether. In addition to the classical marble sculptures that occupied the arched windows, the interior of the garden was peppered with a number of exquisitely trimmed topiary sculptures, including a bear, an elephant, a giraffe, and a horse.

It was in the farthest corner of the garden that the killer had mounted his exhibit, an exhibit that, despite its gruesomeness, Burrell thought looked strangely at home among its marble and spring-green companions—knew instinctively that the killer wanted everyone to see not just Tommy Campbell, not just his statue, but the totality of its *context* as well.

"She's here, Bill," said a voice behind him.

It was Sam Markham.

Turning, Burrell's gaze fell upon a petite, attractive young woman shivering beside the Quantico profiler. He right away pegged the eyes behind the black-rimmed glasses to be Korean—the same as his wife's.

"Can I have one of my people get you a cup of coffee, Dr. Hildebrant?" he said, dispensing with the formalities of an introduction. Bill Burrell knew his team well; knew that Special Agent Sullivan, who was now speaking with their tech guy by the fountain, had already briefed the art historian as to who he was.

"No thank you. I'd like to see the sculpture."

"This way," said Burrell, leading her across the courtyard. If it had been unclear to Cathy Hildebrant who was in charge of this shindig, the way the sea of blue jackets immediately parted to let Bill Burrell pass left no room for doubt.

Upon the FBI's arrival, the forensic team had quickly set about erecting a bright blue canopy over Tommy Campbell and his young companion, and thus Cathy did not have a clear view of the sculpture until she was directly upon it. And for all her anxiety leading up to this moment, despite the reality of the tableau of death before her, Cathy felt numbly detached and analytical, while at the same time overcome with a buzzing sensation of awe—a feeling eerily reminiscent of the first time she encountered the original *Bacchus* in Florence nearly fifteen years earlier.

Indeed, the reproduction of Michelangelo's marble sculpture was even more—oh God, how Cathy wished she could think of another word for it!—*impressive* than in Markham's Polaroids. The pose, the attention to detail—the lion skin, the cup, the grapes—were nearly flawless, and Cathy had to remind herself that she was looking at a pair of bleached dead bodies. Nonetheless, she automatically began to circle the sculpture as she knew Michelangelo had intended viewers of his *Bacchus* to do—an ingenious artistic ploy woven into the statue's multiplicity of angles that subliminally transmitted the dizzy unsteadiness of the drunken god himself. Cathy's eyes dropped to Bacchus's half-human counterpart, the as-of-yet nameless little boy who had been mercilessly contorted into a satyr. Here, too, the creator of this travesty had captured the essence of Michelangelo's original—that mischievous, goat-legged imp who smiles at the viewer while imitating the god's pose and stealing his grapes.

Cathy continued around the statue, glancing quickly

at the dreaded inscription to her at its base, until her eyes came to rest on Bacchus's groin. Beneath the marble-white paint—if in fact it *was* paint—Cathy noticed the vague outline of what appeared to be stitches where Tommy Campbell's penis had been removed. However, as her eyes traveled up his torso to his face, what disturbed Cathy the most was how accurately Tommy Campbell's killer had captured even the subtlest nuances of the original. It was clear to Cathy that whoever had made this heinous thing had gone to great lengths not only to murder Campbell and that poor little boy, but also to transform them into the *very essence* of Michelangelo's *Bacchus*.

"You see, Dr. Hildebrant," began Burrell. "Our preliminary analysis indicates that the killer somehow preserved the bodies and mounted them on an internal metal frame. This means that whoever did this not only has a working knowledge of taxidermy, of embalming and such, but also knows something about welding. This sound like anybody you know? Maybe one of your students who was also involved in metalworking?"

"No," said Cathy. "I don't know anyone who could do this."

"And you have no idea why someone would want to dedicate this statue to you specifically?"

"No. No idea." In the awkward silence that followed, Cathy suddenly became aware that the entire FBI team—what had to be two-dozen of them—was staring at her. She felt her face go hot, felt her stomach leap into her chest, and then a flash of memory, a dream—the third grade, show and tell, and distant taunts of *"Ching-chong! Ching-chong!"* echoing in her head.

It was Sam Markham who stepped in to save her.

"Dr. Hildebrant, is there anything else you can tell us about the statue before the forensic team removes it? For instance, why Tommy Campbell should be missing his . . . well, why he's missing his penis?"

Cathy had the vague suspicion that Markham already knew the answer to his question—that he was trying to get her to talk about *Bacchus* the same way she talked about Michelangelo in the car in order to calm her. And, for the briefest of moments, Cathy Hildebrant loved him for it.

"Well," she began. "There's some debate about this, but the original is also missing its penis. We know that at some point Bacchus's right hand, the one holding the bowl of wine, was broken off to give the sculpture the appearance of antiquity—as for a time it lived among a collection of Roman artifacts belonging to a man named Jacopo Galli. The hand, however, was restored by about 1550 or so, but the penis, well, some scholars believe that it was never there to begin with, or that it was chiseled off by Michelangelo himself soon after the statue was completed."

"Why?" asked Markham.

"Both the Roman and Greek mythological traditions—the Greeks called their version of the god Dionysus—held that Bacchus was not only the god of wine and excess, but also the god of theatre, and thus possessed all powers apropos to early Greek theatre's original ritual and celebratory purposes. Although scholars still debate the true nature of these early rituals, given that sex was part of the excess over which Bacchus reigned supreme, some scholars conclude that there was a sexual component to these early theatrical rituals as well. Hence, in both Roman and Greek mythology we often see Bacchus represented with both male and female genitalia, and thus the ability to govern the excesses of both male and female sexual desire. It has long been believed that Michelangelo purposely sculpted his Bacchus's body with a fleshy, almost androgynous quality—the swollen breasts, the bloated belly—and some scholars suggest that *Bacchus* was purposely completed without a penis to represent this. I tend to disagree with them, however."

"You ever seen anything like this, Sam?" asked Burrell.

"No. Serial killers sometimes pose their victims—put them on display, if you will—either for their own sick benefit or for the others who come afterward. But no, I've never seen anything like this."

"And the missing penis? That mean anything to you, Sam? Killer's got a problem with his gender? Wants to be a woman or something?"

"Perhaps. Or perhaps he's just trying to make the sculpture look authentic like the one in Florence."

"That would explain why the killer put the sculpture on display here," said Cathy.

"What do you mean?" asked Burrell.

"Agent Markham, you told me that the owner of this property is the CEO of an investment firm?"

"That's right. His name is Dodd. Earl Dodd."

"Michelangelo's *Bacchus* was originally commissioned in 1496 by a cardinal named Riario, who intended to install it in his garden of classical sculptures. The cardinal ended up rejecting the statue—thought it distasteful—and we know that by about 1506 or so it had been given a home in the garden of Jacopo Galli, a wealthy banker."

Burrell and Markham exchanged a look, and Cathy suddenly felt self-conscious again.

"I'm sorry," she said. "Forgive me if I'm playing

detective. Too many nights alone watching *CSI*, I guess."

"What are you thinking, Sam?" asked Burrell.

"Dr. Hildebrant," Markham said, "was *Bacchus* Michelangelo's first statue?"

"Heavens no. He was only twenty-two when it was completed, had sculpted a number of others, but *Bacchus* was indeed Michelangelo's first *life-size* statue—the sculpture that really thrust him into the public eye and garnered him recognition as a talented marble carver."

"Then you're thinking this is an introduction, Sam?" asked Burrell. "The first of more to come?"

"Perhaps."

"But why Campbell?" countered the SAC. "And why this boy?"

"I'm not sure," said Markham, squatting by the inscription at the base of the statue. "But I suspect that's something the killer wants Dr. Hildebrant to tell us."

Chapter 7

The motto on the side of the new Westerly Police cruisers read, PRIDE, INTEGRITY, AND COMMITMENT—to which the police chief always added in his mind, *"Tight-lipped."* Indeed, if there was one quality the citizens of Watch Hill appreciated in their chief, it was that he knew how to keep his men quiet. And as the secluded seaside community had long been a vacation retreat for the rich and famous, there had always been an unwritten rule in the department that officers should turn on their cruiser lights and sirens only when absolutely necessary. Over the years, the Westerly Police had even developed a sort of informal "code" in order to avoid the attention of local reporters, who were constantly monitoring the police bands with the hopes of catching a juicy story.

Yet following the disappearance of Tommy Campbell—the juiciest story to hit Watch Hill in decades—unbeknown to the police chief, one of his officers had jumped "on the take"—five hundred dollars cash, no questions asked, to be paid upon delivery of any "credible, first dibs info" relating to the wide receiver's whereabouts. Thus, when rookie WNRI Channel 9 Eye-Team Investigator Meghan O'Neill's cell phone rang with a tip that Tommy Campbell's body had been found down at Watch Hill, the ambitious young reporter knew that her money had been well spent.

And so it was that, as Cathy Hildebrant concluded her examination of The Sculptor's *Bacchus,* O'Neill and the Channel 9 Mobile News Room pulled up outside of Earl Dodd's wall of high hedges. The stretch of Ocean View Highway in front of the mansion looked to be deserted, and for a moment the Eye-Team's star investigator thought she had been duped. However, when she caught sight of the two Rhode Island state troopers standing guard beyond the iron gate, when she glimpsed the line of unmarked FBI vehicles that snaked up the driveway, Meghan O'Neill called in the confirmation to Channel 9 herself.

Yes, that up-and-coming anchor slot was as good as hers.

And although the Westerly Police Chief would never have believed it, although only a handful of his men had known what *really* was going on in the wealthy investment banker's topiary garden before the state police arrived, as soon as the two troopers saw the pretty redhead scramble out of the van, they knew a local boy had rolled.

"I'll call it in," said one of the officers. "You go tell Burrell." And in a flash his partner was off across the lawn as the other radioed for backup.

"I want to be live in thirty seconds," said O'Neill, straightening her blouse and taking the microphone. "We'll start here on the sidewalk, and then you follow me to the front gate." With only a year on the Rhode

Island beat under her belt, Meghan O'Neill learned early on that it was best to get the cameras rolling as soon as possible—that people "behaved better" when they knew they were being recorded.

And judging from the look on the trooper's face at the end of Dodd's driveway, her two-man crew needed to get things moving fast.

"They're ready for us back at the station," called the driver from the van, and the cameraman began Meghan O'Neill's countdown.

"Breaking news in ten, nine, eight . . ."

Taking her cue, O'Neill positioned herself by one of the stone pillars that flanked the entrance to Dodd's property—her cool exterior betraying none of the nervousness, the excitement raging within her.

"Five, four, three . . ."

The audio cut into her earpiece right on time with the cameraman's silent one count—audio that O'Neill had been waiting to hear ever since she landed the Eye-Team gig fresh out of college:

"—have some very big breaking news. Channel 9 has just learned that Tommy Campbell, the missing wide receiver for the Boston Rebels, has been found dead about a mile from where he disappeared back in January. Let's bring in our Eye-Team Investigator Meghan O'Neill, who is first on the scene, first to break what sounds like a tragic turn of events in this shocking case. What's happening down there, Meghan?"

"Good afternoon, Karen. I'm here outside the estate of wealthy Watch Hill resident Earl Dodd. Although we have yet to receive official confirmation from the authorities or from Campbell's representative, anonymous sources close to the investigation told us that early this morning two bodies were discovered somewhere on the grounds behind me, and that one of these bodies has been identified by relatives as the missing Boston Rebels wide receiver, Tommy Campbell."

"I'm sorry, but you said two *bodies, Meghan?"*

"That's right, Karen," said O'Neill, making her move to the front gate. "All we know right now is that another body was found with Campbell's, but who this person is, if in fact his or her identity is known at this point, our sources could not tell us. I'm not sure if you can see behind me, Karen, but it looks like both federal and local authorities have been on the scene for quite some time now. Keep in mind that information is pretty scarce at present, and given that there has been no official statement made as of yet, we haven't been able to confirm whether or not the authorities believe foul play was involved."

"But this certainly is some incredible news, Meghan. Have your sources told you anything about the circumstances surrounding the discovery? Where or how the bodies were found? Perhaps how the victims died and what connection they have to this—you said his name was Dodd?"

"That's right, Karen. Earl Dodd, a wealthy investment banker whose family has lived in the area for generations. Our sources were unable to confirm such details as of yet, including whether or not Dodd is somehow connected to Campbell's disappearance or the discovery of his body. But here we have a Rhode Island state trooper who's been standing guard by Dodd's front gate. Officer, is it true that a pair of bodies has been found on the grounds inside, and that one of these bodies has been identified as the missing Rebel wide receiver, Tommy Campbell?"

Before the trooper could fumble over a reply, a voice from behind him answered on his behalf.

"The FBI will make a statement later this afternoon," said Special Agent Rachel Sullivan. "We'll keep you updated as to when it's time for a press conference."

A pair of FBI agents hung a blue tarp across the front gate.

"Well there you have it, Karen," said O'Neill, unfazed. "Investigators are still being pretty tight-lipped about what's happening. I'm sure our viewers are aware of the kind of worldwide attention this case has gotten ever since the wide receiver disappeared before the Super Bowl back in January. We have known for some time that, given Campbell's notoriety and the circumstances surrounding his disappearance, the FBI has been handling this case from the beginning. And now, Karen, judging from what our sources have told us and the number of federal agents on the scene, I think it's safe to say that this case has taken a turn for the worse down here in the sleepy seaside community of Watch Hill."

"I think we'd all tend to agree with you, Meghan. And certainly, if what you're saying is true, our thoughts and prayers go out to the Campbell family. Hats off to you and the Channel 9 Eye-Team for being the first to break this incredible story. You'll keep us updated as things progress?"

"Thank you, Karen. And yes, our Channel 9 Mobile News Room will remain here on the scene to bring you the news *first* as it breaks. Back to you for now, Karen."

"Thank you, Meghan. Well there you have it, folks. Meghan O'Neill, first with what is sizing up to be perhaps the biggest story of the year. Keep it tuned to Channel 9 for all the latest news on what appears to be a tragic turn of events in one of the most bizarre cases in recent memory. Once again, for those of you just joining us—"

The audio in Meghan O'Neill's earpiece cut out just as what looked like the entire Westerly Police force—*lights flashing, sirens wailing*—rounded the corner.

"You're going to have to clear away from that gate, ma'am," said the chief of police, emerging from his car. "And get this van the hell out of here."

And while Westerly's finest proceeded to cordon off the street outside of the Dodd estate, little did the chief of police know that—even as Meghan O'Neill and her crew set about removing their equipment—the producers at WNRI Channel 9 and about a half dozen other New England stations were already mobilizing their news choppers.

No, there would be no way to keep things quiet now.

Chapter 8

Back inside the topiary garden, Bill Burrell hung up with Tommy Campbell's father. The SAC called the well-known businessman personally to warn him and his wife that the media had gotten wind of the story, and to once again expect a pack of reporters at the end of their driveway. He would send over two of his men to help keep the wolves at bay—would drop by later himself to offer his condolences in person, and to see if there was anything he could do for them.

Yes, he owed them that.

Thomas Campbell Sr. and his lovely wife Maggie had endured a lot since their son vanished back in January—the least of which being the initial onslaught of reporters who hounded their every movement. Indeed, for a time the elder Campbell had even been a suspect in his son's disappearance—an unfortunate and now ludicrous detail of the investigation about which Bill Burrell still felt guilty. He had gotten to know Thomas and his wife quite well; had often sat with the couple on their porch, drink-

ing hot chocolate and looking out over Foster Cove—
the waters of which divers had combed countless times
in search of Tommy Campbell's body.

But now, all that was over. Yes, now that Campbell's body had finally been found, Burrell felt a
heavy wave of guilt for not having been on the scene
when the boy's parents arrived at Dodd's estate,
when they gave the positive ID of what had become
of their only son.

And what exactly had *become of their only son?*

Burrell watched his forensic team begin the somber
task of removing Tommy Campbell and his young companion from their station in the corner of the topiary
garden. His gaze now and then wandered up to the
sky, on the lookout for the news choppers that he knew
would be arriving any minute. It took three of his
men, three *big* men, almost ten minutes to carry the
shrouded tableau of death across the courtyard and
into the transport van that had been pulled up on the
lawn outside the garden.

Damn, Burrell thought. *Whoever did this really is one
strong son of a bitch.*

And as the heavy metal doors slammed shut, as the
van started on its way across the lawn, Bulldog
heaved a sigh of relief that he had been able to get
the bodies off-site before the vultures started swarm-
ing overhead. Yes, that really was his only break in
the case thus far. That meant the medical examiner
could work in peace, and that Burrell's office would
not have to comment on any press footage of the
scene until the official cause of death had been determined.

Burrell lit a cigarette and telephoned his wife—
told her not to expect him home until late that evening,
perhaps even tomorrow morning. She responded like

she always did—an empty, Korean-flavored *"I'll leave the light on"* that had been hardened by two kids and twenty-five years of marriage to "the life." And as he joined Markham and Cathy in the back of the FBI surveillance van, when he saw the pretty professor's half-Asian features in the soft light of the computer screens, the guilt Bill Burrell had felt for abandoning the Campbells all at once transformed into a longing for his wife.

Yes, at fifty years old, the Bulldog was getting soft.

"Tell me what we got," Burrell exhaled in a plume of cigarette smoke.

"Well," Markham began, "our agents were able to track down a collection of Michelangelo's poetry at the Westerly Library, as well as a copy of Dr. Hildebrant's *Slumbering in the Stone*."

"And?"

"I haven't had a chance yet to go over her book, but Dr. Hildebrant has identified the poem and the quotes."

"The ones Sullivan told me about? The ones that were slipped under Dr. Hildebrant's office door almost six years ago?"

"Yes, sir," said Markham, looking down at a sheet of paper. "We found the three quotes online. And at first glance, they appear to be what Dr. Hildebrant took them as—words of wisdom and support in the wake of her mother's death. This at the very least tells us that whoever gave them to her was aware of her personal life. The quotes arrived in the following order. 'If we have been pleased with life, we should not be displeased with death, since it comes from the hand of the same master,' 'The promises of this world are, for the most part, vain phantoms,' and finally, 'To confide in one's self and become something of worth and value, is the best and safest course.'"

"So what's your take on them, Sam?"

"A definite attempt at intimacy, I'd say, as well an implied understanding by the writer of the grief that Dr. Hildebrant was going through at the time. In this light then, the last quote seems somewhat odd, given that the first two deal with death and the afterlife, and actually contrast this world with the next. Upon further research, however, Dr. Hildebrant and I have found that the third quote is often cited as a continuation of the second. I'm not quite sure what to make of that, but taking it into context with the sonnet, which was the last note she received, perhaps it signifies not only advice on how she should deal with her loss, but also a change of focus—both with regard to where Dr. Hildebrant should now focus *her* energy, and where her admirer should now focus *his*."

"I don't follow."

"The sonnet that came next," said Markham, thumbing through the book of poetry. "The one that was originally written to the youth Tommaso Cavalieri, is a much more intimate correspondence than the previous notes. Yes, like the first two quotes, it implies an unspoken and private knowledge of the other—but this time the sender seems to be speaking from both his *and* Dr. Hildebrant's point of view."

"How so?"

"The first four lines read as follows:

> We both know, my lord, that you know
> I come near to have my pleasure with you;
> And we both know that you know my name;
> So why do you wait to introduce yourself?

"As Dr. Hildebrant had to explain to me, Michel-angelo was a homosexual, and his relationship with Cavalieri—a relationship that was never physically consummated but that was nonetheless reciprocated—caused the artist, and presumably Cavalieri, great anguish. Michelangelo is speaking then for both of them, saying that he knows they *both* love each other, and therefore wants Cavalieri to acknowledge it, too. Given that knowledge—that is, the story *behind* the sonnet—we thus have an overt statement from Dr. Hildebrant's admirer that says in effect, 'Not only do I know what you're thinking, but I also know that you know what *I'm* thinking.'"

"'I come near to have my pleasure with you,'" repeated Burrell. "So the person who wrote the note is admitting that he had gotten physically close to Dr. Hildebrant?"

"Maybe," said Markham. "But it could be meant to be taken figuratively, as in close to her through her work—her book, which was published about six months before the notes began arriving."

"But the line about knowing his name, isn't that an overt statement as well? That the writer of the note is saying, literally, you know who I am?"

"Perhaps," said Markham. "But again, her admirer could be speaking figuratively—given the context of the original sonnet to Cavalieri, that it was a sort of homosexual code for something else, a spiritual love that could not be named. If we were to take the first four lines literally, the line, 'So why do you wait to introduce yourself?' seems inappropriate in any context other than Dr. Hildebrant avoiding an advance from someone. And as she has told me nothing like that happened before the notes were delivered, I am inclined to think there is some hidden meaning *be-*

hind the first four lines, as there was for Cavalieri in Michelangelo's time. What that meaning is for Dr. Hildebrant, I can't be sure. But given the rest of the sonnet, I would tend to think that Dr. Hildebrant's admirer, like Michelangelo himself, meant the poem as more of a spiritual overture than an actual love note—that is, in appreciation of her soul rather than her beauty." Markham turned to Cathy. "You said that your admirer made no attempt in his correspondence to change the subject of the poem—a man, a *lord*—to a lady, is that correct?"

"Yes," said Cathy.

"An odd choice if Dr. Hildebrant's admirer meant the correspondence to be a love sonnet. Wouldn't you agree, Bill?"

"Read me the rest of it," he said.

"The next section does in fact seem to support the idea of a figurative, spiritual attraction rather than a physical one. It reads

> If your gift to me of hope is true,
> As true as the desire I've given you,
> May the wall between us crumble down.
> For nothing is more painful than hidden sorrow.
> If I love in you, my lord, only that
> Which you yourself do love, do not despise
> The spirit for the love it bears the other.

"Here again, as in the original, Dr. Hildebrant told me her admirer addressed her as 'lord.' There is also the obvious statement of their spirits loving each other. However, given *that* context—that is, the context of a love, a desire that is not physical, not sexual—the last three lines seem out of place. They read

What I wish to learn from your beautiful face
Cannot be understood in the minds of men:
   He who wishes to learn can only die."

A heavy silence fell over the tech van.

"May I see that?" asked Burrell finally. Markham handed him the book of poetry. "'He who wishes to learn can only die,'" the SAC read out loud.

"Yes," said Markham. "At the very least a strange coincidence—given the recent turn of events, that is."

"But it doesn't make any sense," said Burrell. "'What I wish to learn from your beautiful face cannot be understood in the minds of men. He who wishes to learn can only die?' Do you really think, Sam, that Dr. Hildebrant's admirer told her that he was planning to kill someone? That he actually *waited* five and a half years to carry it out?"

"I don't know, Bill."

"And what does Michelangelo mean in his poem when he says what he wants to learn cannot be understood in the minds of men?"

"Michelangelo is saying that people not only misunderstand him," said Cathy, "but also the kind of love he feels for Cavalieri. He is telling Cavalieri that, although their contemporaries could not comprehend of Michelangelo's desire for him as anything other than lustful and sinful, in reality it goes far beyond that into the realm of the divine—a love that can only be fully understood when one dies, when one comes to know God."

"I guess that's what I don't understand," said Markham. "Why those last three lines are so troubling to me—that is, if this poem was meant only as a spiritual overture. Although the foundation of Michelangelo's love for Cavalieri went much deeper than just the physical, from what you've told me, Dr. Hildebrant, there *was* a sexual, homoerotic component to it as well. Is that right?"

"Yes."

"So the line about the beautiful face," interrupted Burrell. "Are you saying, Sam, that that line doesn't make sense in conjunction with the rest of the poem unless Dr. Hildebrant's admirer is a homosexual? Unless she's a woman?"

"Perhaps. That is, if Dr. Hildebrant's admirer did in fact understand the original context of the sonnet, the history behind it. And banking on my experience in such things, I think it's safe to assume that he or she did."

"But then that means Dr. Hildebrant's admirer and Campbell's killer could not have been the same person. Judging from the size of those footprints in the sand, Campbell's killer was well over six feet tall. Any six-foot-five lesbians in your department, Dr. Hildebrant?"

"I'm afraid not."

"And that sculpture weighed a ton—was almost impossible for one person to handle—and there's every indication that it was brought to the location intact. You saw for yourself, Sam. It took three of my guys ten minutes to load that thing into the van. That means that the person who carried it all the way from the house next door and up the hill out back is one strong SOB—and we know it was *one* SOB from the single set of footprints in the sand, a set of footprints that went back and forth only *once*."

"Yes."

"So what's your opinion now, Sam? You still think the person who sent Dr. Hildebrant those notes is the same person who killed Tommy Campbell? And that this person has to be a homosexual?"

"Perhaps a homosexual," Cathy interrupted. "But not necessarily a woman."

"What do you mean?" asked Markham.

"Agent Markham, you said that you thought Michelangelo's line about coming near to me might not have been meant to be taken literally, right? That maybe my admirer was referring to my work, specifically to my book?"

"Yes."

"Well, maybe then my admirer was referring not to *my* face, but to someone else's."

"What are you talking about?" asked Burrell, but Cathy saw that Special Agent Markham understood. His eyes at once dropped to the book in his lap, to the copy of *Slumbering in the Stone* which had been checked out for him at the Westerly Library.

On its cover was the face of Michelangelo's most famous sculpture.

On its cover was his *David*.

Chapter 9

The Sculptor stepped out of the shower and tow-
eled off in the middle of his studio. His skin smelled
clean, industrially so—like hospital disinfectant, *like
a job well done.* Yes, the only thing out of order now
was the pile of dirty clothes in the slop sink. He
would not don them again, would not even *touch*
them until it was time to go back to the house. Then
he would drop them in the washer and give his father his supper. The Sculptor would not put on a
fresh set of clothes either, for The Sculptor loved
being naked—looked forward to remaining that way
well into the evening, when he would sit in the dim
light of the parlor watching his *Bacchus* plans burn in
the fireplace as he sipped his Brunello.

But first The Sculptor needed to check his technology, needed to see if his premiere exhibit had
made the news yet. He had been patient, had resisted
looking at his monitors until he was finished tidying
up his workspace. And so the man once called Christian rode the mortician's table up to the second
floor—the gears of the winch system much quieter

now that he had oiled them. He turned off the audio feed from his father's bedroom—the A-side of Scarlatti now on its fourth time through—and sat naked at his desk, flicking on the sound of the flat-screen TV just as the Fox News Channel was turning over the broadcast to its local affiliate.

The Sculptor did not recognize the pretty young woman with the red hair and emerald green eyes—for The Sculptor never watched the local news, almost never watched TV at all—and thus did not consider it anything special when the Fox News anchor mentioned that WNRI's Meghan O'Neill had been the first to break the story. And of course, like the rest of Channel 9's loyal viewers, there was no way he could have known about the reporter's anonymous source inside the Westerly Police Department. If he had, he might have decided to wait; might have decided to let O'Neill's man tell her what she needed to know. But just as The Sculptor was in the dark with regard to that, so was Meghan O'Neill. Her five hundred dollars had landed her only *half* a story—a rookie, like herself, who was on the periphery of the investigation; one who got his information secondhand back at headquarters, and who was kept out of the loop about the specific details regarding Campbell's remains.

And so The Sculptor felt somewhat disappointed to learn from the breaking news report that—unless they were doing a good job of hiding it—all the media seemed to know thus far was that the bodies of Tommy Campbell and an unidentified person had been discovered down at Watch Hill, and that both of them had been moved from the site to an "undisclosed location." And from the way the pretty redhead and the Fox News anchor were trading theories as to Campbell's connection with Dodd—a connection that The Sculptor knew went only as far as the millionaire's lovely topiary garden—The Sculptor *also* knew that the media had not captured any footage of his exhibit—not even a picture! That was unfortunate; that was not part of his plan; for that meant it might be days, perhaps even a whole week before the details of his *Bacchus* were made public. And although The Sculptor was a very, very patient man, the idea that the media might miss something suddenly did not sit well with him.

However, it was not impatience that influenced his decision to telephone the pretty young reporter's home station, but the sight of a familiar face *behind* her—more of a grainy shadow, really—in the front seat of what he knew to be an unmarked FBI vehicle. The glimpse of her lasted only a millisecond—would probably have gone unnoticed even by the art history professor's ex-husband—but could not escape The Sculptor's keen eye. No, as Meghan O'Neill directed her cameras across the street to Dodd's front gate, just as it was opening three Chevy Trailblazers emerged from behind the high wall of hedges. And for the briefest of moments The Sculptor was sure he had spied the figure of Cathy Hildebrant through the windshield of the lead car. And despite his excitement, despite his joy that Dr. Hildy had *finally* seen his work, The Sculptor was at the same time struck with an idea.

He would make the telephone call from his cell phone, with a Wal-Mart calling card that still had plenty of minutes left on it. His number would be blocked anyway, but this was just a little more insurance. And of course, there was no need to worry about the ping off the local cell tower. No, he himself had designed the phone's encrypter to cloak all his calls in and out of the carriage house just in case. Yes, for as much as The Sculptor hated technology, he had resigned himself long ago that he would have to master it in order to complete his work. And so, after a quick search online—a search with a rerouted IP address, of course—The Sculptor muted the television and placed his call.

"Thank you for calling the WNRI Channel 9 Eye-Team Hotline," droned the recorded voice on the other end. *"Your call is important to us, but due to the heavy amount of traffic at present, your wait time to speak with an investigator is approximately—se-ven mi-nutes."*

The Sculptor refreshed his computer screens; whistled Scarlatti's *Sonata in D Minor* as he read the headlines on the Drudge Report and CNN.com. While he had been tidying up his studio, a spokesperson for the FBI had confirmed with the Associated Press that the body of missing Boston Rebels wide receiver Tommy Campbell, as well as another unidentified person, had been found on the property of a wealthy businessman in Campbell's hometown of Westerly, Rhode Island—*blahdy-blahdy-blah*, details to follow in a press conference at 5:00 P.M.

That's good, The Sculptor thought. *A little over two hours to plant the seeds; a little over two hours to make sure the press would ask the right questions come conference time.*

The broadcast on the Fox News Channel switched to an aerial view of Dodd's estate, and as the line of FBI vehicles snaked down the driveway, The Sculptor could make out the handful of agents and state troopers who still littered the scene. His *Bacchus*, however, was gone—already on its way to the medical examiner's office, no doubt. The Sculptor shivered with excitement, felt his nipples grow hard at the thought of the FBI analyzing his work, of them dismantling his exhibit and deciphering the connection between his *Bacchus* and Dr. Hildy's *Slumbering in the Stone.* Yes, it was only a matter of time before everyone would begin to understand the message behind his work; only a matter of time before everyone would begin to finally *wake up*.

The Sculptor knew, of course, that the media and the FBI would soon brand him a serial killer, for like Michelangelo himself, his contemporaries did not have a name for what he *really* was; could not begin to grasp the depth of his tortured soul—that fountain of love and anguish, of beauty and divine insight from which his genius flowed, and from which his artistry craved release. Yes, they would think him a monster; would group him with other monsters and misinterpret his work as some demented, selfish pursuit in the vein of a Dahmer, a Gacy, or a Nilsen. The Sculptor had understood that from the beginning; had long ago resigned himself to the fact that only *after* his death—perhaps hundreds of years after— would the true nature of his artistry be fully comprehended by everyone.

Everyone, that is, except Dr. Catherine Hildebrant.

Yes, here in the present, only one person possessed an understanding, a *genius* on par with his own. And that person would soon become his mouthpiece—the vehicle through which he would get his message out to the world; the vehicle through which The Sculptor would wake them all from their slumber.

"Eye-Team Hotline," said the voice on the other end of the phone—a deep, *male* voice that The Sculptor immediately found alluring.

"Greetings," said The Sculptor. "And congratulations to WNRI and the Eye-Team for being the first to break the news on the discovery of Tommy Campbell. Judging from the amount of time I had to hold the line, I assume your operation there in Providence is being flooded with calls about the case, am I correct?"

"What can I do for you, sir?" said the voice impatiently—an impatience that The Sculptor found endearing.

"Perhaps you should be asking what *I* can do for *you*," chuckled The Sculptor. "You see, my friend, as a reward for WNRI's tenacity, I would like to offer you some information pertaining to the case—a *tip*, as those in your line of work are apt to call it."

"May I have your name?"

"If it's all right with you, my friend, I would like to remain anonymous. Surely that is par for the course on a day like today—a day when a lot of tidily-squat about what's what must be clogging up the pipes down there at W-N-R-I." The manner in which The Sculptor sang the station's call letters, like a cheesy radio announcer, had the unintended effect of irritating the investigator on the other end.

"Look, pal, we got a lot going on down here. I don't have time today for nonsense—"

"Now, now, let's not get testy. I could always call one of your competitors, and just think what your superiors would do to you if they found out you turned your back on perhaps the biggest story in your station's history."

"All right," sighed the investigator, unimpressed. "What have you got for me?"

"The FBI has brought in an expert to assist them with their investigation of Tommy Campbell's demise.

Her name is Dr. Catherine Hildebrant—H-I-L-D-E-B-R-A-N-T—and she is a professor of art history at Brown University."

"I'm sorry, you said art history?"

"That is correct. This can easily be confirmed by a quick tour of the school's Web site, and if you hurry—that is, if you're a real *go-getter* like that pretty redhead on the beat—you can confirm for yourself Dr. Hildebrant's involvement in the case. An unmarked FBI vehicle, a black Chevy Trailblazer I believe, will soon drop her off at her place of residence. If you review your latest footage of the crime scene, you'll be able to see the truck exiting the property. From what I can tell, the good doctor left Watch Hill not even ten minutes ago, and unless our friends with the Federal Bureau of Investigation have more goodies in store for her today, I expect that the same Chevy Trailblazer will put her back at 311 East George Street in about forty to fifty minutes—depending on traffic, of course."

"You said 311 East George Street?"

"I most certainly did."

"Why would the FBI be consulting an art history professor?"

"The bodies of Tommy Campbell and his companion were found in that wealthy banker's garden painted white like marble and posed upright in the form of a classical sculpture. Michelangelo's *Bacchus*, to be exact."

"I'm sorry, could you repeat that?"

"I'm sorry, I *cannot.* Hopefully, the powers-that-be at W-N-R-I are smart enough to record their hotline. Therefore, I suggest you review the tape and that footage and get a reporter over to Dr. Hildebrant's house as soon as possible. The arrival of the black FBI vehicle will be confirmation that I'm not full of poop."

The Sculptor hung up. His pulse had quickened— not because he was worried about getting caught; not because he was excited about all those pointed questions he imagined the press would soon be asking the FBI. No, The Sculptor's heart knocked at his chest because of his conversation, his flirtation with the man on the other end of the hotline—a man whose voice had aroused him greatly.

Indeed, The Sculptor was already erect—could feel the hard nakedness of his penis pressing against the underside of the desk. And like a blushing-pink Priapus he sauntered over to the mortician's table. From the space underneath, he unfolded a three-sectional arm, at the end of which was attached a small, flat-screen television. The Sculptor maneuvered it into place—adjusted the arm so the screen hovered about three feet above the head of the mortician's table— and then uncoiled the accompanying cables. He laid them carefully on the floor, plugging one into the wall and the other into a monitor on his computer desk. The screen above the mortician's table at once flickered into life, its image the same as the monitor before him. The Sculptor minimized the CNN.com Web site and double clicked on one of the desktop icons—a marble hand holding a bowl titled "*Bacchus2.*" The screen went blank for a moment, and then the countdown began—thirty seconds, grainy black and white that The Sculptor had designed to look like an old, wipe-style film countdown.

30 . . . 29 . . . 28 . . . 27 . . . 26 . . .

The Sculptor turned on the baroque guitar music

from his father's bedroom and flicked off all the monitors—all except the monitor above the mortician's table.

Then he turned out the lights.

19 . . . 18 . . . 17 . . . 16 . . .

The Sculptor crossed the darkened room and slid under the television screen onto his back—the cold steel of the mortician's table sending a shiver through his buttocks; the black and white numbers above him wiping into each other like circle ghosts on a clock.

11 . . . 10 . . . 9 . . .

The Sculptor smiled, took his shaft in his hand, and waited.

At *"2"* the screen went blank—the room, black—and a second later, just as it had materialized for Tommy Campbell, The Sculptor saw what he had been waiting for: a statue, dirty white against black, so that it appeared to be floating just inches above his face. However, whereas it was Michelangelo's *Bacchus* that had emerged from the darkness for Tommy Campbell, before The Sculptor now was *HIS Bacchus, HIS* creation. And as the marble white effigy of the Rebels wide receiver and his satyr companion began to rotate, unlike the mortician table's former occupant, The Sculptor felt no fear, no confusion at all.

No, in the three months since he had taken the life of Tommy Campbell—*especially in the last few weeks*—The Sculptor had been in this position many, many times.

The Sculptor began to stroke his penis—hard, but slow at first, as he had learned to do in order to time things *perfectly*. And just as Michelangelo's *Bacchus* had done for Tommy Campbell, the image before The Sculptor suddenly morphed into a close-up of the statue's head: the grapes, the leaves, the curly hair surrounding the wide receiver's drunken face—a gleaming white face with blank, porcelain eyes and a half-open mouth. The camera then panned down over Campbell's chest, over his bloated belly, and finally to his groin—to the place where The Sculptor had carefully removed the young man's penis.

And in a fortuitous stroke of timing—an almost *divine* coincidence that The Sculptor did not fail to notice—as the all-enveloping sound of Scarlatti's *Sonata in D Minor* faded into his *Sonata in E,* the image on the screen above faded into something else as well. Now it was just the face of Tommy Campbell—strapped to the table—filmed with a second, stationary camera that The Sculptor had set off to the side of the mortician's table.

"Pop, you there? Did I fall on the porch? They got me in traction or something?"

Once again there was the look of confusion on the star Rebel's face as the video above him commenced, as he tried to comprehend what he was seeing there in the darkness. The Sculptor instinctively focused his attention on Campbell's neck—had learned over the past month to watch his jugular vein, to time the strokes of his penis with the beating of the young man's heart. He kept his rhythm steady, mimicking Campbell's pulse while the wide receiver watched the image of Michelangelo's *Bacchus* rotate and morph above him.

"That's it," The Sculptor heard himself say off camera. *"Shake off your slumber, O son of Jupiter."*

The Sculptor literally skipped a breath when he saw Tommy Campbell attempt to turn his head—actually felt his stomach spasm with delight when he saw the young man's heart begin to beat faster in his neck.

"Who are you? What am I doing here?"

The Sculptor's breathing quickened as he watched Campbell begin to panic, watched him struggle against the straps. The Sculptor knew that the image above the muscle-bound footballer was moving again, panning down over Bacchus's chest, over his belly, to his hairless groin—to the place where his penis should have been.

"What the hell is going on?"

The Sculptor increased the speed, the intensity of his stroke—did not pause at the point in the video when the image above Campbell changed, when the young man finally saw *himself,* the clusters of grapes and vine leaves surrounding his face.

"What the fuck is—"

And as Tommy Campbell began to tremble violently on the screen above him, the heavy pounding of The Sculptor's hand finally joined him with his Bacchus's heart.

"This can't be happening. I must be dreaming!"

"No, my Bacchus. You are finally awake."

And thus, as he had done so many times before, at the precise moment of his Bacchus's release, The Sculptor once again released *himself* into the darkness of their divine communion.

Chapter 10

The two of them were alone again, and when Special Agent Sam Markham finally spoke to her, Cathy Hildebrant felt as if she had been interrupted while watching a primetime crime drama—one of those woodenly acted, corpse-ridden soaps with which she had become so infatuated, and which she was so embarrassed to admit to her colleagues she actually *followed*. Even upon hearing Markham's voice, even upon recognizing the traffic light at which they were stopped—a traffic light that subliminally spoke to her of the silent twenty minutes she and the FBI agent had traveled from Watch Hill—Cathy still had only a vague, detached awareness that the movie she had been watching in her mind had been real and that she had been its *star*.

"You ever been there?" Markham asked.

"I'm sorry, what did you say?"

"The University of Rhode Island. Sign back there said you make a left at the light. Your head seemed to follow it as we passed."

"I'm sorry. I didn't realize I was looking at it."

"College town means there's probably a Starbucks nearby. Interested in a cup of coffee? Want me to check the GPS?"

"No, thank you."

The light turned green and Markham drove on.

"Yes," Cathy said after a moment.

"Change your mind?"

"No. I meant, yes I've been to the University of Rhode Island. Only once. As a guest speaker a few years back when my book came out."

"You had a lot of speaking engagements? After your book was published, I mean?" The FBI Agent made no attempt at delicacy; no attempt to conceal that he was looking for yet another connection between Dr. Catherine Hildebrant and the killer in the movie of her mind. And all at once the weight, the reality of the last few hours came rushing back to her; all at once the tears overwhelmed her eyes.

"I'm sorry," said Markham. Cathy swallowed hard, and turned again toward the window. A long, uncomfortable silence followed.

"Been almost fifteen years since I was there last," Markham said finally. "At URI, I mean. Hardly remember it, really. Like you, I was there only once. With my wife, for homecoming during the fall. She was a graduate of their oceanography program. Had a real love for that school. Wasn't too crazy about it myself—football stadium was kind of dinky, I thought. I guess it was supposed to be a pretty good one back then—their oceanography program, I mean. Not sure what the story is now, though. Lot can happen in fifteen years."

Cathy suddenly realized that the FBI Agent had opted to take the longer route back to Providence—

Route 1 instead of I-95—and more than the sincerity of his attempt at small talk, more than his disclosure of something personal, what settled Cathy's tears was Sam Markham's tone—a tone that for the first time that day was hesitant and awkward; a tone that for the first time that day made him seem *human.*

"That's an interesting pairing," said Cathy—surprised at the sound of her voice, at how eager she was to talk about anything but the day's events. "How does an FBI agent end up marrying an oceanographer?"

"I wasn't with the Bureau back then. Was actually a high school English teacher when I met my wife."

"Aha. So *that* explains it."

"Explains what?"

"The sonnet."

"The sonnet?"

"Yes. I thought your analysis of Michelangelo's poetry seemed a little too erudite, a little too *insightful* even for an FBI profiler." The special agent nodded his approval—playfully and with exaggerated admiration. "My first clue should have been during our initial drive to Watch Hill, when you asked me if the sonnet that I received had been numbered like a Shakespearean sonnet."

"Nonetheless," said Markham, smiling, "an admirable analysis of the evidence, Dr. Hildebrant."

Cathy smiled back.

"I have to admit," he continued, "I'm a bit ashamed that I didn't know about Michelangelo's poetry. Perhaps I did at one time—way back when. But I've been with the Bureau for almost thirteen years now, and I guess you forget all that stuff if you don't keep up with it."

"You forget it even if you *do* keep up with it. At least that's the way it's been for me since about thirty or so."

"Forty's no better."

"You don't look it."

"I still got four months."

"I've got one year, six months, and twenty-three days."

Markham laughed—and, unexpectedly, Cathy joined him.

"Ah well," the FBI agent sighed. "I guess I'll buy a convertible. Or maybe a motorcycle. Isn't that what you're supposed to do when you turn forty?"

"I'm not going to find out—going to stop counting at thirty-nine."

"Sounds like a plan. But I'd buy twenty-nine from you in a heartbeat."

Cathy was unsure if Markham had meant his last comment as a compliment—that is, if he was saying he would peg her for twenty-nine-years-old, or that he would figuratively "purchase" the age of twenty-nine from her for himself. And suddenly Cathy was transported back to college, to those rare but awkward one-time dates with men who mistook her shyness for aloofness, her intellect for arrogance. And despite the anxiety such memories brought with them, Cathy could feel herself beginning to blush as the FBI agent drove on in silence.

She hoped he didn't notice.

"So how does a high school English teacher end up marrying an oceanographer?" Cathy asked at the next traffic light—her need to keep the conversation going, to push through her discomfort outweighing her usual bashfulness.

"I wish I had a romantic story for you, Dr. Hildebrant—"

"Please, call me Cathy."

"All right. I wish I had a more romantic story for you, Cathy. But my wife and I met at a cookout in Connecticut—one of those mutual-friend-of-a-friend deals. She was still in graduate school at the time, but was working at the Mystic Aquarium in their Institute for Exploration. I had just landed a part-time teaching job in a little town nearby. You know the story. 'Hey, I've got a friend I want you to meet,' one thing leads to another, the hand of fate and all that. You get the idea."

"Sounds familiar, yes."

"Same for you?"

"Oh yes. My boss, Janet Polk. The woman you met this morning—the hand that pushed *me*."

"Aha."

"Twelve years ago. She was the friend of my husband's friend who introduced us—my soon to be *ex*-husband, I should say."

"I'm sorry about that. Dr. Polk didn't come right out and say what happened, but I put two and two together when we traced your address to East George Street. You've always kept your maiden name? Never took your husband's for professional reasons?"

"Never took it, no—partly for professional reasons, partly because my mother always kept her maiden name. Korean tradition. Most Korean women keep their family name. She never asked me, but I knew it would make her happy. So, like she had done for her father, I kept my father's name. Nonetheless, an admirable analysis of the evidence, Agent Markham."

The FBI agent smiled with a *touché*.

"Please, call me Sam."

"All right then, Agent Sam. And please don't be sorry. Best thing to happen to me in ten years of marriage will be my divorce decree next month. Janet's the one for whom you should feel sorry. Really. She feels worse about it than I do—almost like she's the one who's responsible for the whole thing. Even asked me if I wanted my ex's legs broken. And you know what? I think she meant it, too—think she meant to do it *herself*."

Markham laughed.

"Don't let her size fool you. She's a real ass kicker, that Janet Polk. Didn't get to where she is today on just her smarts, I'll tell you that much."

"A bit protective of you, is she?"

"Oh yes. Been that way from the beginning—ever since I was her assistant at Harvard. And when my mother died . . . well . . . let's just say Janet was the only one who was really there for me." Cathy felt her chest, her stomach tighten at the thought of Steve Rogers's ultimatum; the teary-eyed, whimpering "end of his rope" speech that he delivered not even two months after her mother's death, when the length and depth of Cathy's grief had simply become too much for him.

"I'm begging you, Cat. You've got to snap out of it. I'm at the end of my rope with you. This isn't good for us. You've got to try to move on, get past it. For us, Cat. For us."

It wasn't so much what her spineless excuse for a husband had said that still bothered Cathy, but that she, a Harvard educated PhD—perhaps *the* foremost scholar on Michelangelo in the *world*—had actually *bought into* his selfishness. Yes, what really set Cathy's blood boiling there in the Trailblazer was the thought that, at the very moment when her husband should have been there for her, she abandoned her mourning to take care of *him*—not because he needed her, but because she was afraid of losing him.

That was the beginning of the end. Should have handed the selfish motherfucker his balls back right then and there.

"May I ask how it happened?"

"He cheated. With one of his graduate students."

"I'm sorry. But I meant your mother."

"Oh," Cathy said, embarrassed. "Forgive me—my mind is going in a thousand different directions. Breast cancer. Fought it for years, but in the end it took her quickly. I suppose you could say she was lucky in that respect. You know, the statistics say that Korean women have one of the lowest incidences of breast cancer in the United States. I guess nobody got around to telling my mother that."

"I'm sorry, Cathy."

"Thank you." Cathy smiled, for she knew Markham was sincere. "Anyway, Janet was the one who really helped me get through it all, from the time my mother was first diagnosed until the end—and afterward, of course. Helped me stay on track to get the book published, to get tenure and all that. Even before everything happened, I always thought of her as sort of a second mother."

"And what about your father?"

"Retired military. Army. Lives somewhere down in North Carolina now with his second wife—the woman with whom he was cheating on my mother. They divorced when I was in the third grade—he and my mother, I mean—right after she and I moved to Rhode Island."

"So you grew up around here?"

"Since the third grade, yes. My mother had a

cousin who lived in Cranston—helped the two of us get settled—and she ended up getting her degree in computers. Carved out a nice little life for the two of us. Before that, I moved around like the typical Army brat. We were all stationed in Italy, near Pisa, when my father met his second wife. She was Army, too. It was after all that went down that my mother and I settled back in the States."

"Italy. Let me guess. Is that where you first became interested in Michelangelo?"

"Yes. My mother was only eighteen when she married my father—met him while he was stationed in Korea. Ever since she was a child she had wanted to become an artist, but back then things weren't so easy for Korean girls. And being one of five sisters, well, her parents were more than happy to marry her off to an American GI. Anyway, ever since I can remember—since the day I was born, I think—no matter where we were stationed, she used to take me along with her to all the local museums. And during the two years we were stationed in Italy, well, you can imagine the time we had together. I don't remember much from our first trip to Florence, but my mother used to say that the first time I saw Michelangelo's *David* I actually started crying—that I thought the statue was a real man, a *giant* who had been frozen in ice, and that I cried for him out of pity."

Markham laughed.

"It was funnier to hear her tell it. She was a lovely woman, my mother—very bright, very witty. Never remarried, either. Everything for her daughter. She was only fifty-two when she passed."

"I really am sorry, Cathy."

"I know."

"And your father?" Markham asked after a moment. "You talk to him much?"

"Once in a great while," Cathy shrugged. "Even before my parents divorced we were never very close. Last time I saw him was at the funeral—was surprised he even showed up, to be honest with you. Paid his child support over the years, but that was pretty much the extent of our relationship. Didn't really want anything to do with my mother and me after the divorce. At least, that's how my mother put it. I know my father would probably tell you different, that it was my mother that took me away from him, but . . . well, you know, actions speak louder than words and all that. I haven't talked to him in almost two years now, I think. Has no idea about what happened with Steve."

"Steve?"

"My ex."

"Ah, yes. Of course."

"And what about you? You said you were working in Connecticut when you met your wife. Did you grow up there?"

"Yes. Waterford. Parents are still there, too. Happily married now for almost fifty years."

"And your wife? How long you two been married?"

"My wife and I are no longer together," Markham said flatly. "But we were married just over two years."

"Wish *I* had signed up for the two-year plan. Less investment; less time wasted—get out of it while you're still young. At least you can look at it that way. I do hope yours wasn't like mine, though—hope it ended amicably."

Markham smiled but said nothing, and suddenly Cathy felt as if she had said something wrong—as if she had gotten too personal, as if she had somehow offended the FBI agent. They drove on in silence for what to Cathy seemed like an eternity—her mind scrambling for a segue to continue their conversation. She had just settled her mind on *"I'm sorry"* when Markham finally spoke.

"You must be hungry. Shall I pick you up something before I drop you off back at your house?"

"No, thank you. I have some leftovers in the fridge that I want to finish before they spoil. But thanks anyway."

Markham and Cathy exchanged sporadic small talk for the rest of the trip back to Providence— pleasant for the most part, but lacking the spontaneity, the easiness of their earlier conversation. And by the time Sam Markham reached the Upper East Side, Cathy was filled with a vague sadness reminiscent of those late hours alone in her dorm room at Harvard—that disappointed "postgame analysis" wherein the shy young woman would pick apart her date over and over again in an attempt to figure out why things had gone south. And even though over the course of the day she had hardly begun to think of her time with the FBI agent as romantic, as anything other than professional, when Markham turned onto East George Street, as much as she hated to admit it, Cathy was worried she might not ever see him again.

"I'll be in touch with you soon, Cathy," he said, reading her mind. "Word's already come down from Quantico that I'll be working local for a while. Until the Boston off—"

Had Cathy not been looking at Markham, had she not been so relieved by what the special agent had told her, she most certainly would have spotted the Channel 9 Mobile News Room before he did. And upon following the FBI agent's gaze, Cathy immediately recognized the white van pulling up to the curb about a hundred feet up the street. There, in front of her house, was the obnoxious yellow 9 with the big blue eye at its center—the same big blue eye that had stared back at her so many times from her television set; the same big blue eye that had watched her leave Dodd's estate less than an hour ago.

"I was afraid of this," said Markham, pulling over. "Damn small town police."

Cathy did not need the FBI agent to tell her that the big blue eye had seen them coming, for even before she and Sam Markham emerged from the Trailblazer, a cameraman and a reporter with a microphone had already positioned themselves at the end of Cathy's walkway.

Markham's cell phone rang.

"Yes? Yes, I see them. No, I'll take care of it. Uh huh. Okay."

Markham hung up.

"I'll deal with these clowns," he said, turning off the ignition. "But let's get you inside first. Don't say anything."

Markham put his arm around Cathy and quickly escorted her to her house, shielding her from the reporter's microphone as they passed.

"Ms. Hildebrant," the reporter shouted. "Can you tell us why you were brought in by the FBI to help with the investigation into Tommy Campbell's murder?"

Cathy felt her stomach drop, felt her heart leap into her throat as she and Sam Markham mounted the front steps to her porch.

"Ms. Hildebrant," the reporter called again. Cathy could not see him, but could tell by the proximity of his voice that the reporter was following her up the walkway. "Is it true Tommy Campbell's body was found posed like a statue in Earl Dodd's garden? A statue by Michelangelo?"

Cathy—at the door fumbling with her keys—felt Sam Markham leave her.

"This is private property," she heard the FBI agent say calmly. "Please move back to the sidewalk."

The reporter ignored him.

"Ms. Hildebrant, is it true Tommy Campbell's body was painted white like a statue by Michelangelo called *Bacchus?*"

Cathy did not see Sam Markham push the camera, did not see him make a grab for the reporter's arm as she entered her apartment.

"Hands off the equipment, pal," Cathy heard the reporter say. She turned around only when she was safely behind the storm door, and saw that the Channel 9 Eye-Team was now backing away from Markham down the walkway.

"I'm a federal agent and you're trespassing on private property," said Markham, holding up his ID badge. "If you won't comply with my verbal command, I have the legal authority to escort you from the premises by force. Now I've warned you once. Please stay off this property."

The reporter was unfazed.

"Can you tell us whether or not there is any truth to the claim that the bodies of Tommy Campbell and another person were posed like this *Bacchus?* Are you aware of what this statue looks like? That the other body could be that of a child?"

"I am not at liberty to comment on the case at present. A press conference has been scheduled—might have even started. If you hurry, you might be able to catch it."

Special Agent Sam Markham headed back toward Cathy's house, leaving the reporter on the sidewalk to call after him with a barrage of unanswered questions.

"Sorry about that," Markham said once he was inside. "Someone, a local cop probably, must have leaked your involvement with the case. I didn't expect them to find out so soon—didn't expect them to come after you."

Cathy was shaken; she just stood there in the front hall—arms folded, heart racing.

"Are you all right?"

"Yes," she said, looking at the floor. "I really am involved in this, aren't I?"

"I'm sorry, but yes." Markham reached into his jacket pocket. "Here's my card. Call me on my cell anytime if you need anything—if you get spooked, if you think of something down the road that might help us with our investigation, or even if you just need to talk. We've had some agents watching your place since this morning. That's who called me a few minutes ago—said the news van had arrived only seconds before we did. Bad timing for you and me, but that's just the way things are. Now listen, Cathy, these agents are going to keep an eye on you for a while—for your safety, and in case Tommy Campbell's killer tries to approach you. You most likely will never see them, so please try to forget they're around, okay?"

"Forget? You mean, you're saying you think Tommy Campbell's killer will come after me now? And you want me to forget?"

"No. Actually, Cathy, I don't think he'll come after

you at all. In fact, judging from my experience, I would say that the circumstances suggest just the opposite. Campbell's killer went out of his way to draw attention to you. The last thing he'd want now is to see something happen to you. No, he'll most likely stay away from you for a while now that he's finished his work and now that other people are aware of his connection with you. All this is just a precaution, Cathy, in case he tries to make contact with you, to leave you another note—that is, if the notes you received five years ago are related to Campbell's murder to begin with."

"They are, Sam. You know they are."

"I can't be sure—might be just a strange coincidence. However, since it's all we have to go on right now, we'll see how far that road leads us. Now listen carefully, Cathy. Even though the press somehow got wind of what happened to Campbell and that boy, and even though they know you've been brought into the investigation, I'm not sure if they know yet about the inscription at the base of the statue. Hopefully we'll be able to keep that detail quiet for a while. That said, even after the press conference this afternoon, I suggest you don't say anything to anyone about the case—more for your own sake than for the integrity of the investigation. Say you've been advised not to discuss the case with the press. That'll usually send them packing after a while. Trust me, Cathy, the last thing you want right now is for the press to know the extent to which you're involved in this. In fact, if my gut is right, I think that's just what the killer wants to happen."

"What do you mean?"

"It's obvious that whoever murdered Tommy Campbell and that boy had been planning this crime for a long time—perhaps even years. Although I'm sure there must be a deeper reason as to exactly why the killer chose Campbell for his *Bacchus,* one cannot deny the superficial resemblance between the football player and Michelangelo's original. That means, in addition to my earlier theory about the connection with Tommaso Cavalieri, the killer could possibly have selected Campbell simply for the reason that he *looked like Bacchus.* He wanted to use him, like Dodd's topiary garden, specifically for aesthetic purposes, and was willing to go to great lengths to do so—would not settle for a more, I hate to say it, *convenient* victim. So, you see? Even though we're not sure yet of his motives, we can nonetheless conclude that we're dealing with a very patient and methodical individual—obsessively so on both accounts. These types of killers are the hardest to catch because they plan so well—pay so much attention to detail and don't leave many clues behind. And until the autopsy results come back, until we get an idea of exactly how this person murdered and preserved his victims—how he actually created that sick sculpture of his—the only window into his motives right now is *you.* You and your book."

"So you're saying you think this maniac is using me?"

"Perhaps. I'll have a better idea once I read your book. But judging from the great lengths to which the killer went to put his sculpture on display in Dodd's garden—a display that the killer obviously intended as some kind of historical allusion publicly dedicated to you—well, it's clear to me, Cathy, that whoever did this horrible crime thought you of all people would understand his motives. And therefore it would also fall to you to help us—the FBI, the press, the public—understand his motives as well. So you see,

Cathy, it appears the killer wants you to be his mouth-piece."

Cathy was silent, dumbfounded—her mind swept up in a tornado of questions that numbed her into disbelief.

"I'll be in touch very soon, Cathy. And remember to call me if you need anything, okay?"

Cathy nodded absently; heard herself say "thank you" in a voice far away.

A blink forward in time to her cell phone ringing in the kitchen, upon which she realized she'd been zoning in the hall.

However, only when Cathy heard Janet Polk say "Hildy?" on the other end did she realize Sam Markham had left.

Chapter 11

Laurie Wenick stood before the open refrigerator and began to tremble. It had been seven months since her son's disappearance, *seven months* since he failed to come home for dinner one afternoon—a cool, otherwise lovely September afternoon when his friends said they left him playing in the woods around Blackamore Pond. And so it happened that, when Laurie stared down at the cold jar of Smucker's in her hand, when she realized that for the first time in seven months she had unconsciously gone to the refrigerator to prepare her son's lunch for the next day—peanut butter and jelly on homemade bread that her son said made all the other fourth graders at Eden Park Elementary School jealous—more than grief, more than the profound loneliness to which she had grown accustomed, the single mother of one was overwhelmed with a sweeping sense of panic—a premonition that *something very, very bad had happened.*

She had gone to bed at 8:00 A.M. like she usually did on Sundays; had worked the night shift at Rhode

Island Hospital as she had done now for months—
for it was the nighttime, the *darkness* of her Cranston
duplex that had become too much for Laurie
Wenick to bear. And on those rare occasions when
she took the night off, the pretty young nurse would
spend her evenings next door at her father's—alone,
watching TV until the sun came up, at which point
she would return to her apartment and sleep through
the day. She was like "a vampire" her father said—a
rare and ineffectual stab at humor in what for both
of them had become a dark and humorless world.

Indeed, despite her anguish, Laurie had understood from the beginning that her son's disappearance had devastated her father almost as much as it
had her; and over the last seven months the two of
them had often traded shoulders for each other in
their moments of greatest weakness. At first their sorrow had been colored with the hope that Michael
Wenick would be found, for this was *Rhode Island,*
and children simply *did not go missing in Rhode Island,*
did not disappear into thin air *without a trace.* Oh yes,
Laurie had read the statistics, had spoken with the
state police countless times about her son; and as far
as she could tell there was only one missing child
case still unsolved in the Ocean State—and that one
went all the way back to the mid-1980s.

However, as the days then weeks plodded on, as
divers scoured Blackamore Pond a second and then
a third time, as the volunteer searches ended and the
pictures appeared on the news less frequently, the
statistics that claimed young Michael Wenick would
return to Laurie and her father safe and sound were
soon overshadowed by the grim reality of the contrary. And when the months began to pile up, when
Christmas came and went without a single clue to

her son's whereabouts, Laurie and her father fell deeper and deeper into a state of numb detachment. It was as if the two of them existed in a zone somewhere between life and death—a pair of zombies, Laurie thought, who had the unique ability to watch themselves as they mechanically went through the motions of living.

Ever since Michael Wenick was born it had been just the three of them in that duplex on Lexington Avenue—the cute, two-story one at the bottom of the hill not even fifty yards from the shores of Blackamore Pond. Laurie's parents divorced when she was in kindergarten, but she had only lived with her father since her senior year of high school—moved in with him when her mother threw her out of the house for getting herself pregnant. Laurie's boyfriend, Michael's father, took off to live with relatives in Florida never to be heard from again—a bit of pretty luck for which John Wenick was always secretly thankful. The burly ex-club boxer never liked his daughter's boyfriend—that rap-loving, baggy-panted punk with the license plate GNGSTA1. In fact, John Wenick had actually gone after the son of a bitch with a baseball bat when Laurie showed up in tears on his doorstep—her boyfriend, she had said, had denied the baby was his. Yes, John Wenick would have buried his Louisville Slugger deep in the scrawny Eminem-wannabe's head had he found him; most certainly would have ended up in jail for murder. And only after he calmed down, only after the little fucker ran away to Florida two days later did John Wenick wonder if it also hadn't been a stroke of luck that "Gangsta Number One" had been off getting stoned with his friends when he had gone looking for him.

John Wenick worked for the state; had been a supervisor at the landfill for over twenty years. And after his grandson was born, he scraped enough of his savings together to place a down payment on the duplex at the bottom of the hill—the same duplex in which he had lived ever since his divorce from Laurie's mother. Between himself and his ex-wife, John Wenick knew that he had always been Laurie's favorite, for he had a special bond with his daughter that his alcoholic ex could never understand. And even though Laurie's mother retained custody of her after the divorce, their relationship at best had always been strained. And so it was only natural that Laurie should have spent the majority of her time at her father's—that is, until she started hanging out with Gangsta Number One. And so it was *also* only natural that John Wenick should have felt somewhat responsible for his daughter's predicament—that if only he had kept an eye on her, if only he had kicked Gangsta Number One's ass at the beginning, all this would never have happened. Hence, John Wenick decided to let Laurie live with him *for good*—was more than happy to set up his daughter and little Michael next door; actually considered it his duty to look after the boy when Laurie enrolled in nursing school.

But more than a sense of responsibility, more than a sense of obligation, John Wenick looked after his grandson because he loved him as if he were his own. And ever since little Michael was five years old, almost every Saturday morning during the summers the two of them could be found fishing at the end of the short driveway that branched off from Lexington Avenue to the woody banks of Blackamore Pond. Without a doubt, Michael Wenick loved to fish more than anything else in the world—even more than the Nintendo *Wii* his grandfather had bought for him the previous Christmas. And how thrilled Michael had been when, the summer before he disappeared, his grandfather took him fishing on a boat off the coast of Block Island! For young Michael Wenick it had been the experience of his short lifetime; for his grandfather, it had been only one of the many happy chapters fate had written since his daughter moved in with him for good nine years earlier.

And so it came as an unfathomable shock to the Wenicks—to the entire community, to the entire state—when on a cool September afternoon sometime between 4:30 and 6:00 little Michael Wenick vanished without a trace from the woods around Blackamore Pond. The Wenicks and the people of Lexington Avenue could never have dreamed of such a thing happening in their neighborhood—in the very woods where their children played; in the very woods where they *themselves* had played when they were children, too. No, the Wenicks, the police, the people of Cranston had no idea that a stranger had entered their midst; had no idea that The Sculptor had been watching little Michael Wenick for weeks—ever since he randomly spotted him walking home from the Cranston Pool one day with two of his companions. Yes, The Sculptor knew immediately that the boy's slight, somewhat small-for-his-age torso would be *perfect* for the upper half of his satyr. And whereas Laurie and John Wenick would never have been able to comprehend the possibility that fate would soon snatch their little Michael from their lives, The Sculptor had understood upon the sight of him that he and his satyr had been destined to come together that day.

And so The Sculptor studied his satyr's movements—followed him home, always at a distance, at first from the pool during the summer, and then from Eden Park Elementary School in the fall; watched him from across the water as he fished with an older man with forearms like Popeye; spied on him with binoculars while he played with his two friends by the big drainpipe in the woods at the northern edge of Blackamore Pond. The satyr was the smallest of the three boys, but he more than made up for his size in daring. Someone, perhaps an older kid, had attached a rope to one of the larger branches, and on many occasions The Sculptor watched the two bigger boys look on in awe as his satyr swung like Tarzan farther and farther out over Blackamore Pond. One afternoon, the tallest of the three boys brought some firecrackers, and The Sculptor could not help but laugh out loud when he saw his satyr drop one into an empty beer bottle and then dive behind a tree.

Yes, The Sculptor had thought. *My satyr certainly is a mischievous one.*

And perhaps it was ultimately Michael Wenick's mischievousness that brought him and The Sculptor together on that cool September afternoon. The Sculptor had discovered that often his satyr would remain behind in the woods after his companions had gone home for dinner, whereupon he would throw various objects out into the water—usually just large stones, but sometimes bottles and cans, and once even a rubber tire. But always his satyr stayed close to the big drainpipe, or to the tiny, open shoreline beneath the high cement retaining wall of one of the backyards that directly overlooked the pond. And so The Sculptor decided that the safer of the two areas would be by the big drainpipe, for in order to capture his satyr he could not allow himself to be seen; yes, in order to acquire the first figure for his *Bacchus* he would have to be very, very careful.

The Sculptor had studied the satellite imagery of Blackamore Pond many times on *Yahoo! Maps*, but the first time he actually set foot in the surrounding woods was at night—after the older kids who smoked cigarettes and drank beer by the retaining wall had all gone home. He parked his blue Toyota Camry—one of two cars he owned in addition to his big white van—on a street nearby and used his night vision goggles to negotiate his way through the dense terrain.

The mouth of the drainpipe was large enough even for him to crouch into, and with his night vision The Sculptor had no trouble seeing down almost half the length of the shaft. He slipped a plastic bag over each of his sneakers, a plastic glove over each of his hands, and entered the pipe. The smell was not too bad—musty and swampy—but the air felt uncomfortably thick and damp in The Sculptor's lungs. Fortunately, The Sculptor had to go only about forty yards before he found what he was looking for: the manhole cover and the runoff opening to the adjoining street. Here, in the storm drain at the end of the pipe, The Sculptor could stand up straight; could see his tires through the narrow slit in the curb—right where he parked his car not even fifteen minutes earlier. And with a heavy push, The Sculptor lifted the manhole cover and peeked out.

The location was perfect.

As he had learned from *Yahoo! Maps*, the storm drain was located at the end of a street named Shirley Boulevard—a quiet, middle-class lane just two blocks over from Lexington Avenue, the street on which his satyr lived with the Popeye-armed fisherman and the pretty blond nurse who drove a Hyundai. The Sculptor had cased this part of Shirley Boulevard during the daytime; knew that most of the people did not return home until around 5:15 P.M.; knew that even in broad daylight the surrounding foliage would conceal him from the nearby houses when he emerged from the manhole—a manhole that was just big enough for the massively muscled Sculptor to squeeze through. There was no sidewalk here, only a concrete slab that capped the sewer opening. And thus The Sculptor also knew that he would be vulnerable only from across the street; knew that it would be safer to get in and out of his car from the passenger's side, upon which he could drop directly into the manhole.

It was almost too good to be true.

And so it was that The Sculptor waited in the drainpipe on four different occasions before he finally abducted Michael Wenick. Yes, there was always the chance that the satyr and his companions might venture into the drainpipe and discover him. And even though in the weeks that The Sculptor had been watching the boys he never once saw them step into the mouth of the dank, dark tube—*probably already conquered that fear years ago*, The Sculptor thought—nonetheless he was prepared with his night vision goggles and the silencer on his Sig Sauer .45 just in case. He did not want to kill the satyr's companions—did not want to waste good material that others might want to use someday. However, The Sculptor had resigned himself from the beginning that he would do whatever was necessary to capture his satyr. Most of all, if he did as a last resort have to kill the satyr himself before he could get him back to the carriage house, he would try to aim for the back of his head. Yes, more important than his satyr's awakening was The Sculptor's desire not to damage his material.

Besides, The Sculptor thought, *it is only through* Bacchus's *awakening that the world shall be enlightened.*

In the end, however, The Sculptor's contingency plan was unnecessary. For on the last of the four consecutive afternoons in which he had waited in the sewer, when he saw by his watch that it was 4:35, when he crept to the edge of the shadows just shy of the entrance to the pipe, The Sculptor had a clear view of his satyr a few yards away at the shore. Finally he was alone—had thrown a beer bottle filled with dirt into the water and was trying to shatter it with rocks before it sank into the murky, polluted depths of Blackamore Pond. And before poor Michael Wenick had time to turn around at the sound of footsteps behind him, like a snake The Sculptor snatched him from the woody shoreline and pulled him back into the drainpipe.

The boy tried to scream, tried to struggle against his abductor's grip as the darkness of the drainpipe closed in around him, but the catcher's mitt–size hand over his mouth, the vicelike grip around his neck and torso was too much for him—so much so that by the time The Sculptor got Michael Wenick back to the storm drain at the other end the boy was already dead.

No, not until he released Michael Wenick and the boy's lifeless body fell to the ground did The Sculptor realize that, as he had struggled and twisted with his satyr down the drainpipe, he had inadvertently snapped the boy's neck; no, not until that very moment did The Sculptor truly understand his own strength. And just as he had not needed to use his .45 on the satyr's companions, the nylon cord and the bottle of chloroform that he had brought with him would now be unnecessary also. The Sculptor thus stuffed the boy's body in a duffel bag and slid off the manhole cover. The coast clear, he pushed the bag onto the concrete slab and lifted himself out of the sewer.

In less than a minute The Sculptor had gathered his things and was speeding away down Shirley Boulevard—his satyr stowed safely in the duffel bag on the backseat. And although he was somewhat disappointed that his little satyr would not be able to see what lay in store for him, would not be able to awaken before the image of what he was to become, as The Sculptor drove back to his home in East Greenwich, he nonetheless felt a bit giddy that the first part of his plan had been so successful.

Yes, it had almost been *too easy.*

Had Laurie Wenick known at that moment exactly what had happened to her son; had she known on that cool September afternoon that her little Michael had been spared the terror, the *brutality* of The Sculptor's plans for him back at the carriage house, she most likely would not have been comforted. Indeed, as she stared down at the jar of Smucker's jelly in her hands, the pretty young nurse felt all at once as if the ordeal of the last seven months was suddenly tumbling down on her. She began to hyperventilate, to tremble, and nearly dropped the jar of jelly before she fumbled it onto the counter.

Something had happened. Something was wrong.

Laurie could *feel* it.

She had not turned on the television since before going to bed that morning—had been sleeping her vampire's sleep when the news of Tommy Campbell made the headlines. And so it happened that, as she stood shivering with panic in the kitchen, Laurie Wenick was entirely unaware that the star Rebel's corpse had been discovered down at Watch Hill. Even if she had been watching TV when the story broke; even if she had learned that *another* body had been found along with Campbell's, Laurie would not have made the connection with her son—for the state police, the FBI had long ago ruled out any link between the disappearance of Tommy Campbell and that of little Michael Wenick. In fact, the authorities had insisted on just the *opposite*, and even though she was more than willing to believe them, in the months following the wide receiver's disappearance Laurie began to resent the constant media attention given to the case—a case that completely overshadowed her own. Indeed, the Campbell case made Laurie feel as if her son had been abducted all over again— even if it was only from the minds of her fellow Rhode Islanders.

On any other day, had Laurie Wenick not reached for the jar of jelly, had she gone instead for her coffee and settled herself in front of the television as she usually did before work, the press conference that was beginning on the steps of the Westerly Police station might have actually come as a relief to her—for now, with the discovery of Tommy Campbell, the authorities and the media would once again focus on the search for her son. Today, however, in the wake of her panic, in the wake of her *premonition*, had she had time to get to the remote before the doorbell

rang—despite what the authorities had told her in
the past, despite all the assurances that the disappearances of Tommy Campbell and her son were not
related—Laurie Wenick would have understood at
once that the unidentified body of which the FBI
Agent was speaking was her son Michael.

Instead, Laurie stood frozen before the refrigerator
as the doorbell dinged a second time—the chimes
from the other room clanging in her ears like church
bells. And like an egg, Laurie's mind suddenly cracked
with the numb realization that it could not be her father—that it was too early for him to have returned
from hunting crows in Connecticut with her uncle.

Here again was the zombie—her movements not
her own, watching herself as she made her way to the
front door. Through the peephole, she saw two
men—*serious looking men* with short hair and blue
jackets. Laurie did not recognize them—*had never
met them before*—but knew them nonetheless; had
seen many others like them in the last seven months.
A voice somewhere in the back of her mind assured
her that the storm door was locked just in case (for
her father taught her *always* to lock the storm door)
and Laurie watched herself—*that woman in the bathrobe,
that woman who looks so tired and hollow*—turn the dead
bolt.

"Yes?"

The man on the front steps held up his ID. His lips
were moving but Laurie could not hear him through
the glass; for upon the sight of those three little letters—*FBI*—Laurie Wenick went deaf with the overwhelming terror of understanding.

No, little Michael Wenick's mother did not need
the FBI, the press conference in Westerly to tell her
why she had reached for the jar of jelly. She would

have been unable to hear them anyway; for just as her fragile eggshell mind cracked again under the weight of her anguish, the once pretty young nurse watched herself collapse into the black.

Yes, all at once Laurie Wenick fainted, for all at once she knew that her son was dead.

Chapter 12

Bill Burrell sat with Thomas Campbell Sr. in his den, their coffee long gone cold. Neither of them had drunk much, for their cups were only props in a scene they had played many times over the last three months. The set was the same—the comfy leather chairs, the bookcases, the warm paneled walls peppered with family photographs. Today, however, the mood, the *color* of the scene was different, for today the wealthy businessman had finally learned what had become of his only son. And as Special Agent Rachel Sullivan concluded her press conference on the television in the corner, as if on cue a thud was heard above Burrell's head.

"She'll be fine," said Campbell, clicking the remote. "Her sister is up there with her. Probably dropped something is all."

In the awkward silence that followed, Burrell took a sip of his cold coffee. Instant. Bitter. Maggie Campbell did not make it for him today; did not brew her special blend of Sumatra as she usually did on the SAC's visits. No, Burrell had learned from Agent Sullivan that, upon identifying her son, upon seeing him frozen white in the horror that was *Bacchus*, Maggie Campbell had gone first into shock, then into a fit of inconsolable hysteria—so much so that by the time Burrell arrived at the house on Foster Cove later that afternoon, Tommy Campbell's mother had since collapsed into her bed upstairs, exhausted from her bout with borderline madness. And save for the handful of reporters that still lingered at the end of the driveway, the house in which Rhode Island's favorite son grew up was as quiet as a tomb.

"Someone was found dead on this property, too," Campbell said. "Did you know that, Bill?"

Burrell looked up from his coffee. Thomas Campbell was staring back at him blankly—his eyes like slits, red from weeping; a haggard shell of the man standing with his son in the photograph on the bookshelf behind him.

"In the summer of 1940," Campbell continued. "Out on the front lawn, a caretaker for the family who owned the house before us. Story goes he was attacking their boy, and a couple of strangers just happened to be passing by. Stabbed the guy dead and then took off. The boy was there the whole time— saw the whole thing. Went on to become a famous movie director—made all those horror pictures in the sixties and seventies. Died last year. Remember him?"

Burrell nodded vaguely.

"Saw a bunch of his movies when I was a kid— scared the hell out of me. We bought the house from his uncle—gosh, going on almost thirty years ago now. Nice old fella—his uncle, I mean. A lot of those old-timers around here still remember all that—the story about the murder and all. Tommy had heard that story, too. When he was a kid. And for years he used to swear that there was a ghost in this house. You know how kids are. But you know what, Bill? I remember him telling me, even when he was little, that he wasn't afraid—that he hoped they could be friends someday, he and the ghost. Isn't that something? A little kid not being afraid of ghosts?"

Burrell nodded, looking down again at his cup.

"That's the kind of boy my Tommy was," Campbell said, his voice beginning to break. "A good friend to everybody. Not afraid to love even a ghost."

"I know, Tom. He was a good kid. The best."

"It's why they took advantage of him out there in that world of his—those people, that slut model he asked to marry him. He was so trusting. He just thought that everybody who smiled at him meant it the same way he did when he smiled back—that's why that whoring cunt was able to break my boy's heart."

Burrell was silent. They had been over it before—had long ago exhausted the possibility that Tommy's ex-fiancée, Italian supermodel Victoria Magnone, was somehow involved in the star Rebel's disappearance. Even before Burrell had met Tommy Campbell's father, even before the wide receiver had gone missing, the SAC had followed the young couple's very public romance and breakup in the media—couldn't help but hear about it every time he turned on the TV or clicked on his goddamn *Yahoo!* homepage to check his stocks. But what the media hadn't told him, what Burrell hadn't learned until he met Tommy Campbell's father, was the degree to which the ending of their relationship had broken the boy's heart. Only after spending time with the Campbells at their house on Foster Cove, only after learn-

ing about the loving son *behind* the image portrayed
of him in the media did Bill Burrell begin to feel
guilty. For as many times as he had watched him play
for the Rebels on TV, as many times as he had seen
his image splattered across the Internet and on the
covers of magazines, only *after* Bill Burrell met the
missing footballer's grieving parents did he start to
think of Tommy Campbell as *human.*

"Tell me, Bill—tell me you know why somebody
would want to hurt my boy."

Burrell could say nothing—could only drop his
gaze back into his cup—for now that Tommy Campbell had been found, now that the moment for which
they had waited three months had finally arrived, incredibly the SAC could not bring himself to comment, let alone ask his friend any more questions.
Thomas Campbell Sr. thus turned once again to the
television—his eyes as blank as the screen on which
only moments before Rachel Sullivan had confirmed
for the rest of America what he already knew.

Special Agent in Charge Bill Burrell was satisfied
with the way his girl had fielded the press's questions,
but at the same time he was deeply disturbed—
angry, of course, because they had to put on the
fucking sideshow in the first place and because the
news of Tommy Campbell's murder had been leaked
to the press before he gave the go. Oh yes, he would
find out who opened his mouth; and when he did,
Bulldog would take great pleasure in *personally* shutting it for them.

However, it was the flurry of questions at the end
of the press conference that really bothered the
SAC—questions that seemed to bother even the reporter who asked them. Burrell, of course, had no
way of knowing that O'Neill had just been fed the in-

formation through her earpiece. He had no way of knowing that the reporter was at the same time irritated that her five hundred dollars had failed to yield this little tidbit of information: that Tommy Campbell and the unidentified person with whom he was discovered had been posed to look like a statue. A statue by Michelangelo. A statue by the name of *Bacchus*.

Even though only a handful of Westerly policemen knew the details about the statue, even though over a dozen state troopers had been brought in immediately to help secure the area around Dodd's estate, it had been the FBI who—upon their initial forensic inspection of The Sculptor's exhibit—discovered the dedication to Dr. Hildebrant beneath a light covering of beach sand on the base of the statue. And so it happened that, prior to Burrell's arrival at the crime scene, Special Agent Sam Markham had given strict orders not to mention the art history professor's name in the company of anyone other than federal agents. And so, as Burrell had watched Rachel Sullivan refuse to comment on the WNRI reporter's questions, one thing became painfully clear: that even if a policeman, local or state, had recognized the statue to be a reproduction of Michelangelo's *Bacchus*, it would have had to have been one of *his* guys that spilled the beans about Hildebrant—unless, of course, the killer had telephoned the media himself.

Either way, neither option sat well with him.

The only bonus about the whole mess, however, was that the WNRI reporter asked no questions about the inscription itself—did not seem to know exactly why Dr. Catherine Hildebrant had been called to the crime scene other than as an expert consultant. That was good, for that meant the FBI still might be able to do their job without a bunch of media attention on Hildebrant and her book. The media might leave her alone once the initial story blew over. Burrell liked the pretty professor—not because she reminded him of his wife, but because he could tell by the way she examined the bodies of Tommy Campbell and the boy that she was strong. Burrell liked that. Yes, indeed. One could say that Bill Burrell even *admired* her.

Thomas Campbell, on the other hand, was oblivious to Dr. Catherine Hildebrant—did not even ask Burrell who she was when Meghan O'Neill mentioned her name. In fact, Tommy Campbell's father seemed to accept the media frenzy in front of the Westerly·Police station as simply the next necessary step in the mourning for his son; did not even question Burrell as to how the information about the statue leaked out to the public—information that he himself had known since early that morning. No, his thoughts were only for his son—his son and someone else's.

"Once they see that statue," Campbell said, staring at the empty television screen, "the real one, I mean. Once they look it up online and see that the figure behind my son looks like a child, they—the people of Rhode Island at least—they're going to know it's that Wenick boy."

"I know. We've got some people at her house now. Just glad they got there before all this about the statue came out."

Although in the creation of his satyr The Sculptor had significantly altered Michael Wenick's face—the tiny horns atop his forehead, the pointy ears, the mischievous half grimace of his mouth on the grapes—it had been a Rhode Island state trooper who, upon the

FBI's arrival, had first alerted them to the boy's possible identity. And after the obligatory search of the missing person databases, after all the pictures and physical descriptions had been compared and analyzed, all signs did indeed point to little Michael Wenick. Burrell knew, however, that they had to be sure before they approached the boy's mother, and that they would then need a positive ID from her before any information could be presented to the public requesting their assistance.

But how do you tell a mother her son has been sawed in half? How do you tell a mother her child has been given a pair of goat's legs and been stuffed to look like a devil? What's even worse, how do you *show* her? And although Bill Burrell had initially felt guilty for arriving at Dodd's estate after Thomas and Maggie Campbell had left—after it took two state troopers, in addition to Thomas and his sister-in-law, to get the hysterical mother back home—now, sitting as he was in the den with the man who had in three months become a valued friend, the SAC felt even guiltier for his secret relief at not having had to break the news to the Campbells *himself*.

No. Even after twenty years with the Bureau, things just never got any easier.

"She's sleeping now," whispered a voice from the hall. In the doorway was Maggie Campbell's twin sister—*or a ghost*, Burrell thought. *A ghost of what Maggie Campbell looked like before her son's disappearance, before she lost all that weight.* He had met the woman before—had mistaken her once for Maggie—but for the life of him could not remember her name.

"Anything else I can do for you, Tom?" she asked. "Before I lay down for a bit?"

"No. Thank you, love. Please, get some rest."

The ghost smiled wearily, nodded to Burrell, then disappeared back into the shadows outside the den.

"She's a good girl," Campbell said. "Been a big help to us from the beginning."

Tommy Campbell's father offered nothing more about his sister-in-law—no name to bail Burrell out of his embarrassment for forgetting.

No, the sad-eyed father with the snow white hair just stared silently into the empty television screen as if he were waiting for a commercial to finish—the prop that was his coffee cold and unmoved in his lap as it had been now for almost an hour.

No, Burrell thought. *After twenty years with the Bureau it just never gets any fucking easier.*

Chapter 13

"Here you go, Hildy," said Janet Polk. "This is the stuff I was telling you about—the stuff my friend over in Anthropology gave me. It smells funky, but it'll relax you. I promise."

Cathy held the cup of tea to her nose—a powerful odor reminiscent of curry making her wince.

"Just drink it, wimp."

Cathy took a sip. It tasted wonderful. "Thank you," she said.

"First fix is free," said Dan Polk. "That's how she rolls. Gets you hooked, then pimps you out on the street like the rest of us bitches."

Cathy smiled for the first time since she left Sam Markham—had almost called him when the reporters began showing up at her door. But, as usual, it was Janet who came to her rescue; Janet who packed up her things and brought her back to her place across town. Cathy always liked coming to the Polks' house in Cranston, especially in the evenings—the way the muted lamplight played off the antique furniture, off the leaves of their countless plants and the richly colored wallpaper that enveloped everything. But more than the house itself, more than coming back to the neighborhood where she grew up, Cathy just liked being with the Polks. She instantly became calm and centered around them—ol' Jan n' Dan, her best friends and surrogate parents. Dan was a retired real estate broker—an odd match for the brainy Dr. Polk, but somehow they made it work. Married for almost forty years, no children, but one of the happiest couples Cathy had ever met. And not since her mother's death had Cathy felt so grateful to be with them.

"You're going to have to talk to them sooner or later," Janet said, settling herself next to her husband on the sofa. "You know that, right?"

"Yes," said Cathy.

Janet had insisted on picking Cathy up after seeing the clip of her and Sam Markham on the news; got a little taste of media attention herself when she backed out of Cathy's driveway and a reporter—the last remaining holdout after Cathy turned off her lights—asked her who she was. "None of your damn business!" she had snapped. And despite the gravity of the situation, Dan Polk could not help but laugh out loud when he saw *that* clip on CNN later that evening.

As was the case for the majority of Americans that evening, Cathy and the Polks sat glued to their television set as the media once again devoured their scraps of Tommy Campbell. The identity of the second body was released to the public around eight o'clock. Michael Wenick. The boy who had gone missing back in September, who had lived seven streets away from the Polks—only *two* streets away from the street on which Cathy grew up!

Unlike the rest of Rhode Islanders, Cathy had followed that story only superficially—did not watch or read much news the previous fall; had spent way too much time on her latest journal article. And in the months following her separation from Steve and the disappearance of Tommy Campbell, she had simply forgotten all about the little boy who had vanished from the woods around Blackamore Pond—the very same woods in which her mother forbade her to play as a child.

For *that*, for *forgetting*, Cathy felt ashamed.

What Cathy found even more disturbing was that she had not put two and two together when she saw the heinous sculpture in person. Had the figure in the background been only incidental to her? Had she been that overwhelmed by Tommy Campbell, by Bacchus, by the *star* of the exhibit?

And so, while the Polks watched the news in stunned silence, Cathy sat across the room staring past the TV—her mind secretly scrolling with passages from *Slumbering in the Stone*. She had not told Janet about the inscription at the base of the statue or about the possible connection between this nightmare and her book—a book that she had written not only as a testament to Michelangelo's genius, but also as a critique of a celebrity obsessed culture asleep on a featherbed of mediocrity. Had her experience with the sculpture down at Watch Hill been a mirror of that very dynamic? Had she been so taken, so fascinated with Tommy Campbell—the football player, the *celebrity* she had once made time for on Sundays—that she did not even *think* about little Michael Wenick, the little boy whose disappearance got nowhere nearly as much attention as Campbell's, and who ultimately, *literally* ended up taking a backseat to him—both in the minds of Rhode Islanders and the tableau of death in which he played a supporting role?

In essence, Cathy thought, *is this psycho, the sculptor of this* Bacchus *trying to say the same thing I was? Is he holding up Michelangelo's genius as the standard by which everything else should be judged? Is he, too, saying, "Shame on you world!" for accepting, for worshipping anything less?*

Worship, Cathy said to herself, turning the word over and over again in her mind. *They once worshipped Bacchus, god of wine, of celebration and theatre, of sexual excess; and now they worship Tommy Campbell, god of a meaningless game, of empty celebrity hookups and breakups, and now the worst of all media excesses.*

Perhaps, answered another voice in Cathy's head—a voice that sounded a lot like Sam Markham's. *But perhaps you're looking too deeply in the wrong direction. Perhaps the killer not only chose his victims because they looked like the figures in Michelangelo's original, but also because only the death of a public persona like Campbell's, or the incomprehensible death of a child, could draw the kind of media attention you're witnessing now. Maybe it takes that much nowadays to get through to us. Maybe the killer is trying to show us not only where our values are, but also, by virtue of his actions, how much it will take to wake us up.*

Wake us up. Yes. Wake us up in some sick way to remind us of our own potential.

What do you mean? asked Sam Markham in her mind.

The deeper message in Slumbering in the Stone—*the quote by Michelangelo upon which the title of the book is based.*

Of course. The quote.

"The *quotes*," Cathy said out loud.

"What'd you say, Hildy?"

"Excuse me, Jan. Is it okay if I use my cell phone in the kitchen?"

"Is everything all right, dear? Do you want us to turn off the television?"

"No, no, please," Cathy said. Had she known that the FBI agent had already finished reading her book in his hotel room, that he, too, had drawn his own conclusions about the killer's motives, Cathy might have had second thoughts about calling him. "I just remembered something I forgot to tell the FBI. But I'd like a little privacy. Is that okay, guys?"

"Of course," said Dan Polk. "And while you're in there, call the escort service for me. Tell 'em to send over Helga. Tall, blond, and a little Hulk Hoganesque is what I'm craving this evening."

Janet elbowed him and Cathy disappeared into the kitchen—found her purse on the table and re-trieved the FBI agent's card. *Samuel P. Markham,* it read beneath the official seal. *Supervisory Special Agent, Behavioral Analysis Unit-2.*

"Markham," Cathy said to herself à la James Bond. "Samuel *P.* Markham. The *'P.'* stands for *'Pretty Damn Cool.'*" Cathy smiled—felt the blood go warm in her cheeks—and dialed the number.

"Hello?" said the voice on the other end.

"Hello, Sam?"

"Yes."

"It's Cathy. Cathy Hildebrant."

"Hi, Cathy. I was going to call you to see how you were doing, but I didn't want to bother you. You've had quite a day. The reporters have left you alone, I take it?"

The FBI agent sounded different, Cathy thought—his voice tired and tight.

"Yes," Cathy said. "I'm spending the night in Cranston with Janet Polk and her husband." Markham did not say anything, and Cathy had the sneaking suspicion he already knew. "Anyway, we were watching TV and I saw they released the identity of that boy—the one who was murdered along with Tommy Campbell. Michael Wenick is his name."

"Yes. We suspected it was him from the beginning, but couldn't alert the public until we got confirmation from the medical examiner and the boy's mother. It all came together shortly after I dropped you off."

"He was a local, Sam—grew up in the same neighborhood as I did. And I feel awful for not recognizing him when we were down there at Watch Hill. It's why I'm calling you."

"What's up?"

"I just remembered that, when we were talking about the anonymous quotes in connection to my book, well, I forgot to mention that the title of the book itself, *Slumbering in the Stone,* was also taken from a quote by Michelangelo."

"'The best artist has that thought alone which is contained within the marble shell,'" Markham said. "'Only the sculptor's hand can break the spell to free the figures slumbering in the stone.'"

"Yes, that's it," said Cathy, flustered.

"I have your book right here in front of me. Just finished skimming through it about a half an hour ago. Interesting stuff."

"Thank you," Cathy said, suddenly nervous. "Well, you see, Sam, upon its initial publication, *Slumbering in the Stone* was met with quite a bit of controversy in academic circles—beginning with my interpretation of that quote. What I mean is, the traditional translation of Michelangelo's Italian held that the word 'only' in the last half of the quote came after the word 'can.' Thus, for years the statement was thought to have read, 'The sculptor's hand can only break the spell to free the figures slumbering in the stone.' I won't bore you with the details, but through my research I discovered that the word 'only' should actually come at the *beginning* of the sentence. Therefore, the quote should really read, '*Only* the sculptor's hand can break the spell to free the figures slumbering in the stone.' You see how it changes the meaning?"

"Yes," said Markham—distantly, studying the quote. "It changes the emphasis entirely. The sculptor himself becomes of supreme importance, making him much more *special*—that he and *only* he has the power to release, to awaken the figures from their sleep inside the marble."

"Exactly. Of course, Michelangelo is speaking metaphorically of the potential in a block of marble to become something beautiful, as well as the fact that only through the lens of true genius can this potential be seen. But the artist is also speaking of the magical, nothing short of *divine* connection that he felt between himself and his creations, for it was from God that Michelangelo received not only his talent and inspiration, but also his torment."

"Go on."

"The classical tradition in which Michelangelo's artistry is steeped—that is, the humanistic tradition hearkening back to the ancient Greeks—held that the male body was aesthetically superior to the female. It is a well-known fact that homosexuality was an integral part of ancient Greek culture, but not in the way we think of homosexuality today—or during Michelangelo's time, for that matter. And remember, of course, that we are just talking about *men* here, for women in ancient Greece were viewed as little better than livestock. You see, although pretty much any type of sexual exploit was open to the male, *exclusive* homosexuality was actually frowned upon in ancient Greece. And they most certainly didn't define a man by his sexual orientation the way we do today. In fact, sexual relations between men—usually between an older man and an adolescent boy between the ages of thirteen and nineteen—were not necessarily seen as a sexual act at all, but as an educational rite of passage into manhood. It was through the exploration of the male body that Greek men could experience the highest form of divinely inspired beauty—a realm, if you will, in which they could walk in the light of the gods. Sometimes the relationship between two males evolved into the deep, spiritual connection of love, and it is for this reason we see in Greek mythology love between two males much more highly prized than love between a man and a woman.

"We see such a dynamic in Michelangelo's sculptures as well—the majority of which are *male*. The figure of the woman is only incidental for him, and Michelangelo's lack of understanding of the female anatomy—such as his awkward placement of breasts and the rendering of female figures with large, manly frames—is evident throughout his career. For example, in another one of his famous sculptures, the *Rome Pietà*, we see the Madonna not only with oddly shaped breasts and an unusually large frame out of proportion with the Christ figure, but the entirety of her body is covered in heavy robes—almost as if Michelangelo is *hiding* her."

"Yes," said Markham. "You have some lovely photographs of it in your book."

"I'm sorry if I'm getting off track, Sam, but what I'm saying is that the male figures in Michelangelo's work are always exquisitely rendered with a kind of detail and authenticity out of proportion to the female—detail that indisputably proves the artist's obsession with the male anatomy. And so it is also through such flawless rendering that we see the classical dynamic of ancient Greece played out not only in the final execution of Michelangelo's sculptures, but also in his experience of sculpting them, for it was only through his work that Michelangelo could come close to communing with what he saw as divinely inspired beauty—a beauty, for him, accessible *only* by the sculptor's hand."

"So, if I follow you, you're saying that, for Michelangelo, it was as much the experience of carving as it was the finished product?"

"Yes. Think of the torment the artist must have gone through, born as he was with an inherent appreciation, an inherent love for the male—both spiritually and sexually. A love that he saw bestowed upon him by God and intrinsically woven into the very nature of his gift—that miraculous gift, given *only* to the sculptor, to release the figures slumbering in the stone. And thus it was the very nature of this gift that was both Michelangelo's sanctuary and his prison. This was a gift bestowed upon him by a God who at the same time forbade him to commune with his figures in the flesh—a God who condemned the kind of deep, spiritual love that Michelangelo so desperately craved with Tommaso Cavalieri; a God who gave Michelangelo the power to create beauty, but, in essence, not the permission to touch it."

"So then Michelangelo is also speaking about himself. That he, too, is a figure trapped in the stone—a figure imprisoned in the marble shell of his homosexuality, and that only through the act of carving could he, for lack of a better phrase, make love with another man."

"You could put it that way, yes."

Markham was silent for a long time—a silence in which Cathy thought she could hear the special agent's brain ticking; a silence that made Cathy so uncomfortable that she told Markham the gist of her Socratic dialogue on the sofa—neglecting, of course, to tell him that he had played Socrates to her Gorgias.

"Yes," said Markham when she had finished. "In your book you quite often contrast Michelangelo's artistry, as well as the world of the Italian Renaissance, with the artistic output of our culture today—specifically with regard to the media. How it dominates our culture, how it dictates what is important, but most significantly, how it physically shapes our intellect—literally, our physiological capacity not only to process information, but also to appreciate beauty. You speak of the detrimental effects of the Internet, of television and movies, and how they are altering, actually conditioning our brains not only to focus for shorter periods of time and with less efficiency, but also to accept a standard of excellence that gets progressively lower and lower. In essence, you are saying that, today, the quality of the marble from which we as human beings are shaped is meager stuff compared to the metaphorical marble of Michelangelo's time."

"That's a lovely way of putting it, yes."

"And only the sculptor's hand—whether it's Michelangelo's or the twisted psychopath's who murdered Campbell and Wenick—can free us from the marble prison that is the media. Our society today, we children of this celebrity infatuated culture, *we* are the figures slumbering in the stone."

"Yes, Sam. That's exactly what I'm saying."

"That would explain why he chose Campbell, and perhaps even that little boy. Or maybe, as you experienced in your examination of the statue, why he chose to portray them as Michelangelo's *Bacchus* in the first place; a sculpture in which the god, the *celebrity*—by virtue not only of his size and orientation but also of the mythology he carries with him—dominates our thoughts."

"It would also explain his contacting me via the quotes, don't you think? Like the sculpture, the medium itself was part of his message—just as the quote at the beginning of my book was part of mine. In essence, the killer was saying to me, 'I understand.'"

"And so the inscription on the base of the statue could just be the killer's way of simply saying, 'Thank you.'"

"Yes, I guess it could."

Sam Markham was silent again—the flipping pages on the other end of Cathy's cell phone the only sound.

"Thank you for calling me, Cathy," he said finally. "You can't imagine what a help you've been. I'll be back and forth between Providence and Boston over the next few days while the autopsies are being performed. Procedure dictates that we collect as much evidence as possible and then send it off to our labs at Quantico for analysis. The way these things go, it's better for the families to get their loved ones interred as soon as possible. I'll be in touch. Try to get some rest, okay? Good night, Cathy."

"Good night, Sam."

Click.

Cathy stood in the kitchen feeling more at ease than she had all day, and despite the topic of their conversation, Cathy hated to admit that she had actually *enjoyed* talking to the FBI agent.

Must be the tea, said the voice in her head, and Cathy promptly told it to fuck off.

The Polks' phone rang, and Cathy could hear Janet in the living room telling Steve Rogers that yes, Cathy was there, and no, she didn't want to talk to him. *Prick must have seen me on TV,* Cathy thought. Then she smiled, for the scene playing out in the living room was one she had seen many times over the last few months. Yes, Janet knew all too well that, no matter what the occasion, when Cathy retreated to her home the last person in the world she would ever want to speak with was Steve Rogers.

"For the last time, Steven," she heard Janet say. "I'm not going to give you her number. Now good night!"

Cathy returned to the living room to learn the Associated Press had confirmed that Tommy Campbell and Michael Wenick had indeed been found painted and posed like Michelangelo's *Bacchus*. And as Janet and Dan followed the details with shock and disgust, Cathy was secretly relieved when nothing was mentioned about the little dedication to her at the base of the statue. However, after CNN showed a picture of Michael Wenick on a split screen next to a close-up of Michelangelo's satyr, the reality of what had happened that day once again came rushing back to her.

And tea or no tea, Cathy knew that, when the lights were out in the Polks' guest room, it was the marble face of Michael Wenick that she would see hovering over her in the darkness.

Chapter 14

It was not Michael Wenick that Sam Markham saw when he closed his eyes that night, or even the Bacchanalian visage of Tommy Campbell. No, there in the gloom of his Providence hotel room was only his wife Michelle. She came to him as she usually did, her presence inextricably linked with his solitude; a jigsaw puzzle of memory—some of which was jumbled into fuzzy pieces, while other parts fit together in segments of some larger picture, the border of which was never quite finished. Tonight, however, the memories of his Michelle brought with them the dull but crushing pain of longing—a pain that was always there for Sam Markham, but that most often lurked only in the deepest catacombs of his hardened heart.

It had been fourteen years since his wife's murder at the hands of a serial rapist by the name of Elmer Stokes. Stokes—a brutish-looking but charming singer whose specialty was traditional sea shanty songs—had been performing for the summer at Mystic Seaport when he saw the pretty, twenty-six-year-old "scientist lady" taking some water samples with her colleagues. Stokes would later tell police that he had followed "the bitch and her scientist friends" back to the Aquarium, where he waited for her in his car until long after dark. His intention, he said, had only been to watch her, to "get a feel for her." But when he saw the lovely Markham emerge from the Aquarium alone, he was overcome with the irresistible urge to take her then.

Elmer Stokes stated in his confession that he wore a ski mask and "pulled a pistol on the bitch." When he ordered Markham into the backseat of her car, she screamed, and Stokes tried to subdue her. Michelle Markham fought back—kicking Stokes in the groin and biting him hard on his forearm. She managed to tear off the ski mask, and Stokes said it was then that he panicked. He shot her twice in the head and fled the scene in his beat-up '85 Corolla. A coworker at Mystic Seaport spotted the bite marks on the shanty man's forearm a couple days later and called the police. At first Elmer Stokes denied any involvement in the murder—a murder that rocked the sleepy little town of Mystic, Connecticut, to its core. However, when police recovered the pistol from the trunk of Stokes's car, the lovable singer who had been such a hit with the kiddies that summer confessed. The authorities were eventually able to tie Elmer Stokes to nine rapes in four states going back over a decade.

Michelle Markham, however, had been his first and only murder.

It was Sam Markham who discovered his wife's body lying next to her car in the Mystic Aquarium parking lot—had gone looking for her when she didn't come home that night. The couple was less than a week shy of their two-year wedding anniversary, for which Markham had saved enough money from his meager English teacher's salary to surprise Michelle with a weekend in the White Mountains of New Hampshire. Their courtship had been brief—a six-month whirlwind of passion and romance followed by an elopement and the happiest two years of their lives. And so it was inevitable that, as Sam Markham sat cradling his wife's head in a pool of blood, his entire world imploded into a downward spiral of grief.

Under Connecticut law, for the murder and attempted rape of Michelle Markham, Elmer Stokes received the death penalty. It was of little consolation to Sam Markham, who sat numb-eyed in the courtroom while his parents and Michelle's family wept with relief at the judge's sentence. Years later, when Markham's sorrow had leveled, he would look back on that time following the trial of Elmer Stokes and invariably think of a crappy Disney movie he saw as a boy called *The Black Hole*, in which the main characters, protected by a special spaceship designed to resist the gravitational forces of the title entity, get sucked down into a hokey and ambiguous sequence where they travel through Heaven and Hell, only to emerge on the other side of the black hole in what appears to be another dimension.

And so it had been for Markham, for the black hole that had been the year following his wife's murder compressed time into a confusing and hazy journey in which he felt like a bearded spaceship drifting aimlessly through the universe of his boyhood bedroom at his parents'. And although, unlike the characters in the Disney movie, Markham could remember little of the black hole that had been his mourning, he emerged on the other side with a decision to apply for a career as a special agent with the Federal Bureau of Investigation.

Yes, a new dimension in Markham's life had begun.

With his newfound sense of purpose, the physically fit and always intellectually superior Markham quickly moved to the head of his class at the FBI Academy at Quantico. After graduation, over the next few years he followed the normal routine of rotating assignments until, while working as a special agent with the Tampa Office, he single-handedly brought down Jackson Briggs, the man the press had dubbed "The Sarasota Strangler"—a vicious serial killer and rapist who had been terrorizing Sarasota retirement communities for almost two years, and who, by the time Markham caught up with him, had a string of seven victims to his credit. Markham's efforts not only earned him a citation of merit from the FBI director himself, but also secured his position as a supervisory special agent in the Behavioral Analysis Unit at the National Center for the Analysis of Violent Crime in Quantico.

Yet through it all, Sam Markham walked alone. Thought simply a solitary man by some, perhaps aloof and arrogant by others, life for the special agent was his job and only his job. Unlike those who knew him, however, Markham was keenly aware of his own psyche—knew that it was his work that brought him closer to his wife; knew that, like a character in a movie, he was on a mission to avenge her death by sparing others the heartache he had suffered. And it was for this very reason that Sam Markham watched himself in his role as an FBI special agent with the same sense of detached cliché and boredom with which he had watched *The Black Hole* as a child. For underneath it all was a nagging sense of futility; an inherent cynicism and understanding that, even at the end, the movie would simply not pay off. Yes, when it came right down to it, Sam Markham knew as well as anybody that, no matter how many serial killers he brought down, he would never find peace until he joined his wife in the afterlife.

And so—even though it had been almost fifteen years since his wife's murder and he had learned to accept his grief—Markham found it strange that, as he watched himself lying there in his Providence hotel room, the jigsaw puzzle that was the memory of his wife had been scattered across a tabletop of guilt. For tonight, mixed in with the images of Michelle were pieces from *another* puzzle—one that took Markham completely by surprise.

Of course, there had been other women over the last few years, but the FBI agent never allowed himself to get too close, never allowed himself to betray the memory of his wife in his heart. But now, with this art history professor from Brown, Markham was aware that something had happened; that something *else* besides his grief was stirring deep down in the catacombs of his heart—a something, for all his self-awareness, Markham did not quite understand, but at the same time in the role of detached moviegoer knew all too well. And so it was that, as he gazed down at the picture of Cathy Hildebrant on the back cover of *Slumbering in the Stone*, Markham watched himself for the first time long in his heart not only for his wife, but for another woman as well; and so it was that the FBI agent had also watched himself swallow his tears of guilt upon the art history professor's phone call—a detail, Markham thought, that only added to the cliché of the movie that had become his life.

By the time he hung up with Cathy, however, Markham's mind was back on his work. The conversation—as much as it had settled him, as much as he had actually enjoyed speaking with the art history professor—confirmed for him the conclusion he had drawn from reading *Slumbering in the Stone*: that the murderer of Tommy Campbell and Michael Wenick was sending a *message* that was part of a much larger purpose—a purpose that involved the public. But rather than delving back into Cathy's book, rather than contemplating the merits of Dr. Hildebrant's theories as to just what that purpose was, after he closed his cell phone Markham found himself unable to take his eyes off the book's cover—specifically, the close-up of *David*'s piercing but delicately carved eyes. Indeed, for almost ten minutes did Sam Markham become mesmerized by the visage that was Michelangelo's *David*—so much so, that when his cell phone startled him from his trance, it took a moment for Markham to remember where he was.

"Yes?"

"You see the news?"

It was Bill Burrell.

"Not in the last couple of hours, no. I've been reading Dr. Hildebrant's book."

"Damn press," grunted Burrell. "Already calling the son of a bitch 'The Michelangelo Killer.' And worse than all the pictures of that goddamn statue floating around is the word getting out about Hildebrant, about her involvement in the case. You think one of our guys could have rolled?"

"It's possible. But I wouldn't be surprised if the killer notified the press himself."

"What makes you say that?"

"Well, it's obvious that he wants attention, obvious that he's sending a message, and that he wants the public to understand this message via the lens of Hildebrant's book—almost like he intends *Slumbering in the Stone* to be some sort of owner's manual for his creation. He went through a lot of trouble to execute this, Bill—to plan the murder of a celebrity like Campbell, to construct his *Bacchus* down to the minutest details, and to risk being discovered while installing the sculpture in Dodd's garden. Consequently, I don't think the killer would want to run the risk of the public misinterpreting his efforts."

"All right, what have you got for me?"

"Half textbook, but the other half is unlike anything we've ever seen before. Beginning with the boilerplate stuff, he's of the highly organized, highly intelligent variety. Other than what we'll learn as a result of the autopsies, the only evidence the killer has left behind so far are those footprints—but he anticipated the possibility of a tread match and took the time to cover them. However, unless he was intentionally wearing bigger shoes, judging from the size of those footprints I'd peg him to be between six-three and six-six—most likely a white male, probably in his mid-to-late thirties, and definitely a loner. Would need a lot of time to accomplish his work, as well as a space in which to do so—perhaps a cellar or a garage. He'd also need a truck or a van to transport his creations. I would say that's where the stereotype ends, however."

"Go on."

"The fact that he carried his statue alone tells us that he's a man of incredible strength—probably either holds a job doing some kind of menial labor, or is perhaps a bodybuilder. I would tend to lean toward the latter, for not only is the killer very bright and apparently well educated, but also his apparent identification with Michelangelo in terms of both the artist's homosexuality and his genius as a sculptor might indicate a desire for the same aesthetic quality in his own physique as well."

"So you're saying now you *do* think this guy is gay?"

"I can't say one hundred percent, Bill. But judging from my conversations with Dr. Hildebrant and my cursory reading of her book, my gut tells me yes."

"That's good enough for me. What about the motive?"

"Well, barring any connection between Campbell and Wenick of which we're presently unaware, again we have a situation where our man does not fit neatly into the usual categories. Other than the fact that both his victims were male—perhaps, one could argue, only an incidental criterion that Michelangelo's *Bacchus* demanded of him—on one level, the killer seems to have chosen Campbell and Wenick simply because they looked like the figures in the original."

"What's the other level?"

"The killer's message. Why he went through all the trouble to kill *specifically* Tommy Campbell and Michael Wenick in the first place. Why he juxtaposed the wide receiver's body with that of the boy's, and then made the effort to exhibit his *Bacchus* in the garden of a wealthy banker down at Watch Hill—an obvious historical allusion to the exhibition of the original."

"And the message you're talking about is what?"

Markham gave Burrell a quick rundown of his conversation with Cathy, as well as their theories about the killer's motives—that deeper message that The

Michelangelo Killer had chiseled out of Cathy's book: *Only the sculptor's hand can free the figures slumbering in the stone.*

"So you think then that he's a type of visionary killer?" asked Burrell. "You think he's delusional? That he read into Hildebrant's book a deeper message that told him to make statues out of people?"

"I wouldn't go so far as to call him entirely delusional, Bill. Too much self-control, too much patience. No, I'd peg him somewhere between the visionary and missionary type, for I think *Slumbering in the Stone* clarified an urge to kill that was already there to begin with. It gave him a sense of purpose—not only, as I explained to you, in terms of 'waking us up,' but also, in light of his attempt to mimic the historical context of the original's exhibition, perhaps to usher in a new Renaissance of thought. Maybe he's trying to shock our culture into its next stage of evolution by harkening back to what he sees as an intellectually superior point in history. Perhaps he's reminding us of a standard of excellence that has been lost, or at the very least, in his eyes, clouded by the mediocrity of media worship and empty celebrity."

"And you *don't* think sexual gratification is a factor?" asked Burrell, frustrated. "Even though both the victims were male and the killer, as you say, is a homosexual?"

Markham could tell by the sound of Burrell's voice that the SAC did not want to entertain his hypothesis. Either all this intellectual nonsense was going over Burrell's head, or the scope of Markham's theory on The Michelangelo Killer's intentions was just too much for Bill Burrell to wrap his mind around.

"I hate to say this, Bill, but in a way I hope there *is* a sexual component to these murders—might actu-

ally make them easier to solve if we could follow a
more visceral motive as opposed to an intellectual
one. Yes, I think the killer does receive some kind of
psychological gratification from his work, but the
pattern of behavior thus far seems to indicate something else, something beyond his own, selfish inter-
ests—the totality of which we've never seen before.
If, as I explained to you, the killer is in some sick way
trying to imitate Michelangelo through his creations,
then, although he may be sexually attracted to them,
it would be inappropriate for him to consummate his
relationship with them via the sexual act itself. Of
course, I could be wrong. We won't know for sure if
there was any sexual assault until the autopsies are
finished, let alone exactly *how* Campbell and Wenick
were killed. And even then, given the state of the
bodies, given the amount of chemicals and preserva-
tives the killer must have used to achieve his goals,
we might never know exactly what this guy did to his
victims—if in fact Campbell and Wenick were his first
victims."

"You think he may have killed before?"

"Maybe not a human being, but I would be willing
to bet the farm that the goat—the one from which
he got the legs—had been the first to go. I'd also be
willing to bet that the killer has a couple of cats and
dogs to his credit, too. He knew what he was doing,
Bill—chose Campbell and Wenick not only because
they fit the vision of his *Bacchus* perfectly, but because he was *ready* for them. I don't think he would
let all the planning, all the effort he put into finding
the perfect specimens go to waste unless he was completely sure that, at least in theory, his sculpture
would work. Remember, Michelangelo had been
carving reliefs and smaller sculptures for years be-

fore he broke onto the scene with his first life-size statue."

"So what are you saying, Sam? You think this nut job is going to kill again? You think his message, as you say, goes beyond Campbell and that boy?"

"I hope to Christ no, Bill," said Markham, flipping through his book. "I hope the same warped sense of purpose that caused him to murder Campbell and Wenick will also magnify in his mind the cultural significance of his creation to the point where he thinks he's achieved his goal—that he thinks he's done enough. But I'll tell you this—if our man is in fact intent on killing again, it'll be against the canon of Michelangelo's sculptures from which he'll select his victims. And, although I may be wrong, there's a good chance those victims will be male. I just hope we can nab him before he begins his next project."

Burrell was silent for a long time.

"I'm heading back to Boston as we speak," the SAC said finally. "But I'll be in the Providence office tomorrow. We got our team working with the state medical examiner on those autopsies, so hopefully we'll get some solid leads to follow in the next couple of days."

"Okay."

"I assume Washington is going to put you on reassignment—that you'll be joining us here at the Boston office for a while?"

"You know how those things go. If Gates feels I can better serve the investigation at Quantico, he'll want to keep me there to help oversee things. Depending on what happens, there's a good chance they'll eventually want me back."

"Then, off the record, it's square with you if I personally ask Gates to have you reassigned to the

Boston office, have you set up to work out of the Resident Agency in Providence—temporarily, that is?"

"I'd rather be local—do my best work on the street, yes."

"Good. We're going to need you on this one."

"Okay."

"And thanks, Sam."

"Okay."

Burrell hung up, but Markham did not bother to close his cell phone. No, once again the special agent found himself instantly transfixed by Catherine Hildebrant's *Slumbering in the Stone*—only this time it was not the determined eyes of *David* that had captured his gaze. No, there on the page to which he had intentionally flipped during his conversation with the SAC was a picture of Michelangelo's *second* major sculpture.

Yes, there lying in Sam Markham's lap was the *Rome Pietà*.

Chapter 15

Stretched out naked on the divan, The Sculptor let the last of his Brunello play over his tongue—the smoothness, the fruit driven warmth of the Sangiovese grape a nice pairing, he thought, with the remaining heat from the fireplace before him. It was late and he was sleepy; he felt so relaxed, as if he were floating—the soft classical music surrounding him like a saline bath drawn especially for him. The Sculptor had allowed himself that evening a celebratory meal of lamb and risotto—a nice change of pace from all the protein shakes and nutritional supplements that made up the majority of his diet. Yes, he had *earned* this indulgence—the fatty lamb, the sugary wine, the carb-ridden risotto—but that meant he would have to work doubly hard in the cellar tomorrow, putting an extra ten pounds on each side of the bar during his bench press, for Monday was his chest, back, and shoulders day.

With the last of the fire fading, with the plans for his *Bacchus* long ago in ashes, The Sculptor heaved a heavy sigh at the thought of having to rise. The grandfather clock in the corner chimed its warning for the half hour—*11:30*—but The Sculptor wished to stay on the divan *forever;* wished to bask in his moment of triumph just a little bit longer.

Oh yes, it had been a lovely evening. After giving his father his supper and putting him to bed, while his lamb cooked and his risotto simmered on the stove, The Sculptor spent over an hour in the library—sat back naked in the big leather chair with his feet on the desk, sipping the last of some Amarone and nibbling from a hunk of Parmigiano-Reggiano. Quite a few books passed through his fingers, mostly older volumes in Italian, the pages with The Sculptor's favorite passages long ago dog-eared—Boccaccio, Dante, Machiavelli. He read them slowly, sometimes twice—savoring the language with a sip of wine or a bite of cheese—and then moved on to others amidst a serenade of classical music by Tomaso Albinoni. It was the old routine The Sculptor relished, but one he had neglected as of late due to his work in the carriage house; and the library was filled with stacks of books in some places as tall as The Sculptor himself.

It was well after eight o'clock by the time The Sculptor finally sat down in the parlor with his lamb and his Brunello—the fire roaring, all but *begging* him for his *Bacchus.* And thus it was with no particular ceremony that The Sculptor threw the twisted log of plans into the flames—for his mind was already on his next sculpture. And there he sat alone for over three hours, eating his lamb and sipping his wine as the music from the library became a soundtrack for his thoughts—for what he imagined to be happening outside now that the world had received his *Bacchus,* and for what he imagined would happen in the future when the world received his next creation.

Soon, The Sculptor thought. *Very, very soon.*

His dinner done, his dishes washed, and the parlor clean, The Sculptor stepped out into the night—the cool April air popping his naked flesh into goose bumps as he made his way across the flagstone path toward the carriage house. He had not been back there since telephoning WNRI and communing with his *Bacchus* atop the mortician's table. No, The Sculptor had wanted to prolong the anticipation of checking his technology until the very last minute, when he knew the totality of his exhibit would dominate the news. And as he climbed the stairs to the second floor, with every step The Sculptor's heart beat faster and faster with excitement.

He entered the carriage house and immediately went for the computers. While they were booting, he turned on the television—Fox News, some blond lady live in front of Dodd's estate *blahdy-blahdy-blahding* about a possible motive for the murders, about a possible connection to Earl Dodd. Yes, he had expected something like that—*only a matter of time before that theory is put to rest,* he thought. But when the *blahdy-blah* was soon accompanied by a picture of Michelangelo's *Bacchus,* The Sculptor's heart leapt with joy into his throat.

And so, instead of moving on to the Internet, The Sculptor waited—listened for the one word in the *blahdy-blah* that would confirm for him his triumph; the one word that would give him permission to proceed with his next project the following morning.

And after about ten minutes, it fell from the blond
lady's lips like an angel from Heaven.

Hildebrant.

Yes, the blond lady was saying that a Brown University professor by the name of Catherine Hildebrant—*"an expert on the works of Michelangelo"*—had
been brought in by the FBI as a consultant for the investigation. And although she could not be reached
for comment, Hildebrant, the blond lady explained,
had written one of the most widely read books on
Michelangelo to come along since Irving Stone's *The
Agony and the Ecstasy.* The blond lady also explained
that, even though *Slumbering in the Stone* had been
met with some controversy in certain academic circles, it was a good primer for anyone interested in
the artist and the relevancy of his work today.

It's almost too good to be true, The Sculptor thought.

The Sculptor had known from the beginning
that he would have to play the Hildebrant card carefully, for although he had wanted the media to
know of her involvement in order to draw attention
to her book, The Sculptor also knew that his plan
might backfire if the public knew that *Slumbering in
the Stone* had been the inspiration for his *Bacchus.*
Yes, The Sculptor wanted to thank Dr. Hildy for all
her help; yes, he wanted her to speak publicly about
her book; but The Sculptor understood that if too
much attention was paid to *Slumbering in the Stone* itself—that is, if the book became inextricably woven
in the public consciousness with the murders as the
Beatles' *White Album* had over the years become
with the demented intentions of Charles Manson—
then the simplicity, the clarity of his message would
be lost.

In addition, such a bombardment of misguided media attention might cause the shy Dr. Hildy to retreat from the public eye entirely. And how much better would it be if she didn't? How much better would it be if the pretty art history professor went on television to talk about Michelangelo and perhaps about her book, too? Thus, the reason for the sand over the inscription at the base of the statue—a detail The Sculptor hoped would be discovered by the forensic teams *after* the police arrived; a detail that The Sculptor hoped could be kept from the public for a while—or at least until the interest in *Slumbering in the Stone* and Michelangelo had solidified.

Besides, The Sculptor thought, in the grand scheme of things, it was unimportant that the general public should catch on to—let alone understand completely—the deeper meaning, the deeper genius of his work in connection with Dr. Hildy's book. No, of supreme importance was the public's interest in the *murders*, for only through that interest could they be drawn closer to Michelangelo; only then could The Sculptor begin—*without them even knowing it*—to chisel away at the marble of confusion and misguided values that had become their prison.

Yes, only The Sculptor's hand could free them from their slumber in the stone.

And so The Sculptor double-clicked on the desktop icon labeled *Yahoo!* The headlines, as he expected, were about the murders of Tommy Campbell and Michael Wenick. That was wonderful, but he would read them later—perhaps tomorrow morning after his 6:00 A.M. workout and before commencing the research for his next project. No, what The

Sculptor was interested in at present lay in the bottom right hand corner of the *Yahoo!* homepage in the box titled, *Today's Top Searches.*

At *Number 2* was *Tommy Campbell.*

At *Number 1* was *Michelangelo.*

The Sculptor smiled.

It had begun.

EXHIBIT TWO
The Rome Pietà

Chapter 16

In the week and a half following the discovery of Tommy Campbell and Michael Wenick, Sam Markham spoke with Cathy Hildebrant only twice: once on Thursday to ask her if she had any insight into the coroner's preliminary findings; once the following Wednesday to tell her that the FBI was temporarily reassigning him to the Boston Field Office and to ask her to join him there the next morning.

In their Thursday conversation, Markham told Cathy that the internal organs of both Campbell and Wenick had been removed by the killer—Wenick's through the lower half of his severed torso, Campbell's through a previously undetected incision running from the base of his testicles through his rectum—and the resulting cavities were found stuffed with a mixture of tightly packed sawdust and hay. Both the victims' heads were shaved and their hair replaced with special "wigs" sculpted from an epoxy compound. The killer had also removed the victims' brains from what was clearly a postmortem-drilled hole at the base of each of their skulls. Wenick, Markham said, most

likely died from a broken neck, for even though both
the bodies had been contorted and mounted on a
zigzagged iron bar that ran up through the wooden
tree stump, through Campbell's buttock and into his
torso, only the bones in Wenick's neck showed signs
of trauma that occurred *prior* to death.

Markham went on to explain that Campbell's
penis appeared to have been removed while he was
still alive, but because of the missing organs—and because both the bodies had been drained and the
veins and tissues embalmed with some kind of
preservative that needed further analysis—the wide
receiver's cause of death was still to be determined.
The final results of the autopsy, Markham stressed,
would not be in until the following week, and everything—the white lacquered paint, as well as the
epoxy sculptured wigs, the fake grapes, and other ac-
coutrements that adorned the bodies—would require further analysis. Markham told Cathy that all
pertinent forensic evidence—including the entire
base of the statue—had already been flown to the
FBI Laboratory at Quantico for testing. That was
good, Markham said, for that meant the detail about
the inscription to Cathy could be kept out of the
public eye a bit longer.

And that meant that Cathy could be kept out of
the public eye a bit longer, too. Immediately following that fateful Sunday, Dr. Catherine Hildebrant was
met with an onslaught of messages on her University
voice mail asking for an interview—so many, in fact,
that she had to instruct her students to contact her
only via e-mail. And even though it had been the end
of the semester and she could finish up most of her
work at Janet's, by Friday of that first week—when

other art historians and so-called experts had already been making the interview circuits for days—the media seemed to have forgotten all about the pretty art history professor who had initially been brought in as a consultant on the case, and who subsequently refused all their requests for an interview.

However, even though by Friday of that first week interest in Cathy had waned, interest in her book had not. Amazon and Barnes & Noble quickly sold out of their few remainder copies of *Slumbering in the Stone,* and both placed a large backorder with Cathy's publisher—a small, academic press which in turn informed their star author to expect some hefty royalty checks in the months to come. Other books on Michelangelo began to sell out, too; and by that first Friday, *The Agony and the Ecstasy* had cracked the number 10 spot on Amazon's bestseller list.

While both professional and amateur sleuths alike waxed philosophical on the deeper meaning, the deeper cultural significance *behind* the murder/sculpture of Tommy Campbell and Michael Wenick—some of whom actually referred to *Slumbering in the Stone* while postulating their theories of The Michelangelo Killer's motives—none made the connection to Cathy's book as a possible inspiration for the killings—a fact that Sam Markham in his second conversation with Cathy did not find surprising. Without the knowledge of the inscription at the base of the statue, he explained, without the knowledge of the quotes and a direct connection between the killer and herself, there would be no reason for the public to make a connection with her book more than any other the killer might have read, including literature not necessarily related to Michelangelo.

Thus, following a number of carefully calculated comments by Special Agent Rachel Sullivan in her press conferences that week—comments that suggested Cathy had been consulted by the FBI simply because of her geographic proximity to the crime scene—by that first Friday the media seemed to have moved on from Dr. Catherine Hildebrant.

Markham, however, had not. Had he known how many times Cathy had wanted to call him just to chat—and had he known how often she had Googled his name on her laptop while at the Polks'—the FBI agent might have better understood the turmoil that fate had awakened in both their hearts. During his first conversation with her that week, Markham had assured Cathy that it was better for her if he should keep his distance until the media attention died down. She needn't worry, he said, for even though she was staying with the Polks, she was still under constant surveillance by the FBI. And so Markham felt a certain amount of relief that he had an excuse to stay away from Cathy Hildebrant. But even though the demands of the investigation actually warranted his distance from her, coupled with his relief was a mixture of guilt and shame—guilt because his nagging preoccupation with the pretty art history professor often took his mind off his work; shame because he felt dishonest for not admitting even to himself how often his thoughts of her made him smile.

Markham spent the majority of that week and a half traveling between the Boston Field Office and the Resident Agency in Providence. Most of the time he was alone, but sometimes Rachel Sullivan accompanied him, as on the two occasions when they attempted to speak with Laurie Wenick. Both times they had to settle for her father; for Laurie—who had tried to stab herself in the neck with a butcher's knife upon learning what had become of her son— was presently being held under a strict suicide watch at the Rhode Island Institute of Mental Health. Thus, it had fallen to John Wenick to perform the grim task, the grim *technicality* of identifying the upper half of his grandson—that is, once little Michael Wenick had been removed from the rocky cliff and separated from the goat's legs. John Wenick could offer nothing to help Markham and Sullivan with their investigation other than a tearful oath that he would one day see "whoever did this to my grandson dead at my feet."

And so, while the remaining pieces of The Sculptor's *Bacchus* were being processed and analyzed back at the FBI Laboratories at Quantico, and while Rachel Sullivan and her team began following up on the class rosters obtained from the Registrar's Office at Brown, Special Agent Sam Markham immediately set about pursuing leads gathered from the plethora of physical evidence The Michelangelo Killer had left behind—the most promising of which so far being the hindquarters of the goat.

The first element of the killer's *Bacchus* to be examined at the FBI Laboratory, DNA testing quickly determined that the goat which The Michelangelo Killer had selected for the bottom half of his satyr was a medium-sized adult male of the Nubian variety: a short-haired, somewhat muscular goat distinguished by its floppy ears and what breeders called its distinctively "Roman" nose—a characteristic that Markham, given what he knew of The Michelangelo Killer so far, did not treat as a coincidence. Indeed, through his research, Markham also discovered that, as far as goats go, the Nubian was one of the most sociable, vocal, and outgoing of all the different breeds. *Outgoing,* Markham said to himself over and over. *The same word John Wenick had used to describe his grandson.* Another coincidence? *Perhaps,* but Markham could not help but think otherwise.

The special agent began his investigation by surfing the Internet and telephoning the handful of farms in the New England area that either featured the Nubian breed, or had Nubians among their livestock—beginning with and working his way outward from the farms closest to the area where Michael Wenick was abducted. He got lucky on his second try: a farm called Hill Brothers Homestead in Burrillville—a rural, heavily wooded town located in the northwest corner of Rhode Island. Markham followed up with calls to the other farms as well, but only Louis Hill, owner of Hill Brothers Homestead, confirmed that one of his Nubians had indeed gone missing the previous fall.

"Mr. Hill?" said Markham, emerging from his car.

"One of 'em, yes," said the old man in the beat-up Boston Red Sox hat. He stood on the porch of his small farmhouse with his hands in the pockets of his baggy overalls. "If you're looking for my brother, he's a ways down the road. You'll have to shout, though, as he'll have a hard time hearing ya from six feet under."

"I spoke with you on the phone, Mr. Hill," said Markham, showing his ID. "Special Agent Sam Markham. Federal Bureau of Investigation."

"I know, son. Just giving you a hard time. Louis Hill. A pleasure to meet you."

"Likewise."

"About time someone got up here about Gamble."

"Gamble?"

"The buck I told you about on the phone. Reported it to the police back in November, but nobody done shit since. Didn't think they'd get the FBI on it, though. You boys got a missing animals division or something?"

"Mr. Hill, you said on the phone that Gamble was the only one of your goats to go missing last year?"

"Yep. Hadn't had a goat go missing in over a decade. And as far as I know, never had one stolen neither. Had big plans for that boy. Shoulda seen him—was a *be-ute* of a stud."

"And you said Gamble was stolen at night, in the dark sometime between eight o'clock and five the next morning?"

"Had to have been, yeah. Grandson checked on the goats and locked the barn as he usually does before he goes to bed. All present and accounted for. Went to feed them the next morning, lock on the barn was busted open and the door to Gamble's stall ripped off the hinges."

"May I see the barn?"

"Sure thing."

Hill led Markham from the porch around to the back of the farmhouse. In addition to the large barn and a pair of smaller buildings at the rear of the property, Markham spied about two dozen Nubian goats in a nearby paddock—many of whom raised their heads and approached the fence as the men passed.

Outgoing indeed, Markham thought.

"Settle down, children," said Hill. "Don't go begging the government for no handouts now."

The large swinging doors were propped open, the inside of the barn empty, but the lingering smell of livestock—of hay and manure and sawdust—suddenly bombarded Markham with memories of a petting zoo to which his father had taken him as a little boy—a ramshackle affair at the local mall where a llama once nibbled at the collar of his shirt and made him cry. The barn itself was typical in its layout—a single corridor flanked by stalls for the animals. The horse stalls, of which there were four, came first; followed by six stalls on each side that Hill said were reserved for the goats. These—unlike the horse stalls, which had high wooden doors and barred windows—were enclosed by chain link gates and were separated from each other by 2 x 6s that Hill said could be removed to make the pens bigger.

"They usually go three or four to a stall," said the farmer. "Sometimes more if a doe is weaning. And in the winter we can take down those walls and house more together, separating them by size, age, and sex if we need to. But Gamble always had his own stall down at the end year round. He could get a bit ornery, but he was smart, and would try sometimes to push the latch—why his was the only stall that was padlocked. He got the job done when it came time to getting with his honeys, though. That's what a special boy he was. Goddamn shame if you ask me."

Hill and Markham reached the opposite end of the barn.

"See there?" asked Hill, pointing to his prized buck's former stall. "My grandson and I fixed it, but you can still see where the sons of bitches pulled the gate off. Didn't even bother with the other goats—coulda gotten to *them* easy. Nope, no padlock or nothing was gonna stop these guys. Guess they had their sights on Gamble from the beginning—just pulled the goddamn thing right outta the frame."

Markham squatted down and ran his pinky finger along the wooden beam—along the outline of the gate hinges' former position.

"Cops took fingerprints and everything," said Louis Hill, spitting. "But they found nothing—not even any pry marks. Said it woulda taken three or four men to pull that gate off its hinges. First I thought it mighta been kids—local boys playing a prank or something. Then I got to thinking it mighta been somebody who wanted to breed Gamble. I mean, these guys went to a lot of trouble to get him. I tell ya, that boy was a real *be-ute* of a—"

"Mr. Hill, you said Gamble went missing back in *November?*"

"Yep. Two weeks before Thanksgiving. I remember cuz my grandson had a game. He's only a sophomore but he's a starter. Quarterback. Gamble going missing messed up his head bad for that one. Felt like it was his fault. Good kid, my grandson. Always loved those—"

"And you never saw anyone suspicious lurking around the property?"

"I'm telling ya what I told the police. Have no idea who woulda wanted to take Gamble other than what I already told ya."

"Mr. Hill, the FBI has reason to believe that Gamble may have been found."

"He's dead, ain't he?" said Hill, spitting again. "Where'd they find him?"

"You been following the news at all lately, Mr. Hill? You've heard about the murder of Tommy Campbell and that boy down at Watch Hill? You know what happened to them?"

A look of grim realization suddenly washed over the old man's face.

"I saw the picture of that statue on the news—the one they said looked like the thing the killer made outta those bodies. You mean to say that the bottom half of that boy is a *real* goat? You mean to say that you think it's *Gamble?*"

"There's a very high probability of that, yes."

"So you're telling me the fella who did that to those boys was here? On my *property?*"

"We won't know for sure until I send a team here to get some DNA samples from Gamble's offspring. We're also going to need to question your grandson."

"What's he got to do with any of this?" asked the old man, his voice trembling.

"He was the last one to see Gamble alive. And the one who subsequently discovered him to be missing. He might be able to tell us something the police overlooked." Markham had no intention of telling Louis Hill that his grandson could be a suspect in the case. No, he would let Rachel Sullivan and her team handle that; let them spring the search warrant on the old man if he refused to cooperate.

"I'll do whatever I can to help," said Louis Hill.

Markham left the farmer staring blankly into Gamble's empty stall. But more than being disturbed at the incredible amount of strength it would have taken The Michelangelo Killer to rip the gate off its hinges—if in fact it *was* The Michelangelo Killer who had done so—what *really* bothered Sam Markham as he sped away down the shady country road was the date when the crime occurred.

November, Markham said to himself over and over again. *The killer acquired the bottom half of his satyr after he already had the boy. That means the killer was confident enough in his technique for preserving humans* before *he murdered Michael Wenick. That means Michael Wenick might not have been his first. That means I was wrong about the timeline.*

That means I was wrong.

Chapter 17

It was after she hung up with Sam Markham on Wednesday, May 6th—the afternoon on which she learned she would be accompanying him to the Boston Field Office the next day—that Cathy also received word that her divorce from Steven Rogers was official. Cathy took the news with no more emotion than if she had been listening to the morning weather report—a forecast that called for cloudy skies but with only a twenty percent chance of precipitation. And be it due to the previous week's events, or that she had long ago exhausted any love she had left for her ex-husband, Cathy closed the book on her ten-year marriage to Steven Rogers with a sense of numb resignation.

Her ex-husband, on the other hand, seemed to have had a last minute change of heart. On the Friday before their divorce was to be final, Rogers showed up on the Polks' doorstep virtually in tears, demanding to see his wife. And after a quick back and forth between Janet and the man to whom she would always regret introducing her best friend, Cathy emerged onto the Polks' front porch.

"Can we talk, Cat?" Steve shouted over Janet's shoulder. "Please?"

"It's all right, Jan," Cathy said, and Janet scowled her way back into the house.

"I've been following that story all week on TV," Steve began. "Been worrying about how you've been holding up through it all. I begged Janet for your new cell number, but she wouldn't give it to me."

"That's the point of the unlisted number. We agreed that any communication between us would go through our lawyers."

"You wanted that, not me. I wanted to work things out but you didn't want to deal with it. You wanted this divorce, Cat. Remember that."

"What are you doing here, Steven?"

"Well—it's just that—they talked to me, too, you know. The FBI. The day after it all happened. They asked me if I had any students that might fit the profile of the guy they were looking for. Christ, I couldn't give them anything—don't know why the fuck they'd want to talk to me, other than my association with you. Is there something I should know about, Cat? Some other reason why you're involved with this bullshit?"

"They're probably just covering their bases," Cathy lied—it hadn't occurred to her that the FBI might question her ex-husband.

But he's still in the dark. They must not have mentioned the notes.

That was good.

"Christ, Cat. It's been a pretty fucked-up week. I've been seeing all that stuff on TV, been hearing about what happened to Soup and that little boy and . . .

well . . . being sort of involved in a way, and hearing
your name all the time mentioned in that context—
well, it's really been messing with my head, Cat.
Made me realize how foolish I was to let go of the
person that meant the most to me in this world. And,
I don't know, with the finality of it all, our divorce
staring me right in the face, I just thought that
maybe—"

"She dump you, Steven, your little graduate student?"

"Catherine, please," said Steve with a hand through
his thick curly hair. "This has nothing to do with her.
You know I'll never feel the same way about her, about
anybody, as I felt, as I *still feel* about you."

"You should have thought about that before you
got your dick stuck in her thesis. I have nothing more
to say to you. Good-bye, Steven."

Only after she was back inside, only after she
heard the sound of Rogers's BMW Z4 roadster speeding off into the distance, did Cathy realize how much
the events of the previous week had changed her. For
the first time in their twelve-year relationship, Cathy
had not the slightest impulse to give in to Steve
Rogers—not the slightest. That meant that it was
truly over; she had grown stronger—so much so that
when she hung up with Sam Markham the following
Wednesday, Cathy felt secure enough to resign herself to the feelings for him that had already begun to
blossom in her heart.

Of course, Cathy knew very well that her interest
in Markham began with their first encounter; but
Cathy was also smart enough to realize that her feelings toward him had been confused not only by the
overwhelming totality of the previous week's events,
but also by her acute self-awareness of her still-

vulnerable broken heart. But while Markham had been pursuing leads all over New England, after quietly finishing up the spring semester at Brown, after dealing with her ex-husband and retreating with the Polks to Bonnet Shores for the weekend to help them ready their beach house, despite a somber self-consciousness that her actions were playing out in the shadow of the murders of Tommy Campbell and Michael Wenick—murders that, still unbeknown to the general public, had been dedicated to *her*—Cathy also felt a gnawing premonition that a door to a new life had been opened, and that it was Sam Markham who would carry her over the threshold.

In addition to speaking with Markham only twice since telling him about the opening quote to *Slumbering in the Stone,* Cathy received a telephone call from Special Agent Rachel Sullivan the morning after she arrived at Janet's. Sullivan advised Cathy to make an official statement to the Associated Press telling them she could offer nothing more than confirmation that the bodies of Tommy Campbell and Michael Wenick had indeed been found posed like Michelangelo's *Bacchus.* Sullivan also advised that Cathy stay clear of any interviews—not only to maintain the integrity of the investigation, but also in the event the information about the inscription was ever leaked to the press. Cathy heeded Sullivan's advice, and by Friday of that first week, the messages on her voice mail had dwindled down to one.

And so, with the worst seemingly behind her, on the morning after her divorce from Steve Rogers—a bright May morning that whispered of the coming summer, her first as a single woman since her midtwenties—Cathy sat waiting on the Polks' front porch amidst a haze of dread and excitement. Yes, now that the semester was over, now that Rogers was out of her life for good, the void that should have been the beginning of her new life was overwhelmed by a constant preoccupation with two people: The Michelangelo Killer and Sam Markham. That both of them should be inextricably tied together was to Cathy Hildebrant both a blessing and curse. Although she could not rid her mind of The Michelangelo Killer's *Bacchus*, of the terror of knowing that her book had been the inspiration for that heinous crime, by that same token such thoughts invariably brought with them the presence of Sam—a presence far away but at the same time close to her in the dark, a presence that helped her through those long nights alone in the Polks' guest room.

"Nice to see you again," said the FBI agent as Cathy climbed into his Trailblazer. Cathy smiled— the residue of her daydream on the porch making her blush. "You're holding up okay, I take it?"

"All right, I guess. And yourself?"

"I'll brief you in a bit."

Markham drove off.

Cathy thought the FBI agent seemed chipper, more at ease than during their trip from Watch Hill, when the sudden awkwardness between them had taken Cathy completely by surprise. But today, rather than second guess herself, Cathy knew at once that Sam Markham really did think it was nice to see her. And being in his presence again, Cathy was suddenly filled with a buzzing sense of gratitude and guilt at the thought of the circumstances, of the man who had brought them together.

"Sorry I'm late, by the way," Markham added. "But I had to pick up some documents at the Providence office and got caught up for a sec."

"Probably a good thing. We should be past all the traffic by now."

"Yes, I've become quite the regular in that mess this past week."

"So where exactly are you now, Sam? I thought you were working in Boston."

"I am. The Boston Division oversees FBI operations in Massachusetts, Rhode Island, Maine, and New Hampshire, but we have smaller satellite offices scattered about in every state. These are called Resident Agencies. We've got one in Providence, and they've set me up with a computer and my own office there so I can be local—easier for me to get somewhere fast if I need to. However, I still answer to Bill Burrell in the Boston office, and have been traveling back and forth this past week for meetings and to go over evidence."

"I see."

"The Boston office is located right in the heart of downtown, and the facilities are much bigger and more high tech than what we have in Providence. The totality of our operations there demands it— everything from public corruption and organized crime divisions to fraud and counterintelligence. Burrell was reassigned there last fall as the special agent in charge, and also to assist in the restructuring of their Violent Crime Division. I was sent up from Quantico to run a seminar on the latest research and forensic techniques being developed at the National Center for the Analysis of Violent Crime."

"So that's where all the profilers hang out?"

"Actually, there's no such thing. The FBI does not have a job called a profiler—just a term that has sort of evolved in popular culture."

"Forgive me. My television education, I'm afraid."

"No, no," Markham smiled. "Don't feel silly—just one of the many public misconceptions about the Bureau. The procedures commonly associated with what has come to be known as 'profiling' are performed by supervisory special agents like myself back at the NCAVC in Quantico, so it was really only a coincidence that I was nearby when this Michelangelo Killer made his spectacular entry into the public eye."

"Yes. He really has thrown us for a loop, hasn't he? The whole country. Can't turn on the television or even check my e-mail without seeing a picture of *Bacchus* in the headlines—can't even look at it now without thinking of Tommy Campbell and that poor little boy. So does that mean The Michelangelo Killer has gotten what he wants, Sam? Does that mean in a way he's won?"

"As far as turning people on to the works of Michelangelo? I would say yes. Yes he has."

Cathy was silent, lost in thought as Sam Markham pulled onto the Interstate.

"I know what a strain this has been on you," Markham said, glancing toward the Providence skyline. "And I can't tell you how much I appreciate you agreeing to join me today for this teleconference."

"I just hope I can be of some help," Cathy sighed. "Like I told you on the phone, I've been wracking my brain this past week trying to come up with more insight into *Slumbering in the Stone*, but I feel like I've come to a dead end."

"The insight you've given me so far has been invaluable in helping me get a bead on this guy, Cathy. Also, the way you've handled yourself with the press has been more than admirable. It's why I'm taking you to Boston today. It's why I've asked Bill Burrell to bring you in as an official consultant on this case."

"What?" Cathy said—her heart dropping into her stomach. "You mean you want me to work for the FBI?"

"That's exactly what I mean, Cathy. And not for free, either. The Bureau is ready to negotiate a consultant's salary with you."

"But Sam, I—"

"A lot has happened in the eleven days since we first drove together to Watch Hill, Cathy—specifically with regard to the developing profile of our killer. I told you on the phone about the goat—about how The Michelangelo Killer obtained the bottom half of his *Bacchus*'s satyr."

"Yes."

"Well, since our conversation about *Slumbering in the Stone,* and since concluding that The Michelangelo Killer most likely used your book as a springboard for his murders, Rachel Sullivan and her squad have been following up on those class rosters. Now, even though you can't recall any of your former students who fit the physical and psychological profile we've identified for the killer thus far, from the outset Sullivan and her team have been working from the premise that the killer may have been associated with you indirectly—that is, perhaps via one of your students. She thus focused her attention first on all the male students that were listed on your rosters for the three years leading up to the publication of your book and, shortly afterward, your receipt of the anonymous notes—the latter of which, and you'll forgive me, you told us happened shortly after your mother passed away, correct?"

"Yes."

"And you told Sullivan that you did not start requiring your book for your classes until the year after it was published—the following fall, right? Almost a year after you received the quotes and the sonnet?"

"Yes, that's right."

"That means that, even though the killer had to have read your book in a context outside of the classroom, back then he still had to be a local—a student or otherwise—and familiar enough with the campus to be able to drop off the anonymous notes undetected. Just to be safe, Sullivan took into account your class rosters for the following two years as well—which, in theory, would give us the most practical cross section of male students from which to begin drawing a link to potential suspects. As your classes during this time frame were comprised only of majors and graduate students, and as you were teaching only two classes per semester, the actual pool of potential suspects who might have had direct contact with you is quite small. The fact that the vast majority of these students, both undergraduate and graduate, have been *female*, only whittles this number down even further."

"Sam, please don't tell me that this psychopath actually sat in front of me in one of my classes."

"No, no," said Markham with a raise of his hand. "But most likely someone who knew him did."

"What do you mean?"

"Does the name Gabriel Banford mean anything to you, Cathy?"

"Gabriel Banford? Yes, of course, Gabe Banford. I remember Gabe. He was an undergraduate with us for a time—gosh, going back about seven or eight years now. I don't really remember him other than

his jet black hair and his clothes—a little bit more extreme than the usual Goths that sometimes litter the
List Art Center. One of those lost soul types—bright
from what I heard, but no direction. I had him
briefly in class when he was a freshman but he ended
up dropping out and transferring to the Rhode Island School of Design the following fall. His parents
were not happy about it—that I *do* remember. Janet
told me about it later—said they were trying to
blame the department or something. I guess he had
a lot of psychological issues, and later a drug problem from what I heard. I got all this secondhand, of
course, from Janet. I hate to say this, but the only reason I remember him is because of what she told me
happened to him afterward—after he dropped out
of RISD and got involved with the wrong crowd."

"So you know about how he died?"

"You're going to have to forgive me, Sam, but all
of this happened around the same time as my
mother—was in a bit of a fog when Janet told me
about it. But, if I remember correctly, it was a suicide,
right? Drug overdose?"

"That was the official ruling, yes. But before we
talk about that, let me back up a sec. You see, given
the small number of male students in the initial suspect pool—a pool that Sullivan treated from the beginning as potentially comprised of direct and indirect
suspects in terms of their relationship to you—it didn't
take her squad long to track down the whereabouts
of your former students, most of whom are now living out of state. Serial killers, especially the types who
hang on to their victims for an extended period of
time, tend to almost always hunt their prey in a relatively small area in close proximity to their home. If
we take into account the distances between the areas

where Tommy Campbell and Michael Wenick were abducted, the chance of the killer's home lying *beyond* each area in either direction goes down exponentially the farther you travel out of state into Massachusetts and Connecticut. Understand?"

"Yes. Because the murders of Campbell and Wenick occurred in Westerly and Cranston—cities on almost opposite sides of Rhode Island."

"As did the murder of the goat."

"Of course. You said the goat was stolen from a farm in Burrillville, which is even farther away from Watch Hill—sort of up in the northwest corner of the state."

"Right. So we have *three* murders from which we can begin to plot a possible location where The Michelangelo Killer might live. If we include the anonymous notes that you received five and a half years ago, that actually gives us a fourth location to which we can tie the killer. If we plot The Michelangelo Killer's home in the middle of these four points, this would most likely place his home south of Providence—closer to Providence and Brown University if we work from the premise that serial killers of this resident type, the type of which The Michelangelo Killer undoubtedly is, most often first become active in areas closest to their homes—i.e., the notes."

"You mean it's like they get braver as time goes on? Sort of like an animal that ventures out for food farther and farther from his cave?"

"That's exactly what I mean, yes. The need for food, if I may use your analogy, begins to overshadow the risk of getting it. Serial killers have a comfort zone from which they like to work just like anybody else. It's why, as so often is the case, the farther away they get from their comfort zone the easier it is for us to catch them—why so often it's their *later murders* that lead us to them. They start to slip up, get sloppy because oftentimes their need for victims clouds their fear of the risk involved, and thus it's that very risk that ends up being their undoing."

"But what does all this have to do with Gabe Banford?"

"Even though you claimed that none of your former students fit our psychological and, more important, *physical* profile of The Michelangelo Killer, following up on your class rosters, Gabe Banford immediately caught Sullivan's attention because, of all your male students for the time frame we're looking at, Banford was the only one who was deceased. This automatically ruled him out as a potential suspect. However, a closer examination of his case file opened up the possibility of him being a victim—perhaps The Michelangelo Killer's first."

"But how do you conclude that? His death was nothing like Campbell's and Wenick's."

"The case file on Banford paints quite a sad picture of the boy—bright, from a moderately wealthy family in New York City, but psychologically disturbed, in counseling since he was eleven and distant from his parents. The classic example of what we at The Bureau like to call a PEP-child."

"PEP?"

"Pill for every problem—a kid of the Adderall-Ritalin generation. Throw in some Paxil and Zoloft, and you get a good idea of the stew bubbling in Banford's head. To make a long story short, yes, before dropping out of RISD Banford became involved with a group of disenfranchised intelligentsia types who were not only regulars at a gay club in downtown Providence called Series X, but who also dabbled in recreational drugs—marijuana and coke mostly, but sometimes they'd snort heroin and pop hallucinogens, too. The police report in Banford's case file includes a number of statements from his friends claiming that, prior to his death, Banford's heroin snorting was slowly evolving into a habit of the *Trainspotting* variety. And in addition to a monthly stipend from his parents and a string of part-time jobs from which he was fired, Banford's friends told police that they suspected he had begun to support his budding needle habit by *other* means as well—if you take my meaning."

"Gabe Banford?" Cathy said in disbelief.

"Yes. Banford's friends stated to the police that Gabe would often hook up with older men at Series X with the understanding that he would be paid for his services. There was also an ambiguously worded posting on the Men Seeking Men board on Craigslist that the police were able to trace back to Banford when they looked into his computer."

"But why do you think he was connected to The Michelangelo Killer?"

"Although there were high traces of heroin discovered in his system on the night he died, the autopsy report stated that the cause of Gabriel Banford's death was not from an overdose of heroin, but of epinephrine—more commonly known as adrenaline."

"Adrenaline? I don't understand."

"Hear me out. Banford lived with two roommates on the East Side of Providence—both of whom were either complicit in, or at the very least, turned a blind eye to Banford's burgeoning drug use. Banford would most often shoot up in his bedroom where—and I quote from the police report—his roommates said, 'He'd just sit and chill to music and art DVDs.' And so it was in Banford's bedroom that one of his roommates found him the next day when he wouldn't answer his cell phone. Police found a number of syringes and narcotics besides heroin—cocaine, some low grade acid, a little pot—but no prints on anything other than Banford's and his roommates', both of whom had alibis at the time of the boy's death. And so, the police chalked up Banford's overdose of epinephrine either to suicide or as simply a bit of drug experimentation gone bad. The autopsy report stated that the epinephrine itself was of an extremely high concentration per cubic centimeter, but could not be traced to any legitimate source. Probably was manufactured in a homemade lab—which is possible if you have the know-how."

"But what does this have to do with the murder of Tommy Campbell?"

"The autopsy results for both Campbell and Wenick were finalized yesterday. And although his internal organs were removed, with the help of the state medical examiner the FBI labs were able to isolate in some of the tissue samples what appeared to be traces of highly concentrated compounds of both epinephrine and a diazepam-ketamine mix, the latter of which could have been used as a tranquilizer. Thus, the official ruling now stands that Tommy Campbell's death was a result of a myocardial infarction caused by an overdose of highly concentrated epinephrine."

"Oh my God."

"Yes. Strange, isn't it?"

"But, Sam, couldn't this be just a coincidence? I mean, if I follow you correctly, don't you need more evidence to tie The Michelangelo Killer to Banford than just the epinephrine and the fact that he was gay? And why didn't the police investigate the possibility that Banford's death could have been a homicide to begin with?"

"They had nothing to go on other than what they found in the boy's bedroom. No fingerprints, no sign of a struggle, nothing suspicious in his e-mails or on his computer—nothing to indicate that anything was out of the ordinary with regard to what they knew of Banford's life at that point. Banford's friends told police that he had often talked about killing himself, and all signs in his bedroom seemed to point to just that, or perhaps an accidental overdose—the way he was sitting up in bed under the blankets, the DVD player still on, the open book on his nightstand. But as far as *someone else* being involved, well, Banford's roommates testified that when they arrived home later that evening—the evening on which, unbeknown to them, Banford was already dead in his bedroom—the door to the apartment was locked as usual and nothing seemed out of the ordinary."

"So then perhaps it *was* a suicide—or an accidental overdose."

"Perhaps," said Sam Markham. "But there were two interesting details listed in the evidence inventory of the crime scene that, up until now, most likely would have gone unnoticed—or at the very least, deemed irrelevant. The first being the DVD that was found in Banford's room at the time of his death, a DVD that he was most certainly watching when he OD'd—a DVD his roommates told police was stolen from the bookstore where Banford had worked briefly, and from which he had been fired the week earlier. It was a DVD that, along with the other stolen items from the bookstore, the police didn't think unusual for him to have in his room—the room of a former art history and RISD student who, according to his friends, still thought of himself as part of the drug-enlightened intelligentsia."

"What was the DVD?"

"A documentary entitled, *Michelangelo: A Self-Portrait.*"

"Dear God," said Cathy—then suddenly it struck her. "Sam, you said there was another detail. Please don't tell me you were talking about the open book on Banford's nightstand."

"Yes, Cathy. Just published that spring. The first edition of *Slumbering in the Stone.*"

Cathy's head began to spin, but through her confusion there emerged an obvious flaw in the FBI agent's reasoning.

"Wait a minute. What you're saying doesn't make any sense. If, in fact, you're telling me that Banford somehow met The Michelangelo Killer either at Series X or on Craigslist, how on earth could this psychopath have connected Banford to me—to his having been in my class? I mean, the kid wasn't even in the department for a whole semester, and had been out of Brown for over two years at the time of his death."

"I am aware of that, yes."

"And why would The Michelangelo Killer have stolen my book from the bookstore where Banford worked? Why would he have left it in Banford's room?"

"I never said the killer stole the book."

"So you're saying that *Banford* stole the book, too?"

"That's exactly what I'm saying."

"Sam, please, I'm confused. Are you saying then that Gabe Banford might have stolen the book and the DVD for The Michelangelo Killer?"

"No, Cathy," said Markham—his eyes off the road

and on her for the first time during their drive. "What I'm saying is this: I think there is a strong possibility that The Michelangelo Killer connected Banford to you only *after* he met him. He might have spotted him at Series X or contacted him on the computer or perhaps even first saw him in the bookstore. Might have singled him out for any number of reasons—maybe because The Michelangelo Killer was sexually attracted to him, maybe because Banford represented to him everything about today's cultural excesses that The Michelangelo Killer so despises. We might never know, as the club has been closed for three years now and Banford's computer long ago destroyed. But if I'm right about this, I think The Michelangelo Killer was going to murder Gabriel Banford anyway. I think, for whatever reason, he had chosen this boy to fulfill some sick desire— perhaps even a sexual one at the beginning—but it was *you and your book* that gave him a greater understanding of the true nature of that desire—a desire rooted in his homosexuality. Maybe through your book he found a parallel between his relationship with Banford and that of Michelangelo and Cavalieri. And so it was you, Cathy, who thus focused him on his greater purpose."

"I don't understand."

"This past week, in addition to scoping out the countryside surrounding the farm in Burrillville, I checked out the Campbells' property down at Watch Hill, as well as the woods surrounding Blackamore Pond in Cranston. At first I thought there might be some connection to Campbell and Wenick having been abducted near a body of water, but then I realized that all three areas, including the farm in Burrillville, can be viewed unobstructed from at least one vantage point located a relatively long distance away: the Campbells' porch from across the water on the banks of Foster Cove, the spot in the woods where Wenick was abducted from the opposite shore of Blackamore Pond, and the paddock in which the goats are kept from atop a nearby hill. This means that The Michelangelo Killer could have watched his victims undetected for any length of time. That means he could have studied them and planned his movements accordingly.

"Now, once we learned about Banford, I checked out the location of his old apartment on the East Side. And what do you think I found? Yes, the same thing—an unobstructed vantage point from a few blocks away that gave a clear view of what used to be Banford's corner bedroom on the top floor of his three-story walkup. This means The Michelangelo Killer could have known when Banford was in his room or perhaps, more important, when he *wasn't* in his room."

"You mean the killer broke in while he was away? You mean he was waiting for him when Gabe Banford came home?"

"I have no idea, Cathy, but the coincidence of the epinephrine and the Michelangelo material is just too startling to ignore. And when you think about it, it actually makes more sense that The Michelangelo Killer would have found out about you and your book after he had already decided to kill Banford—I mean, given what we know about him so far, there is no question that he is very selective when it comes to choosing his victims in conjunction not only with your book, but also with what he sees as his greater purpose. And the way the Banford murder played out—the fact that he left the body there, the fact that it wasn't posed in any particular way—indicates that his purpose at that time may have not been fully realized.

"So you see, when it comes right down to it, we're most likely looking at one of two possible scenarios in terms of Banford being the link between you and The Michelangelo Killer. The first, that Banford knew his killer and that they had some kind of relationship and Banford told him about the book, or perhaps about how you used to be one of his professors. The other scenario is that The Michelangelo Killer might have been in Banford's room sometime *before* he killed him, and ended up having some kind of an epiphany. That by seeing the DVD and your book only by chance, by coincidence, by being in the world of his victim, he suddenly understood why the hands of fate had brought him and his victim together. He got lucky in a sense just like we did when we stumbled onto Banford while exploring your class rosters for a suspect. That Banford should have been on one of your rosters *and* in possession of *Slumbering in the Stone* might have been a detail of which the killer was entirely unaware.

"Then there's the night he died. With Banford high on heroin and whatever else, The Michelangelo Killer could have easily climbed up the fire escape and subdued the boy without a fight. Who knows, in his drugged-out state, Banford might have even opened the damn window for him—might have actually welcomed him into his room thinking he was the Tooth Fairy or something. But my point is, just as I'm convinced that it was Banford who somehow turned The Michelangelo Killer on to you, I am also convinced that The Michelangelo Killer was not only in the boy's room on the night he died, but also that it was he who injected Banford with the adrenaline while forcing him to watch the DVD on Michelangelo's life."

"But why would he make Banford watch the DVD?"

"To free him from his slumber, of course. The same reason The Michelangelo Killer uses epinephrine to murder his victims."

Cathy stared at Markham blankly.

"When do we as human beings produce the most adrenaline?" he asked.

"When we're excited—no, when we're afraid, of course."

"And what do most people fear more than anything else?"

"I guess that would be death."

"Perhaps. But one could argue the opposite—that our fear of *life* is more terrifying than any other we as human beings ever experience, and thus produces the most adrenaline. It is a fear, however, that we have forgotten; a terror that is fleeting, yes, but perhaps so powerful, that the only way our minds can deal with it *is to forget.* And that is the fear of leaving the womb, a child's fear at the moment he is born."

"'What I wish to learn from your beautiful face,'" Cathy said absently, "'cannot be understood in the minds of men.'"

Markham finished the quote.

"'He who wishes to learn can only die.'"

"So that means that—when he kills them—he wants them to have the same revelation, the same *understanding* that he has. And through their fear they are reborn. The Sculptor's hand has awakened

them, freed them from their slumber in the womb—
in the stone."

"Yes. Tommy Campbell was alive when his penis
was removed and alive when his flesh was stitched
back together. That means The Michelangelo Killer
wanted him to see what he had become and thus
wanted him to understand the true nature of his re-
birth."

"He had already killed then, Sam," Cathy said suddenly. "When he sent me the sonnet—The Michelangelo Killer had already murdered Gabe Banford
months earlier."

"Yes, Cathy. So maybe the quotes and the sonnets
were more than just an attempt to make contact with
you. Maybe The Michelangelo Killer was not only
telling you he understood, but also was trying to say
'thank you' in a way for showing him why he wanted
to murder Banford, for showing him his true purpose—a purpose that he simply stumbled upon in
what he must have seen as a stroke of divine providence."

Cathy felt a shiver run across her back, but what
Sam Markham said next terrified her more than her
thoughts of the faceless Michelangelo Killer.

"I was wrong about this guy, Cathy. I was wrong
about the timeline, about when the goat was killed in
relation to the murder of Michael Wenick, and thus
about the killer's progression from animals to humans. It's something that I should have seen from
the beginning, simply because it would have made
more practical sense for the killer—and forgive me
for putting it this way—to get the top half of his satyr
first, and then fit the bottom half, the goat legs, onto
it. What I'm saying is, The Michelangelo Killer was already confident enough in his technique of 'sculpt-

ing' the bodies of his victims *before* he abducted
Wenick and Campbell—bodies that he intended to
put on public display. That I didn't see the obvious
practicality of acquiring Wenick first was an amateur
mistake on my part, clouded by the fact that this
Michelangelo Killer's modus operandi is unlike any
we've ever seen. It's why I need you on this case with
me, Cathy, why I need your insight into the mind of
Michelangelo to help me get into the mind of this
killer."

"I'll do what I can to help you, Sam," said Cathy—
the words falling from her lips before she had time to
think.

"Thank you," said Markham. There was a long silence—the low hum of the Trailblazer's tires the only
sound.

"You mentioned something a moment ago," Cathy
said finally. "You said the killer was already confident
in his technique of sculpting. Are you saying, Sam,
that you think The Michelangelo Killer might have
even more victims? That he might have killed others
in the five-and-a-half-year gap between Gabriel Banford and Michael Wenick—others that he used simply to experiment and develop his technique? Like
an artist?"

"I hope I'm wrong, Cathy, but I can't get the pictures from your book out of my mind—the pictures
of Michelangelo's early sculptures; the reliefs and
the smaller statues that he made before he broke
onto the scene with his first life-size sculpture, his
Bacchus. And even though serial killers usually have
what's called a 'cooling off' period, even though this
Michelangelo Killer is a very calculated and patient
man, five and a half years seems like a long time for
him to merely jump from a murder like Banford's to

the type we see with Campbell and Wenick. Yes, it's important that his victims looked like the figures in Michelangelo's *Bacchus*, but if we take into account what happened to Banford—and, as I suspect, what also happened to Campbell—of equal, perhaps even more importance is the awakening of the *figures themselves*, not just the public's interpretation of their deeper message. My only hope is that—since this guy is so patient, since he is so obsessed with detail that he was willing to risk murdering a public figure like Tommy Campbell for his *Bacchus*—he might not have wanted to risk being caught while experimenting on other victims."

"Then Gabriel Banford might have been an experiment, too."

"Either that, yes, or as I suspect, part of a larger plan yet unformed. We might never know if Banford was The Michelangelo Killer's first murder, but from what Rachel Sullivan's investigation into the criminal databases has told us thus far, it most likely was the first in which he used epinephrine—no records going back over the last ten years list a suspicious death due to an overdose of epinephrine."

"But if The Michelangelo Killer did indeed develop his technique like an artist," Cathy said, "if he has experimented with the use of adrenaline and the preservation of other bodies over the last few years in secret, there could be no way of telling how many people he killed before Campbell and Wenick, before the creation of his *Bacchus*."

"That's what I'm afraid of, Cathy. That's exactly what I'm afraid of."

Chapter 18

The FBI Field Office. Boston. Ten minutes past ten.

Bill Burrell sat at the conference table scowling into his coffee. He needed a smoke—*needed it bad*—but did not want to step outside and risk missing the linkup with Quantico. Markham and the art history professor were running a little late—an accident on the inbound artery, Sullivan had told him. *A little luck*, Burrell thought, as the Boston office was having an embarrassing bit of interference with their video feed that day—something about sunspots, his tech guy had said, or a faulty coaxial cable. Either way, Burrell was not in the mood to be understanding. No, the briefing from Rachel Sullivan that morning—the news about Gabriel Banford, about the adrenaline link—did not sit well with him. And the SAC knew instinctively that the upcoming teleconference with Quantico would be no better, for whereas Sam Markham was still holding out hope that the FBI had only three victims on their hands, Bulldog Burrell had a bad feeling that this son of a bitch Michelangelo Killer had more than just the blood of Banford, Wenick, and Campbell on *his*.

"Sorry, Bill," said Markham, entering. "Had to stop by in-processing to get the paperwork started for Dr. Hildebrant. Cathy, you remember Special Agent in Charge Bill Burrell?"

There were others seated around the large conference table, but only Burrell and Rachel Sullivan rose to greet her.

"Yes, of course," Cathy said. "A pleasure to see you again. And you, too, Special Agent Sullivan."

"Call me Rachel."

"And you can call me Bill," said Burrell. "Please, be seated."

An FBI agent to whom Cathy was introduced— and whose name she immediately forgot—vacated his seat for her at the far end of the table, and Cathy and Markham took their places across from Burrell and Sullivan—a large video screen on the wall before them. Cathy suddenly noticed another man on all fours—his rear poking out of a closet that seamlessly blended in with the rest of the walnut paneled walls.

"You'll have to forgive us," began Burrell, "but we're having a bit of technical difficulties this morning. Can I get you something to drink? Coffee or something?"

"No thank you. Sam—I mean, Special Agent Markham already offered."

"Then he already briefed you on what to expect today?"

"Yes, he did."

"Good," said Burrell. "First off then, on behalf of the Federal Bureau of Investigation I would like to officially welcome you on board. I want to also thank you personally for all your help thus far, and for agreeing to work with us as we move forward on this case. You've been an invaluable asset to us in developing the profile for this killer, Cathy. I assume that, on your ride up from Providence, Sam here brought you up to date on where things stand at this point? Told you about the development regarding your former student Gabriel Banford, and the possibility of his being linked to this psychopath the press is calling The Michelangelo Killer?"

"Yes."

"Rachel here is overseeing that end of things. She will be working on the Banford case file with the hopes of finding a more concrete link between him and the killer—mutual acquaintances, Internet records from the postings on Craigslist, that kind of thing. Her team will also be looking into all the unsolved missing person cases in Rhode Island and its immediate vicinity dating from the Banford murder to the present— cases involving other young men who this Michelangelo Killer might have abducted and experimented with before he got to Wenick and Campbell."

"You see, Cathy," said Markham, "serial killers tend to consciously select their victims from one particular demographic—victims who meet certain criteria that, for whatever reason, gratify the serial killer's deeper psychological motivations to murder—motivations of which the killer might be either unconscious or sometimes fully aware."

"That's right," said Burrell. "And given the profile that you and Markham have developed for this Michelangelo Killer so far, the murder of young males most likely is this guy's MO. Therefore, Sullivan and her team will be specifically looking into the disappearance of young male prostitutes and drifters who were known to reside in Rhode Island and the surround-

ing area over the last six years. Not only does this fit
the profile of Gabriel Banford, who we know had
begun stealing and prostituting himself to help support his drug habit, but also these types of victims
tend to be safer targets for serial killers in that, because so many of them move around from one place
to another, their disappearances usually go unreported—and thus, in this case, would draw little attention to The Michelangelo Killer while he
developed his craft."

"Yes," said Sullivan. "As Agent Markham probably
informed you, we're going to begin working from
the premise that, after the Banford murder, The
Michelangelo Killer would have wanted to develop
his technique for preserving and painting his figures
before the public unveiling of his *Bacchus* nearly six
years later. However, we have another team working
from the angle that the killer might have already
been familiar with embalming, and thus they'll be in-
vestigating funeral parlors, morticians, taxidermists,
and others who not only would have that kind of
working knowledge, but who would also have access
to the types of chemicals needed to preserve a
corpse. It's those preliminary findings from the FBI
labs at Quantico on which we'll be briefed today.
Once we have an idea of exactly how the killer went
about preserving Campbell and Wenick, we'll have
much more to go on."

"All set, Chief," said the man whose behind had
been sticking out of the wall. Cathy recognized him
from Watch Hill—the "tech guy" who had set her up
with the laptop that day.

Burrell nodded and the large video screen on the
wall flickered to life—two men seated at a table, one
in a suit, one in a white lab coat.

"We got a visual on you now, gentlemen," said Burrell. "How about you?"

"Yes, Bill," said the man in the suit. "We can see you fine."

"Good. You know everybody else here, Alan, but I want to introduce you to Dr. Catherine Hildebrant. She's agreed to come on board as a consultant in the case and will be assisting Sam down in Providence. Cathy, this is Alan Gates, chief of Behavioral Analysis Unit-2 at Quantico. Next to him is Dr. Gilbert Morris. He heads up the Chemistry Unit in Scientific Analysis back at the FBI Laboratory."

The two men nodded their hellos.

"What have we got, gentlemen?"

"I talked to Special Agent Markham earlier this morning, Bill," said Unit Chief Alan Gates, the man in the suit. "He's updated me on the latest developments, so I'll defer to him for the rest of this conference. Sam is officially in charge now from our end, and has expressed his utmost confidence in your team there—specifically Agent Sullivan and her outstanding work as coordinator between your office and the NCAVC."

"Good," said Burrell. "Dr. Morris?"

"Thank you, Bill. I've been instructed to tell you that the scientists in the Trace Evidence Unit will be submitting their report on the wooden base and the tree stump to your offices later today."

"Fine."

"With regard to Scientific Analysis, one of my assistants is preparing a breakdown of the specifics from each subunit as we speak, but I'll give you a general overview of what we've found thus far." The man in the white lab coat shuffled a pile of papers. "First off, we've found nothing more in the chemical makeup of the epoxy compound that was used to sculpt the lion skin, the bowl, and the figures' hair that would identify it as anything other than the TAP brand *Magic-Sculpt* commonly sold on the Internet or in the arts and crafts stores in your area."

"Good," said Burrell. "I've already got people working on that angle."

"The Toxicology Unit, in conjunction with the state medical examiner in Rhode Island, has confirmed that the high concentrations of synthetic epinephrine found in Tommy Campbell's tissue did indeed lead to his death. Five years ago, we might have missed this, Bill, as the chemicals the killer used in the preservation process altered the base cell structure significantly. However, we still might not be able to get a pure enough sample of the epinephrine to allow us to trace the drug to a specific source. The same goes for the high-powered diazepam and ketamine. We'll keep you updated as that investigation progresses."

"Right."

"Here in our labs at Quantico, we've been able to determine that the killer preserved his victims building on a technique called Plastination—a process where water and lipid tissues are replaced by curable polymers."

"Plastination?" asked Burrell.

"Yes. A process of anatomical preservation being used more and more around the world, but first developed in the late seventies by a German scientist named Dr. Gunther von Hagens. There have been a number of his Body Worlds exhibitions in the last decade or so, but a similar show from a Chinese company recently drew a lot of worldwide attention and criticism. I've included those details in my report, but the general character of both the German and Chinese exhibitions is the same—a group of skinless, sometimes partially dissected cadavers posed in life-like positions and put on display for public viewing. Individual plasticized body parts are also sold to medical and veterinary schools all over the world, but are nonetheless quite expensive."

"So what do you think, Alan? Our man might have once been a med student? Might have even worked for one of those companies?"

"Maybe," said Unit Chief Gates. "But unfortunately, Bill, the information about the Plastination process is readily available on the Internet. Anyone with a basic knowledge of chemistry and the desire—as well as the time and means to fulfill that desire—could, with a little trial and error, figure out the process himself."

"That's right," said Dr. Morris. "It appears the killer preserved his victims by first removing their internal organs and then embalming them with a formaldehyde solution. Then the body was placed in a bath of acetone, which—under freezing conditions—would draw out the water and replace itself in the cells. Next would come the bath of the liquid polymer, in this case silicone rubber. By creating a vacuum, the acetone will boil and vaporize at a very low temperature, drawing the liquid polymer into the cells behind it. While the bodies were still supple, the killer then stuffed the cavities, stretched the bodies into the desired position on the metal frame—probably using wires to help him pose his figures—and left them to dry. Keep in mind, Bill, that the plastic must be cured, and most likely the killer hardened it using heat or ultraviolet light."

"Jesus Christ," said Burrell.

"Yes," said Gates. "Our boy has quite an operation going. He has a large space—a studio, if you will—in which to work. Must also have quite a lot of money socked away. I suppose some of the equipment such as the ultraviolet lamps and the vacuum sealed tub needed for the acetone and polymer baths could be jury-rigged, but the amount of time for experimentation, as well as the time it would take to preserve each body, even under ideal conditions, is staggering—estimated anywhere from eight to twelve hundred man hours."

"So we're looking at a guy who has a lot of time on his hands? A guy who is perhaps independently wealthy?"

"Probably," said Gates. "If you take into account the timeline between Campbell's disappearance and the appearance of the bodies down at Watch Hill, you're looking at a total of just over three months. Even with all that time off, needless to say, our boy hasn't been getting much sleep lately."

The room was silent.

"Sales or thefts of large quantities of acetone," said Gates, "as well as the silicone rubber needed for the Plastination process will be a good place for our teams here to begin. We'll take care of tracking things down on that end."

Burrell nodded.

"Next," Dr. Morris began again, "the Paints and Polymers subunit found a match in our database for the chemical compound of the paint used on the figures of Campbell and Wenick—a mixture of Starfire brand acrylic enamel auto paints, including a primer and a clear coat. Like the epoxy, this brand of automotive paint can be found at many dealers throughout the country and on the Internet. The paint was clearly applied to the bodies in many layers, and by using some type of sprayer. However, mixed into the paint was a white powder that the General Chemistry subunit identified as ground marble."

"Marble?" asked Burrell. "You mean like the kind of marble used in statues?"

"Yes, that's exactly what I mean, Bill. Nonfoliated, calcite-based metamorphic rock with the molecular makeup, color, and density identical to what our databases identified as unique to and originating from a specific quarry in Italy."

"Carrara," said Cathy absently, impulsively.

"That's right, Dr. Hildebrant," said Gilbert Morris. "The ground marble found in the paint was undoubtedly quarried from Carrara, Italy."

"How did you know it was Carrara, Cathy?" asked Burrell.

"Well," she began, "Carrara is a small town in Italy about sixty miles north of Florence. The marble quarried there has been a favorite of sculptors dating back to Ancient Rome, and many of the city's greatest monuments were carved from it—as were countless sculptures during the Renaissance. Even more so than his own quarries in Pietrasanta, Michelangelo prized Carrara marble above all other types of stone because of its beauty and consistency. Indeed, it was from blocks of Carrara marble that Michelangelo carved his most famous masterpieces."

"And they're still quarrying marble there today?" asked Rachel Sullivan.

"Yes. As far as I know, Carrara marble is still regarded as the finest, and statues carved from it are exported all over the world. However, the marble itself is very expensive."

"So," said Burrell, "it appears this Michelangelo

Killer went through a great deal of effort and expense not only to get Tommy Campbell for his *Bacchus,* but also in acquiring the marble powder from Carrara. This might be our best lead so far. Sullivan, you'll assign someone to start looking into the import records for all the Carrara marble coming into Rhode Island? See if you can track down sales records for vendors who deal specifically with Carrara marble statues?"

"Will do."

"You should probably look into any reports of statue or marble thefts in the area over the last six years, too. Maybe our man got his marble that way—stole a statue or something and ground it up himself."

"Right."

As Dr. Morris went on to give the report from the Metallurgy subunit on the sculpture's frame, Cathy glanced uneasily over to Sam Markham. Among his paperwork from the Providence office, Markham had also brought with him his copy of *Slumbering in the Stone.* Cathy could not see to which page he had turned, but she knew exactly what he was looking for. And as if reading her mind, Markham looked up from his book to meet its author's gaze.

"I think Dr. Hildebrant would like to say something," he said. "Go ahead, Cathy. It's about Michelangelo's *Bacchus,* isn't it?"

"Yes," Cathy said—the room at once was silent. "Although Michelangelo carved his most famous sculptures from blocks of Carrara marble, for his *Bacchus* he used a flawed block of *Roman* marble. That is, marble that was *not* quarried from Carrara."

"So?" asked Burrell. Cathy looked to Markham,

who—nodding understandingly—smiled back at her with his eyes.

"Go ahead, Cathy."

"Well," she said, "given what we know about The Michelangelo Killer thus far—about his obsession with detail, about his desire to embody his *Bacchus* in the historical milieu of the original—it seems strange to me that he would knowingly and erroneously use Carrara marble powder for his statue when other types of flawed, low-grade marble of the Roman variety would be readily available to him for much cheaper."

"I don't follow," said Burrell. "And what's the difference really? The guy is obviously so obsessed with being like Michelangelo that he wanted to use the Carrara marble powder simply because it was Michelangelo's favorite. Maybe he wanted to improve upon the original—make his *Bacchus* from better stuff than Michelangelo's."

"What Dr. Hildebrant is saying," said Markham, "is that The Michelangelo Killer wouldn't do that."

"Why?"

"Because, from what we can tell about this guy, if he had originally planned on acquiring marble powder for his *Bacchus,* he would not have settled for anything other than a type of marble powder more in line with that of Michelangelo's original. Thus, Dr. Hildebrant is telling you that The Michelangelo Killer used the Carrara marble most likely because he already had it—most likely because he had originally planned on using it for something else. Something more appropriate."

"What?" asked Bill Burrell.

As Sam Markham held up his copy of *Slumbering in*

the Stone, Cathy and the rest of the room saw the page to which he had turned.

It was just as Cathy had suspected.

Sam Markham was holding up a picture of Michelangelo's *David.*

Chapter 19

That afternoon The Sculptor was Christian again. With the females he had called himself Mike or Michael, sometimes Angelo—but now that he was with the boys, it would be Christian. *Chris* for short. Yes. *Had* to be Chris—seemed only fitting, unquestionably more *appropriate*.

Chris.

Chris, Chris, Chris.

Chris sat in his Toyota Camry about three blocks away from the Providence hotel where he had told RounDaWay17 to meet him. This gave Chris a clear view of Kennedy Plaza, where he knew his consort would soon be arriving. Chris had told RounDaWay17 he would compensate him handsomely for the bus trip from Boston, told him he was a businessman from New York City in Providence only for one night, and RounDaWay17 was just what he was looking for. RounDaWay17 told Chris that his real name was Jim; told him that he was twenty-one, but from his pictures, with his shirt off and all, he *really* appeared to be around sixteen or seventeen—probably

of Hispanic descent; lean, but not too slight of
build—of perfect proportion for The Sculptor's next
project. Of course, The Sculptor would not know for
sure until he saw RounDaWay17 in person. Nonetheless, the man who today called himself Chris felt
more than satisfied with his choice.

True, it had been hard to tell with the females,
and when it came right down to it, both Michael and
Angelo never really *understood* the females—never really
knew what they were getting even though they had
met the ladies in person first, had picked them up at
night off the streets of South Providence. However,
back then The Sculptor was not nearly as skilled as
he was now; he did not know how to cloak his IP address while shopping for his material on Craigslist as
he would for clothes at the Gap. Yes, when it came
right down to it, back then The Sculptor was little
more than an amateur.

Now, however—almost six years after he first spotted the angel in black at Series X, almost six years
after he followed, watched, and *freed* him from his
slumber—yes, almost six years after the Goth named
Gabe brought him and Dr. Hildy together, The
Sculptor had had more than enough time to prac-
tice.

And so the man named Chris was elated to see
RounDaWay17 step off the bus at Kennedy Plaza and
begin heading toward the hotel. Chris rested his
elbow on the door and surreptitiously raised a small
spyglass to his eye—he did not worry that it was daytime, or that someone might see him. No, the windows of his Camry were tinted and the license plates
today were phonies—the car hardly noticeable amidst
the countless others that crowded the busy streets of
downtown Providence. And as RounDaWay17 made

his way across the street with his overnight bag—passing right by the blue Camry—Chris was nearly brought to tears. The Sculptor had chosen his Jesus well—he would be the perfect size to complement his Mary. True, his Mary was not yet complete, but that was something he would take care of this weekend while the material for Jesus cured in the carriage house, in the big stainless steel hospital tub.

The *Pietà* would come together much more quickly than his *Bacchus*—would take much less planning, for the *Pietà* would not require the kind of hard-to-find material that had been needed for *Bacchus*. No, now that he had gotten the world's attention, now that they had all begun to awaken from their slumber, The Sculptor understood that he could use the material that was readily available to him—*bargain* material that would serve the purpose just as nicely.

Besides, the most important part of his *Pietà* involved Dr. Hildy. Oh yes, he would have to thank her in some way for all her help; he would have to show her how truly grateful he was by giving her something much more than just an inscription on the base of a statue—an idea that seemed kind of silly to him now. Yes, The Sculptor hated the Internet, hated television and the media, but had understood from the beginning that part of his work would have to include the daily monitoring of the sales of *Slumbering in the Stone* and other books on Michelangelo, as well as keeping track of the public's growing interest in the artist as a whole—the specials on the documentary channels, the magazine articles, the talk shows, the search engines, etcetera, etcetera. And although Dr. Hildy had not yet granted any interviews, although she had not yet spoken in public about her book, The Sculptor was thrilled nonetheless at the

snowballing success of his *Bacchus*—success that only
The Sculptor and perhaps the FBI knew was due in
large part to good ol' Dr. Hildy.

Yes, Chris said to himself as he started his car. *There
will be time to thank her later. That's what this weekend is
for.*

His mind back on his prey, Chris let RounDa-
Way17 disappear down a side street before pulling
out into traffic and looping around the block to in-
tercept him. He slid into a parking spot at the curb
and adjusted the rearview mirror—a hand over his
slicked blond hair and a nudge of his glasses in as he
waited for the young man to approach from the sidewalk.

"Jim?" called Chris, rolling down his window. Roun-
DaWay17 stopped—startled, his eyes narrowing. Michael and Angelo had seen that look with the females,
too—that red, hungry look of desperation, suspicion, poor judgment. From RounDaWay17's pictures,
however, Chris did not think the boy liked needles in
the way the Goth named Gabe had, or like some of
the females he found in South Providence. Of course,
he wouldn't know for sure until he got RounDaWay17
back to the carriage house, but hoped that—if in fact
RounDaWay17 did like needles—the marks would be
on the back of the legs like with the females.

But then again, those females had been bad material all around.

"It's me, Jim. *Chris.*"

A light flickered in the young man's eyes. Instinctively he scanned the street, then glanced quickly at
Chris's license plate. The females had done that, too.

"Oh my God," said Chris as RounDaWay17 approached his window. "I'm so glad I ran into you before you got to the hotel. I was just going to leave a

message for you at the front desk, but you saved me the trouble. They screwed up my reservation. I know I told you the Westin but I'm going to be staying at the Marriott instead. It's over on Orms Street. Hop in."

RounDaWay17 scanned the street again—the instinct, the suspicion.

"Or I can just meet you there," Chris said, smiling. "It's a bit of a walk, so you'll have to grab a taxi. It's up to you."

RounDaWay17 hesitated only for a moment, then quickly made his way around to the passenger's side—his overnight bag in the backseat.

Then they were off.

"I have to say, Jim," Chris began after a moment. "You're much better looking than your pictures."

RounDaWay17 smiled thinly. Chris could see that the young man was nervous; he knew that he would soon start telling him how he hadn't been at this long—perhaps might even say that this was his first time, as some of the females had. But just as Michael and Angelo had been smart enough to know that the females were lying, Chris was also smart enough to know that—if in fact RounDaWay17 *did* leap into such a narrative—the young man most likely would be lying, too.

Chris stopped at the traffic light for the on-ramp—Cranston, Route 10.

He was first in line.

That was fortunate.

"You ever been there?" asked Chris, pointing past RounDaWay17 to the Providence Place Mall.

"Coupla times," said the young man.

"Maybe when we're finished I'll get you something nice."

RounDaWay17 smiled again—wider, more relaxed.

The light turned green. Chris headed for the on-ramp.

"We going to Cranston?" asked RounDaWay17.

"You see the sign for that new clothing store up there?" Chris replied. And as RounDaWay17 craned his neck to look out the passenger side window—unwittingly baring his jugular—in a flash The Sculptor hit his target.

The *hiss-pop* of the gun startled the young man more than the pain of the dart, and RounDaWay17's hand automatically went to his neck—his fingers closing around the dart at the same time he met his attacker's gaze. But the damage was done, and just before RounDaWay17's eyes glazed over, The Sculptor could see in them the grim flicker of realization, of *fear*.

Then the boy was out—slumped over and sleeping soundly in the passenger seat before The Sculptor even reached the highway.

The Sculptor pulled the dart from the boy's neck, removed his wig and his glasses, and put everything under the seat. He looked in the rearview mirror—a hand over his bald shaved head.

Now again he was The Sculptor. And now again he was smiling; for The Sculptor knew that the next time RounDaWay17 opened his eyes, he would awaken in the arms of divine release.

Chapter 20

"What's bothering you, Cathy?"

It was late in the afternoon, and they were stuck in traffic at the Route 93/95 interchange—had hardly spoken a word to one another following the teleconference, the paperwork, and Cathy's long orientation with Personnel.

"My life," Cathy whispered suddenly. "My whole life has been dedicated to the work of Michelangelo. And now I'll never be able to look at his statues, teach a class—never will be able to even *think* about him the same way again—I mean, without thinking about . . ."

Cathy trailed off into a quiet stream of tears. And as the Trailblazer inched slowly forward, Markham reached out his hand for hers. She let him take it—felt her fingers melt into his.

"I'm sorry," was all the FBI agent said.

But for Cathy Hildebrant, it was enough. And once the Trailblazer found its way onto Route 95, once the traffic picked up and they were on their way again, Cathy realized her tears had dried.

The two of them drove the rest of the way to Cranston in silence.

Sam Markham, however, did not let go of Cathy's hand.

"I'll be flying off to Washington tomorrow," he said, parking in front of the Polks' house. "Official business and to gather the rest of my things—will be back Monday morning. We've still got people looking after you, but I want you to call me if you need anything. Even if you just want to talk. Okay, Cathy?"

"Only if you promise to do the same."

Markham smiled.

"I promise."

"Okay. I promise, too."

Then Cathy did something she had never done before in her life: unsolicited and of her own accord, she leaned over and kissed a man on the cheek.

"Thank you, Sam," she said, and was gone.

Only when she was safe inside the Polks' kitchen, only when Janet asked her how her day had gone, did Cathy realize what she had done. And just as the shy art history professor began to giggle, back on the road Markham checked his face in the rearview mirror.

He was still blushing.

Chapter 21

"Shake off your slumber, O son of God."

Why is Papa speaking English?

The seventeen-year-old runaway from Virginia Beach smiled—happy to be home again. But for some reason his bed was cold and hard this morning, and he could feel his heart pounding in his back and in his side against—

The bus station floor. I fell asleep again at the bus station.

Paul Jimenez cracked his eyes—a bright ball of light stinging them to slits.

No, he thought. *Something else. I can't wake up.*

"Bad shit," he heard himself whisper. "Eliot, you motherfuck—"

But then Paul Jimenez remembered that he didn't talk to Eliot anymore—had not even seen him in over six months, ever since the pigs picked him up for stealing those checks. And Paul never used that shit like Eliot did—never used that shit *at all* anymore. He had been lucky with that, had been warned about that shit almost a year ago on his first day in town by the guy he met at the Boston Public Library; the guy who smiled a big gold-tooth smile when Paul said he was clean; the guy who told him about the big bucks a kid like Paul could make on Arlington Street as long as he stayed clean.

"You start taking that shit, though," the guy had said, *"and you're done, son. Hawks ain't gonna drop that kinda coin for a junkie. Fresh and clean. Remember that."*

Paul's eyes fluttered wide, and amidst a bright white haze the young man suddenly understood that he was not on the bus station floor; he was not even on the floor at Brian's—that cold hardwood floor on which he had been crashing with his friends for the last couple of months, and on which a roach tried to crawl in his ear. But he was lying down—yes, could feel something steel-hard on his back and buttocks. And he was groggy, felt like he couldn't move—*had to be doped up on something.* Yet at the same time he felt his veins pumping with energy, with the light above him, with the heart pounding beat of—

Music? Somebody slip me shit at the club? Some bath- room floor in Chinatown?

For a moment Paul thought he could see the dance floor, the lights flashing on the college boys— some looking for it for free, some looking to make some extra money to get their Abercrombie & Fitch fix. All the same.

Roofie motherfuckers.

"That's it," said the man's voice—a voice that Paul recognized from someplace. "Come forth from the stone."

Paul tried to speak, but his throat hurt—felt like he had swallowed a glass full of needles. Then he felt a dull prick, a tug on his forearm. His heart was rac- ing—even more so than when he confessed to Papa that he liked boys; even more so than when Papa shut him in the hotel room with that prostitute hoping that he would come out a man; even more so than when Papa drove him to the Greyhound station, bought him a bus ticket to Boston, and told him never to come home again. But this was a different kind of heartbeat—harder, *more painful*—a heartbeat that he could feel all the way down to his fingers and toes, the tips of which felt like they wanted to pop.

"Where am I?" Paul asked, his voice cracking. The edges of the light before him solidified into a white rectangle—

Must be the Strand, he thought—the shit-bag movie theatre where, as "Jim," he used to meet his clients in the back row for a quick swallow or no swallow—ten percent of either going to the theatre manager, of course. But that was before he started using the computer at the library; that was before he set himself up in business online—where the *real* money was. Yeah, he still worked Arlington Street sometimes, but only in a pinch; only when—

No, Paul thought. *It ain't the Strand*—screen was too sharp, too close to his face in the darkness. And then Paul's senses, Paul's memory came back to him in one big rush—the images in his beating blood filling his brain like water in a balloon.

The man in the car. The big man in the suit. Chris. Was going well. Was buying Jim's innocent act. Then he spit at me—no, pinched me in the neck; smiled at me when I—

Instinctively Paul tried to sit up, tried to separate himself from the cold steel behind him—but his head would not move, would not even turn from side to side. And he felt something on his shoulders—hairy and itchy. Paul tried to lift his hands, but his wrists were tied down; and although he could not see his chest, his thighs, or his ankles, he understood all at once that the man named Chris had strapped him down to a table.

Naked.

It's finally happened, Paul thought, his mind scrambling for what to do. *I finally got myself in with a* loco.

Sure, during his year on the streets of Boston, Paul had run into his share of freaks—had even let a hawk dress "Jim" up in a diaper once and whip him with a belt. Probably should have gone to the hospital after that one, but the money from that gig was so good he was able to rest up at Brian's for a couple of weeks before going back to work. But now something was *really* wrong. He had been slipped something—could feel it in his chest, in his hands and feet, pumping hard, pumping *painfully.*

He had to think. *Fast.*

"I'll roll which-you, lover," he said as Jim. "But you gotta tell me what's what first. Turn on the lights so I can see you, baby." Paul's voice felt sharp, clear, but seemed to disappear in front of him—sucked up dead into the darkness. Then suddenly the screen above him flickered into life.

The image floating before Paul's eyes was that of a statue—dirty white marble against the darkness, floating just inches from his face. Paul recognized it immediately. It was the Jesus and Mary statue from atop his mother's dresser; the small white figurine that she'd had since before he was born—the one he was never allowed to touch; the one she used to look at when she'd say her rosaries.

The Pietà, Paul said to himself. *That's what she used to call it. The* Pietà.

Yes, there was Mary, draped in her flowing robes and staring down at the crucified Jesus in her arms—

the very same version of Jesus that Paul had stared at
so many times when his parents were out working.
The memories came flooding back to him at once:
the strange excitement at first; then, when he was
older, the guilt he felt upon looking at Jesus' body—
a virtually *naked* body that even by the age of six had
already begun to cause a strange stirring in his
Toughskins.

"I gotch-you," said Paul, said Jim. "This is what
you're into, it's cool. But let's talk business first so we
can enjoy ourselves. Okay, lover?"

"Ssh," said the voice again. "Look at the screen, O
son of God."

Paul knew it was Chris—the guy from the car, the
guy from the Internet. Paul could feel himself beginning to panic—his mind racing in time with his
heart. He had to stay calm, had to think clearly, had
to fight the shit this prick had slipped him. Then suddenly the image of the statue shifted, and began closing in on the face of Jesus.

"That's it," said Chris from the darkness, from
somewhere off to Paul's right. "Shake off your slumber, O son of God."

As did Tommy Campbell on the mortician's table
three months earlier, Paul tried to turn his head,
tried to find the owner of the voice, but could see
nothing except the image of the statue before him,
which now had settled on a close-up of Jesus' face. It
was just as Paul remembered it, but better—*much
more detailed than the cheap souvenir copy that had been
his mother's.* A face that was serene, at peace with
death. A face that, even in his panic, Paul could not
help but find simply beautiful.

"Seriously, lover—I getch-you. We can do whatever
you want, but that shit you gave me is hurting me in-

side. And I gotta clean myself in back, baby. Know what I mean?"

Paul was telling the truth about the painful pounding in his veins, but as far as *getting* with this guy? *No way.* Soon as this *loco* untied him he was *out*—would kick him hard in the balls and make a dash for the door. Yes, Paul would take his chances naked outside. After all, even *Jim* could tell this guy was *fucked up.*

Paul strained hard against the straps when the image before him began to move again. And just as Tommy Campbell had become transfixed by the body of Bacchus scrolling before him, Paul Jimenez watched as the screen slowly panned down over Jesus' chest—to the subtle indication of the wound in His side, to the small nail mark in His right hand, down His legs, and coming to rest on the wounds in His feet.

Suddenly—be it from the instincts of a hustler, the shit pumping through his veins, or both—all at once Paul understood. Yes, all at once Paul was overcome with the sweeping terror of knowing deep down that Chris—*or whatever the fuck his name really was*—meant to kill him.

"You motherfucker!" he screamed, his skin breaking out into cold sweat. "You let me go now and I won't say nothin'. I got friends. They gonna know who you are, you dumb motherfucker! I told them where I was going! They gonna find you on the computer, you stupid fuck!"

No reply—except the painful pounding of his heart. The image on the screen flickered and changed, and then Paul saw only himself, *saw only his face* as he struggled against his restraints. He did not pause to ponder the strap and the wig of long wavy hair that had been placed on his head—the wig of long wavy hair that he knew right away was meant to look like Jesus' hair.

"Help!" Paul screamed as the image on the screen began to pan down over his body. "Somebody help me!" Paul did not care to look for the camera, did not try to see who was filming him. No, for Paul there was one thought and one thought only: *Get me the fuck out of here or I will die!*

Paul pulled frantically at the straps, watching the screen with pounding terror as the camera moved down his body. He strained harder when he saw the strap across his chest, and as he did so, he saw the wound in his side split open and begin to run red down his rib cage. Instinctively he stopped. No pain, but the feeling of something warm and wet in his hands. And thus, even before the camera reached them, Paul knew what he would see. He began to cry.

"Please, God," he said—the sight of the gaping holes in the back of his hands making him nauseous. "Don't do this to me, please! I'll go straight. I promise! I don't wanna die. I wanna go home. I promise you, God."

Paul began to convulse—the shit, the fear pumping through his veins now one and the same. His eyes felt like they would burst. He tried to shut them, tried to keep them in their sockets, but an invisible touch from behind overpowered him.

"Keep watching," said Chris—his fingers resting gently on Paul's eyelids and propping them open. "Keep watching and you will understand. Keep watching and you will be *free.*"

The image on the screen had come to rest on Paul's feet—jerking, bleeding profusely from the holes that The Sculptor had spiked in them. Paul tried to turn his head, tried to look away from the horror of what had been done to him, but the tears in his eyes seemed only to make the image before him clearer.

"Please, God—I don't wanna go to Hell . . ."

And as his heart exhausted itself in a final surge of adrenaline, more than from the terror of succumbing to The Sculptor's chisel, the spirit of Paul Jimenez took flight on the wings of—

No one knows my name.

No one knows my name.

Chapter 22

In tears, Cathy Hildebrant closed her laptop and flicked off the bedside lamp. It was late, and she was tired. *Overtired,* she thought, *and perhaps a bit over-emotional as well.* Yet despite her rational side's whisper of reassurance, Cathy could not help but feel profoundly disturbed upon finishing the online *Providence Journal* account of Tommy Campbell's funeral—not because she was so touched by the fact that the entire Rebel team had flown in for the private, closed-casket ceremony down in Westerly; not because she was so moved by the line quoted from the eulogy given by Campbell's childhood best friend: *"He made a career of catching passes, but a lifetime of catching hearts."* No, what had driven Cathy to tears were the two lines at the end of the article—a little blurb, almost an afterthought, mentioning that a small private ceremony had been held in Cranston on Sunday morning, too.

And so Cathy cried herself to sleep with thoughts of Michael Wenick—a nagging voice in the back of her mind that wondered if The Michelangelo Killer hadn't also read the article; a voice that at the same time taunted her with, *"See? He was right!"* even as it cried, *"Shame on you, World! Shame on you for not seeing the satyr behind the Bacchus!"* But Cathy *did* see the satyr—could not think of the Wenicks sitting in St. Mark's Church without seeing that distorted face, that ghoulish smile munching on the stolen grapes. Yes, Cathy saw the satyr *all too well*—saw it floating next to her in the darkness of the Polks' guest room as clearly if she had crawled inside Michael Wenick's coffin with a flashlight.

It was just after midnight when Cathy awoke with a start. She had been dreaming of her mother—her heart still pounding from the chase down the street, from her close call with the van.

Mom was supposed to pick me up at school, Cathy thought. *But she drove right past me in that strange, long black car. Somebody else was driving—she screamed to me out the window. I tried to run after her—ran out into traffic. But my legs were too heavy. Would have gotten killed by that van if I didn't wake up.*

For as often as she thought of her mother, for as much as she missed her mother, Cathy rarely dreamt of her mother. And more than she feared those memories of her encounter with The Michelangelo Killer's *Bacchus* down at Watch Hill—memories that for two weeks now had been her constant companion in the dark at bedtime—Cathy was so disturbed by the strangeness of her nightmare that she turned on the light.

Cathy's eyes landed on her copy of *Slumbering in the Stone* on the nightstand. Her dream quickly evaporating, the residue of her fear, however, remained.

And for reasons Cathy Hildebrant would never quite understand, she instinctively opened *Slumbering in the Stone* to a page she had dog-eared the night before—just one of the many she had marked with the hopes of later finding a key into The Michelangelo Killer's mind.

The photograph at the top of the page was a detail of Michelangelo's *Night,* one of six marble figures the artist carved from 1520–1534 for the Medici Chapel in the Church of San Lorenzo, Florence—for the tombs of Dukes Giuliano and Lorenzo de'Medici specifically. The two marble façades were almost identical in their conception—each with an idealized marble statue of the Medici duke seated in a shallow niche above the sarcophagus that contained his remains. Two nude allegorical figures reclined on each of the curved sarcophagi lids—*Night* and *Day* for Giuliano, *Dusk* and *Dawn* for Lorenzo. The text to which Cathy had unconsciously turned read as follows:

With regard to *Night* specifically, scholars have long pondered over the unusual shape of the figure's left breast. As I mentioned previously in our discussion of the proportional ratios in the *Rome Pietà,* art historians—and more recently, even plastic surgeons—have long argued that the execution of *Night*'s left breast once again reflects the artist's supposed unconcern or unfamiliarity with the nude female figure. True, as in all of Michelangelo's females, the breasts are misshapen and awkwardly "slapped onto" an undeniably masculine torso. However—even though there is a consensus amongst modern scholars that the unusual appearance of *Night*'s left breast is intentional and not a result of an aesthetic error or the statue's slightly unfinished state—in a recent study of the figure, an oncologist with the Cancer Treatment Centers of America found in *Night*'s left breast three abnormalities associated with locally advanced breast cancer: a large bulge to the breast contour medial to the nipple; a swollen nipple-areola complex; and an area of skin retraction just lateral to the nipple—all of which indicate a tumor just medial to the nipple.

As the noted oncologist accurately points out, these abnormalities do not appear in the right breast of *Night* or in the companion figure of *Dawn*—or in any other of Michelangelo's female figures for that matter. Hence, the evidence strongly suggests that Michelangelo used for his model a woman—dead or alive—with advanced breast cancer, and thus accurately reproduced the physical anomalies in marble.

Yet, despite the detail of the diseased breast itself, curiously, once again we see both breasts awkwardly joined with a masculine frame—as if Michelangelo's understanding of the female could go no further than a narrow and objective appraisal of the "parts" which differentiate the two sexes, but could never quite grasp how those parts worked together within the whole. Then again, there is the theory that Michelangelo might have *intentionally* sculpted his female figures as such—masculine with female parts—simply because, as we discussed earlier, he viewed the male body as aesthetically superior.

Nevertheless, given that Michelangelo depicted lumps in only one of the four naked breasts that adorn the Medici Chapel—and given that *Night,* the "darkest" and most allegorically omi-

nous of all the figures, should be the one depicted with the ravaging disease—there can be
no doubt that Michelangelo not only recognized
the lump as not just an aesthetic anomaly, but
also intentionally sculpted *Night*'s "disease of the
breasts"—a disease during the Renaissance which
was thought to have been caused by an excess
of *black* bile—as just one of the many subtle details that comprise the metaphorical statement
of the façade as a whole. However, the degree
to which Michelangelo *understood* the disease as
a form of cancer—that is, if he understood the
reason behind the lumpy breast in a context other
than traditional Renaissance "humor-based"
medicine—is still open for debate.

Against the collage of disjointed images that had
been her dream, Cathy sat up in the Polks' guest bed
searching the photograph of *Night* for a long time.
She remembered vividly the circumstances surrounding the picture—a picture she had snapped on
her old Nikon while still a graduate student at Harvard. At the time she had *never* thought she would
use it for a book, let alone in such a prophetic context with regard to the disease that murdered her
mother. Indeed, it was on the very afternoon that
Cathy dropped off the film of *Night* at the photo lab
in Florence that her mother dropped the terrible
news over the telephone.

"I don't want you to worry, Cat," Kyon Kim had said.
"We Korean women are strong. I'm gonna be just fine."

More than the pain her memories brought with
them, more than the wicked irony of the chapter she
had written while her mother was undergoing treatment in Boston, which since had become an inadver-

tent testament to her as well, Cathy could not shake the terrible feeling that something *beyond* her dream— something that *went much deeper* than the lasting image of her mother screaming as the long black car raced past Eden Park Elementary School—had compelled her to turn to the section on *Night* and breast cancer.

"Yes, Dr. Freud," Cathy said aloud. "I see the blatant symbolism. The long black car is cancer. The long black car belongs to Mr. Death. He's the driver I can't see—my mother sitting in the passenger seat beside him as he whisks her away. I don't want him to take her."

But the statue of Night, *replied a voice in her head. Your compulsion to turn to the photograph taken on the very same day your mother told you she had breast cancer. Quite a coincidence, wasn't that, Cat? But you didn't make the connection back then, did you? Back in Florence? Only years later when you were working on your book—when your mother had already taken a turn for the worse—did you realize the irony of that day. Almost as if the gods were trying to warn you back then, Cathy—but you were incapable of hearing them.*

"Are you trying to warn me of something, Mom?" Cathy asked. Her eyes fell back to the page, to the text below the detail of *Night*.

> Hence, the evidence strongly suggests that Michelangelo used for his model a woman— *dead or alive*—with advanced breast cancer, and thus accurately reproduced the physical anomalies in marble.

"A woman, dead or alive," Cathy said to herself. Again, she read and reread the text which followed, so sure that she was missing something, so sure that there was a hidden connection between her dream and the statue of *Night,* between the circumstances surrounding the evolution of the chapter and the words on the page to which she had turned—words that held a clue into the mind of The Michelangelo Killer.

A message within a message, Cathy thought. *See it before it slips away.*

Mother, coincidence in Florence, breast cancer, Night.

Dream of Mother, compulsion to look at Night, *breasts, The Michelangelo Killer.*

"What's the connection?"

Yet, despite the detail of the diseased breast itself, curiously, once again we see both breasts awkwardly joined with a masculine frame—as if Michelangelo's understanding of the female could go no further than a narrow and objective appraisal of the "parts" which differentiate the two sexes, but could never quite grasp how those parts worked together within the whole.

"Parts within the whole," Cathy whispered, scanning frantically the words she had written over seven years ago. "Parts, parts, parts . . ."

Then again, there is the theory that Michelangelo might have *intentionally* sculpted his female figures as such—masculine with female parts—simply because, as we discussed earlier, he viewed the male body as aesthetically superior.

Masculine with female parts, Cathy said to herself. *The male body as aesthetically superior.*

A statement, intentional, a message to the viewer? A message from Michelangelo, from The Michelangelo Killer? A dream, a message from Mom?

What the fuck?

Mom. A woman. Dead or alive? Night. A woman. Dead or alive?

No.

Mom. Mom's cancer. Disease. Breast cancer. Breasts? Breasts? The Michelangelo Killer and breasts?

Am I going crazy?

Perhaps, replied Sam Markham in her mind.

Cathy closed the book and returned it to the nightstand—her thoughts now a jumbled mess; the connection between her dream and her search for The Michelangelo Killer—a connection of which she had been *so sure* upon turning to *Slumbering in the Stone*—quickly fading into a gnawing sense of foolishness.

You're a psychic now, too? asked a mocking voice in her head—a voice that sounded a lot like Steve Rogers.

Cathy dismissed it and turned off the light. She lay there a long time, unable to sleep—her mind racing with the jigsaw puzzle that had become her life.

"We're missing something," she whispered in the dark. "Aren't we, Mom? Sam and I, the FBI—*all of us.* There's something right there in front of us—just below the surface like the lump in *Night*'s breast. We see it but we don't understand. We see it but we look right past it. Is that what you're trying to tell me, Kyon Kim? Please, Mom, help me understand."

As if chiseled from the lips of its marble namesake, the brutal silence of night was Cathy's only reply. She had the urge to call Sam Markham, but because of the hour resolved to wait. Yes, best to talk to him after he gets back today—after she had time to sort things out. And so, with thoughts of Samuel P. Markham—the *"P."* standing for *"Professor Hildy Has a Crush On"*—Cathy Hildebrant fell asleep.

Chapter 23

As Cathy finally drifted off to sleep, Sam Markham—at home in his study with his feet on his desk—felt not the slightest bit sleepy when the clock in the bookcase ticked past 3:00 A.M. He would be flying back to Rhode Island in a few hours, and would have plenty of time to once again look over the material from Thursday's briefing in the FBI plane that would transport him from Quantico to Providence. But something was bothering him; something wasn't right; something needed to be addressed now.

In his lap was the report on the Plastination process from Dr. Morris—much of which had been taken from the Body Worlds/Institute for Plastination Web sites. And after carefully reviewing the entire printout, Markham had to agree with Gunther von Hagens, the inventor of Plastination, who said in his introduction that, like most successful inventions, Plastination is simple in theory.

Simple.

That was the word that kept bothering Markham.

Simple.

Yes, with the right equipment, it seemed to Markham that—at least on the surface—the Plastination process would be "simple" enough for *anyone* to execute. After decomposition was halted by pumping formalin into the veins and arteries, the key, as von Hagens said, was having the means to pull the liquid polymer into each cell by a process he called "forced vacuum impregnation," wherein, after the initial fluid exchange step—the step in which water and fatty tissues are removed by submerging the body in an acetone bath—the specimen is placed in a vacuum chamber and the pressure reduced to the point where the acetone boils. The acetone is then suctioned out of the tissue the moment it vaporizes, and the resulting vacuum in the specimen causes the polymer solution to permeate the tissue. This exchange process is allowed to continue until all of the tissue has been completely saturated—a few days for thin slices; weeks for whole bodies.

Weeks.

And simple in theory, yes. But even if The Michelangelo Killer *did* have the money and intelligence to set up his own Plastination lab, unless he had a bunch of body parts lying around—

Yes. It was *that* little detail that was bothering Sam Markham the most. The printout from the Body Worlds Web site made it abundantly clear where the Institute for Plastination (IFP) in Heidelberg, Germany, "acquired" its specimens—the majority of which came from its "donation program," wherein IFP donors legally signed over their bodies to be Plastinated by von Hagens and his crew after their deaths.

"But who *are* these people?" Markham asked out loud. "What are their names?"

Markham sifted through the printout again, unable to find the names of donors anywhere. *Yes.* It was the feel of the information he was reading; the feel of the whole von Hagens/Body Worlds/Institute for Plastination mind-set. A mind-set that, despite a brief and somewhat hollow overture of thanks to its donors both dead and alive, spoke of their bodies simply as a commodity, as *material* for the wide-ranging industry of anatomical study—an industry that was sorely in need of plastinated supplies. ·

Having been around many dead bodies himself, Sam Markham understood the need for objectivity in the world of medicine and anatomical study as much as he did the need for it in his line of work—understood all too well the need for detachment when looking at a murder victim in order to get his job done. So, yes, Markham could on one hand see the practicality of the industry—the need to treat the donated bodies simply as material. However, it was also clear to Markham that, with regard to the Body World exhibits themselves—exhibits in which its skinless subjects were posed sipping coffee, throwing karate kicks, even riding horses—the creators were subconsciously sending a message to the public that they should see the figures not only as "frozen in life," but at the same time were asking them to look at just the body itself, completely divorced from the real life that had once activated it.

No, we should never ask who these people really were.

Markham thought of The Michelangelo Killer—of the kind of mind, the kind of spirit it would take to create the horror that was his *Bacchus.* Over his thirteen-year career with the FBI, Markham had learned there was always a certain amount of objectification that went on in the mind of a serial killer with regard to the perception of his victims. But with The Michelangelo Killer, things seemed quite different.

Tommy Campbell and Michael Wenick were just material for his exhibition, he said to himself. *Just as the epoxy compound and the wood and the iron and everything else was. Just one component of his art, of his message, of his quest to wake us from our slumber.*

Material.

Markham flipped to the page in *Slumbering in the Stone* that he had dog-eared a couple of hours earlier—to the quote from Michelangelo which he had underlined in red: *"The more the marble wastes, the more the statue grows."*

Marble. Michelangelo's material—some of which he would transform into works of artistic brilliance; some of which, depending on its location in the block itself, he would damn to the studio floor, to the garbage heap. Hence, both a reverence for the material itself, but yet the understanding that some would have to be discarded.

Dead bodies. The Michelangelo Killer's material. He *had* to have experimented on others before Campbell and Wenick, had to have used humans before perfecting his technique—some of whom, perhaps just pieces at first, he transformed into plastinated works of art; others he simply discarded as waste. Hence, both a reverence for the material, the male figure as aesthetically superior, and the understanding that he would need to waste some of his victims to achieve greatness.

Marble. Material. Waste. Dead bodies. The male figure as aesthetically superior.

Something didn't quite add up.

Something that was so close, so *simple,* yet still just so far out of reach.

Markham sighed and flicked off his desk lamp. He would force himself to sleep, to think about something else for a while. And as he crawled into bed, his thoughts immediately ran to Cathy Hildebrant. Markham hated to admit how much he had missed her over the last three days; he hated even more to admit how much he was looking forward to seeing her again. However, what really bothered Markham was the nagging suspicion that he was missing something very important; something that might put the art history professor in danger; something that might make him lose someone he cared about all over again.

Chapter 24

Steven Rogers prided himself on his youthful appearance. At forty-five and with a head full of curly brown hair that he dyed regularly, the handsome theatre professor was still sometimes carded at the bars along with his graduate student girlfriend—a rare but flattering enough experience to which he actually looked forward, specifically, the patented double take from the doorman or waitress upon seeing the age on his driver's license. Blessed in part with good genes, it was really his deep-seated sense of vanity that kept him looking so young—coupled with an unconscious desire to always be appealing to the opposite sex. Yes, Steven Rogers ran six miles five times a week; watched his fat and carb intake; still used the Bowflex that his ex-wife bought him for his fortieth birthday; and still lived whenever possible by the old adage his doting mother hammered into him as a child: *"Early to bed, early to rise, Steven, makes a man healthy, wealthy, and wise."*

Healthy? Yes. Wealthy? He couldn't really complain. But wise? Well, even Steve Rogers would have to agree that the jury was still out on that one.

Yes, Rogers had done a lot of dumb things in his forty-five years on this planet—the dumbest of all, perhaps, leaving those e-mails from Ali on his computer. It had been an honest mistake. He had to uninstall then reinstall his AOL software, forgot to change the "save mail to computer" setting, and his wife found everything a few months later. *That was the worst part,* Steve thought: The e-mails had been on there for months before Cathy happened to come across them.

Stupid stupid stupid.

No, Ali Daniels was not Steve Rogers's first indiscretion during his twelve-year relationship with Cathy Hildebrant—his first *student,* yes, but not his first affair. There had been a handful of others of which his ex-wife was entirely unaware: a summer theatre actress here and there and a regular fling with an old girlfriend he ran into twice a year on the conference circuit. The latter had been going on since before both of them got married, so Rogers did not feel the slightest bit guilty about that one. Besides, *she* was the one with the kids.

In fact, Rogers was actually proud of himself for the degree to which he had remained "faithful" to Cathy Hildebrant over the course of their twelve-year relationship—for in his bachelor days he had been quite the satyr. Indeed, Steve Rogers always had a sneaking suspicion that if he had put as much effort into his acting career as he had into getting laid, he might have been the next Brando—or at least the next Burt Reynolds. He had often been compared to the latter in his youth—a comparison that he downright resented while at Yale; and later, one that he used to his advantage in his early thirties as a second-rate regional theatre actor.

Oh yes, Rogers was very, very vain. But more than his vanity, Rogers carried with him an unconscious yet subtle resentment for the hand that life had dealt him. True, on paper he had much to be proud of—after all, he was a graduate of the prestigious MFA in Acting Program at Yale University, and he was a tenured faculty member and *the* senior acting instructor in the Department of Theatre, Speech, and Dance at Brown University. Nonetheless, Rogers secretly felt like something of a failure—felt that for some reason the deck had been stacked against him from the beginning. It really had nothing to do with his mediocre acting career. No, even before entering Yale at the age of twenty-two, Rogers had already begun to feel as if he was somewhat unappreciated by his constituents, as if nobody *really understood* the depth of his talent. But rather than grow into a sense of bitterness, Steve Rogers's perception of his place in the world evolved over the years into a sense of entitlement, of being owed something—so much so that when he cheated on Cathy Hildebrant, he actually felt like he *deserved* some recreational pussy for giving in to the concept of marriage in the first place.

Yes, cheating was one thing—*getting caught was another.* It was as if for Rogers only an acknowledgment of the act itself by the betrayed could *really* define it as adultery—*If a tree falls in the forest and no one is there to hear it, yada yada yada.*

And so, more than the hurt he had caused his ex-wife, more than the guilt of his failed marriage, Rogers would forever curse himself for being *so stupid* as to let fate get the best of him once again. Sure, Cathy could have screwed him; she could have really taken him for a bath if she had wanted to—so yeah, he had to concede his good fortune with regard to the painlessness of his divorce. However, Steve Rogers could not help but feel somewhat the victim—could not help but feel somewhat abandoned. When it came right down to it, Rogers hated to admit to himself that he wished Cathy had fought just a little bit harder, been just a little bit more aggressive and spiteful to him over the last four months—for that would have proven that he really had meant something to her.

Yes, as his career as a second-rate actor had taught him, the only thing worse than hate was *indifference.*

Ironically, it was with a certain amount of indifference that Rogers held Ali Daniels—that great piece of graduate student ass whose *MySpace* generation *I-have-to-get-an-e-mail-from-you-every-day-now-that-we've-fucked* neediness ruined his good thing with Cathy. True, Steve Rogers had loved Cathy Hildebrant as much as he could possibly love someone other than himself—probably still did, in a way. And true, he was self-aware enough to realize that he had been jealous of her at times—of her PhD, of the success of her book and, most recently, of the attention she had received as a consultant *or whatever-the-fuck-she-was* on that nutbag Michelangelo case. Nevertheless, Rogers understood that he would miss Cathy and the routine, the security, the practical convenience of the life they had carved out as a couple. If only he had heeded his working-class father's advice like he did his mother's; if only he had lived by *that* credo, perhaps none of this nonsense would have happened to begin with.

"Remember, Steven, you don't shit where you eat."

Looks like all that shit is blowing over now, anyway,

Rogers said to himself, his feet pounding the pavement.

And so, despite his brief moment of weakness the week earlier, Rogers peacefully resigned himself to the fact that it was now time to move on for good—from both Cathy Hildebrant and the annoyingly needy, pseudo-intellectual Ali Daniels.

Now that she's graduated, Steve thought, *now that she's got her fucking useless Masters it'll be easier to just let it drop. Won't say anything unless I have to—maybe tomorrow when she calls from her new digs in New York City. Or maybe I'll break the news to her in an e-mail. Wouldn't that be a little poetic justice?*

Rogers checked his time and kicked his pace into high gear as he usually did during the last mile of his morning run. He was ahead of schedule—might even make it home before it was light. *That was good.* More than anything else—*even more than sex*—Steve Rogers loved that feeling of having finished his run before most people were even awake; of having a leg up on the day ahead of him—a leg up on all those fat lazy slobs who stayed up the night before watching Letterman. It was a feeling that helped to ease the unconscious but palpable resentment that fate had forced him to be an actor; moreover, that fate had forced him into the actor's schedule, into those late hours at the theatre which sometimes prevented him from staying ahead of the game the next morning.

"Early to bed, early to rise, Steven, makes a man healthy, wealthy and wise."

Rogers rounded the corner onto the street that would loop him back to Garden City Center—the outdoor shopping mall in Cranston to which he made a special seven-minute drive from his house five mornings a week, and where he always parked his BMW Z4 roadster by the big gazebo at its center. Rogers had been coming here for years; the uneven terrain and low traffic of the surrounding middle-class neighborhood was ideal for his strict running regimen. Yes, he was making *incredible* time today, would make it back to the big gazebo, would sit on the bench, and breathe the cool May air and drink his Gatorade before any of the other runners even arrived—perhaps even without having seen a single light flick on in the kitchens of the houses as he passed. It was Monday morning. The people in this neighborhood worked. And it gave Steve Rogers a great sense of satisfaction to know that he had already accomplished more in a little over an hour than they would all week.

Depending on what time he started, the last leg of Steve Rogers's run had the potential to be the darkest—especially in the winter, when he would reach the poorly lighted loop around Whitewood Drive well before sunrise. On this particular morning, Steve had risen at 4:00 A.M., was on the pavement by 4:15, and thus hoofed it onto the heavily tree-lined street just as the sky was beginning to change color out of sight beyond a jagged curtain of oaks and pines. Now that the semester was over, now that he had made the decision to move on from *both* the women in his life, Rogers kicked off his first official summer as a bachelor right on schedule. He had honored his pact with himself that he would have to work extra hard to get himself back on the market for some younger pussy. Yeah, he was going to take his buddy back in Chicago's advice: he was going to try the Internet dating scene; would make a profile and shave ten years off his age and play the field of late-twenty-to-early-thirty-somethings in Boston for a while. Yeah, better to play that game on the road than to damage his reputation on his home turf any further.

"Remember, Steven, you don't shit where you eat."

His heart pumping powerfully, his thoughts clear and precise, Steve Rogers was deep in the zone when he came upon the blue Toyota Camry. The car was parked between the streetlights, at the side of the road in the shadow of a large oak tree—just one of the many cars he had passed that morning. No, the avid runner and born-again bachelor did not even give the blue Toyota Camry a second glance as his Nike Air Max sneakers carried him into the shadows and straight into the arms of The Sculptor.

It all happened so fast—so fast that Steve Rogers barely had time to be afraid. Out of the corner of his eye he thought he saw movement, then the flash of a red dot. A man stepped out from the thicket, from behind the bushes next to the large oak tree.

Hiss-pop!

Rogers felt a sharp pain in his shoulder—his trapezius muscle. He whirled around but kept running—backward—his hand instinctively reaching for the pain. His fingers found something, tugged, and pulled it free just as he entered the pool from the streetlight. Between his thumb and forefinger he saw a small yellow dart—about the size of a house key. He was about to cry for help when suddenly—

Hiss-pop!

Another sting—this time in his neck, in his jugular—as if the big blue bug on top of the New England Pest Control building had suddenly swooped down from the dark and bitten him. Again Rogers reached for the pain—his fingers closing around the dart just as he saw the man coming for him—a man in a tight black T-shirt, a big *bald* man with funny goggles and a wide white-toothed smile.

And as the shadows and the light from the street lamp began to iris inward, as his fingers went numb and his knees began to buckle, Rogers thought of Mr. Clean—and that he needed to wash the bathroom floor and get rid of Ali's blond hair before he brought any new women home.

Chapter 25

Over a week and a half passed before Steve Rogers would finally be reported missing by his distraught girlfriend, who had hopped a bus from New York City after her repeated e-mails and telephone calls went unanswered. Ali Daniels arrived at Rogers's home to find his mail piling up and the previous week's issue of *The Providence Sunday Journal* lying in the middle of his unkempt front lawn. Rogers's BMW Z4 roadster was nowhere to be found—had already been impounded after the groundskeeper who maintained the big gazebo in Garden City reported it abandoned, and Cranston's finest simply hadn't gotten around to notifying its owner yet.

To top things off, it would be twenty-four hours after Ali reported her boyfriend missing before the Cranston Police would finally connect the dots to Rogers's impounded roadster. And although Rogers had long been dead by the time the authorities began treating him as a missing person, the self-centered theatre professor might have taken comfort in knowing that fate had been kind to him in the end. For if he had dumped Ali before his meeting with The Sculptor, who knows how long his disappearance might have gone unnoticed, as it was not unusual for his colleagues, his family, and his friends not to hear from him for weeks at a time—especially after the end of the semester, when he and Cathy would sometimes vacation before summer theatre rehearsals began at Brown.

The Cranston Police, of course, were entirely unaware that *another* man had been recently reported missing in Boston—a young man known as "Jim Paulson," or simply as "Jim." And despite the cryptic description of Mr. Paulson's lifestyle given by the young man's friends, it soon became clear to the Boston Police that lover boy Jim and his constituents dwelt in that world where people rarely ask your last name, let alone your *real* one. Yes, the Boston Police were very familiar with the way things worked on Arlington Street. And given that—wherever he had gone—Mr. Paulson had taken with him almost everything he owned, until anything told them differently the Boston Police would treat Mr. Paulson as they had treated so many other boys whose cruel fates led them down the great white way of drugs and prostitution: Mr. Paulson either moved on or jacked too much shit; either way, he'd turn up eventually; either way, it wasn't their problem.

And even if Paul Jimenez's friends had known about his online persona as RounDaWay17, The Sculptor had long ago taken care of that loose end—had long ago hacked into Jimenez's e-mail account, the most recent activity of which would have shown Jimenez taking care of business as usual from an IP address at the public library in Dayton, Ohio.

Yes, The Sculptor was very, very thorough.

It was late in the afternoon when Cathy received the call from the Cranston Police on her cell phone— an unknown number she immediately muted into voice mail. She and Markham were on their way to an interview—a scenario she had become quite familiar with since Markham's return from Quantico, one quite different than what she had expected via her television crime drama education. The people Cathy and Markham spoke to could use a good scriptwriter; they were not nearly as articulate or helpful as those witnesses on TV—who, after a string of three or four of them, always led the authorities straight to their man. Indeed, the handful of people who the FBI questioned with regard to the Gabriel Banford connection did not help at all. And the investigation into any other possible murders/disappearances that fit The Michelangelo Killer's victim profile, as well the leads derived from the forensic evidence on which she and her new colleagues at the FBI Field Office in Boston had been briefed two weeks earlier, had all so far turned up nothing.

All, that is, except one curious clue: the Carrara marble dust found in The Michelangelo Killer's paint.

"Except for the Carrara marble," Markham said, pulling into the parking lot, "it seems almost as if The Michelangelo Killer had all that other stuff just lying around. The amount of formaldehyde, of acetone, the silicone rubber needed for the Plastination process—never mind the drugs—strange that we're not able to get a lead from any of it, where this guy got hold of the large quantities of chemicals and equipment he would need to get his job done."

"Unless he made the chemicals himself," Cathy

said. "Unless he distilled them from products that
were much more readily available."

"Yes. Like the acetone—the primary ingredient in
paint thinner and nail polish remover. But then there's
the formaldehyde. Not something you can pick up at
Lowes or Home Depot. And from what I've read, not
only does it have a short shelf-life, it's much more difficult to manufacture from other base products—
that is, unless we've got a chemist with a large lab on
our hands."

"This man is very bright, Sam, and very thorough.
He knew that the first thing the FBI would look into
would be the unusual forensic evidence—wouldn't
have used anything that could be traced directly back
to him. And given the fact that The Michelangelo
Killer has been active for at least six years, he could
have acquired his equipment and replenished his
chemicals gradually. He could have even broken into
any number of funeral parlors and stolen just enough
formaldehyde here and there so it wouldn't be noticed. I mean, the time and planning it took to prepare
and display his figures—it's almost as if The Michelangelo Killer also planned on what forensic evidence
he would leave behind."

"Nothing is left to chance."

"The Carrara marble dust."

"Yes. An interesting detail that I have a feeling The
Michelangelo Killer wanted us to find. Let's hope
this interview turns up something."

Despite the inconvenience that Carrara marble
was still exported all over the world and in many
forms—from blocks of raw material, to cheaply fash-
ioned souvenirs, to large pieces of exquisite detail—
Rachel Sullivan stumbled upon a police report from
three years earlier that would eventually provide the

FBI with their first real lead, their first big break in the strange case of The Michelangelo Killer.

Reverend Monsignor Robert Bonetti, who would be celebrating his eightieth birthday in less than a week, had served as resident pastor of St. Bartholomew's Church in Providence longer than any other in parish history—twenty-nine years by his count—and had no plans on retiring anytime soon. This was *his* parish, *his* neighborhood, for not only had he grown up only a couple of miles away on Federal Hill, the Reverend Bonetti had over the years repeatedly turned down opportunities for promotion in order to remain among his people. And even though "St. Bart's" was staffed by the Scalabrini Fathers—a Roman Catholic Holy Order that traditionally transferred its priests from parish to parish every ten years or so—because of Bonetti's age, his impeccable record, his outstanding work within the community, his expansion of the church itself, and his desire to go on ministering to the masses long after he could have retired, the Scalabrini Fathers made an exception in his case and allowed him to stay on at St. Bart's for as long as he wished.

The tall and lanky priest met Cathy and Markham on the front steps of St. Bart's—a much more modern-looking structure than the traditional Romanesque Neo-Gothic churches that dotted the working-class neighborhoods in and around Providence. Cathy, as a professor in Brown University's Department of History of Art and Architecture, immediately pegged the church as having been built—or at least renovated—in the late sixties or early seventies.

"You must be Agent Markham," said the Reverend Bonetti, offering his hand. "Which means that you, my dear, are Doctor Catherine Hildebrant."

"Yes, I am. A pleasure to meet you, Father."

"Likewise—the both of you."

"You spoke with Special Agent Rachel Sullivan on the phone," said Markham. "She explained why we wanted to talk to you?"

"Yes," smiled the priest. "Ostensibly about our *Pietà*. But you see, Agent Markham, I've been around long enough to know that things aren't always what they seem. The FBI wouldn't trouble themselves with a curious little theft that happened three years ago— that is unless they felt it was somehow connected to something much more important."

There was nothing condescending in the priest's tone; nothing sarcastic or off-putting. No, the Reverend Bonetti spoke with the simple sincerity of a man who did not wish to play games; a man whose gentle, bespectacled eyes and thick Rhode Island accent spoke of someone who had *indeed* been around long enough to know what's what.

"This is really about that Michelangelo Killer, isn't it?" asked the priest. "About what happened down there at Watch Hill?"

"Yes, it is," said Markham.

For the first time the Reverend Robert Bonetti's gaze dropped to the ground, his mind entirely somewhere else. And after what seemed to Cathy like an interminable silence, the priest once again met Markham's eyes.

"Follow me," he said.

Once inside the dimly lit church, the good reverend led Cathy and Markham to a small chamber off the main church—the devotional chapel dedicated not only to a large pyramid of votive candles, but also to a series of marble statues that lined the surrounding walls. The statues were of various saints and were themselves also bordered by smaller stands of candles, and the sweet smell of scented wax made Cathy feel queasy. Behind the pyramid of votive candles, at the rear of the devotional chapel, Cathy and Markham were surprised by what they found: a large, exquisitely carved replica of Michelangelo's *Rome Pietà.*

"Exactly like the one that was taken three years ago," said the Reverend Bonetti. "That one had been donated by a wealthy family a number of years before I arrived here at St. Bart's. It was hand carved to the exact proportions of the original, as well as from the same type of marble Michelangelo used five hundred years ago. Carrara marble, it is called. And as is the case with the statue you see before you, our other *Pietà* was made by a skilled artisan in Italy whose studio produces only a couple dozen statues per year— usually ranging in size, like this one, from about three to four feet high. His name is Antonio Gambardelli, and his statues are much more accurate, much more expensive than any other replicas on the market not only because of their attention to detail, but also because of their proportional accuracy. Indeed, at least three years ago, a Gambardelli *Pietà* of this size was valued at close to twenty thousand American dollars. I know this because whoever took our statue not only left us with instructions on how to replace it, but also left us the means to do so."

"Wait a minute," said Markham. "You're telling me that the thief left you *twenty thousand dollars?*"

"Twenty-*five* thousand to be exact," smiled the priest. "A little detail that I neglected to tell the Providence Police upon their initial investigation. You see, Agent Markham, when you've been around as long as I have, you begin to understand something of human nature. The person or persons who took our

Pietà left the money in cash, in an envelope addressed to me right there on the pedestal, so that I could replace it—not so that I could redecorate the evidence room at the Providence Police Station, if you take my meaning."

Sam Markham was silent, his mind spinning.

"The extra five thousand was undoubtedly intended for us to cover the shipping costs of the statue, as well as to repair the damage from the break-in and to compensate us for our trouble."

"Why report the theft at all then?" asked Markham, his voice tight. "Why not just take the money, replace your statue, and not be bothered—that is, since you intended not to cooperate fully with the authorities to begin with?"

"I was the only one who knew about the money, Agent Markham, as I was the first one in the church on the morning after the break-in. However, the damage to the side door and the absence of the statue itself could not be hidden from my fellow Scalabrini, let alone the congregation. You see, Agent Markham, the money was addressed to me—twenty-five thousand dollar bills in a sealed envelope. There was no need to report it, as whoever took our *Pietà* seemed to want it, seemed to *need* it more than we did here at St. Bart's. And even though I may not have understood that need, I took the gift of the money as an act of faith, as a confidential act of penance. And up until the telephone call from the FBI, took the person who left the twenty-five thousand dollars in the statue's place as a man with a conscience."

Sam Markham was silent again, his eyes fixed on the *Pietà*.

"But now," the Reverend Bonetti continued, "I see that my silence may have been misguided, for now I see that the FBI thinks the man who took our *Pietà* three years ago might be the same man who murdered those two boys—the same man who made them into that horrific sculpture down at Watch Hill."

"The envelope," said Markham, turning to the priest. "The sheet of instructions on how to replace the statue—I don't suppose you saved them?"

The Reverend Robert Bonetti smiled and reached into the inside pocket of his black blazer.

"I hoped this might help you forgive me for not telling the authorities about the money sooner. But now I hope even more that it'll change your opinion of me being just a simple and foolish old man."

The envelope that the priest handed Markham had scrawled across it in neatly looped cursive the words, *For Father Bonetti*. Inside, Markham found a brief handwritten note not only giving instructions on how to obtain another *Pietà* from Gambardelli, but also a short apology for any inconvenience the thief may have caused Father Bonetti and his parish. Markham showed the note to Cathy. She recognized the handwriting immediately.

Flowery. Feminine. *Precise.*

The same handwriting from the notes she received five and a half years earlier.

She nodded.

"The man we are looking for is tall, Father Bonetti," said Markham. "About six-three to six-six. And very big, very *strong*—would have been able to lift the statue off its base and carry it from the church himself with no problem. Most likely a bodybuilder or someone who's into power lifting. Anybody you know fit that bill, Father?"

"Most of the men in our congregation are working

class, Agent Markham—skilled laborers or others who work with their hands. They are mostly Italians, but we have a growing Hispanic population as well. Yes, a lot of these men are powerfully built, but only a few that tall. And I know of none who have twenty-five thousand dollars to blow on a statue."

"You ever see anyone strange hanging around the church? Not a regular parishioner, but someone just dropping by once or twice to poke around?"

"Not that I remember, no."

"No unusual confessions that I should know about?"

The priest smiled thinly.

"Even if there were, Agent Markham, I'm not at liberty to tell you."

"Is there anything else you might be able to tell us, Father Bonetti?" asked the FBI agent. "Anybody you might know that would have knowledge of the statue and also the means to pay you twenty-five thousand dollars for it?"

"We used to have quite an extensive picture gallery on our Web site," said Father Bonetti. "Since the theft, however, most of the pictures have been taken down. They were mainly shots of the church interior. One of them, of course, contained our Gambardelli *Pietà*. Perhaps your man simply recognized it and targeted us that way."

Cathy and Markham traded glances.

"Thank you, Father," said Markham. "You've been a great help."

"I'll walk you out," said the priest. And once they had exited the church, once Cathy and Markham reached the bottom of the front steps, the Reverend Robert Bonetti called after them.

"I was down there, too, you know."

Markham and Cathy turned to face him.

"Down at Watch Hill. At the Campbells' house on Foster Cove. Last time was over thirty years ago, before they owned the place. Used to belong to the family of a friend of mine—famous movie director, he was. Grew up with him. Even spent some time with him down at Watch Hill when we were kids. Lovely town, but a lot of evil lurking underneath. Never seen anything good come from that place. You best keep that in mind."

Cathy and Markham exchanged an uneasy silence.

It was starting to rain.

"Everything is connected," said the priest finally. "Remember that, you two. Everything is connected."

And with that the Reverend Robert Bonetti disappeared back into the darkness of St. Bartholomew's.

Chapter 26

"Are you thinking what I'm thinking?" asked Cathy once she and Markham were on their way.

"I'm thinking a lot of things."

"Twenty-five thousand dollars for a statue that he planned on destroying. It wasn't just the marble, Sam. The Michelangelo Killer wanted a flawless replica of the *Rome Pietà* itself—a Gambardelli *Pietà* specifically—and was willing to pay above market value for it when he could have just stolen it. Why?"

"Because money is no object for him. The only reason The Michelangelo Killer didn't buy one directly from Gambardelli himself is so the statue couldn't be traced back to him. And besides, to have simply stolen the statue would have been rude—self-centered and crass—just one of the many aspects of our culture that I suspect The Michelangelo Killer is trying to change."

"But it's the *Rome Pietà*, Sam. If we stick to the premise that The Michelangelo Killer used Carrara marble dust for his *Bacchus* because he had originally planned on using it for something else, that he should have stolen the *Rome Pietà* would indicate it was the re-creation of *that* statue—not Michelangelo's *David*—that had originally been the killer's goal."

"And the Carrara marble from which that statue was carved, the specificity of that *form*, would help him—in an undoubtedly spiritual, even magical way—achieve the same kind of likeness, the same kind of proportional fidelity for his *Pietà* that we saw in his *Bacchus.* Hence, there would also be a connection between his material—the human bodies that would comprise his work—and the material that comprised Michelangelo's work both in form and substance."

"But, since he used the dust from the *Pietà* for his *Bacchus,* that means then that his plan did in fact change."

"Yes. Perhaps he figured out another, even more intimate way for his victims to connect with the statue that they were about to become. Perhaps he scrapped his initial idea of the magic being in the marble itself. Perhaps he gained a deeper understanding of the opening quote to your book—that the magic lies *only* in the sculptor's hand."

"But, Sam, then that means—"

"Yes, Cathy," said Markham, swerving onto the highway. "I was wrong about the profile for this killer. I had an inkling of this when I was back at Quantico, when I was going over the information on the Plastination industry, but couldn't put my finger on it. There's little if any self-gratification for The Michelangelo Killer in the actual act of murdering victims. Murder is only incidental for him—a means to an end in acquiring material for his sculptures. However, as we saw with Gabriel Banford, and as was surely the case with Tommy Campbell and his severed penis, it is crucial that The Michelangelo Killer's victims, his material, become aware of their fate *themselves*—to awaken from their slumber, if you will, in order to truly become one of his creations. And I suspect that any self-gratification on the killer's part would come from that. Yes, there may be a sexual component to this, but I suspect it arises out of a more intellectually and spiritually complex connection with his creations than simple, base-level sexual gratification—a connection that the killer would see as akin to Michelangelo's connection with *his* creations. I've suspected from the beginning that The Michelangelo Killer is not seeking only some kind of self-gratification—sexual, spiritual, or otherwise—and always thought of him more in the context of a mission killer, that is, a killer with a specific goal. However, I see now that I made a crucial mistake with regard to his victims."

"It's why Sullivan and her team have been unable to establish a pattern," Cathy said. "Why they've been unable to find any murders or disappearances of young men in Rhode Island that fit the profile of Banford or Campbell or Wenick. We've been looking in the wrong place, Sam. We've been looking only at *men.*"

"Yes, Cathy. *Humans* are The Michelangelo Killer's material—both men *and* women. The killer has both a reverence for his material and the understanding that some of it has to be wasted. And just as I am sure he considers the male of the species as aesthetically superior, I am also sure now that, if he had to waste material in the experimentation with and development of his Plastination technique, he would focus solely on females. I suspect that if we start looking into the disappearance of female prostitutes in the last six years, we might come up with something."

"So he had planned in the beginning on using a female for his *Pietà*?"

"It looks that way, yes."

"And then for some reason he abandoned that project and began focusing on Michelangelo's *Bacchus*? Perhaps because he saw the similarity between *Bacchus* and Tommy Campbell? Perhaps because he also found a better way of getting his message across to the public?"

"Perhaps."

"But the breasts . . ." Cathy said absently.

"What's that?"

"I'm not sure, Sam. Something's been bothering me for almost two weeks now—something, like you, I can't quite sort out."

As Cathy and Markham sped across town toward the East Side of Providence, a brown paper wrapped package—bundled neatly with the rest of her mail into a folded Pottery Barn catalog—sat waiting patiently in Cathy's mailbox.

Even the postman had thought it a curious-looking parcel—felt bubble wrapped, about the size of a DVD case—but with no return address, and covered with far too many stamps—of various denominations, ten dollars worth in all—as if the sender did not want to go to the post office, but wanted to make sure it arrived at its destination. But what was even more curious to the postman was the way in which the sender saluted its recipient—a neatly written phrase above the street address which read simply:

Especially for Dr. Hildebrant.

Chapter 27

Miles away, The Sculptor wiped the spittle from his father's chin. Instead of seating him as he usually did in the big chair by the window, The Sculptor had served his father his supper in bed that evening. He had played a few episodes of *The Shadow* on the CD player inside the old Philco and thought he saw the left corner of his father's mouth curl up ever so slightly during the introduction.

Then again, The Sculptor could not be sure. His mind might be playing tricks on him, for he was tired—*very* tired. And he had been working very, very hard lately. His *Pietà* was completed—had come together in just over two weeks from the afternoon he picked up RounDaWay17 at Kennedy Plaza in downtown Providence. Then again, in a way he had cheated, for The Sculptor had finished off many components of his *Pietà* over a year ago—the metal frame, the rock of Golgotha on which the Virgin would be seated, the contours of her flowing robes. And of course, the most important parts of the Virgin herself—her head, her hands, her breasts—had been preserved, articulated, and painted long before Bacchus and his satyr went into the pressurized tub of chemicals.

Back then, when he first started experimenting with pieces of the women, the Plastination process took much longer than it did now—just as long as it still took von Hagens and his team over in Heidelberg, Germany. But The Sculptor had made improvements on von Hagens's methods; he found that he could speed up the process considerably by alternating pressure and energy currents through the solvent, as well as by inserting thin "conductor tubes" at key points around the body between the various tissues. And unlike von Hagens, who skinned his subjects to display the muscles and internal organs, The Sculptor, who had no need for the insides, found that hollowing out the torso and placing a single conductor tube along the spine would help speed up the process even more. And so, whereas it took von Hagens months, sometimes a whole year to prepare and then pose a figure, it now took The Sculptor—working diligently, around the clock—just a little over a week.

Yes, The Sculptor could have made quite a bit of money patenting the improvements on von Hagens's Plastination process if he wished. But then again, The Sculptor was not concerned with such base matters as *money*.

Ironically, it was the skin that had always given The Sculptor the most trouble, for during the process of preparing his figures The Sculptor found that, after dissolving the hair with depilatory cream and removing the lipid tissues from underneath, the skin became loose and slippery and very difficult to work with. And only through trial and error with the pieces of the

women did he finally find the right balance of traditional tanning techniques and the methodology he
adapted from von Hagens. The result gave him a tighter
surface through which he could articulate the veins
and muscle tissue underneath for desired definition
and detail, yet the skin remained porous enough so
that his mixture of special paint bonded with it nicely.

Indeed, once you got past all the trial and error,
all the experimentation with this or that much of *yada-
yada-chemical,* the rest of the process was pretty straight-
forward. After The Sculptor hung and drained his
material from a large hook he had attached to the
bottom of the mortician's table—and after the internal organs had been discarded and the preliminary
embalming of formaldehyde complete—The Sculptor
followed his improvements upon the Plastination
process until it was time to pose the prepared figures
and let the silicone harden in a bubble of plastic sheeting heated by UV lamps. Unlike with his *Bacchus,* the
appendages of which required a much more complex articulation process to get the positional ratios
correct, the *Rome Pietà* did not take nearly as long. The
Pietà was much tighter, much more compact in the way
the original figures' limbs had been carved from the
marble. The real trick had been getting the angles
right—the Virgin's arms, the tilt of her head, the degree of incline of Christ on her lap.

As with his *Bacchus,* The Sculptor discovered that
he could save himself a lot of trouble if he got the angles of the iron frame right first. And since the Virgin's body would be almost entirely hidden under
her robes, there was really no need to worry about
damaging that material. Thus, The Sculptor had
much more room for error, much more room with

which to play in terms of manipulating the figure onto the frame. Then once both of the bodies were cured, stuffed, and mounted—and once the Virgin's head and her hands and her breasts had been attached and the last of her robes laid on and starched into the right pattern of folds—The Sculptor adjusted Mother and Son's plastinated limbs by tying them off and suspending them at various heights from rows of smaller hooks that he had fixed to the underside of the mortician's table: After enclosing the statue in a ring of clear plastic sheeting running from the underside of the table to the floor, and after the silicone rubber had hardened under the heat of the UV lamps, all that he needed to do was sculpt the epoxy compound for Christ's hair and his beard, let it dry, then layer his paint on with his pump sprayer until he achieved the desired finish.

The last of the paint had gone on that morning.

And even though he was tired, even though he had worked feverishly for days with little or no sleep, as The Sculptor pulled the blankets up to his father's chin, he was nonetheless pleased not only with how quickly his *Pietà* had come together, but also with how beautiful it had turned out in the end. *Even better than my Bacchus,* he thought, smiling. The Sculptor could not help but feel giddy when he imagined what Dr. Hildy's reaction would be—knew that when it was all over she would thank him when she saw, when she understood how his work had changed the world. Yes, very soon she would learn to *appreciate* him.

Of course, in the end, it was really he who appreciated *her.* Oh yes, The Sculptor had much to thank her for. And hopefully, when she saw the DVD he sent her, when she understood just one of the many reasons why fate had brought them together, maybe she would already start to appreciate him.

Just a little.

The Sculptor knew that Dr. Hildy would most likely receive the DVD today or tomorrow—might have already watched it, for that matter. He hoped she had, for the information she and the FBI would get from watching it would help him in his plan. The Sculptor had wanted to deliver the DVD personally— had wanted to slip it in her mailbox *himself* just like the old days when he used to sneak into the List Art Center to deliver the notes, his heart pounding with fear and excitement. But now things were different, and he dared not get too close. Yes, The Sculptor knew the FBI was probably still watching Dr. Hildy very closely; which was why, since the unveiling of his *Bacchus,* he had driven by her place on the Upper East Side only twice—in disguise; in his third car, his '99 Porsche 911. The Sculptor always used his Camry to drive by the Polks'—much less conspicuous in that neighborhood. The Sculptor could tell by the metal mailbox next to Dr. Hildy's front door that she was still picking up her mail even though she was staying with her friend Janet—the older woman, the one who looked like that tennis player from the 1970s, Billie Jean King.

Tennis players. The Sculptor *hated* tennis players.

As the Shadow set off in pursuit of this week's villain, The Sculptor watched his father closely. And when he saw his eyes begin to flutter, The Sculptor removed the syringe from his forearm and dabbed the needle mark with an alcohol swab. He had given him just enough of the sleepy juice to keep him dreaming until morning. Yes, The Sculptor knew deep down that his father dreamt—*had* to be dreaming from the way his face jerked and his eyes twitched when The Sculptor sat in the big chair by the window watching him when he himself could not sleep. Indeed, The Sculptor had conditioned himself over the years to sleep very little—had no need for it other than to repair and rebuild the torn muscle tissue from his strenuous workouts in the cellar. And unlike his father, as far as The Sculptor knew, as far as he could remember, he *never* dreamt himself.

The Sculptor replaced his father's colostomy bag, washed his own face and hands in the upstairs bathroom, and lay down naked on his big four-poster bed. He had many years ago redecorated the room in the baroque style of which he had always been the fondest, but his bedroom still carried with it the memories of his youth, especially memories of his mother who, sometimes—when his father was away on business and she had had too much to drink— would crawl into bed naked with him to *apologize,* to *warm him up* from the ice baths into which she often plunged him facedown when he was naughty.

The Sculptor reached for the remote control and pressed the On button—the DVD player and the big television in the armoire flickering to life simultaneously. There was no TV reception here—no cable hookup in the main house. No, The Sculptor merely thought of the big TV in the armoire in the corner of the room as his "memory box." Yes, he would relax for a while in the old routine—he might even allow himself to take a little nap before the big night ahead of him.

Play.

The Sony DVD logo dimmed, then was replaced with the trip to Niagara Falls—the first of the eleven

3-minute-long Super 8 films The Sculptor had strung together and digitized onto DVD. The trip to Niagara Falls was silent—shot in 1977 when the boy named Christian was only two years old. There he is in his mother's arms, waving to the camera by the old-style, coin-operated observation binoculars—the falls misting like ghosts far off in the distance behind them. The mother—a lovely looking woman with large lips and a yellow scarf around her neck—whispers something in the boy's ear. He laughs and waves again.

Cut to—

The boy is now in his father's arms, standing next to the same coin-operated binoculars. He waves happily as his father bounces him up and down. No, unlike the man in the room next door, the father has no trouble moving—looks young and handsome and strong in his tight white polo shirt. And his *eyes*—so full of life, of love for his son and the woman out of sight behind the camera. He blows her a kiss. Does it again. Speaks to his son, and then they *both* blow her a kiss.

Cut to—

Panning across the falls.

Cut to—

Close-up of the mother at the railing. She gazes out at the scene before her, unaware that her husband is filming. She looks happy, but lost in thought. And The Sculptor, watching from his bed, wonders, as he has done now for many years, what she was thinking at that moment—knows that it is too early for her to be thinking about the tennis pro, the man with whom she would have an affair years later. The mother realizes she is being filmed, smiles, and mouths to the camera shyly, *"Eddie stop!"* But her husband goes on filming. The wind blows her hair, her yellow scarf, as she tries to look natural. She starts to speak—

Cut to—

The mother with the boy looking out over the falls. The boy has his thumb in his mouth and is snuggled tightly against his mother's bosom. He seems somewhat afraid—is not crying, but looks only at the camera while his mother speaks to him.

Cut to—

The mother—smiling, holding the sleeping boy in her arms—gets into the passenger side of the white Ford LTD.

Cut to—

The mother, again with the sleeping boy—darker, this time filmed inside the car from the driver's seat. The camera zooms on the boy named Christian—his thumb still in his mouth.

Cut to—

The father driving, laughing, and speaking to the camera as his wife films him.

Cut to—

A quick series of shots of the road, of the scenery, and then the first reel ends.

The rest of the Super 8s—shot over the next three years—follow the same happy pattern: Lake George, the Story Land theme park in New Hampshire, a trip to the beach at Bonnet Shores. But only the *last* of the eleven has any sound—shot in 1980, when the boy named Christian was just five years old.

It is his birthday party, in fact, filmed outside in the backyard, against the woods on a bright sunny day of ice cream cake and pin the tail on the donkey. The boy named Christian opens some presents—a soccer ball, a Tonka truck—while other children and people whose names The Sculptor has long forgotten look on with oohs and ahs. The Sculptor knows all the dialogue by heart; he has watched this film many, *many* times.

"What's my *present gonna be, Mary?"* asks his father from behind the camera, to which his mother smiles and replies, *"How about a fat lip?"*

The partygoers laugh.

There are a couple of quick shots of the boy named Christian kicking the soccer ball across the lawn with a little girl, then finally the scene The Sculptor has looked forward to for thirty-three minutes—the scene for which he always waits *so patiently.*

The boy named Christian is sitting alone outside at the table—the open canisters of blue and green Play-Doh barely noticeable amidst the paper cups and frosting covered plates that litter the plastic *Empire Strikes Back* tablecloth. He is hard at work on something—entirely unaware that his father is filming him.

"What are you making, Christian?" asks his father from behind the camera.

"My friend David," says the boy perfunctorily, not looking up.

"Who's David?" whispers another man off camera.

"His imaginary friend," the father whispers back. *"Says he lives out back in the carriage house."*

The unidentified man off camera mumbles something inaudible. And with the sounds of partygoers, of happy children echoing off in the distance, just as the camera begins to zoom in on the boy named Christian and his blue-green Play-Doh sculpted man, the home movie of The Sculptor's fifth birthday party abruptly cuts to black.

Chapter 28

Cathy Hildebrant and Sam Markham sat in silence outside her East Side condo—the intermittent sound of the windshield wipers swiping in time to the dull *tick-tick* of the Trailblazer's idling motor. Since his return from Quantico, they had been in this position many times—sitting like teenagers in the car outside the Polks' in what Cathy had come to think of as their stereotypical "awkward end of the date scene."

Unlike the afternoon two weeks earlier when she had kissed him on the cheek, Cathy had yet to make such a bold move again. Upon his return from Quantico, Markham seemed distant—much more professional and much less apt to reveal anything personal. Even on the handful of occasions when they had been alone in his tiny office in downtown Providence, working on his computer and studying the printouts from Boston late into the evening, Special Agent Sam Markham always made sure that he was occupied away from her, always made sure that he did not get physically too close to his new partner. And on the one occasion when he accidentally brushed up against her—the only time their eyes met and their faces were so close that Cathy was sure he'd kiss her—instead, Markham only smiled and turned his flushed cheeks away from her.

But worse than anything, Cathy thought, was that in all their interviews, in all their trips around New England in the Trailblazer to question this person or that, Special Agent Sam Markham had yet to reach for her hand again.

Something was wrong; something was holding him back.

Deep down Cathy understood this—could feel it in a way that she had never felt before—but her conscious, rational side simply could not sort it out, did not know what to do with this knowledge, this newfound perception into a man's heart—a man who seemed at once so close but yet still so distant from her.

"You're going to be all right staying alone now?" Markham asked finally.

"Yes. Janet and Dan are leaving for the beach tomorrow. They want me to go with them, of course—and I will visit this summer—but I need to cut the cord and get back on my own. I'll call them once I get inside and let them know I'll be staying here tonight. After all, this is my home now."

"I don't want you to be afraid of anything, Cathy. We'll still have people watching you around the clock. I'll make sure they know you're back here. And you know you can always call me, too."

"I know."

The awkward silence again.

"What is it, Sam?" The question had fallen from Cathy's lips before she realized she was speaking, and Markham looked taken aback.

"What do you mean?"

"It's just that, well, I thought—" As she met his gaze, when she saw behind his eyes what she knew to be his feelings for her retreating once again, suddenly Cathy felt foolish—felt like she wanted to cry, like she had to get out of there.

"I'm sorry," she said, gathering her things. "It's just me being stupid. Just give me a call when you need me again."

"Cathy," Markham said, "Cathy, wait."

But she had already slammed the door—her heels clicking noisily on the cement walkway as she made her way to the porch. Markham sat frozen, helpless behind the wheel. Then, in a flash of impulse, he was out—caught up to her just as she stepped inside. The bundle of mail fell to the floor; and when Cathy turned to him, when Markham saw the tears in her eyes, he finally gave over to his heart and kissed her.

There, into the evening, they made love amidst a sea of cardboard boxes—all the while oblivious to the muted phone calls that went on *Für Elise*-ing in Cathy's handbag.

Chapter 29

If Steve Rogers had known that the two Cranston Police detectives had missed his ex-wife at her East Side condo by only a matter of minutes, had he known that Janet Polk had unintentionally misinformed them that her best friend would be staying with her in Cranston that night, the vain and self-centered theatre professor most certainly would have thought that fate had gotten the best of him once again. His only consolation might have been the pretty redhead who—albeit with selfish motives herself—had inadvertently taken up his cause. Meghan O'Neill—chief of the newly appointed, three-man WNRI investigative team whose sole purpose was to look into leads and develop stories in connection to The Michelangelo Killer—got an unexpected break that evening. Her team had been patiently monitoring the police bands for weeks now with the hopes of hearing one of two words: Michelangelo or Hildebrant. And so, when news came across the wire that the Cranston police were having a hard time locating the latter for questioning in the disappearance of her ex-husband, O'Neill scrambled her three-man crew into the Eye-Team van and headed for the East Side.

"If Hildebrant is home," she told them, "we'll shoot the segment there. If not, we'll move to Cranston and use Rogers's house as a backdrop."

Either way, O'Neill's team understood: *she* would be the one to break the story.

The house was dark, and Cathy—lying naked on the sofa in Markham's arms—was just drifting off again when the doorbell startled her awake. Markham put his finger to his lips and, reaching for his gun, moved silently out into the hall. The doorbell rang again, but even before the FBI agent reached the peephole, the light filtering through the blinds told Cathy who was standing on her front porch.

Spotlights, she thought, covering herself with a blanket. *Another news crew. What do they want now?*

"Reporters," Markham whispered, and signaled for Cathy to stay put. He stood leaning in the archway to the hallway with his back to her—his gun at his side as if he were considering whether or not to ambush them. Cathy smiled—*wished he would*—and despite the interruption, despite the sudden longing for the sanctuary that had been the Polks', Cathy could not help but be aroused at the sight of Markham's muscular physique—the back and shoulders, the buttocks and thighs that looked to her in the milky gloom like nothing less than sculpted marble.

The spotlight went out and Markham again disappeared into the hallway. Cathy heard the sound of a car starting, then speeding off outside. And after a moment, the FBI agent returned with their clothes. He placed Cathy's handbag and the bundle of dropped mail on top of a cardboard box.

"They're gone," he said. "What they could want from you at this point is beyond me."

"Maybe they wanted to know what kind of lover you are."

Markham laughed, embarrassed, and the two of them got dressed in the dark—silently, a bit awkwardly, but with the unspoken certainty of a long-awaited love affair just begun. And soon they were in the kitchen, sipping tea at the table in the warm glow of the stove light. Markham held Cathy's hand, but they spoke to each other only in spurts—funny stories and details about their lives separated by long periods of silence—neither of them really knowing what to say, but nonetheless content simply to be in each other's presence.

"I should probably get going," said Markham when he saw the clock on the stove tick past nine o'clock. "Will be in Boston all day tomorrow to brief Burrell and to coordinate our findings with Sullivan's team and my people back at Quantico."

"On Saturday?"

"Sucks, huh?"

"You can spend the night here if you like," she said, the words coming from her like another language—the first time in twelve years that she had invited a man to spend the night at her place. "Is that proper etiquette? You'll have to forgive me, Sam. I don't usually do this."

"Neither do I," said Markham. And then he did something unexpected. The FBI agent took her hands and kissed them. "I'm sorry about before," he said. "About closing off from you. I know you noticed. I know you felt it, and it wasn't fair of me—to pretend like that or to make you feel vulnerable and silly. That's not me, Cathy. I don't play games. It's just that, well, this kind of thing is hard for me—it's just so new and out of the blue. I'll tell you about it another time, but know that, despite the circumstances in which I found you, and no matter what happens and how stupid I may act, all this is real—you and me, Cathy, and the way you know I feel about you, it's real. Just be patient with me, okay?"

Cathy's heart skipped a beat, and then she kissed him—long and passionately—and when they parted, Markham smiled.

"I could do this all night. But if I were you, I'd call your Auntie Janet. It's getting late and she's probably worried sick about you."

"Shit," said Cathy, her eyes darting around the kitchen. "I forgot all about her—thinks I'm staying there tonight. My bag. Where'd I put my bag?"

"Relax. I put it in the living room. First cardboard box on the right."

In a flash, Cathy disappeared out into the darkened hallway and was back with her handbag, her cell phone already at her ear. She plopped her bag and the banded bundle of mail onto the table.

"Five missed calls from her. And looks like two voice mails. She's got *me* worried now."

Markham finished his tea and placed his cup on the table—noticed right away the curious-looking parcel sticking out part way from the Pottery Barn catalog.

"Hey, Jan, it's me," said Cathy behind him, drifting back out into the hallway.

It was not the plethora of stamps that caught the FBI agent's attention, but the partially visible handwriting—the familiar, flowery, and precise way the sender had written *Providence, Rhode Island 02912*.

"I know, Jan, I'm sorry. I'm at my place. Was working late and—"

Markham snapped off the elastic band and removed the brown paper wrapped parcel from the
bundle of mail.

"What?" he heard Cathy say from the hall.

Markham rose from the table—studied the handwriting in the light from the stove: *"Especially for
Dr. Hildebrant."*

"When was the last time she heard from him?"

Markham removed from his back pocket the envelope that had been given to him by the Reverend
Bonetti. He compared it to the brown paper wrapped
parcel—the handwriting was identical.

"All right, all right," Cathy said, returning to the
kitchen. "Don't worry, Jan, I'm fine—yes, will call
them right now. Okay. I'll let you know. Love you,
too." Cathy closed her cell phone. "It's Steve, Sam.
My ex. Janet said the police want to talk—"

The look on Markham's face told her everything—stopped her cold like a slap. And as the FBI
agent held up the brown paper wrapped package—
when Cathy saw the envelope from the Reverend
Robert Bonetti in his opposite hand—all at once the
pretty art history professor knew something very,
very bad had happened to her ex-husband.

Chapter 30

Her heart beating wildly, the opening of the DVD player sounded to Cathy like thunder—the Sony logo on the television screen casting the darkened living room in the light blue wash of a gathering storm. Markham had opened the brown paper package in the kitchen—used a paring knife to slice the tape and handled the bubble wrapped contents carefully with a paper towel. The DVD case, like the disc inside, was eerily blank—no writing or any other distinguishing marks—and still carried with it the scent of newly minted plastic. Markham placed the disc into the DVD player and took his seat next to Cathy on the sofa.

The screen dimmed, went black for a moment, and then a countdown began—four seconds, grainy black and white in the style of an old film countdown. Black again, and then a gentle whisper in the darkness of: *"Come forth from the stone."*

Cathy's heart dropped into her stomach when she saw Steve Rogers's face fade into the frame—a strap across his forehead and what appeared to be two stubby leather pads by his ears holding his head in place. He was sweating badly, his eyes blinking hard.

"Oh my God, Sam," Cathy cried. "It's Steve."

"What the fuck?" said her ex-husband on the television screen before them—his voice hoarse and gravelly.

"That's it," said a man's voice off camera. *"Shake off your slumber, O Mother of God."*

"What the fuck is—"

Cathy and Markham watched like gaping zombies as Rogers struggled then abruptly stopped with a look of confusion across his face. The light on his shiny cheeks had changed ever so slightly, and he seemed to be watching something above him—his eyes widening and narrowing in an eerie silence.

"That's it," said the man's voice again. *"Shake off your slumber, O Mother of God."*

Rogers attempted to turn his head toward the voice.

"Who are you? What the fuck you want?"

The light on Rogers's face changed again, and he stopped straining. In their stunned silence, Cathy and Markham could tell that something had caught the man's eye. Rogers's breathing seemed to quicken all at once, when suddenly the camera angle shifted—a bit jumpy now, filmed directly above him.

"He's using two cameras," Markham said absently. "One stationary, the other handheld."

The continuity of the cut was seamless as the camera began to pan slowly down from Rogers's face to his neck. And just as the first of the bloody stitches scrolled upward from the bottom of the screen, Steve Rogers began to scream.

"What the fuck! What the fuck you do to me!"

"Dear God, no," Cathy gasped when she saw the

breasts—plump and white and stitched like eggs at awkward angles onto her ex-husband's muscular chest. She cupped her hand to her mouth as Steve Rogers went on screaming on the screen.

"I'm sorry, Cathy!" she heard him yell. *"I'm sorry!"*

And as the camera continued to pan down over her ex-husband's stomach, over the thick leather strap which held him down to the steel table, Cathy felt like her head would explode. It was as if she had already seen in her mind what was coming next— knew deep down that she couldn't bear the sight of it. And in a flash she was up off the sofa and vomiting in the hall as Markham, frozen in horror, watched the bloody stitches where Steve Rogers's penis *should have been* rise onto the television screen.

The screaming stopped for a moment. Another edit. Then the last part of the scene played again from the angle of the stationary camera—the screams of her ex-husband echoing once again through the walls of Cathy's East Side condo; the soul of Steve Rogers taking flight before Sam Markham's eyes just as Cathy fainted into black.

Chapter 31

Bill Burrell raced down Route 95 at over ninety miles an hour—the colored lights of the Friday night traffic parting before his state trooper escorts like Christmas wrapping paper at a pair of scissors. Rachel Sullivan was about a half-hour ahead of him. She would meet him in Dr. Hildebrant's room at Rhode Island Hospital after her team's preliminary sit-down with the Cranston Police.

Son of a bitch, he thought. *No way getting around the locals now.*

It had all come together so fast—it was his wife who actually told him about the breaking news story down in Rhode Island only seconds before he got the call from Markham. It was all just too bizarre, he thought—yes, just like the media was already fucking calling it: "A bizarre twist in the case of The Michelangelo Killer." The news-fuckers didn't know about the DVD or that Steve Rogers was already dead. No, the simple fact that there was another disappearance in Rhode Island—the disappearance of the ex-husband of Dr. Hildebrant, that Brown University professor and resident expert on Michelangelo who had been associated with the case at the beginning—was enough meat for the vultures to chew on.

For now.

Son of a bitch, Burrell said to himself as he whizzed across the Rhode Island–Massachusetts border. *Only a matter of time before the whole thing explodes, before they learn of Hildebrant's connection to everything—not just this nutbag Michelangelo Killer, but to us.*

But more than worrying about how the pretty art history professor who so reminded him of his wife would handle everything; more than worrying about how all the media attention she would soon receive was going to impede the FBI's investigation; as he sped toward Rhode Island Hospital, Special Agent in Charge Bill Burrell could not ignore the sinking feeling that—even with this newest development—the strange case of The Michelangelo Killer would continue on and on as it had all along.

Cold.

Chapter 32

Sam Markham's brain sizzled like a slab of bacon—his thoughts sputtering and popping inside his skull with the panic of what to do next. Cathy had suffered a mild concussion, but would be okay—he knew that deep down. But as he sat beside her hospital bed, his anxiety fired back and forth between his need to go looking for The Michelangelo Killer, and his concern, his *gnawing guilt* for the woman he loved.

Sullivan's team would be the ones to scramble on the information he'd gleaned from the DVD, for Markham knew he had to be there when Cathy woke up. He had heard the smack of her head on the hardwood floor when she fainted—a dull thud out in the hallway that could have been prevented had he been there to catch her, had he not been so transfixed by the horrible DVD death of Steve Rogers. But worse for Cathy than the fall was when Markham revived her—the shock at first, then the hysterics that followed when her mind attempted to wrap itself around what she had just witnessed.

"Mother!" she had screamed in the ambulance.

"You were right, Mother! You tried to warn me but I didn't listen! I'm sorry, Steven!"

The EMTs had to strap Cathy to the gurney and administered a sedative on the ride over to the hospital. And as Markham held her hand, as she started to calm, Cathy whispered to him what he already knew.

"The *Pietà*, Sam. The breasts. He used Steve for the body of his *Pietà*."

From his reading of *Slumbering in the Stone*, Sam Markham knew all about the *Rome Pietà*—knew that Michelangelo had ingeniously sculpted the Virgin Mary out of proportion to Jesus in order to get the correct visual relationship between the two figures. He also knew right off the bat that the real *Rome Pietà* was still on display in St. Peter's Basilica in Vatican City, and thus instinctively ordered Sullivan to mobilize the local police forces outside of every church named St. Peter's in Rhode Island, southern Massachusetts, and northern Connecticut. But deep down Markham knew it wouldn't be that easy—knew that The Michelangelo Killer wouldn't tip his hand to Dr. Hildebrant and the FBI *just like that*.

Perhaps he was even trying to throw them off the trail.

Nonetheless, before climbing into the ambulance with Cathy, Special Agent Sam Markham had the good sense to grab from the Trailblazer his now ragged copy of *Slumbering in the Stone*. He had pored desperately over the chapters on the *Rome Pietà* at Cathy's bedside while she slept—learned that the statue was originally commissioned as a grave marker by the French cardinal Jean de Billheres. Its first home had been the Chapel of St. Petronilla, a Roman mausoleum located in the south transept of

St. Peter's which the cardinal had chosen for his funerary chapel. There it had lived for a short time until the chapel was demolished. The *Pietà* occupied a number of locations around St. Peter's when finally, in the eighteenth century, it came to rest in its current location in the first chapel on the right of the Basilica. Markham relayed all this information to Sullivan, but her subsequent Internet search came up empty. She could not with any certainty link these details (St. Peter's, St. Petronilla, funerary chapels, Cardinal Billheres, etc.) to any specific site in Rhode Island—in all of New England for that matter.

And so Sam Markham felt helpless. He felt that he could see the future rolling, unstoppable, toward him in his mind—could see *so clearly* The Michelangelo Killer's upcoming *Pietà*: a heinous sculpture with a woman's head and hands and breasts sewn onto Rogers's body à la Frankenstein. As a result of his research into the Plastination process, Sam Markham's rational side told him that—even if The Michelangelo Killer had already murdered his Mary and his Jesus long ago—the killer would not have had nearly enough time to preserve Rogers's body. His *gut*, however—that intuition that all the best "profilers" learn to follow despite "the facts"—told him otherwise.

Yes, Markham knew in his gut that not only was he missing something very important, but that he was also running out of time.

He needed Cathy—needed her to wake up and to talk to him calmly.

An agent from the Resident Agency poked his head into the room. "Burrell is on his way," he said, and Markham nodded. There were two Providence agents posted outside the door, and Markham knew

Burrell would square the FBI protective custody for Cathy himself. That was good; it would be much better than the surveillance they had placed on her—the depth of which Cathy had no idea. Yes, although the FBI had watched Cathy's every move now for almost a month, although she was most certainly never in any real danger, Markham felt nonetheless ashamed that Cathy had been used involuntarily as bait.

That couldn't be avoided.

But now things *had* to be different; now The Michelangelo Killer had killed for her *personally*—murdered her ex-husband, used him specifically for his *Pietà* in what was undoubtedly a gesture of gratitude to Dr. Hildebrant for all her help. Hence, Markham understood there was no other way now except for Cathy to go into hiding. But for how long? And would Cathy even want to once the reality of what had happened sank in? How many times, Markham wondered, had she secretly wished for Steve Rogers to get run over by a truck or to slip on the ice and split his head open? And now, would she ever be able to forgive herself? Would she ever be able to get over the guilt that she was somehow responsible for her ex-husband's death?

As Markham studied Cathy's face in the dim light of the hospital room, he thought of Michelle. He wanted to spare Cathy *that pain*; he wanted to untie the canvas straps that held her down and just carry her away from it all.

Then Markham thought of Steve Rogers strapped down to his bed—the steel table on which The Michelangelo Killer had most likely operated on him, the steel table on which he filmed Rogers's last breath.

The epinephrine, Markham thought. *The killer gives them a heart attack while they stare at themselves—at the statue they are about to become, above them on a television screen. It's important they understand—just like Gabriel Banford had to understand way back when. And through the terror of that understanding, the terror of being born again, they awake from their slumber and are freed from the stone—just as Cathy and I suspected.*

Markham's mind began to wander.

There were chains running up from the side of the table. Looked as if it was suspended from the ceiling—perhaps so it could be raised and lowered like in those Frankenstein movies. A high ceiling. Yes. A winch system—would have to be hooked on a ceiling too high for a cellar. A garage or a warehouse maybe. Money. The killer has money. Lots and lots of money—twenty-five G to blow on a statue.

The Pietà.

"*Exactly like the one that was taken three years ago,*" he heard the Reverend Robert Bonetti say in his mind. "*That one had been donated by a wealthy family a number of years before I arrived here at St. Bart's.*"

A wealthy family . . .

"*We used to have quite an extensive picture gallery on our Web site . . . One of them, of course, was of our Gambardelli Pietà. Perhaps your man simply recognized it and targeted us that way.*"

Markham looked at his watch: 1:03 A.M. Too late to wake up the old priest on a hunch—not even a hunch. A *long shot.* And a desperate one at that. And besides, he was running out of time; he knew instinctively that something was going to happen this weekend, maybe even tonight—if it hadn't happened *already.* If only he knew *where.*

Where, where, where!

"Cathy," he whispered in her ear. "Cathy, I need you now."

Her eyes fluttered, and Markham's heart leapt into his throat.

"Sam?" she said groggily—the sedatives fighting to keep her under.

"Yes, Cathy, it's me. You're safe. Everything is going to be all right now."

"Where am I? I can't move my—"

"You're all right, Cathy." Markham said, untying her wrists. "You're in the hospital. You bumped your head, but you're fine. The doctors strapped your hands to the bed so you won't hurt yourself—because you were hysterical. But there, you see? You're free now. I'm here, Cathy. I won't let anything happen to you."

"It was Steve, Sam," Cathy sobbed. "It's all my fault—"

"Ssh, Cathy. Stop it now. It's not true. Don't think like that."

"But the *Pietà*. He made Steve into the *Pietà* for *me*."

"Ssh. Cathy, listen to me. You've got to stay calm. You've got to be strong for me. We don't have much time. The Michelangelo Killer wouldn't have sent you that DVD unless he was sure that it wouldn't hinder his plan, unless he was convinced that it wouldn't lead us to where he was about to exhibit his *Pietà*—at least until it was too late for us to catch him."

"St. Peter's," Cathy said, swallowing hard. "The real *Pietà* is in St. Peter's."

"I know, Cathy, but that's too easy. I've got those bases covered, yes, but my gut tells me we're going in the wrong direction. This guy is too smart for that. You've got to think of someplace else the killer might want to exhibit his *Pietà*."

Cathy was quiet for a moment, her eyes locked with Markham's—the love she saw reflected in them giving her the strength to continue.

"The statue was originally located in the Chapel of St. Petronilla."

"Yes. St. Petronilla. I read about it in your book—commissioned for the tomb of a French cardinal by the name of Billheres."

"The chapel itself was initially an old Roman mausoleum that had been converted by the Christians on the first site of St. Peter's—before the church was redesigned and rebuilt in the early sixteenth century by Donato Bramante, a famous Italian architect. The chapel in its Roman form no longer exists, and there is much debate as to what it originally looked like before Bramante got his hands on it. However, if you take into account how Michelangelo designed his *Pietà* for that space specifically, one thing is certain."

"What?"

"If the *Pietà* is lit by natural light falling from above, as it would have been in the Old St. Peter's, the Virgin's face is cast in shadow, while the body of Christ is fully illuminated. The metaphorical implications are obvious—the light, the eternal life in the dying flesh of the Savior, etcetera. But you see, one has to ultimately remember that the statue was originally intended to be a *funerary monument*, not just a devotional image—although it is that, too. The overall design of the *Pietà*—the way the Virgin's gaze and open arms direct our attention first to her Son, then to the mortal remains buried beneath her—in its original installation, in its original lighting, it demanded that we see the statue as Michelangelo intended, that is, a context in which the viewer not only reflects on Christ the Savior, but also on our own mortality, as well as that of Cardinal de Bill-heres."

"So you think then that the light from above is the key to the overall effect of the statue?"

"Yes. If you look again at the pictures in my book, you will notice in the close-ups a fine line inscribed in the Virgin's forehead. Seen at a distance under light from above, this line creates the illusion of a thin veil—an ingenious device, yes, but one that re-quires the trick of the light in order to be seen. Other-wise, it looks like just a line in her forehead."

"So," said Markham, "it's not so much about the connection to St. Peter's as it is to a chapel, perhaps even a mausoleum, where the light would hit the statue from above. That means then that the location itself is very important to the killer in terms of how it relates to the viewer's overall experience of the sculp-ture. Like the killer's *Bacchus*. Dodd's topiary garden served as more than just a historical allusion, a re-contextualization of the statue's original location. Yes, perhaps the killer exhibited his *Bacchus* in Dodd's garden because it would subliminally mimic a Renaissance viewer's experience of Michelangelo's *Bacchus*—an experience that The Michelangelo Killer wanted to provide for us just as it was five hundred years ago."

"I don't know, Sam," Cathy sighed, her eyes again welling with tears. "I don't know anything anymore."

"Ssh," said Markham, kissing her forehead. "Know that I care about you, Cathy. Know that I'm going to take care of you, now. I won't let anything hurt you."

Cathy felt her heart melt, felt her eyes about to overflow in unexpected streams of joy. She wanted to tell Sam Markham she loved him, but a voice from across the room interrupted her.

"Sam?"

Markham and Cathy turned to see Bill Burrell standing in the doorway.

"I have to go now, Cathy," Markham said, kissing her again. "I'll call a nurse to see if you need—"

"Don't leave me, Sam."

"I have to, Cathy. You'll be fine. The place is crawling with FBI agents. You just sleep for a while and I'll be back before you know it."

Cathy turned away.

"I'm going to catch this guy for you," Markham said, turning her face back to him with a gentle finger on her chin. "I promise you that, Cathy. It's personal now."

Cathy smiled weakly—the sedatives dragging her down again.

"Thank you, Sam," she whispered.

Markham laid his hand on her cheek. And when he saw that she had fallen back to sleep, he joined Bill Burrell out in the corridor.

"She's doing all right?" the SAC asked.

"Yes. She'll be fine."

"We'll take care of her now."

"Yes."

"Where's the DVD? I want to see it."

"Forensics has got it—analyzing the paper, the tape for trace evidence—but they won't find anything, I'm sure. He's too smart for that. Nonetheless, they're going to dump it onto the computer to see if we can pick up anything through digital enhancement. They'll dupe you a copy and you can take a look at it shortly."

"Good. Now tell me you got something more for me, Sam."

"Something's going down this weekend—soon, maybe in the next couple of hours if it already hasn't."

"What makes you say that?"

"The DVD. It was meant to confuse us, yes, but it's also a challenge from the killer—a dare to try and stop him."

"You're sure?"

"Yes, I am. But I need to get on the Internet—need to get on a computer right now here in the hospital."

"Why?"

"I'll explain it to you on the way. But I'm telling you, Bill, I have a very bad feeling The Michelangelo Killer plans to unveil his next exhibit tonight. And if I can figure out where, we might be able to get there before he does."

Chapter 33

The Sculptor backed his big white van out of the carriage house, made a three-point turn, and drove slowly down the tree-lined dirt driveway. This was the only area of his family's property that The Sculptor never maintained—thought it best to leave it grassy and overgrown in case any unwanted visitors happened to take a wrong turn off the paved driveway at the front of his house. About halfway down, he stopped the van and got out to move the large tree trunk that he usually left lying about for added protection. No need to replace it once he passed, however; for it was late, and he did not have to worry about any unwanted visitors at this hour.

In no time The Sculptor was back in his van and on his way. He emerged onto the darkened road through the break in the old stone wall that lined his family's property. There were very few streetlights here, and no sidewalks; most of the homes in The Sculptor's wealthy East Greenwich neighborhood were, like his own, set back off the road among the trees. Most of the lots were also enclosed by the fieldstone walls that weaved their way for miles through the surrounding woodlands. Indeed, as a boy, The Sculptor and his father had often followed them for hours—sometimes running into their neighbors and chatting with them along the way. But those days were gone, and The Sculptor and his father *never* spoke to their neighbors anymore.

The Sculptor reached the main road on which he would have to travel for some time. The overall distance was relatively short—and he would drive for the most part along the back roads just to be safe—but here, in the light, with the occasional car passing, he knew he was the most vulnerable, had the greatest chance of being spotted by the police. Such a risk could not be avoided, however; and thus The Sculptor was prepared with an adequate stockpile of loaded weapons under the passenger seat—his Sig Sauer .45 and the double barrel shotgun that had been in his family for years. He also had with him his tranquilizer guns—both the pistol and the sniper's rifle he had used on Tommy Campbell—just in case he ran into some irresistible bargain material along the way.

Such a prospect, however—as well as his having to use the guns—The Sculptor knew was slim, for when it came right down to it, The Sculptor was not really worried that the police might *ever* pull him over— even in the daylight. Indeed, the police might actually want to *avoid* him, for one of the first things The Sculptor had done when he was experimenting with the women was to purchase some additional colors of Starfire auto paint that would enable him to duplicate exactly the Channel 9 Eye-Team logo on the side of his van.

Chapter 34

Sam Markham sat at the doctor's desk—the harsh, speedy pulse of the fluorescent lights battering his tired eyes as he typed the words *"topiary garden"* and *"Rhode Island"* into the *Google* search engine.

"But Sam," said Bill Burrell, leaning over his shoulder, "what makes you so sure The Michelangelo Killer discovered the location for his *Bacchus* on the Internet?"

"Something the Reverend Bonetti said about their stolen *Pietà*—that they used to have a picture of it on their Web site. Just bear with me—I'm sort of working backward here."

Markham clicked on a couple of links; then, unsatisfied, he typed the words *"Earl Dodd"* and *garden Watch Hill* without quotes—but still came up empty. Markham thought for a moment, then flipped through his copy of *Slumbering in the Stone* to the page on the history of Michelangelo's *Bacchus*.

" 'The *Bacchus* was originally commissioned by Cardinal Raffaele Riario,' " Markham read aloud. " 'Who rejected it upon its completion on the grounds that the statue was distasteful. We know that by 1506, the *Bacchus* had found its way into a collection of ancient Roman sculptures belonging Jacopo Galli, Michelangelo's banker. There the *Bacchus* lived for some seventy years, weathering the elements at Cancelleria in Galli's Roman garden, until it was bought by the Medici family and transferred to Florence in 1576.' "

Markham typed the words *Roman garden* and *Rhode Island* into the search engine.

"Bingo," he said, and clicked on the sixth result from the top. The link brought him to a Web site titled, *Homes of the Elite.* A couple more clicks and Special Agent Sam Markham found exactly what he was looking for: a single photograph of Earl Dodd's topiary garden—no name, no address, just a caption that simply read, *"A lovely Roman garden in Rhode Island—overlooking the sea!"*

"Jesus Christ," said Burrell. "He must have driven around for weeks just trying to find the fucking place."

"And must have thought it nothing short of divine providence when he learned that the owner of his Roman garden was in finance like Jacopo Galli—wouldn't have settled for anyplace else, I suspect. It's why he went through so much trouble to display the statue there."

Markham flipped to Cathy's chapter on the *Rome Pietà.* He skimmed, then read aloud, "'In such a fashion, with the body of Christ illuminated by the natural light falling from above, the *Pietà* in its original installation must have seemed to the visitors at the Chapel of St. Petronilla as physically accessible yet at the same time untouchable; material yet undoubtedly supernatural—like the Savior himself, corporal yet divine.'"

"You're searching like he would," said Burrell. "You're using Hildebrant's words to find your destination like you think he did."

"The light," whispered Markham, typing. "It has to do with the light."

Natural light falling above chapel Rhode Island.

Nothing.

Light above chapel Rhode Island.

Nothing.

Chapel Rhode Island.

Nothing—too many.

Markham backtracked through Cathy's section on the *Rome Pietà*—his finger tracing along the text like a lie detector needle.

The *Pietà* is thus an expressive and decorous funerary monument, but at the same time perhaps the greatest devotional image ever created: a private memorial built for one man, but a public donation of faith intended for all of mankind.

"But you see," Cathy said in Markham's mind. *"One has to ultimately remember that the* Pietà *was originally intended to be a funerary monument, not just a devotional image."*

Markham typed, *Rhode Island funerary monument private memorial public.*

Nothing.

Funerary, Markham thought frantically. *Odd word.*

Impulsively, he changed his search criteria to, *Rhode Island cemetery monument memorial public faith.*

Markham clicked on the first of his search results. What he saw next made his breath stop in his throat.

The first photograph was an exterior shot of a small, circular structure that appeared to be built from marble, and that reminded Markham of the columned temples of Ancient Rome. The columns themselves were situated around an interior wall, through which there appeared to be only a single entrance. Beneath the photograph was the caption:

The Temple of Divine Spirit is located at the heart of Echo Point Cemetery. Its circular design—inspired by the "round" Temple of Hercules in Rome—is intended to represent an all-inclusive memorial for those who have passed on, as well as a monument to those who have been left behind. It is a place of prayer and contemplation open to the public and people of all faiths. On your next trip to Echo Point Cemetery, please feel free to remember your loved ones in the Temple of Divine Spirit.

Beneath this text was another photograph—this one of the temple's interior.

Markham did not bother to read the accompanying caption.

No. The single shaft of sunlight streaming down from the oculus in the temple's ceiling told him everything he needed to know.

Chapter 35

As Sam Markham and Bill Burrell scrambled to gather their agents, as Rachel Sullivan frantically alerted both the local and state police to get their asses over to the remote Echo Point Cemetery in Exeter, Rhode Island, The Sculptor was already installing his *Pietà* under cover of darkness. The rain had stopped earlier that evening, but the skies remained cloudy—the air humid enough to break The Sculptor's face into sweat beneath his night vision goggles. The distance he needed to carry his *Pietà* was much shorter than the distance he'd carried his *Bacchus* a few weeks earlier—a straight shot of only about twenty-five feet from the back of his van. But his *Pietà* was much heavier than his *Bacchus*—was much more awkward and difficult for the muscular Sculptor to maneuver due to the delicacy of the painted starched robes. However, once he managed to carefully load the statue onto a dolly that he constructed over a year ago specifically for this purpose, The Sculptor ultimately had no trouble dragging his

Pietà down the flagstone path and up the steps into the Temple of Divine Spirit.

The Sculptor methodically unloaded his *Pietà* into place directly beneath the temple's oculus—that opening in the ceiling which The Sculptor knew would mimic perfectly the original visual dynamic in the catacomb which the Christians had renamed the Chapel of St. Petronilla. The "veil effect" he had created in the Virgin's forehead with a strand of tightly tied fishing line was breathtaking, but The Sculptor paused only briefly to admire his work—dared to stand only for a minute in the cavernous temple with his night vision goggles and ogle over the aesthetic divinity created by the downcast, cloud-filtered moonlight.

Yes, the nameless material he had harvested from the streets of South Providence, the whore's head that he had chosen to be his Virgin's, had turned out perfectly—her youthful visage sad but serene, full of loving and longing but at the same time at peace with the knowledge that her Son will soon triumph over death. And the RounDaWay17 material had turned out brilliantly, too; it was perfectly proportioned to the Virgin's body, and, as seen through the night vision goggles, reflected as planned the supernatural luminescence of the falling moonlight—*just as Dr. Hildy described in her book.*

Oh yes, The Sculptor could stand there gazing upon his *Pietà* all night, but The Sculptor knew that that would be foolish, or at the very least would be a waste of time.

As The Sculptor had hoped, in addition to their regular duties, the local and state police—*at the FBI's request*—had been spread out on stakeouts of churches all over Rhode Island—none of which happened to be near Echo Point Cemetery. And so The Sculptor took his time gathering his things back into the van entirely unaware that an FBI agent named Sam Markham had discovered the location for his latest exhibition. Back in the driver's seat, The Sculptor relaxed for a moment before turning the key in the ignition—was just about to shift into drive when the reflection of flashing blue lights on the headstones caught him completely by surprise.

Bad luck, he said to himself. *Someone must have called the police.*

His heart all at once beating fast, The Sculptor removed his night vision goggles—knew the approaching headlights would temporarily blind him if he didn't—and reached under the passenger's seat. The Sculptor's fingers immediately closed around his Sig Sauer .45, and when he again looked out the windshield, he could see the two police cars winding their way among the headstones from the opposite side of the cemetery.

Only two, The Sculptor thought. But he knew instinctively that more would follow—knew instinctively that he had only *one chance.*

Yes, The Sculptor said to himself. *Only one chance to take them by surprise then get out of here.*

The Sculptor climbed out the passenger door and quickly made his way around to the back of the temple, darting behind the headstones as he backtracked his way toward the road. The Channel 9 Eye-Team logo would be the bait—would hopefully lure the policemen out of their cars and thus buy him enough time to sneak up behind them and put a bullet in their heads. The Sculptor hid himself behind a nearby tree and removed a black ski mask from his back pocket, pulling it tightly over his bald head, his sweaty face.

Then he waited.

And soon, just as he expected, the two Exeter police cars—*locals, thankfully*—pulled up in front of the temple. The Sculptor could see from the flashes of light off the van, off the white marble of the temple and surrounding headstones, that each car held only one officer.

That was fortunate.

"You guys can't be here," he heard one of them shout upon emerging from his car. And as the two officers approached the van—their guns not even drawn—The Sculptor was upon them before they even had a chance to turn around.

As was the case when he went shopping for his material with the tranquilizer guns, The Sculptor did not pause when he shot them. However, instead of aiming for their necks, he pointed the red dot from his laser sight just underneath their police hats—one silenced bullet in each of their heads, then two more once they hit the ground just to be safe.

The Sculptor hopped back into his van and drove quickly away from the scene. He did not mourn the fact that he had just wasted good material or whether or not the police dash-cams had recorded the whole event. His face was covered, of course, and he could always repaint the van. He would have it safely hidden away again in the carriage house before the police had time to review the video. And so The Sculptor opted to take his chances on the highway rather than risk being cornered by the police on the back country roads. He had just kicked the van up to sixty-five when he saw the state police cars and the black FBI vehicles speeding past him down Route

95—in the opposite direction, *toward* the Echo Point Cemetery exit.

The Sculptor smiled. He had no way of knowing, however, that Sam Markham and Bill Burrell saw him, too—had no idea that they both cursed aloud when they spotted the Channel 9 Eye-Team van whizzing past, both of them furious at the local cop who had rolled this time.

"Fucking vultures," the SAC grunted.

Oh yes, if The Sculptor had heard that little comment, he most certainly would have giggled.

Indeed, many of the local and state authorities would see The Sculptor's Eye-Team van that night, but just as The Sculptor had hoped when he first painted the logo on its sides, their only wish had been to avoid it.

EXHIBIT THREE
Toward David

Chapter 36

Two weeks later

Sam Markham sat at his desk in downtown Providence. He felt sick as he watched the police video for at least the hundredth time—pausing, rewinding, and playing in stop motion every move The Michelangelo Killer made. As with the video of Steve Rogers, the team in Boston had immediately set about enhancing the footage, and Markham could see everything that had happened in front of the Temple of Divine Spirit—not only the calm, methodical way in which The Michelangelo Killer slaughtered the two policemen, but also the Channel 9 Eye-Team logo streaking out of camera range.

Markham remembered seeing the van on the highway that night—*oh how he remembered!* Felt the urge to vomit every time he thought about how close he had been to the killer—just a few yards across the grassy median. But more than watching over and over again the brutal murders of the two Exeter policemen—murders for which the supervisory special agent felt partly responsible—what *really* made Markham sick was that, as was the case with the video of Steve Rogers, he could get no clues from it—could not determine anything other than the make of the van and the killer's size and height.

Yes, even though The Michelangelo Killer was dressed entirely in black—a black ski mask, black gloves, and a tight fitting long-sleeve black shirt—Markham could clearly make out the killer's physique against the white of the phony Eye-Team van: about six-five and *very* muscular—a bodybuilder, just as the celebrated profiler had suspected all along.

Of course, in the two weeks following the shocking exhibition of The Michelangelo Killer's *Pietà* down at Echo Point Cemetery, the ballistics tests on the killer's .45 caliber bullets and the leads on the van—a Chevy 2500 Express model that most likely was the same one reported stolen three years earlier—had so far turned up nothing. In addition, a still from the police video had been released on the Wednesday following the discovery of the Michelangelo Killer's *Pietà*, but the public had given the FBI nothing but red herrings.

The public.

Markham sighed and closed his computer's video player. And just as he expected, when he clicked on the Internet Explorer icon, the first picture on his AOL homepage was of Michelangelo's *Pietà*. The media firestorm that followed the discovery of the grisly scene in Exeter made the fallout from The Michelangelo Killer's *Bacchus* seem like a snowball fight. Indeed, as soon as the real Channel 9 Eye-Team van showed up outside of Echo Point Cemetery, it seemed to Markham as if a war had broken out—the news choppers hovering above and the media frenzy outside the cemetery gates reminding him of a scene right out of *Apocalypse Now.* There was no keeping anything from the press this time—not even the most telling details of The Michelangelo Killer's *Pietà*, which the killer had actually *signed.*

Yes, unbelievably, The Michelangelo Killer had chiseled another message into his work—this time not to Catherine Hildebrant, but to the public in general. Markham remembered from his reading of *Slumbering in the Stone* that the *Rome Pietà* was the only work Michelangelo ever signed—the legend of which claimed that, upon overhearing a visitor to the Chapel of St. Petronilla attribute the statue to another artist, Michelangelo returned later that night and chiseled in Latin a message on the sash across the Virgin's chest: *"Michelangelo Buonarroti, Florentine, made this."* Hildebrant went on to state in her book that the legend was fictional, and that the signature had been there from the beginning. *"A bold stab at fame,"* she had called it. *"Michelangelo's most blatant attempt ever for public recognition."* And although Sam Markham had since learned from Cathy that there was still much scholarly debate as to the reason why Michelangelo signed his *Pietà*, both of them agreed that there could be no doubt as to the reason why "The Sculptor" had signed his.

"The Sculptor from Rhode Island made it."

"Just like the legend," Cathy had said to Markham when she first laid eyes on the inscription. "He's telling the press what to call him. He's *correcting* them."

And the press obeyed.

They called him "The Sculptor" now in the papers and on TV, on the Internet and on the blogs and the

sick homepages that had sprouted up in dedication
to him since the discovery of Tommy Campbell. Indeed, the media seemed to talk of nothing else; and
Markham felt a palpable anxiety every time he
turned on his computer and his television. Worst of
all was the public's infatuation with Catherine Hildebrant—the woman Sam Markham now knew he loved;
the woman that the *public* loved for her now indis-
putable connection to The Sculptor. Yes, once the
media got wind that the pretty art history professor's
ex-husband had been used for the body of The Sculptor's Virgin Mary, the FBI knew they could no longer
keep her sheltered from the press, knew they could
no longer mask the connection between the killer
and her book. And thus, the FBI also knew they could
no longer use her effectively as a consultant on the
case.

At least not in public.

Cathy had recovered quickly from her knock on
the head—seemed to awaken with a newfound strength,
a newfound understanding of the role she must now
play in catching the man who had become so obsessed
with her. She had insisted on seeing The Sculptor's
Pietà at the morgue in person, had examined it with
an even more discerning eye than she had the *Bacchus* down at Watch Hill—even though she was well
aware it was her ex-husband's body holding up the
Virgin's flowing robes. Markham was in contact with
Cathy a dozen times a day—spoke to her on his cell
phone during the countless hours she spent doing
research for him on the computer, while he followed
up on his leads all over New England. Yes, Cathy seemed
to be holding up well, but Markham was very worried
about her. She was safe, of course, in protective cus-

tody—had been moved immediately upon her release from the hospital to an FBI safe house just outside of Boston. But Markham was afraid of the toll the ordeal was taking on her, was worried about that moment when the totality of what happened to her ex-husband—what happened to the others as a result of her book—*really* hit her.

Don't worry, whispered a voice in his head. *She's a fighter—just like her mother.*

Rachel Sullivan had given a statement to the press in Boston a week earlier, in which she officially released the names of the victims whose body parts The Sculptor had used for his *Pietà*.

There were four in all.

Of course, the FBI knew from the beginning about Rogers, whose headless, handless body—sans breast augmentation—was still awaiting release to be flown back to Chicago for burial by his family. As for the other victims, once the medical examiner removed the paint from the victims' fingertips and forensics was able to get some solid prints, the FBI's Integrated Automated Fingerprint Identification System (IAFIS) returned a match on the Virgin's hands and those of the Christ figure—respectively, Esther Muniz (aka Esther Munroe, Esther Martinez) twenty-eight years of age at the time of her disappearance, a resident of Providence, and Paul Jimenez, eighteen (aka Jim Paulson) from Boston and Virginia Beach.

Both were known prostitutes.

The fourth victim was also a prostitute, and after the FBI Forensic Science Unit released a photograph of the Virgin's head—digitally altered and colored to make the victim appear as she might have been "in life"—authorities quickly confirmed an anonymous tip that the victim's name was Karen Canfield (aka Karen Jones, Joanie Canfield)—originally from Dayton, Ohio—nineteen years old when she disappeared off the streets of Providence three years earlier. DNA testing matched her head to the breasts found on Steve Rogers's torso.

Of the two women, only Muniz had been reported missing by an abusive boyfriend who, shortly after his girlfriend's disappearance, had died in a botched drug deal. In addition to being a prostitute and a convicted felon, Muniz was also on the books as a habitual drug offender, and had three children by as many fathers.

All of her children had been in foster care since the day they were born.

Canfield, aged fourteen at the time she ran away from Dayton, was last seen by her alcoholic mother five years before her disappearance. Canfield's mother told the FBI that she had no idea her daughter was even missing—and from what Markham could gather, most likely would not have lost any sleep even if she had. As was the case with the movements of Paul Jimenez in Boston, the details of Karen Canfield's life in Providence were at this point still sketchy—the sad but typical nowhere story of a runaway-turned-underage-stripper-turned-crackhead-turned-prostitute—and a week's worth of investigation had turned up enough for Markham to see the *Dead End* sign at the end of *that* street. Indeed, the handful of Canfield's former acquaintances with whom the FBI had so far spoken claimed that she had often talked about getting clean and going to live with an aunt in North Carolina; and thus, when she stopped appearing on the streets of South Providence, they had just assumed that their friend had moved on—never even thought to report her missing.

The one bright spot in the tragedy that had been Karen Canfield's life was that her estranged mother requested her daughter's head and breasts be sent back to Dayton when the FBI was through with them.

Paul Jimenez's family, on the other hand, wanted nothing to do with him; and thus, the FBI would hang on to his body and Esther Muniz's hands indefinitely.

Markham quickly scanned his e-mails, promising himself he would get to them upon his return from Boston—after the teleconference with Quantico, in which he and Burrell's team would once again be briefed on the ongoing forensic and coroner's reports, as well as the joint investigations that had begun into the lives of the latest victims. Yet Markham could not ignore the nagging feeling that it was all a waste of time; he could not ignore that little voice in the back of his head that told him The Sculptor was too smart to allow himself to be caught *that way*—that is, by allowing himself to be traced to his *material*. Indeed, it seemed to Markham that The Sculptor had thought of everything: from the phony license plates and the fake satellite dish on his Eye-Team van, to the way he left absolutely no trace evidence in the material he used for his sculptures—other than that of which he was obviously consciously aware.

But there must be something *he's overlooked,* Markham thought. *Something that perhaps goes all the way back to the murder of Gabriel Banford, or to the theft of the Pietà at St. Bart's; something that The Sculptor had done when his plan was not yet fully formed—or perhaps something from the period when he was still experimenting.*

Yes, Markham felt instinctively that The Sculptor's latest exhibit had somehow gotten him off course—that he'd had enough information to catch The Michelangelo Killer from the beginning.

Slumbering in the Stone, Markham said to himself. *It was Cathy who led me to the exhibition of The Sculptor's* Pietà—*her book that got me so close I could have spit on him that night. Perhaps everything I need to catch him is right there.*

Suddenly Markham understood that he did not need to hear anything more from Quantico. He already knew that the preliminary coroner's reports would show that Steve Rogers and Paul Jimenez had died from an overdose of epinephrine, and that the glossy white Starfire paint which had covered The Sculptor's *Pietà* would show traces of finely ground Carrara marble—marble that undoubtedly had been pulverized from the stolen *Pietà* at St. Bart's. Perhaps something might be learned from the heavy starched canvas The Sculptor had used for the Virgin's robes, or the rock of Golgotha.

But still . . .

Slumbering in the Stone, Markham said to himself. *The key has to be in* Slumbering in the Stone.

Markham checked the time in the corner of his computer screen—would have to leave soon if he was going to make the meeting in Boston. He was torn; he felt like he needed to stay in Providence—*just knew* that the answer to catching The Michelangelo Killer was right there on his desk, right there in the book in his briefcase. But Markham also knew he needed Cathy; and Christ was he tired—couldn't think straight. He had slept for only a couple of hours in his office between working on his computer and reading over and over again the printouts from Boston and Quantico. He had spoken to Cathy before drifting off—had whispered her to sleep with "I miss you" and "I'll see you tomorrow" instead of the three words he had really wanted to say—those three words he had not said to another woman since the death of his Michelle. They had slept together in the same bed only once in the two weeks since they first made love at Cathy's East Side condo, stealing kisses and passionate exchanges here and there when the coast was clear at the safe house. If Bill Burrell and his team knew about his affair with Cathy Hildebrant, if they thought it improper, they weren't saying. And to be honest, Sam Markham didn't give a shit if the whole fucking Federal Bureau of Investigation knew. No, in the two weeks since he first began to admit to himself his love for Cathy Hildebrant, Markham began to feel more and more that he was working not for them, but for *her*.

The only e-mail Sam Markham chose to open that morning was from Rachel Sullivan. He responded with a short *Yes* to her question as to whether or not he wanted to donate to the fund she was organizing for the slain officer's families. She was a good egg, that Sullivan, and a damn fine agent—would soon be a SAC herself, Markham thought; she was doing a bang-up job of scraping the shit from the toilet bowl that was South Providence. No doubt she would be giving a presentation today on her missing persons report—had already informed Markham that, after weeding through the databases, she was presently working with a list of at least eight names of prostitutes who were known to have disappeared from the Rhode Island area in the last six years, and whose circumstances might tie them to The Michelangelo Killer.

Eight, Markham had said to himself. *How many are The Sculptor's? And how many others went unreported?*

Markham felt his stomach knot at the thought of The Michelangelo Killer going shopping for material on the streets of South Providence like it was Wal-Mart. *But a smart place to buy,* Markham thought—a typical hunting ground for serial killers because so many of their victims go unnoticed. But whereas Markham knew that most serial killers hunted out of the need to satisfy some kind of selfish sexual or psychological urge, he also knew that The Sculptor only hunted out of a need for supplies.

"Put me down for 500," Markham added in his e-mail, and then shut down his computer.

Five hundred dollars, he said to himself. *Two hundred and fifty each for their lives. Pathetic.*

At that moment, Markham would have given his whole salary to the policemen's widows. But at the same time he understood that anything more than his five hundred dollars would make him and the FBI look guilty. He had attended the double funeral that week—actually wept when he saw the slain policemen's children place their flowers on their fathers' caskets. In hindsight, it had been foolish for the FBI to put out an APB—foolish to unleash the cunning Sculptor on a couple of unsuspecting locals.

But then again, two weeks ago, how could the FBI have known what they were really dealing with?

A killing machine, Markham thought. *Built like the fucking Terminator, and who won't stop until he finds his man.*

Yes, as vivid as were those teenage memories of Arnold Schwarzenegger blasting his way through the streets of LA in pursuit of Sarah Connor, Special Agent Sam Markham could see so clearly the man for whom The Sculptor would be searching next—a dark and grainy movie in his mind, in which a ski-masked Terminator chased a marble white statue through the streets of downtown Providence.

A movie starring Michelangelo's *David*.

Chapter 37

The plan from the beginning had always been *David,* but it was the *Pietà* that had inspired him to actually start *working*—yes, the *Pietà* around which the development of his skills had evolved. And so, that it should have been the *Pietà* that ended up causing him so much trouble bothered The Sculptor greatly.

In the two weeks since his second exhibit—in the two weeks since he had been *almost caught*—The Sculptor followed attentively every single story about him in the media. Yes, he saw many times the still photographs of him that had been taken from the police dash-cam, the ludicrous FBI composite sketch of what he might look like under his ski mask, the details of his height and weight, the pictures of the make and model of his van—all that *blahdy-blah-blah.*

In the end, however, such details did not worry The Sculptor, for in the end The Sculptor knew such details would not hurt him. No, what really got under The Sculptor's skin was his understanding that—although he wasn't quite sure *how*—the police and the

FBI had one way or another figured out where he was going to exhibit his *Pietà*. And even though it had quickly become obvious to him that the authorities had made their discovery only at the last minute, The Sculptor—putting two and two together from the media reports—nonetheless had a good idea who might have tipped them off.

Dr. Hildy. It had to have been Dr. Hildy.

The Sculptor threw the weight bar back onto the rack with a loud clang. He had benched more than ever today—was well aware that he was channeling his frustration into his workouts in a way that was unusual for him. The Sculptor's workouts in the cellar were normally quite methodical—steady, calm, and unemotional. But today, The Sculptor felt restless, felt helpless—like he *needed to be working*. Everything was all ready for his *David*—the video, the base and frame, the epinephrine, the formaldehyde, the chemicals for the Plastination process. He had even repainted the van—had disposed of the phony satellite dish—and would start working on switching it out for something else once he got his new material. All he really needed now was the *right* material. But because The Sculptor could not figure out exactly how Dr. Hildy and the FBI had managed to guess the location for his *Pietà*, instinctively The Sculptor felt it was too dangerous to go shopping just yet.

And just where would he go shopping? Not on the streets of South Providence anymore; not on the Internet, or up in Boston where the FBI now knew the RounDaWay17 material had come from. No, the FBI would be looking for that. Besides, The Sculptor had understood from the beginning that, with the unveiling of his *Pietà*, he would no longer be able to use that kind of material anyway; he understood that he would have to go back to shopping for material as had done for his *Bacchus.*

True, the news reports erroneously claimed that The Sculptor had found his material for the Christ figure on Arlington Street in Boston. And if the FBI did in fact know about RounDaWay17's Craigslist account, they most certainly hadn't revealed it to the press. No, The Sculptor was not worried about *that*— knew that it would be impossible for them to trace RounDaWay17's online activity now that The Sculptor had hacked into, changed, and deleted the young man's account.

No, it was the gnawing not-knowing of exactly *how* Dr. Hildy and the FBI had figured out the location of his *Pietà* that worried him the most.

At least everything is ready, he said to himself. *That's some comfort.*

In the beginning, when he first began experimenting with the pieces of the women, The Sculptor would travel all over New England picking the locks at the backs of funeral homes and stealing just enough formaldehyde to get him by—just enough so it would not be missed. But The Sculptor observed in his travels that many of the funeral homes produced their own formaldehyde, and later, after he accidentally stumbled upon a picture of Rhode Island native Tommy Campbell on the Internet—when he saw the resemblance to Michelangelo's *Bacchus,* when he understood that it was his *destiny* to have the wide receiver for his first exhibit—in addition to putting his *Pietà* on hold, The Sculptor decided to start producing his own twenty-nine percent formaldehyde solution in the small lab he had set up off the wine cellar to manufacture his epinephrine and his high-powered tranquilizers. Using a technique of methanol conversion that he learned on the Internet, there in the cool damp bowels of his family home he could prepare and store not just his formaldehyde, but all his chemicals; and when he was ready, he could transfer them to barrels and wheel them up and out of the back hatchway door for use in the carriage house.

It was a very efficient system.

However, as was the case with the Plastination process in the carriage house, more than the actual acquisition of his chemicals—the majority of which had been either distilled from common household products or stolen barrel by barrel from warehouses that weren't even locked—the biggest problem for The Sculptor in his cellar lab was always the ventilation. And despite the numerous exhaust vents that he had installed, despite the gas mask that he always wore, after working for long hours in his cramped laboratory The Sculptor would sometimes begin to feel dizzy. And on those rare occasions when he would accidentally touch the epinephrine—highly concentrated *synthetic* epinephrine that he had also learned to manufacture from his hours of study on the Internet—he would start to sweat, would feel his heart speed up and his head go all loopy. The Sculptor, however, did not mind such temporary changes within his body—the dizziness, the speedy heartbeat—as in a way, he thought, it helped him connect to his creations.

But The Sculptor did not like the change he felt within his body today; nor did he like the emotions bubbling up inside of him when he thought of Dr. Hildy. And as he slid two more plates onto his weight bar, The Sculptor could not help but feel as if the pretty art history professor had betrayed him.

The Sculptor had been smart enough to know from the beginning that Dr. Catherine Hildebrant would be at the very least an unwilling accomplice in his plan. But after all *he had done for her*, after he had specifically used her ex-husband for the body of his Virgin as a *favor* to her—that same man who had betrayed her, that same poopy-head who The Sculptor had followed for years, who *he knew* was having sexual relations behind the good doctor's back—yes, Dr. Hildy could have *at least held off* on telling the FBI about his *Pietà* until it was in place.

The Sculptor blasted out six more reps on his bench, and when he returned the bar to the rack, it was as if his mind at once had cleared. And in a flash of insight, The Sculptor suddenly understood the brutal but simple reality that, if indeed it had been Dr. Hildy who had led the FBI to his *Pietà,* then there was a good chance that Dr. Hildy might do the same with his *David.* Hence, although it had never been part of his original plan, The Sculptor understood all at once that the best thing to do in order to guarantee a smooth exhibit of his *David* was to get rid of Dr. Catherine Hildebrant.

And much to his surprise, The Sculptor suddenly felt *a lot better.*

Chapter 38

"I want to go back to Providence," said Cathy Hildebrant. She and Sam Markham stood before Burrell's desk like a pair of high school delinquents in the principal's office—contrite, fearful, yet defiant.

"I can't allow it," said Burrell. "That would be like throwing you to the wolves."

"I don't care. I can be more help to you working with Sam on the street."

"But Cathy, you've been watching the television these last couple of weeks—been reading the papers and the news reports online. You know the press is looking for you, is dying to pick your bones."

"I'm not worried about that. I'll keep a low profile."

"But with the murder of your ex, don't you see that they all blame you? We can't protect you from them anymore. It's an entirely different situation now—they don't want to just talk to you about The Michelangelo Killer, they want to get closer to him through you. I know you've been following the news.

The press and the public are just waiting for The Sculptor's next exhibit. They all know what it's going to be—the goddamn statue of *David*. Christ, it's only a matter of time before every young male with muscles in Rhode Island starts going into a panic, starts going into hiding."

"I understand that but—"

"I can't guarantee your safety down there, Cathy," Burrell said, rising. "Hell, I shouldn't even have you as a consultant on the case anymore."

"She'll be fine with me, Bill," said Markham. "We can set her up in a room in my building—I'll be personally responsible for her, twenty-four-seven."

"Both of you were at the teleconference today, Sam. Both of you understand now what this guy is all about. We can tie him to at least nine murders, including Gabriel Banford and the two policemen. That's at least nine. Who knows how many of Rachel's missing prostitutes are his. Who knows how many more there are that we don't know about—prostitutes, young men, women, children. He doesn't hunt in one demographic, Sam. He chooses his victims according to some sick plan that parallels the artistic output of Michelangelo. I mean, Christ, what's to say he won't come after Cathy next?"

"I can't stay in hiding all my life," Cathy said.

"No, but you can goddamn well stay there a little longer."

An awkward silence fell over the office as the SAC turned his back on them—staring absently out his window to the Boston skyline.

"I understand what you've been going through, Cathy. I understand that you've been cooped up with us for almost two weeks now. I know it must make you feel isolated, helpless, and a little stir crazy—

being away from the people and the places you love. That's to be expected. But at least there's the buffer of distance between you and the killer; at least the press doesn't know where you are. If you go back to Providence, if you start working the streets with Markham again, someone might spot you, might notify the press. And if the media finds out where you are, then The Sculptor might find out, too." Burrell turned to face her. "Look, Cathy, if you can just hold out a little longer, if you can just sit tight until we get something solid—"

"You can't hold me here against my will."

"You're right," said Burrell. "But I can fire you from the case if you choose to leave protective custody. Is that what you want me to do?"

Both Cathy and Markham knew the SAC was bluffing, but it was the FBI agent who called him on it.

"If she goes, I go."

Burrell looked at him incredulously.

"I mean it," Markham said. "I'm done—I'm through with the Bureau for good. You can't fire me, Bill, but I can quit. I can fly back to Quantico and hand in my resignation first thing in the morning."

Bulldog's cheeks flushed red.

"Leave us alone," he said.

Cathy looked uncomfortably to Markham. He nodded, and she quietly left the room.

"Bill, I know what you're going—"

"You don't know shit," Bulldog bellowed, his fists clenching. "You think you can scare me with ultimatums? You think I give a *fuck* if you resign?"

"Yes I do," Markham said calmly. "I think you know how bad it would look if word got out that your obstinacy got in the way of this investigation. And I think you know how bad it would look if I let it be known how close we were to catching this guy, and that you of all people let him get away."

"Close, my fucking ass—"

"I can catch this guy," said Markham, leaning on the SAC's desk. "But I can do it only with your full support and that means Cathy's support, too. I can't do it without her."

The bulldog just stood there—fuming.

"It's in her book, Bill. The answer is in her book. *I know it.* It was Cathy who got me close to him that night—Cathy who figured out it was the lighting, the key to the parallel between the environments that was so important for The Sculptor's exhibition. Don't you see, Bill? Together we can catch him. You just have to trust me on this."

"I'm not an idiot, Markham. I know you two have been playing patty cake these last few weeks. And girlfriend or no girlfriend, I'm telling you now that if anything happens to her, you're done. Meaning, I'll see to it personally that you're demoted to the fucking mail room. You understand me?"

"Yes, I do."

Burrell turned his back to him—his eyes once again falling to the Boston skyline.

"We'll set her up in your building for two weeks—change her hair color and give her contacts. At the end of those two weeks we'll reassess the situation. Understand, however, that if at any time I decide it's too risky—if the press finds out about her, if the location of the safe house is blown, whatever the fuck the reason—if I don't like the way things are playing out and you two balk, then she's out and you can do whatever the fuck you want."

"I understand."

"But let me be perfectly clear on this, Sam. No matter what happens, *you* are the one who's responsible for her. You got me?"

"Yes. Thank you, Bill."

"Now get the fuck out of my office."

Chapter 39

The FBI safe house was the only one of its kind left in Rhode Island; it had been initially set up as a surveillance unit after the terrorist attacks of 9-11, and was located on the second and third floors of a commercial building in downtown Providence, directly across the street from the former law offices of a suspected Al-Qaeda sympathizer who was eventually prosecuted. Its original purpose now abandoned, the FBI had since re-outfitted the property into an operations suite with separate apartments, and only in the last year had begun using it as temporary housing for its itinerant agents. The phony placards in and around the building indicated that the second and third floors were occupied by an import/export business, but the private access of the underground parking lot, as well as the building's card-key security system to the elevator and each floor, made it a doubly safe location for all types of FBI operations.

In an odd way it all felt so normal to Cathy Hildebrant. It looked almost identical to her former digs in Boston, but that she should be staying there with

Sam Markham gave Cathy a sense of being *home*—a feeling of being a newlywed, like when she was first setting up house with Steve Rogers.

Steve Rogers.

Cathy tried not to think of her ex-husband—tried not to think about the images from The Sculptor's DVD that had been branded into her brain. She knew deep down that it was not her fault and that The Michelangelo Killer had begun hunting victims even before he'd ever heard of Dr. Catherine Hildebrant. But more than the degree of her culpability in her ex-husband's death, Cathy tried not to think about the mixed feelings she had now that he was gone. No, she would never have wished what The Michelangelo Killer had done to him even on her worst enemy; but what chewed away at Cathy's guts was the feeling that she had lost him *twice,* and that, as much as she hated to admit it, the first time around had been harder than the second.

There'll be time to sort it out later was her mantra—the same one she had repeated to herself over and over during her mother's battle with breast cancer. Yet instead of following up with encouraging words to stay focused, to finish her book and secure tenure, Cathy now had a new tagline: *after I catch The Michelangelo Killer.*

Cathy stood before the bathroom mirror and pulled her hair back into a ponytail. She did not like how she looked with blond highlights. They made her look cheap, she thought, like a porn star. But it had to be done as part of the deal with Burrell and Boston. What would take more getting used to would be the contact lenses—she had never liked those; they always felt dry and made her eyes look puffy. Again, another necessity, but she would take along her black-rimmed glasses with her just in case. The worst, however, was when she donned her sunglasses. She thought she looked silly. Like a porno-Asian La Femme Nikita.

"You ready?" asked Markham, his head poking through the bathroom door. His presence calmed her, grounded her, but at the same time made her feel ashamed. Yes, despite everything that had happened since she met him, Cathy actually felt happy to finally be alone with him again.

"Yes," she said. "If you don't mind being seen with me."

Markham kissed her neck and left her at the sink. They had spent the night in each other's arms—made love like a pair of adulterers into the wee hours of the morning—and Cathy's nostrils were still filled with the strange scent of her hair coloring and Sam Markham's cologne.

As Cathy brushed her teeth, she suddenly had the impulse to call Janet Polk—to open her cell phone and leave her surrogate mother a quick message saying she was okay. *But that's a no-no,* Cathy thought. Yes, Cathy knew damn well that she was not supposed to talk with anyone other than the FBI until Bill Burrell gave the go ahead—another part of her agreement with Burrell which, like her hair, she regretted. Cathy had not spoken to Janet and Dan since she left the hospital; she had gotten messages to them through Rachel Sullivan, but still she felt guilty, for Cathy knew how worried Janet was since learning about the murder of Steve Rogers.

There'll be time to sort it out later.

Cathy emerged from the bathroom to find Markham standing in the middle of the common area—his copy of *Slumbering in the Stone* open before him as if he were an actor about to give a reading.

"What is it?" Cathy asked.

"Nothing, really. Just trying to gather myself before we go—overtired, I think."

"What do you mean?"

"Well, ever since the teleconference with Quantico yesterday, there's a quote in your chapter on the *Pietà* that's been bothering me—a quote attributed to Michelangelo himself, and related by his contemporary biographer, Ascanio Condivi."

"You mean the quote regarding the Madonna's youthful appearance?"

"Yes. In your discussion of the various reasons as to why Michelangelo might have sculpted his *Pietà* with the Virgin Mary as a young woman, you say that the artist himself told Condivi, 'Don't you know that chaste women stay fresh much longer than those who are not chaste? How much more so then with the Virgin, who never had even the slightest lascivious desire that might alter her appearance?' "

"Why should that bother you?"

"Well, as we saw with his *Bacchus*, The Sculptor is well aware of the baggage the contemporary context of his *Pietà* would carry along with it—that is, how our knowledge of where the pieces came from would affect our perception of it. As we learned with *Bacchus*—where we, the viewer, see both the mythology of the Roman god and the satyr wound up into the lives of Tommy Campbell and Michael Wenick— when we look at The Sculptor's *Pietà*, we see the story of the Virgin and Christ, but we also see the stories of the prostitutes—the lascivious desires of *their* lives. Our minds see the contradiction of the holy and the impure all at once."

"So you think the message in this case is ultimately one of blasphemy?"

"I don't know, but I just can't help thinking there's something I'm missing—something that connects your chapter in *Slumbering in the Stone* to The Sculptor's use of prostitutes for his *Pietà*—something that goes beyond just the convenience of readily available material."

"He didn't only use prostitutes," Cathy said blandly.

"I'm sorry, Cathy. I know that. But—and you'll have to forgive me—but I'm thinking it goes beyond the victims' professions, if you will, to the concept of sin, of *sexual impurity*. In The Sculptor's eyes, you see, all of the victims he used for his *Pietà* were sinners with regard to sex—which brings me to something else you wrote when you spoke of Michelangelo's influences for his *Pietà*. You say, 'Another possible explanation as to why Michelangelo chose to portray his Virgin as a young mother is that he was heavily influenced by Dante's *Divine Comedy*. We know that the artist was not only an admirer, but also a scholar of Dante's work, and therefore must have been familiar with Saint Bernard's prayer in Canto 33 of *Paradiso*, which begins, "Virgin mother, daughter of your son." Here we see the relationship of the Virgin and her Son played out against the inherent contradiction of the Holy Trinity, wherein God exists in three forms: the Father, the Son (God incarnate as Jesus Christ), and the Holy Spirit. Thus, when taken in this undeniably "incestuous" context, if God is both the Father and Son, then the Virgin Mary is both Christ's mother and His daughter, as well as his *wife*. One can then argue that Michelangelo is embodying this contradicting but parallel trinity in terms of the figures' similar ages—a contradiction wherein the father-daughter/mother-son/husband-wife relationship is skewed, existing in a spiritual realm outside of time, wherein physical age is only a "relative," earthly index.' "

"So you think then that the *Pietà* might represent to The Sculptor some kind of warped, confused relationship between a mother and son?"

"I don't know, Cathy," Markham sighed. "Maybe I'm just overtired. Maybe I'm looking too deeply into it all. But when you think about how much trouble The Sculptor went through to get the Gambardelli *Pietà*, it might indicate that we were wrong about its relationship to his victims. Don't misunderstand me, Cathy. I still think the killer wanted the marble of the statue to connect his victims to his sculptures. And although that plan might have changed, might have evolved into something else when he began focusing on his *Bacchus,* we now know that we were correct in our theory that The Sculptor had experimented with women before he moved on to males and full figures. However, even though The Sculptor wanted to use a male for the body of his Virgin to get the proportions and the breast placement correct, as well as to embody Michelangelo's point of view on the female figure in general, I just can't ignore the differences between how The Michelangelo Killer constructed his *Pietà* and his *Bacchus.* When you look at the fact that he used three separate human entities for the Virgin herself, and when you take into account that you discuss in your chapter on the *Pietà* the relationship between the Virgin and Christ as a contradicting yet parallel trinity to the traditional Christian Holy Trinity—well, it's a bizarre coincidence, don't you think?"

"Yes. Yes it is."

"Never mind all the metaphorical and moral implications that go along with such a reading of this parallel, incestuous, *impure* trinity."

"Is that why we're going to see the Reverend Bonetti again today?"

"Yes," said Sam Markham. "I honestly haven't a clue exactly what or why, but something tells me that there's more to The Sculptor's theft of the Gambardelli *Pietà* than we first realized."

Chapter 40

The Reverend Robert Bonetti watched them from his office window—had requested on the telephone that they enter at the back of the church so as not to disturb his parishioners, who would be coming and going all day for confession. When he saw them emerge from the Trailblazer, at first the old priest did not recognize the blond woman with the sunglasses who accompanied the FBI agent named Markham. Only when they passed outside his window did Father Bonetti realize the pretty art history professor from Brown University had finally decided to come out of hiding.

Although Reverend Bonetti rarely watched television or sat in front of a computer screen, and although he preferred to read or watch his tiny collection of old black-and-white movies on the rectory's ancient VCR, even he knew what had happened to Catherine Hildebrant—to her ex-husband, yes, but also to *her*. Bonetti knew that the media was claiming it was her book, *Slumbering in the Stone*, that had inspired The Michelangelo Killer to commit his atrocities; he knew that, since the death of her husband, she had withdrawn from the public eye—probably had gone into protective custody, the papers said. Oh yes, he had read the news stories, had seen Hildebrant's picture many times on Meghan O'Neill's *Special Report: The Michelangelo Killer* series on Channel 9. And now there were the rumors that the first statue—the one with the football player and that poor little boy from Cranston—had originally been dedicated to her, too.

When he heard the outside door slam, Father Bonetti's heart went out to Catherine Hildebrant as it had so many times over the last couple of weeks. But he needed to move quickly, and just as the knock came at his office door, the old priest slipped the copy of *Slumbering in the Stone* that he had picked up a week earlier into his desk drawer.

"Come in."

Cathy entered first, followed by Markham.

"Dr. Hildebrant," said Reverend Bonetti, offering his hand. "Despite the circumstances, it truly is a pleasure to see you again. I won't pretend that I don't know what's happened to you over the last few weeks. But let me first offer my condolences for your loss, and second, my support in this difficult time. If there's anything I can do, you'll tell me?"

"Thank you, Father."

Another round of pleasantries, and the three of them took their seats around Father Bonetti's desk.

"Now," said the priest. "To what do I owe this return visit?"

"I'd like to ask you a few more questions, Father," said Markham. "Specifically with regard to your Gambardelli *Pietà*."

"I'm not sure what else I can tell you. I've seen the police photos, the composite sketches of your man.

There's no one I know who fits that bill, and certainly no one that could afford twenty-five thousand dollars for a statue."

"I understand that, Father. But I was hoping you could perhaps tell us a little more about the statue itself. You said that there was originally a picture of it on your Web site?"

"Yes. It was a photograph of the votive chapel—the one off the main church that I showed you—the one that currently houses our replacement *Pietà*."

"Was there anything on the Web site, however—a caption or an accompanying description—that identified the statue specifically as a Gambardelli *Pietà*?"

"Not that I recall, no."

"The picture then—was it a close-up of the statue, or taken at a distance?"

"I guess you could say it was taken at a distance. It has been a tradition at St. Bart's for many years to move the pyramid of votive candles into the main church after Thanksgiving in order to accommodate the three life-size Nativity statues that occupy the chapel during the Christmas holiday. I believe it was around that time that the photograph was taken. There is no manger to house the Nativity—just the architecture of the chapel itself—so the Gambardelli *Pietà* would have been visible against the wall behind the statues of Jesus, Mary, and Joseph."

"The family who donated the *Pietà*," Markham continued. "What was their name?"

"Well, now," said the priest, leaning back in his leather chair. "For the life of me, I can't remember. If you'll recall, our original *Pietà* was donated a few years before I arrived. There was a plaque engraved with the family's name at its base, but of course that was stolen along with the statue. I'm ashamed to admit, Agent Markham, that—for all the time I've spent in this church—I'm not sure I *ever* knew the family's name. Strange isn't it? How you can pass by something every day and not really see it?"

"And you never had the plaque replaced?"

"No. The family who donated the statue moved away many years ago. Matter of fact, if my memory serves me, they hadn't lived here for decades before I arrived—moved to a wealthier neighborhood—the gift of the *Pietà* being a bit of sentimentality on the part of one of their old matriarchs, I take it. However, our deacon at the time of the theft, a Scalabrini who has since moved on, took it upon himself to track them down. He did find someone—a daughter I think—but the person to whom he spoke said not to bother having another plaque made, as the family did not want to be associated with our church anymore."

Markham and Cathy exchanged a look.

"This deacon," said the FBI agent. "Do you know how he discovered the family's name? Are there records of donations and things of the like in your files?"

"I assume that's where he found it, yes—perhaps also from asking around the congregation."

"And these records, these files—do you still have them?"

"I would think so. But to be honest, Agent Markham, I wouldn't even know where to begin looking for them. Any records older than five years we move to the basement, where they're stacked in a dead files pile along with all the documents that were transferred from the old church after its renovation in the late 1960s—stuff going back almost a hundred years. Ironically, it was the deacon's search for that family's name that was our motivation to start cleaning house down there. However, even if you did find the actual record of the donation, Agent Markham, you might still have to track down the surviving family members like our man did three years ago. If you'd like, I can find out from the Scalabrini Fathers where the deacon is stationed—can ask him if he remembers the last name, where the family is living now, and can get back to you early next week."

"Under normal circumstances, that would be fine, Father. But, with the murder of Cathy's ex-husband, with the discovery of the *Pietà* two weeks ago in Exeter, there is every indication that The Michelangelo Killer is going to kill again—and soon. Hence, we need to follow up on every lead as quickly as possible."

"Yes," said the priest. "I read about it in the papers. The authorities, the media seems to think his next public exhibition will be the statue of *David*. Indeed, I'm willing to bet that sales of your book, Dr. Hildebrant, have skyrocketed with amateur sleuths looking for a way to prevent the crime, to solve the case before the FBI does."

Cathy was silent.

"You're probably right, Father Bonetti," said Markham. "So you see why it's extremely important that we get that family's name as soon as possible."

"If you don't mind my asking, Agent Markham, why would the FBI be interested in a family who donated a statue over thirty years ago? What does any of this have to do with The Michelangelo Killer, other than you think that he stole our *Pietà*?"

"I *know* he stole it, Father Bonetti. And to be quite frank with you, I'm not exactly sure what I might find on the other side of this—that is, if and when I'm able contact the family in question. And to be even more frank, your stolen statue is the only solid lead I have to go on at the moment, the only place for sure I know The Michelangelo Killer was other than the scenes of the murders and the exhibitions of his statues. However, one thing I *do* know, Father, is that the theft was not random—meaning, I don't think the killer saw your *Pietà* on the Internet. No, I think The Michelangelo Killer had known about the statue from the beginning. He may have sat in this church many times over the years—perhaps became fascinated with it as a child. After all, the last time we met, you yourself said that everything was connected."

"Yes I did, didn't I," said the priest, his thoughts far away.

"So please, Father, would you be so kind as to let us look through your records?"

Reverend Bonetti smiled and nodded his consent. He led Cathy and Markham to a stack of boxes in the basement—three deep against a wall, and piled almost to the ceiling in some places.

"You have quite a task ahead of you," said the priest. "The deacon began organizing the files himself with the intention of throwing most of them out. Fortunately for you, as you can see from the labels on the newer boxes, he got only as far as 1994 before he was called to move on. The boxes in the back are from the old church, so you needn't bother with those. I can't guarantee you'll find what you're looking for, Agent Markham, but if the document is still here, and if the deacon did in fact return it to the box in which he found it, I would assume it's in one of these boxes toward the front."

"Thank you, Father," said Markham.

"You'll have to excuse me now, as I must get upstairs for confession. I'll be back down to check on you in an hour. If you find what you're looking for before then, please let yourselves out the back door. I only ask that you leave the original document behind."

"Will do."

"I'll say my farewells to you now in the event I miss you." The old priest took Cathy's hand. "Dr. Hildebrant, may God give you strength and courage in this difficult time."

"Thank you, Father."

Reverend Bonetti smiled and disappeared up the stairs.

Cathy and Markham began in earnest—did not bother with the files that the nameless deacon had already organized. What made their search even more difficult, however, was that many of the boxes contained files mixed from different years—some, from different decades, as if they had been moved to the basement gradually and at random over a long period of time. It was tedious work, and about an hour into their search, Cathy's mind wandered to a bizarre flashback of a game show she used to watch with her mother when she was a child. *The New Treasure Hunt* it was called. She could not exactly remember its premise—just vague images of women looking through presents in search of money—but it starred a guy named Geoff Edwards—*that* she knew for sure. Cathy could recall her mother saying that he was handsome— had not thought of the show or its host in decades. Indeed, she was so taken by this unexpected trip down memory lane that she almost dismissed the document lying limply in her lap.

Cathy found herself sitting on the floor, staring down absently at a long list of names dated for the fiscal year of 1976–1977. On the last page, under the heading, "MISCELLANEOUS DONATIONS," the following entry had been circled:

> Marble reproduction of Michelangelo's Pietà.
> Artist, Antonio Gambardelli.
> Donated in memory of Filomena Manzera.
> Insurance value: $10,000.

But even more telling was the name and telephone number scrawled at the top of the page:

> *Shirley Manzera, 401-555-6641 (E.G.)*

E.G., Cathy thought. *East Greenwich.*

"I found it," she exclaimed, handing Markham the paper.

The FBI agent scanned it hungrily.

"We got lucky," he said finally. "The phone number—Father Bonetti and our mystery deacon have come through for us."

Chapter 41

The Manzeras' home occupied the corner lot on a street named Love Lane. Cathy recognized it as having been built in the 1950s—a sprawling, L-shaped ranch, with a two-car garage connected to the house via a narrow breezeway. At the rear of the house—behind a high, perforated stone wall—Cathy could also make out an Olympic-size pool, as well as a tennis court. Yes, from the looks of things, there was no doubt in Cathy's mind that the Manzeras, whoever they were, could afford a Gambardelli *Pietà*.

Sam Markham whipped the Trailblazer around the grassy median that separated the north and south sides of the street and pulled up under the shade of a large oak tree.

"Remember, Cathy," he said, "sit tight and keep the doors locked. This woman was extremely uncooperative on the telephone—very defensive. I don't want to risk her clamming up if she recognizes you. Only reason she agreed to talk to me is because she thinks the theft of her family's statue is part of some stolen art ring—thinks there might be a reward in it for her."

"I understand."

"I'll be back in a flash," Markham said, and kissed her on the cheek.

Cathy's eyes followed the FBI agent as he made his way up the flagstone walkway and rang the doorbell. She could not see the woman behind the screen door, could not see to whom Markham spoke as he raised his ID—just as he had done for her in another lifetime. And when Special Agent Sam Markham disappeared into the house, Cathy closed her eyes behind her dark sunglasses and waited.

Even if her mind had not begun to wander, even if she had not drifted off into a light afternoon sleep, Cathy most likely would not have noticed the '99 Porsche 911 cruise past on the cross street straight ahead of her—would not have given it a second look even if she had. Not in *this* neighborhood anyway.

The Sculptor, on the other hand, spotted the Trailblazer immediately; he recognized it as not only out of place in front of the Manzeras' house—the house which he drove by *every single day* on route to his own—but also instantly pegged it as FBI from his countless viewings of the news clips from Watch Hill and Exeter. And although he did not dare drive by it a second time, and although he did not dare take a closer look to see if perhaps Dr. Hildy herself was inside, The Sculptor knew nonetheless why the Trailblazer was there.

Yes, not only did The Sculptor finally understand how Dr. Hildy and the FBI had figured out where he was going to exhibit his *Pietà*, but he also understood that he had made a crucial mistake early on in his plan. However, the simple fact that the FBI had gone to the Manzeras *first* told The Sculptor that they had not yet made the connection *to him.*

Not yet.

But they were close.

And even though he was unsettled by his discovery, even though he thought himself foolish for his *silly, silly mistake,* as The Sculptor drove back to his home less than a mile away, he took comfort in the knowledge that fate had given him the opportunity to correct it.

Chapter 42

"Sorry I took so long," said Markham, hopping into the Trailblazer. "But we've got some work ahead of us."

Cathy awoke from her nap disoriented. It was as if time had suddenly leaped forward, and she could not be sure how long the FBI agent had been gone.

"What did you find?"

"Quite a lot. But who knows if any of it is going to help us. Best thing to do now is to get back to the computer—or better yet, get to the library before it closes."

"Why?"

"Well," Markham began, driving off, "first thing I found out is that Shirley Manzera's late husband is the connection to St. Bart's—the Gambardelli *Pietà* was donated in memory of his mother. Mr. Manzera's family was originally from the Silver Lake area of Providence, where St. Bart's is located. I don't know the details, but Shirley Manzera said her husband used to own some kind of construction business. Don't have to be a rocket scientist to figure out that he made quite a killing back in the 1950s, and moved his whole family out of Providence and into upscale East Greenwich. I didn't want to ask how Mrs. Manzera met her husband, but she was adamant about wanting nothing to do with the Catholic Church—particularly St. Bart's and her 'husband's old neighborhood,' as she put it. She's a bit of a snob, quite frankly."

"How did her husband die?"

"Not what you think. I saw some pictures of him on the mantle and asked. Emphysema, the old woman told me. Four years ago."

"I see."

"But hang on. The Manzeras had four children—three daughters and a son named Damon. Damon was the youngest, and judging from the family photos, probably about a ten- to twelve-year spread between him and his oldest sister. All the daughters are married."

"Wait. You said Damon *was* the youngest? Did something happen?"

"I couldn't ask, Cathy. Couldn't pry because of the reason I was there—the stolen art ring. But, did you see the swimming pool, the tennis court out back?"

"Yes."

"Again, I don't know the exact details—but Mrs. Manzera told me that her son Damon drowned in that swimming pool ten years ago."

"And you think his death is somehow connected to The Michelangelo Killer?"

"I don't know, Cathy. But we should look for something in the newspapers first—an article about the drowning, the young man's obituary. If anything seems out of whack, I can get Sullivan on the police and coroner's reports for Damon Manzera next. I may be totally barking up the wrong tree. It may all be just a bizarre coincidence—"

"You don't really think that, do you, Sam?"

The FBI agent gave only a weak shrug of his shoulders as the black Trailblazer emerged from the leafy canopy that was the Manzeras' neighborhood. The silence was long and awkward, but by the time Markham reached Route 95 they were talking again— trading theories as to what to do in the event of a dead end.

Neither one of them noticed the blue Toyota Camry that had entered onto the highway a short distance behind them.

Chapter 43

The Sculptor was careful not to get too close—made sure he left at least six or seven car lengths between him and the FBI vehicle. He had taken a gamble driving back to his house in order to exchange the Porsche for the Camry—did not want to be too conspicuous in case whoever was inside the black Trailblazer spotted him as they exited the neighborhood and made for the highway. It was a gamble that paid off. And now that The Sculptor was onto them, he did not want to ruin this golden opportunity to find out exactly what the FBI was up to—did not want to throw away the stellar hand that fate had finally dealt him.

The Sculptor had spent that Saturday morning in disguise—a moustache, glasses, and a baseball cap—driving around aimlessly in his Porsche, searching for a *sign*—of Dr. Hildy, maybe, or perhaps where he might later go shopping for some material for his *David*. And although he had found neither and was about to return home frustrated, just like the day when he unexpectedly spied his satyr walking home from the Cranston Pool, The Sculptor understood that fate had also directed him to drive by the Manzeras' house just in time.

Yes, perhaps more than anything The Sculptor understood the delicate workings of fate—understood how to recognize the signs of divine providence and negotiate that razor-thin line between predestination and free will. Such insight, such sensitivity was a gift that had been bestowed upon him as a boy—when he was still called Christian—when he first laid eyes upon the *Pietà* in St. Bartholomew's, the church of his mother.

It was there, back in her old neighborhood, that she used to take him on Sundays when his father was away on business. And it was there, in the small chapel off of the main church, that the boy named Christian would often stand for what seemed like hours staring at the marble statue of the Virgin and Her Son.

"A mother's love is the greatest gift a boy can have," Christian's mother would often tell him. "It's why I named you Christian."

"And your name is Mary," the little boy would reply. "Just like in the statue."

"That's right," said his mother. "And I love you more than anything in the whole wide world. Just like in the statue."

Oh yes. Even as a boy The Sculptor *understood*.

And for years on those Sundays at St. Bartholomew's it was only just the two of them—Mary and Christian, mother and son—listening to Father Bonetti read the Mass, and then lingering in the votive chapel to stare at the marble statues long afterward. Mother and son always agreed: the *Pietà* was their *favorite*.

But when the boy named Christian grew a little older—oh, six or seven The Sculptor supposed—his mother began to rest her hand in his groin when she drove him home from the bakery after church—the smell of fresh Italian bread filling the car as his Sunday khakis grew tight beneath the warmth of her hand. It was a strange sensation, the boy named Christian thought, but one that was pleasing to him nonetheless. What was even *better* was when she would sit next to him that way on the sofa. She would let him stay up late on Fridays to watch Victoria Principal—that woman on *Dallas* who was so pretty, and who the boy named Christian thought looked *just like his mother.* On one such Friday, when the boy named Christian asked his mother why she did not sit with him that way when his father was home, his mother explained that it was a secret: a *special secret* from God that was to be kept only between mother and son; a secret that if anyone else knew, not only would the boy's father kill himself, but God would kill her—would turn her into a statue *just like Mary* in the church.

And so the boy named Christian never understood why, all of a sudden one day when he was nine, mother and son stopped going to church. But it wasn't too long afterward that the beatings began, and later, worst of all, *the cold baths.* Even though he did not like the beatings, the boy named Christian always understood why his mother knocked him on the head; he always understood why she slapped him then locked him in the bathroom with the spilled bleach. That only happened when he was *bad*—like the time he drank some of her wine, or the time he tore out some pictures from her old college history books.

But always—when he was *super naughty* as his mother used to call it—when the boy named Christian went down face first into the tub of icy water, he had no idea what he had done to set his mother off. The cold baths came only once every month or so; they were always late at night when his mother had been drinking. "Out!" she would say, bursting into his bedroom—her breath foul with the smell of wine and cigarettes as she yanked him by the hair into the bathroom. The baths were always the same, but the boy named Christian never got used to them. He was sure that every time he went under that *this time* would be the last; he was sure that, as he began to choke, as she pushed him under once more he would never see his beloved father again.

But always, just as he felt that icy tingle down in his chest, his mother would pull him out of the tub. And later, as he lay shivering naked in his bed in the dark, she would crawl under the covers with him—one hand stroking between his legs while she pleasured herself with her other—the warmth of her bare breasts against his skin indescribably magical in its consolation to him.

"A mother's love," she would whisper over and over. "A mother's love."

This too was a secret just between them—a secret with dire consequences for their whole family if revealed.

When he was a little older the baths and the beatings stopped, but his mother would still crawl naked into bed with him at night. She would stroke his penis longer, until the boy named Christian "blew his load" as his friends at school called it. And when he was older still, just before his father sent him off to Phillips Exeter Academy in New Hampshire, Christian's mother began putting his penis between her legs, instructing him with her hands and her body how to make love to her.

"A mother's love," was all she would say. "A mother's love."

And so the boy named Christian wrestled with his mother's love for a long time—never told his father, never told *anyone*. What made it even more difficult for him was that he was *so very bright*. He understood what it meant when his counselor in elementary school said he tested at the "genius" level. He understood every single thing his teachers at Phillips threw at him, even the technology behind the patents his father had developed for his booming software company. Yes, *all that kind of stuff* came easily to the boy, to the young man named Christian. But the one thing he could never wrap his mind around was his mother's love.

That is until he read *Slumbering in the Stone*.

The Sculptor, however, would argue that it all began with his return to St. Bartholomew's. It was a week after his mother's funeral, on the very same day the eighteen-year-old Christian spoke with his father's lawyer—a kind old gentleman who would facilitate the sale of his father's software company and make The Sculptor a millionaire many times over. It was then that the lawyer explained to him the details of the accident and about his mother's affair at the country club with a tennis pro named Damon Manzera—a once promising young player whose career was cut short by injury, and who the lawyer said was only a few years older than Christian himself. Thus, it was after his meeting with the lawyer that the young man named Christian wandered without thinking back to St. Bartholomew's, searching like a zombie in the fog for something to guide him.

And so it was that—even though he was nowhere near to understanding *the bigger picture of it all* quite yet—the young man who would one day become The Sculptor had his first awakening before the *Pietà*, standing there gazing down at Michelangelo's masterpiece as he had done in his mother's arms so many times, so many years ago. However, it was not the statue itself, but the plaque at its base that—like a chisel to a block of marble—cracked Christian's mind with the understanding of why fate had brought him there that day.

Dedicated in memory of Filomena Manzera

Manzera. *Damon* Manzera.

Yes, how many times had the boy named Christian sat in that very same church with his mother, listening to Father Bonetti assure the congregation that our time in this world served some greater purpose of which together we all played a part, that all of mankind's lives were intertwined, that *"Everything was connected."* And after some poking around, the young man named Christian learned that the family who had bestowed upon St. Bartholomew's their gift of the *Pietà* was in fact the *same family* who had bestowed upon the world the tennis pro Damon Manzera—the tennis pro who had killed his mother and turned his father into a vegetable.

And just as the young man named Christian understood that fate had brought his mother and the tennis pro together at the country club in some divine connection to the *Pietà*—a divine connection that had to do with *him*, with a mother's *love for her son*—the young man named Christian also understood that fate had now brought him and the tennis pro together, too.

Oh yes. Christian understood all too well what he had to do next.

And so, after he finished up at Phillips Exeter, between visiting his father at the care facility and going full time to nursing school, the young man named Christian began building up his body—first at the gym, then in the cellar of his parents' home—all the while his mind focused clearly on the duality of his purpose: the caring for his father and his revenge on Damon Manzera. And after the former was safely back at home, for years Christian followed the latter, learning his movements and waiting patiently for a sign from fate that it was time.

Ironically, it all came together so quickly in the end. Damon Manzera, who was still teaching tennis at the country club—and who himself had become quite the drinker after a failed marriage—had moved back temporarily with his parents on Love Lane, where he spent many a warm summer evening in the backyard drinking beer and swimming in the Manzera's in-ground pool. If Damon Manzera ever thought about his former mistress, if he ever felt guilty about the part he played in her death, he gave no sign of it to Christian, who for four years had spied on him nearly every day with his binoculars.

And so, with the permission of fate, the young man named Christian snuck into the Manzeras' backyard through the woods, hopping the high stone wall just after dark and waiting among the trees until Damon Manzera was good and drunk. He did not yet have the night vision goggles or the tranquilizer rifle that he would later use on Tommy Campbell; he did not even have to wrestle the tennis pro under control as he had done when he dragged poor Michael Wenick down the drainpipe. No, for the young man who would soon become The Sculptor, his first murder was somewhat anticlimactic; and in the end he simply lifted the unconscious Manzera off his lounge chair and drowned him with no more effort than it would have taken him to wash the dishes.

Christian was able to hop from the diving board and into the woods without leaving even a single footprint on the cement. When in the weeks that followed it became apparent that he had actually gotten away with his murder of Damon Manzera, the young man named Christian began to feel empty. Yes, the man who was to become The Sculptor wanted to kill again; he wanted to kill more Damon Manzeras—so much so that he actually got an erection when he thought about it.

Indeed, for all his intellect, for all his self-awareness, the young man named Christian never quite understood why—when he was younger, when he was away at Phillips Exeter—he had never shown much interest in girls. He would not get hard when he looked at them in class and would certainly not "jerk off" like his classmates did to the pornographic pictures that were so often passed around. True, sometimes he found his hands absently wandering to his groin late at night when he thought about his mother, but the only time he *really* got hard was when he thought about his male classmates, when he would see them with their shirts off or coming out of the shower stalls, upon which Christian would quickly avert his eyes so as not to become aroused in front of them.

There was only one other boy at Phillips that Christian knew felt the same way—an "experienced" boy who took Christian under his wing, and with whom he would sometimes sneak away to places hidden; places where they could kiss and be naked against each other; places where they could take each other's penises in their mouths, or insert them in each other's behinds. With the death of Christian's mother, however, all that stopped; and long after Christian moved back to Rhode Island, the young man struggled with his desire for male company and the guilt that somehow his homosexuality had contributed to both his mother's death and his father's vegetative state.

Yet with the murder of Damon Manzera, Christian found himself getting hard when he thought about that, too; and thus he understood that fate had directed him to channel his desire into something much more productive. He began fantasizing, began researching and experimenting with different methods. The idea of epinephrine had appealed to him from the beginning because he knew it would mimic his heart-pounding revelation before the *Pietà* at St. Bartholomew's. And when he was ready, when he finally succeeded in producing a highly concentrated solution of the drug himself, the young man named Christian set about finding a proper candidate.

Gabriel Banford was always to have been the first victim of this new method. Christian had followed him for weeks after spotting him at Series X and planned on waiting for him in the dark of his bedroom. But on the evening that he *should* have killed him, when he stumbled upon Banford's copy of *Slumbering in the Stone*, when fate directed him right then and there to flip to the chapter on the *Pietà*, the man who would from that day forward call himself The Sculptor wept under the weight of his divine revelation—a revelation that surpassed the one at St. Bartholomew's. Yes, through this woman Catherine Hildebrant's analysis of Michelangelo's Holy Mother and Son—her brilliant articulation of what she called that "parallel trinity" as embodied in the artist's portrayal of the

Virgin herself—the boy, the young man named Christian not only *finally* understood his love of the *Pietà*, but also his mother's love for *him*.

So overcome was The Sculptor by his revelation that he left Banford's apartment in shock. He left the young man alive only to return a week later—*after* he had purchased his own copy of *Slumbering in the Stone* and read it cover to cover ten times, after he finally understood the totality of his purpose—that is, why fate had led him to Banford, to Dr. Catherine Hildebrant, and to Michelangelo, that man whose work was to become a template for The Sculptor's destiny.

Everything is connected.

And now, six years later, as he followed the black Trailblazer on Route 95 toward downtown Providence, The Sculptor grinned widely beneath his fake moustache. Yes, even though the FBI was getting close to him, even though they had made the connection between the stolen *Pietà* and the Manzera family, The Sculptor knew deep down that fate had once again interceded on his behalf. And although he dared not get too close, The Sculptor also had a feeling that behind the tinted windows of the black Trailblazer sat the person for whom he had been searching all morning.

Yes, something deep down told The Sculptor that he had finally found Dr. Hildy.

Chapter 44

It was just after 5:00 P.M. when Markham and Cathy emerged from the Providence Public Library—their heads hung low, their faces drawn. They had spent over an hour searching the periodical databases for information on the death of Damon Manzera. There wasn't much—the obligatory newspaper blurbs, the obituaries—but nothing that listed the death as suspicious, no evidence of foul play. Indeed, a spokesperson for the medical examiner was quoted many times as being very clear to the contrary, and stated that, at the time of Manzera's death, the young man's blood alcohol level was found to have been "dangerously high." And thus, the coroner had concluded that most likely Manzera either fell asleep in the pool or somehow staggered off its edge into the water. Either way, the official cause of death was listed as accidental drowning; either way, end of story.

"We've now got two options on this end, Cathy," said Markham, sliding into the Trailblazer. "Either I go back and tell Mrs. Manzera the real reason why I was there, see if I can find out anything else about her son, or we start poking around Manzera's circle of acquaintances to see if they know anything—maybe start with his ex-wife, or at the country club, the one in East Greenwich where the newspaper articles said he worked."

"But Sam, this all happened over ten years ago. Wouldn't the police have done that already?"

"I assume so, yes. When we get the police records, we'll be able to see who they questioned. I can only hope they missed something." Markham closed his eyes, rested his head back, and sighed. "I don't know what else to do, Cathy—starting to think this whole Manzera connection to the stolen *Pietà* was a bad idea. I'm starting to think I don't know what the hell I'm doing anymore."

"It's in the book, Sam," Cathy said, taking his hand. "You're right about that. I know it. Everything we need to catch him is right there in *Slumbering in the Stone*. You're just tired, is all. We both are. Why don't we get some takeout Chinese or something—grab a bottle of wine and call it a day. Tomorrow's Sunday. We can sleep in for a bit, maybe take a ride down to the coast—official business, of course. After a good night's rest we'll both be able to think more clearly. What do you say, Special Agent Markham? Is it a date?"

Markham smiled, kissed her deeply, and drove off.

Neither one of them noticed the blue Toyota Camry that had been parked diagonally across the street about a block away.

It pulled out again behind them.

The Camry followed the Trailblazer first to a Chinese restaurant in Cranston, then to a nearby liquor store, and finally back to downtown Providence, where the Trailblazer disappeared underneath an office building via a private driveway. And after about five minutes the blue Toyota Camry passed by—did not turn down the driveway like the Trailblazer. No, the driver of the blue Camry could not miss the two big PRIVATE ACCESS ONLY signs; he could clearly see the video cameras and the steel, card-access security gate—thought there might even be a guard or two prowling around as well.

"So that's where they're keeping her," The Sculptor said out loud.

Despite her new hair color, despite her Jackie Onassis sunglasses, The Sculptor had recognized Dr. Hildy outside the library as soon as she stepped out from the Trailblazer. And while he had waited for her and the unknown FBI agent to finish their research inside—research he knew had to do with the tennis pro, Damon Manzera—The Sculptor concluded he needed to put his *David* on hold.

It was all right. He had done that before with his *Pietà,* when he finally understood the scope, the *message* of his work as something beyond himself, when he finally understood that, in order to really wake the world from its slumber, no material other than Tommy Campbell would be worthy of his *Bacchus.*

Yes, The Sculptor did not mind adapting; he did not resist changing his plans if he felt the hand of fate leading him someplace else.

But exactly where did fate want him to go next?

The Sculptor needed time to think and figure out how he would dispose of Dr. Hildy—perhaps this FBI agent, too. But unlike before, when he could take his time, when his work was still unknown to the world, The Sculptor knew now that the clock was ticking. Yes, he had to move quickly—had to get to Hildebrant and the FBI agent before they got to him. *But how?* It was much too risky under the present circumstances to try to take them at that fortress in downtown Providence—especially since The Sculptor had no idea what it looked like inside.

And so, as The Sculptor drove away from Providence, he resigned himself to wait for the right opportunity to take them on the *outside*.

The Sculptor smiled, for he knew deep down that fate would bring him and Dr. Hildy together very soon.

After all, fate had never let him down before.

Chapter 45

"I thought we agreed we were going to take a break today," said Cathy.

She stood in the doorway to their bedroom—naked, save for the button-down shirt of Markham's which she wore drawn tightly around her. They had spent that Sunday together driving along the coast—had ended up in Newport and strolled along the cliff-walk before taking in a late lunch at a restaurant overlooking the harbor. Upon their return to the safe house, the fax from Rachel Sullivan had already arrived: the coroner's report, as well as a list of names taken from the East Greenwich Police investigation on the death of Damon Manzera—both requested by Sam Markham the evening before. Cathy had made the FBI agent promise to let them wait—convinced him that nothing could be done with the information until the following morning. And after another evening of wine and lovemaking, the once shy art history professor could not help but feel a certain amount of pride that her feminine wiles had won out yet again.

"It's 12:15," said Markham. "*Ante meridiem.* Technically it's now tomorrow—haven't broken my promise to you, have I?"

"I guess not. But you woke me up."

"Sorry."

Dressed in only his underwear, the FBI agent lay on the sofa in the common area—which also consisted of two recliners and a television, two desks complete with computers and printers, a copier and a fax machine, as well as an entire wall dedicated to the twelve video monitors that continually displayed surveillance from the building's exterior, its second and third floor corridors, as well as its parking garage.

Sullivan's fax lay scattered about on the floor—cast aside by Markham in deference to his copy of *Slumbering in the Stone.* Cathy sat down beside him.

"What's got your attention now?" she asked.

"Wasn't able to learn much from the fax, so I started reading again about *David.*"

"And?"

"I guess the thing that keeps jumping out at me is how tall the statue is—seventeen feet, you say?"

"Yes. You can't really grasp its size, its magnificence until you see it in person."

"But the way it was sculpted—the head and the upper torso, the hands slightly out of proportion to the lower half of the body—you say in your book you think this was intentional on Michelangelo's part?"

"Yes. There are a number of theories about this. As I'm sure you've read, the enormous block of Carrara marble from which *David* was originally sculpted had already been worked by a couple of other artists—one of them being a student of Donatello—and then ended up being neglected in a courtyard for almost thirty years before the twenty-six-year-old Michelangelo was commissioned to finish the project in 1501. Some scholars believe that Michelangelo had to work from a figure that had been blocked out earlier. However, I believe that the marble wasn't nearly that far along when Michelangelo got to it. And as the guild that originally commissioned the statue had intended for it to sit atop the buttress of a cathedral—a plan that was later abandoned—when viewed from below, the proportions of *David* would be correct."

"It took him a little over three years," said Markham, reading. "And the statue ended up being installed outside the entrance to the Palazzo Vecchio."

"Yes. A representation of the biblical David whose defeat of Goliath and the Philistines came to symbolize the triumph of the Florentine Republic over its rival city-states, Michelangelo's *David* was initially placed outside the Palazzo Vecchio—a fortresslike palace that served as the old seat of civic government in Florence. It's hard to believe, isn't it? Hard to believe nowadays that the Florentines would have allowed what has become the most famous statue in the world to be subjected to wind and weather and pigeon poop before moving it indoors to the Galleria dell'Accademia almost four hundred years later."

Markham was silent—his eyes fixed on a photographic detail of *David*'s waist.

"You're thinking about where he's going to display it, aren't you?" said Cathy. "You're thinking about what to do in case we don't catch The Michelangelo Killer before he creates his *David*."

"Actually, I'm thinking about where he's going to get his material."

"What do you mean?"

"We know from our investigation thus far that no young males with a physique resembling the statue of *David* have been reported missing—a physique one can assume the killer will have a hard time finding among the population of male prostitutes from which we now know he's drawn."

"Yes."

"Well, as I mentioned earlier, there's the unusual proportions—the relationship of the torso to the statue's lower half. The Sculptor would not be able to accommodate for that the same way he did with his *Pietà*—that is, by using more than one body, piecing it together, and then hiding the joints underneath the figure's clothing. No, like *Bacchus,* the statue is nude, and thus theoretically the killer would have to use only one person—would have to be very selective in choosing his material. And so, ironically, what on the surface would seem like the simplest of the three statues in actuality will be the most difficult for him to achieve."

"Unless he is planning on correcting Michelangelo's intended forced perspective. Meaning, the killer intends to adapt the proportional ratios to be viewed straight on."

"Yes. But the physique, the musculature of *David* is so well known. That in and of itself will take a lot of searching. Much more difficult to come across another famous Rhode Islander on the Internet—the way he most surely saw the figure of his *Bacchus* in the photographs of Tommy Campbell. You saw them, didn't you? The pictures of Campbell taken on that beach in Rio a couple of years ago with his model ex-girlfriend?"

"Yes," said Cathy. "So you're thinking The Sculptor may go looking for his *David* at a local beach? A swimming pool, perhaps—someplace where he would be able to get a good look at his material?"

"Perhaps for the body, yes—but for the other part, most likely no."

"What other part?"

"As I said, one would think that, *theoretically*, The Sculptor would have to acquire a single body that resembled the statue of *David*. However, what about the statue's penis?"

"What about it?"

"It's uncircumcised."

Cathy was silent. She understood.

"As you state in your book," said Markham, "whereas the historical David, being a Jew, would have most certainly been circumcised, Michelangelo was consciously sculpting his *David* in line with the classical Greek aesthetic, which would have seen a circumcised penis as mutilated. Such a detail will thus be of supreme importance to The Sculptor—something he will *have* to account for. So you see, it's clear that it is going to be exponentially more difficult for The Sculptor to acquire a body that both looks like *David* and *also* has an uncircumcised penis. Hence, I'm willing to bet that the killer will be searching for the latter separately, and thus plans on attaching it to his *David* afterward—perhaps beneath an epoxy-sculpted line of pubic hair."

"So you're suggesting then that we try to beat him to his material? That we focus on finding out not only where he's going to find a body like *David*'s, but also a penis like his as well?"

"Yes. Either that, or we try to bring him to *us*."

"What do you mean?"

"From what we know about this guy—his intelligence, the solitary sort that he is, and the fact that he now knows the public is on to him—where would be the safest place for him to go shopping for his *David*?"

"The Internet."

"Yes—a place where he can browse and study his material like he most certainly did with the images of Tommy Campbell."

"So you're saying we might be able to lay a trap for him?"

"That's exactly what I'm saying, Cathy. It's a long shot but—in addition to all the other leads we've been following, including the new Manzera connection—we can post an ad on Craigslist and some of the other Web sites known to be used by gay men. Put a picture up of a guy with a physique like *David*'s, and advertise our John Doe as a local uncircumcised male seeking companionship. I've looked into these sites myself when we were pursuing the male prostitute angle. Some of these men—many of whom are undoubtedly prostitutes themselves—are not shy about advertising the details of their privates, including whether or not they are circumcised. If we make our John Doe such an irresistible target—that is, create a profile for someone who looks like *David* and has the uncircumcised penis to boot—The Sculptor might not be able to resist killing two birds with one stone."

"But how do you know The Sculptor hasn't already acquired his penis?"

"Because, in order to get the proportions right he'll have to find his *David* first. I made that mistake with the *Bacchus*, Cathy—when I thought The Sculptor would have experimented with the goat before acquiring the top half of his satyr. I'm not going to make that mistake again. Of course, it's obvious The

Michelangelo Killer won't be able to find a seventeen-foot-tall man. However, if he finds someone with the right proportions, regardless of his height, he'll have a better idea of what size penis to look for in order to retain the aesthetic proportions of the original. If we can save the killer all that trouble with an ad on the Internet, we might just be able to catch him."

"But do you think The Sculptor would fall for something like that?"

"I don't know, Cathy. But right now, it's the only thing I can believe in."

Chapter 46

The Sculptor followed the black Trailblazer as he had done for the past two days—at a distance, always just out of sight behind a buffer of six or seven cars. Unbeknown to Sam and Cathy, the blue Toyota Camry had been with them almost the entire time since they left the Manzeras in East Greenwich—had followed them the next morning all along the coast, had waited for them to come back from their stroll together in Newport, had accompanied them everywhere they went on their romantic Sunday sojourn. Yes, The Sculptor could tell Dr. Hildy and the FBI agent were an item by the way they touched each other—the way they held hands at the restaurant, the way the good doctor snuggled up to her male companion by the cement wall overlooking the ocean. This was good; this meant it would be easier for The Sculptor to catch them off guard. Indeed, had it been nighttime, had there not been so many people around that day in Newport, The Sculptor would have disposed of the happy couple right there on the cliff-walk.

But to do so in broad daylight would have been too risky.

Yes, The Sculptor would have to wait for fate to give him a *better* opportunity.

And so, early Monday morning, when The Sculptor saw the black Trailblazer emerge from the private underground parking garage in downtown Providence and then head for the FBI Resident Agency a few blocks away, The Sculptor knew that today was a day for business, not pleasure. The good doctor and her male companion were inside the FBI building for almost two hours. And when they emerged again, The Sculptor's hand automatically went to his Sig Sauer .45, which lay next to him under his jacket on the passenger seat.

He had resigned himself to taking them today, but the timing must be *just right*—he had to tread ever so carefully along the fine line between fate and free will.

The Sculptor followed the Trailblazer all over Rhode Island, but only when he saw it pull into the East Greenwich Country Club did he understand just how close they were to finding him.

They're following the old police report, The Sculptor concluded.

Oh yes, the FBI would most certainly want to question him about Manzera—just like the East Greenwich Police did ten years ago, when the tennis pro's parents insisted their son could not have drowned by his own accord. However, luckily for the young man named Christian, the philandering Manzera had made a lot of enemies in his time at the country club. He had banged more than his share of married women, and thus the young man named Christian was only one of a slew of people, including Manzera's ex-wife, who had openly admitted they were happy to see the tennis pro dead. And so, despite Mr. and Mrs. Manzera's insistence to the contrary, with nothing more for the police to go on their son's death was quickly ruled an accident.

But now things were different; now the *FBI* was on the case. They had video of The Sculptor himself and would make the connection between the figure in black at Echo Point Cemetery and his own physique as soon as they laid eyes on him. And unlike ten years ago—when the young man named Christian had yet to become The Sculptor, when the young man named Christian had yet to even *begin* remodeling the carriage house—now there was evidence *everywhere:* the van, the equipment, the lab—not to mention all the excess material scattered about.

No. There was no way of getting around it all now. Once the FBI set foot on his property, it would not take them long to put two and two together.

The Sculptor began to panic—felt his heart beating fast in his chest; he felt the urge to race home, gather up his things, and make a run for it before the FBI arrived. But a short time later, when he saw the black Trailblazer pull out of the country club and head off in the direction of his house, an inner voice calmly whispered to him of the opportunity that had just presented itself. That the black Trailblazer was driving slowly meant that the man formerly known as Christian was just one of many people the FBI had planned on questioning that day—just a name on a list.

That was good.

That meant there was still time.

And so The Sculptor sped off in the opposite direction—took the shortcut on a dirt road through the woods that he knew would bring him to his house well before the black Trailblazer arrived. Unless The Sculptor was mistaken, fate would deliver Dr. Hildy and her FBI boyfriend straight to his doorstep.

Oh yes. The Sculptor wanted to *make sure* he was there to welcome them.

Chapter 47

After Markham's conversation that morning with Bill Burrell—and after the SAC's lukewarm reception and then reluctant acceptance of his Internet idea—while Rachel Sullivan and her team began putting together a profile for Craigslist and a handful of other Web sites popular in the gay community, a crestfallen and unenthusiastic Sam Markham began knocking off the names listed on the East Greenwich Police report—names of people who had been questioned in connection to Damon Manzera's death ten years earlier, names that Markham was beginning to think were a waste of time.

Not revealing the true nature of their visit, Markham and Cathy first spoke with Manzera's ex-wife, and then with the ex-husband of the woman with whom Manzera had been cheating prior to his divorce. Neither one of them recognized Cathy Hildebrant; neither one of them had anything to offer other than "what they already told the police ten years ago." However, both suggested that Markham and his partner try their luck with the general manager at the East Greenwich Country Club.

"There's still hope, Sam," Cathy had said en route. "The Manzeras suspected all along that their son had been murdered. Just because the police were unable to find anything doesn't mean that we won't."

"Look at the addresses on that list, Cathy—probably a 'who's who' of Rhode Island high society. You saw how cold, how suspicious, and tight-lipped Manzera's ex and that other guy were—just like Manzera's own mother. Yes, like our friends down at Watch Hill, the one thing these people fear even more than The Michelangelo Killer is a good scandal."

Although the general manager of the East Greenwich Country Club explained to Sam Markham that he had in fact heard of Damon Manzera, he also explained to them that—having been in his position for only a year—he felt uncomfortable speaking about rumors regarding his club's members.

"The Manzeras are one of East Greenwich's most respected families," he said. "In addition to his aging mother, Damon Manzera leaves behind three sisters—all of whom have been members of our club since they were little girls. Thus, you will understand, Agent Markham, if out of respect for the family I decline to comment on what is to me nothing more than gossip and hearsay."

"Yes, I understand," said Markham, sliding the list of names across the general manager's desk. "And I hope you understand, sir, that I could make things very difficult for you and your little club if I thought even for a second that you were hindering this investigation. Meaning, I wouldn't think twice about getting a subpoena for your records and having it delivered to your office under full police escort—complete with lights and sirens, of course, and perhaps some television cameras, too."

The general manager was silent.

"Now why don't you take a look at that list of names and see if you've changed your mind about helping me."

"Other than the two names you've already crossed off," said the GM after a quick scan, "the only other name that I can connect for sure to the period of time in which Manzera was employed here is the Bach family. From what I gather, they were members up until about fifteen years ago—some kind of personal tragedy if my memory serves me, although I'm not sure I ever knew the details. But at least they'd have been members when Manzera was employed. You might want to try them. Other than that, I do recollect hearing rumors about Manzera's flings with married women, but as for names, I can't tell you if anybody on this list is a match. And that's the truth, Agent Markham. You have my word on that, for as I've already explained to you, I've only been in my current position for about a year now. However, if you'd like, I can try to telephone my predecessor for you. I'm sure he'd be happy to cooperate, to report on his own firsthand knowledge of the goings on at the club around the time of Manzera's death."

"That'd be fine. Thank you."

While Markham and Cathy waited, the general manager tried repeatedly to contact his predecessor. However, when the latter proved unreachable by phone, the general manager gave Markham the man's Florida address and telephone number and asked to be excused. And for the time being, the FBI agent let him off the hook, added the information to his list, and left the general manager's office in a huff.

"Who's next?" Cathy asked once they were back inside the Trailblazer.

"Just so happens it's the Bach family," said Sam Markham, scanning his list. "The one the general manager mentioned. Specifically, Edward and Christian Bach."

"Any notes on them?"

"Nothing really. Like the others, names have an X next to them—just lists them with the same 'persons of interest' blurb that the cops wrote down for Manzera's ex and that other guy. Looks like they dismissed them as suspects early on in their investigation. Does say, however, that Edward is the father, and Christian the son. Mother listed as deceased. GPS shows their last known address isn't too far from here. Best hit them next and then grab some lunch. What do you say?"

"Sounds good. It's almost two o'clock. I'm starving."

Within ten minutes the Trailblazer's GPS system led them down a winding wooded road, through a pillared fieldstone wall, and up a long driveway to a large, three-story house. On the other side of the driveway, behind a waterless fountain, Cathy could make out a black Porsche 911 and a blue Toyota Camry.

"You must hate these slum assignments," she said, and Markham smiled. Had he noticed the overgrown second driveway, had he been able to see through the trees and the thick underbrush to the carriage house at the rear of the property, Supervisory Special Agent Sam Markham might not have been smiling.

Markham and Cathy exited the Trailblazer and

climbed a set of four wide flagstone steps. They followed the path along the side of the house and then climbed up another four steps to the side door—a door that stood curiously propped open as if the owner of the house had been expecting them. Markham looked inside. He could see into what looked like a mud room, and into the kitchen beyond.

"Hello?" he called, knocking on the open storm door.

Turning, Markham was about to speak when, out of the corner of his eye, he saw movement—then the flash of a bright red dot reflected off the glass.

"Get down!" he shouted, pushing Cathy away from the red dot and inside the house. But the silenced bullet found him anyway—grazed the back of his head and took off a chunk of his right ear as he tackled Cathy onto the mud room floor, the warmth of his blood spattering her face.

The sound of a loud pop on the door frame—then another bullet tore into Markham's thigh. The FBI agent shrieked in pain.

"Move, Cathy, move!" he shouted, rolling off of her and fumbling for his gun. Cathy, her ears buzzing, her muscles tense with fear, scrambled to her feet just in time to see a shadowy figure in the doorway—the sunlight streaming in behind him; tall, bald, and naked as a marble Hercules.

Yes. They had found The Sculptor.

A flash of red light passed across Cathy's eyes. She froze—did not see Markham rise to his feet and grab The Sculptor's arm—only heard the bullet whizzing past her ear. Her vision spotted from The Sculptor's laser sight, Cathy backed away into the kitchen, watching in red blotchy horror as Markham tried to wrestle The Sculptor's gun away from him. Their grunting figures crashed against the walls of the mud room as The Sculptor fired off two silenced bullets into the floor.

Then, with a roar, The Sculptor seemed to explode—his arms flailing outward in a burst of power. Sam Markham went sailing across the room—his back slamming into the darkened door frame behind him.

Only then did Cathy notice the open cellar door.

"Sam!" she cried—but it was too late. As Markham recovered, as he finally drew his gun from his shoulder holster, the red dot again flashed across Cathy's eyes.

Thhhwhip! Thhhwhip!

And then Sam Markham disappeared into a black abyss—the muffled sound of his body thumping down the cellar stairs sucking Cathy's breath from her lungs.

Firing again down into the darkness, The Sculptor moved to the cellar door in a blur. Then he flicked on the light at the top of the stairs. Cathy had not seen where The Sculptor's bullets had hit Markham, but in the light cast from the cellar stairwell, she could see on The Sculptor's face that he was satisfied with his shots. Cathy tried to scream, but her fear held her breath tight in her throat.

The Sculptor whirled his eyes on her—eyes that, in the shadow cast from the cellar, looked to Cathy to be carved from ice.

"It's nice to finally meet you, Dr. Hildy," said The Sculptor, raising his gun. "I wish the circumstances could have been different."

Suddenly Cathy's breath returned, and she became aware that her legs were moving, dragging her forward against the fear that so desperately wanted her to stay put. Another *thhhwhip* of a bullet by her left ear, and then the kitchen, the adjoining dining room flying past her in a rush. Cathy found herself at the front door, her fingers like numb hotdogs against the dead bolt—slippery and useless as the sound of footsteps thundered behind her. Cathy turned to find The Sculptor approaching from the dining room. She made a dash to her left—could see the sunlight down the hall at the back of the house; she was aware somehow that if she followed alongside the grand staircase it would lead her back to the mud room door. But the naked, hairless man who looked like a bald Arnold Schwarzenegger intercepted her. Cathy fell backward onto the stairs, The Sculptor standing over her and leveling the red dot of his gun between her eyes.

"I wasn't expecting this, Dr. Hildy. I hope you won't think me rude."

There was no click like in the movies; only the look of curious disappointment on The Sculptor's face when he noticed his Sig Sauer—its clip spent—had locked itself in the empty position.

Cathy did not wait; in a flash she kicked the heel of her sneaker hard into The Sculptor's naked testicles. The Sculptor howled in pain—his gun dropping on the steps, his hands instinctively going to his groin as his massive frame fell forward, blocking an escape route past him. Like a crab, Cathy pinwheeled her arms and legs backward, found her footing, and scrambled up the stairs—her disorientation, her terror carrying her right past the servants' staircase which, unbeknown to her, would have brought her back down into the kitchen.

No, with The Sculptor fast on her heels, in a haze

of red wallpaper and richly stained wood, Cathy raced down the upstairs hallway in the *opposite* direction.

Streaking past one of the bedrooms, out of the corner of her eye she saw the silhouette of a man sitting by a large window. Instinctively, she ran to him.

"Help me!" Cathy cried, dashing into the bedroom and slamming the door behind her. "Call the police!" But when Cathy caught sight of the man's face, when she looked into the hollow eyes of the helpless, drooling invalid that was The Sculptor's father, her heart sank into her stomach.

"Albert?" the man croaked, his eyes staring past her.

But Cathy did not have time to lament, for a split second later The Sculptor burst into the room behind her.

"Get away from him!" he bellowed, coming for her in a blur of naked flesh. Cathy backed away against the wall—her hands grasping a stainless steel IV stand just as The Sculptor was upon her. She flung it at him, the plastic bag and its metal arm hitting The Sculptor square in the face. The Sculptor's hands went to his eyes, buying Cathy enough time to get away from him across the four-poster bed.

Cathy made a frantic dash for the stairs—had just reached the banister when she felt the meaty slap of The Sculptor's hand on her back. Then suddenly she was flying backward—her feet grazing the top of the railing as she left the floor and sailed through the air. She landed on the hardwood floor with a thud. The pain in her knee, in her buttocks, and in her elbow was excruciating, but Cathy bounced to her feet and ran for the darkened doorway in front of her at the far end of the hall. She made it inside just in time, slamming the door behind her and closing her fingers around the lock just as The Sculptor's shoulder smacked into the door from the other side.

Another smack and Cathy backed away from the door. The room was pitch black, and Cathy tripped—fell to the floor as something crashed beside her. It sounded like metal, but when Cathy reached for it, her hands closed around something round and rubbery—heavy, but also spongy like a Nerf football.

Then the door exploded open—The Sculptor's massive leg still cocked as the light streamed in from the hallway behind him. He flicked the switch by the door, and Cathy gazed down in horror at the object in her hands.

It was Steve Rogers's head—shaved and painted white as marble.

Cathy screamed and threw her ex-husband's severed head at The Sculptor as she backed away on the floor. Then all at once she froze, her eyes finally taking in the totality of the room into which she had entered—a room with heavily draped windows and black painted walls. Dozens upon dozens of body parts were posed and displayed on pedestals and iron frames—hands; arms and legs; severed torsos, some with a head and an appendage still attached; while other heads stood like solitary busts on pedestals of their own. All the body parts were painted white, and had Cathy not felt her ex-husband's Plastinated head herself—had she not known who owned the house through which she was being chased—the world's foremost scholar on the works of Michelangelo would have thought the pieces around her to be made of marble.

Yes, Cathy Hildebrant had found The Michelangelo Killer's sculpture gallery.

Cathy rose to her feet and stumbled backward.

The terror was overwhelming her—the scene eerily quiet as The Sculptor approached, a single line of blood running down his cheek like a scarlet tear. The Sculptor paused briefly to pick up the iron stand on which Steve Rogers's head had been mounted, and as her back slammed against the wall, Cathy watched in terror as he raised the iron stand high above his head.

She closed her eyes.

But instead of the blow she was sure would follow, instead of the pain, Cathy heard the stand drop to the floor—followed by the sound of giggling.

Cathy opened her eyes.

The Sculptor stood before her smiling, his eyes penetrating her own, yet at the same time flickering with the spark of an idea—his fingers resting deviously on his lips like a child who had just played a prank.

"Of course," he said. "How very silly of me."

Cathy could only stare back at him in numb confusion.

"The bullets, the empty gun—fate kept you alive, Dr. Hildy. Don't you see? You were meant to understand, you were meant to be awakened, for only the sculptor's hand can free the figures slumbering in the stone."

And with that The Sculptor was upon her.

Chapter 48

Cathy awakened to the sound of humming, of fingers tapping away on a keyboard. Her vision was blurry, but she could make out something square hovering above her—the light coming from her right accentuating its edges. And her neck hurt—her back and buttocks were *cold* against something steel-hard.

Then Cathy remembered.

The wrestling move; the way The Sculptor had tackled her when she tried to run past him; the way he wrapped his arms around her neck and squeezed her from behind—*Good night Irene,* Steve used to call it when they played around on the bed. *The Sleeper Hold.* But there was never that choking feeling with Steve, never a room clad in black with white arms and legs and heads and torsos jumbling up and turning red, then breaking into snow like a UHF channel on an old TV.

Then Cathy understood.

She was naked, on her back—her head locked staring forward at what was clearly a video monitor;

her arms and legs were immobile, strapped down against what she knew to be a stainless steel mortician's table. And then all at once Cathy understood where she was. She was lying on the *very same table* that she had seen on The Michelangelo Killer's DVD; the *very same table* on which she had watched her husband screaming in agony before what was to become The Sculptor's *Pietà*.

The *Pietà*.

As Cathy thought about the fate of her husband—as she thought about what she knew lay in store for her, too—her mind simultaneously raced along with all the theories, all the knowledge about The Michelangelo Killer that she and Sam Markham had culled together in the weeks since she first accompanied him to Watch Hill.

Sam, a voice cried in her head. *Where's Sam?*

Ssh! replied another voice. *Stay calm. There'll be time to sort it out later.*

The Pietà, Cathy repeated to herself over and over amidst her rising panic. *Sam knew that the answer lay in the* Pietà—*in The Michelangelo Killer's interpretation of it through* Slumbering in the Stone.

Yes, Cathy needed time to think—needed to stay calm, needed to focus on the moment at hand. Although she could not turn her head, Cathy knew that The Sculptor was close. She could hear his humming, the *tippity-tippity-tap* of his typing only a few feet away to her right.

The Pietà. *Sam was right. The* Pietà *was his first—everything revolved around the* Pietà. *Everything BEGAN with the* Pietà.

Tippity-tippity-tap.

Sam was sure he was onto something—just knew he was so close to unlocking the key to The Sculptor's mind. The se-

cret lay in the reason why Michelangelo chose to portray his Virgin as a young mother. Dante's Divine Comedy— *Canto 33 of* Paradiso. *"Virgin mother, daughter of your son." The inherent contradiction of the Holy Trinity; its "incestuous" context; the impure, almost incomprehensible parallel trinity—the father-daughter/mother-son/husband-wife relationship. That warped relationship between a mother and son.*

Tippity-tippity-tap.

Mother and son, mother and son, mother and son . . .

Tippity-tippity-tap.

The son's name is Christian. Christian. Christ. Oh my God. Christ.

Tippity-tippity-tap.

Could it be? Could it be that he sees himself as the Christ—that is, that he sees the relationship to his mother through the Pietà? *The parallel trinity? Some kind of warped relationship between mother and son? Incestuous? Spiritual, otherworldly incest as defined in* Slumbering in the Stone? *Could it be?*

Tippity-tippity-tap.

Sam said the mother was deceased? Was her name Mary? Is it possible? Could it all be true?

Christian! Oh, dear God, Christian!

Cathy suddenly became aware of movement to her right—saw a shadow cross the frame of the video screen above her.

Then came the smiling face of The Sculptor leaning over her.

"You're awake, Dr. Hildy," he said—then began to giggle. "Well, not *totally* awake, as I'm sure you'd agree."

The Sculptor left her again, and Cathy could hear the squeaking of something metal—something rolling on the floor. Her heart was pounding—her mind booming with a voice that said her conclusions *had to be true*—a voice that at the same time told her *what she must do to survive!*

"However," said The Sculptor upon his return to the table, "I need to make some proportional adjustments—need to give you some sleepy juice while I work on your boobies. Then you will awake, Dr. Hildy. Then you will come forth from the stone as fate intended."

Cathy felt something cold and wet on her forearm—knew The Sculptor was prepping her for an injection of some sort.

"But tell me who you are first," he said, pausing, staring deeply into her eyes. "Surely you must know deep down, surely you must *already* understand. Tell me who you are to become? *Night* or *Dawn. Dawn* or *Night?* Personally, with your bone structure, I see you unquestionably as the *Dawn.* However, given your mother's history with her boobies, perhaps *Night* is more appealing to you. Either way, I promise I'll leave it up to you. It's the least I can do. Yes, after all you've done for me. I *owe* you that."

Then, without warning, Cathy spoke.

"My dear Christian," she said—her voice not her own, the subtle flicker of recognition in The Sculptor's eyes giving her the strength to continue. "Oh my son, oh my dear boy—let me hold you one last time."

The Sculptor cocked his head—curiously.

"Mary, Mary, mother of God," Cathy said automatically, an inner force *ordering* her what to say. "Mother and daughter and wife of the Son. Let me hold you one more time, my Christian. Just like in our *Pietà.*"

The Sculptor leaned into her.

"I'm here, my Christian. Your Mary—your mother,

your daughter, your wife. I knew you would understand. I knew you would find me again—my love, my only son."

"Mother?" whispered The Sculptor—his eyes glazing over.

"Yes, my Christian," Cathy said—at once lucid and borderline insane before the foul heat of The Sculptor's breath. "It's your Mary—your wife, your mother. Loosen the straps, my son. Let me make love to you again. Let me make love to you again in that special way, the way no one else understands—our secret. Yes, just like when you were a boy, my Christian. Let me take you in my arms and hold you the way I used to—just like in the *Pietà*."

"Mother?" The Sculptor repeated. "Mother is that you?"

"Yes, my Christian. Let me love you again. Just like in the *Pietà*."

"Just like in the statue, Mother?"

"Yes, my dear Christian. Mary and Christ. A mother loving her son. Just like in the statue."

The Sculptor did not move his face—kept it close enough to kiss her—but Cathy felt his fingers on the straps at her wrists.

"That's it, my son. Let me come forth from the stone. Let me touch you again from beyond the grave."

First her right, then her left—*yes, her hands were free!* The Sculptor lay on top of her—his face nuzzling in her neck, the hardness of his erection pressing against her leg.

"I'm here, Mother."

"That's my little Christian," Cathy groaned—a wave of nausea making her tremble. She swallowed hard and ran her nails down The Sculptor's muscu-

lar back. "The strap on my head, my Christian—
across my chest and on my feet—release me from my
slumber, my son. Let your mother go. Let me make
love to you again after all these years—let me sit up
and hold you just like in the statue."

Outside herself, Cathy watched the scene unfold
before her as if she were sitting in a movie theatre.
She gazed upon The Sculptor with detached terror
as he, zombielike, his eyes locked with hers, unbuck-
led the straps on her head and feet. And when he sat
beside her on the table, when he released the strap
about her chest, Cathy watched herself in numb
amazement as she sat up on the mortician's table
and took The Sculptor in her arms.

"Let me hold you, my son. Let me make love to
you just like in the statue."

The Sculptor lay across her lap—closed his eyes
and suckled at Cathy's breast as the man once called
Christian moved her hand to his groin.

"This makes Mommy sorry?" mumbled The Sculptor. "This makes Mommy love me again?"

"Yes, my Christian," Cathy sputtered—the dam
that was her will, her sanity, about to break. "Mommy
is so very sorry, but don't ever forget that Mommy
loves you."

Her fear, her revulsion rushing back all at once, as
Cathy's left hand closed around The Sculptor's shaft,
the fingers of her right found the IV needle. Without
thinking, without *pausing*, Cathy Hildebrant brought
down the stubby steel barb hard into The Sculptor's
eye—heard a squirty *pop* and felt his penis go limp as
he shrieked in pain, as his hands flew to his face and
he flopped off her lap like a fish.

Cathy dropped from the table, The Sculptor writhing
on the floor only inches away from her—his screams

swallowed up by the spongy black walls surrounding him. Despite her panic, Cathy could not help but notice the computer screen. She did not pause, however, when she saw the figure of Michelangelo's *Dawn* floating in the black like a corpse on the sea. No, instead Cathy immediately went for The Sculptor's video camera—picked up the tripod and brought it down like a club on the back of his head as he rose to his knees. The Sculptor—a hand at his eye, the blood spurting between his fingers—braced his fall with his free arm; he just knelt there stunned for a moment staring at the floor. But as Cathy brought the tripod up again, The Sculptor unexpectedly kicked out his leg like a mule, knocking the video camera from Cathy's hands and sending her flying into the mortician's table. It swung on its chains—gave way to her weight as Cathy fell backward. There was a loud crack—the feeling of the floor giving way beneath her—and suddenly Cathy was falling.

In the split second that it took her to hit the cement below, Cathy understood what had happened—remembered all too well what the mortician's table had looked like from the DVD and knew that she had fallen into a trap underneath. But unlike her intellect, her feet were not so accommodating; and Cathy slammed into the first floor of The Sculptor's studio—her left ankle buckling and twisting in a bright burst of pain. Cathy howled and stumbled against the van—the force of her impact bouncing her backward into a pile of plastic sheeting. Yes, there was light down here cast from a small black-and-white monitor atop the drafting table.

And then there was the *smell*. The strong smell of—

Nail polish remover?

Cathy did not have time to think. She could hear The Sculptor scuttling above her. She screamed and staggered to the garage door—tried to lift it by its handle but it would not budge.

"Help me!" Cathy cried. "Somebody help me!" Like a caged rat, Cathy zigzagged to the rear of The Sculptor's studio—found no exit there either and collapsed at the edge of the stainless steel hospital tub. The smell of the nail polish remover was stronger here; it was coming from inside the tub—a tub that looked to Cathy like a chrome coffin.

The Plastination chemicals, Cathy thought. *The acetone.*

Cathy spied a cup on the ledge of The Sculptor's slop sink and made a limping dash for it. She was back at the tub just as The Sculptor's feet dropped through the trap door in the ceiling. Cathy threw open the lid and plunged the cup into the cold, stingy liquid. Quickly she brought it out again, hiding it from view as she crouched by the tub, as she turned to face her attacker. Her eyes met The Sculptor's as his feet hit the floor. He just stood there, staring at her for what seemed like forever—his one good eye blinking robotically as the blood trickled down from the other's pulpy socket.

Then The Sculptor began to giggle.

Amidst her paralyzing fear, out of the corner of her eye Cathy spied the glow of the garage door button to her left—*two of them*, in fact, across the hood of the van on the opposite wall next to a door.

"All right," Cathy hissed, gripping the cup of acetone. "You can't get it up for anyone but your mother, so I guess you'll have to kill me you sick son of a bitch."

In the shadows, in the dim light cast from the TV

monitor, Cathy could not see the look in The Sculptor's remaining eye. No, all Cathy Hildebrant could make out was the clenching of The Sculptor's fists, the cocking of his elbows and the lowering of his head.

Then, without warning, he charged.

In a flash, Cathy brought up the cup of acetone and splashed it in The Sculptor's eyes. The Sculptor screeched like a cat, his hands flying to his face as he stumbled backward. Cathy climbed over the rim of the tub and lifted herself onto the van—her bad ankle banging painfully against the wall, her naked flesh rubbing raw as she slid across the hood. Cathy made it to the side entrance. She could not see The Sculptor as he cried out again, as something came crashing down out of sight behind the van.

"Help me!" Cathy shouted—her body sandwiched awkwardly between the van and the door as she wrestled with the knob. Then she noticed the dead bolt— one that required a key from *both sides*. But Cathy did not pause, did not look behind her when she heard the driver's side door open, when she realized The Sculptor was coming for her across the front seat of the van. No, her fingers automatically went for the glowing garage door buttons.

But nothing happened.

"No!" Cathy screamed, pressing frantically; and then she began backing away between the wall and the van. Suddenly, the passenger door slammed open into the wall. The Sculptor's massive frame was too big to get through, too big to follow her along this side of the van. But then again, it was clear to Cathy that The Sculptor had no intention of following her. No, in the dim light of The Sculptor's studio, Cathy could see that

The Sculptor had retrieved from the van a double barrel shotgun.

Yes, all The Sculptor really cared about now was his *aim.*

"Bad material," he said perfunctorily.

Then The Sculptor fired.

The shot was sloppy, half-blind. It took out a chunk of Cathy's right arm and spun her against the van, dropping her to the floor. But Cathy kept moving. Another shot, the crack of the pellets ricocheting off of the cement as Cathy rolled underneath the van. The Sculptor howled with frustration as Cathy emerged on the other side and rose to her feet—her arm bloody, her naked body scraped and soiled. Cathy began to shiver, began to weep, but did not cry out when she saw The Sculptor open the van's sliding side door; she did not say a word when she saw him reloading his shotgun. She only backed away until she could back away no more, until her naked body crashed into The Sculptor's drafting table.

The Sculptor did not speak either—only stood in the middle of his studio and raised his shotgun for a clear shot at Cathy's head.

And then time seemed to slow down for Cathy Hildebrant—seemed to *all but stop* as a flowing black angel tumbled from the trap in the ceiling and landed directly on top of The Sculptor. The shotgun fired, wide and wild with a clang to Cathy's left—a hiss and a pop and the instantaneous smell of sulfur. And then time resumed, rushed back to normal speed when Cathy recognized Sam Markham falling back against the van—the blood on his face, on his shirt as black as oil.

"Sam!" she cried, her legs coming to life. But they

did not carry her to him. No, as Markham slumped weakly to the floor, in an instant Cathy found herself running toward *The Sculptor*.

Already dazed and off balance, The Sculptor received her like a domino. He gave no resistance as Cathy slammed into him, knocking him backward, knocking him directly into the stainless steel hospital tub.

The Sculptor hit the acetone with a splash, sending the chemical spraying all over the carriage house as he went under. Cathy was close behind; she fell on top of the coffinlike lid and slammed it closed—her fingers locking only one of its four latches just as The Sculptor pushed up like a vampire from the inside.

Then out of the corner of her eye Cathy saw the flames.

The Sculptor's errant shot had set to sparking what Cathy recognized to be an arc welder, and now the spattered acetone had ignited. Cathy backed away toward the van—The Sculptor's furious movements rocking the stainless steel tub as more acetone seeped out from underneath the partially locked lid. Whirling, the flames mating and multiplying all around her, Cathy spied the van's keys in the ignition.

"Get up, Sam!" she shouted. "Get up into the van!"

Her strength not her own, Cathy Hildebrant lifted the semiconscious FBI agent through the van's open side door—took the driver's seat and turned the key in the ignition as The Sculptor suddenly burst up from the hospital tub in a spray of acetone. And just as she slammed the van into reverse, Cathy saw The Sculptor go up in flames. She saw him point to her and heard him scream like a fiery demon when the hospital tub exploded—its force sucking the wind from Cathy's lungs as the van crashed backward through the garage door in a fireball. Cathy kept her foot on the gas; she slammed into a tree as she tried to back away from the sheet of flames that engulfed the acetone-soaked windshield—the sheet of flames that was eating its way around the *entire van*.

"Sam!" she cried, dragging him out the side door of the burning van. Cathy helped Markham to his feet and supported him on her bad ankle as they stumbled together down the overgrown dirt driveway.

They had only gotten about twenty yards when another explosion sent a wave of heat up their backs and knocked them to the ground. But Cathy did not turn around—did not care to see the carriage house go up in a plume of chemical fired flames. No, all that mattered now was Sam Markham.

"It's over now, Sam," she whispered, holding him in her blood-soaked arms. "It's all over."

Epilogue

Cathy closed her cell phone and just sat on the back porch sipping her coffee and looking out over the river. It had all come so fast, was still all so new, but it still felt like home. However, the conversation with Rhonda, her new literary and publicity agent, had unsettled her, left her feeling numb and confused—so much so that when Sam Markham sat down beside her, Cathy hardly noticed he was there.

"I'm sorry, did you say something?" she asked.

"I asked you if you wanted a refill."

"No, thank you."

"How'd it go?"

"Typical—the usual this and that percentage about the new book deal. But the big news is they want me to fly out to Hollywood to act as a consultant on the film—preproduction meetings and a bunch of other stuff that I didn't quite catch."

"Already?"

"Next week."

"You mean when Janet and Dan are supposed to visit?"

"Yes."

"Damn. They move fast out there."

"I told Rhonda I couldn't, and she said she'd see if they could rearrange things around my schedule."

"That's my little powerbroker," said Sam Markham, wincing as he leaned in to kiss her. Cathy rubbed his shoulder.

"It's bothering you this morning?"

"Nah," he said, smiling. "Just a little sore from moving, I think."

Cathy knew he was lying—knew that her Sam would never complain. She kissed him—the conversation with Rhonda about percentages, about the movie rights to her unfinished book evaporating all at once when she looked into her husband's eyes, when she was reminded *once again* how lucky she was to still have him.

Indeed, The Sculptor's Sig Sauer had done a number on Special Agent Sam Markham, top to bottom—shattered the bones of his left shoulder, collapsed his left lung, and took out a nice chunk of his right leg, too. The doctors said Markham's shoulder would heal up fine—might feel some pain now and then when it rains—but he could expect to have a slight limp for the rest of his life. The bandages for the last phase of the reconstructive surgery on his right ear had come off a week earlier, and Cathy often began to tear up when she caught herself unconsciously stroking that side of his face.

Yes, it truly was a miracle that Sam Markham was alive; truly a miracle the way they ended up saving each other from The Sculptor. That they were married in a small ceremony the previous fall seemed only natural. That Cathy should take his name? Well, she knew her mother would approve. But that Dr. Catherine Hildebrant, *the* preeminent scholar on the works of Michelangelo, should resign her position at Brown University and move down to Connecticut to be with her husband? Now, *that* was giving in to *fate.*

And so it was at moments like these—when they were alone, when they sat together in silence on the back porch of their new home—that Cathy Markham felt at once both guilty and grateful for the man who had changed her life so drastically: The Michelangelo Killer.

When all was said and done, the official FBI report would credit Christian Bach (aka The Michelangelo Killer, aka The Sculptor) with no less than twenty-one murders, including Gabriel Banford and Damon Manzera. The body parts of eleven more women—eight identified as prostitutes from Providence and Fall River, Massachusetts, and three still listed as Jane Does—were discovered on Bach's property: some were preserved as sculptures in Bach's "art gallery," while other discarded pieces were found buried in the woods directly behind the burned-out shell of the carriage house. And even though dogs had been brought in to search the rest of Bach's property, even though they found no more victims beyond the immediate vicinity of what the press had dubbed, "The Michelangelo Killer's Studio of Death," Markham had a gut feeling that Christian Bach's body count might be even higher.

Bach's East Greenwich neighbors, his few remaining acquaintances, and the members of the wealthy circles in which his family once traveled were all shocked and outraged to discover that *one of their own* could have committed such unimaginable crimes. True, they knew the handsome and brilliant young Bach had become something of a recluse after the death of his mother. And true, he had broken off all ties with both sides of his family in order to care for his father. But such a move was not unusual in families where money was concerned, especially the kind of money in Bach's family. Yes, one couldn't be too careful nowadays with relatives looking for a handout or making claim to money that wasn't theirs—an unpleasant fact of life made only clearer by the swarm of vultures that was now trying to get a piece of Christian Bach's father. And besides, the young Mr. Bach had maintained his grounds with such care, had been so kind to the children at Halloween, had been so generous with his donations to his various philanthropic organizations that—well . . .

However, that it should have fallen to Cathy Markham to tell The Michelangelo Killer's story was perhaps the most bizarre twist of all. Never mind that Bach's body was never found—quite a common occurrence in such cases, the authorities assured, cases in which a massive explosion is followed by a longburning, extremely hot chemical fire. After the smoke had cleared and the public resigned itself to the fact that there was absolutely *no way* Bach could have survived, and after the initial media blitz died down and she and Sam Markham were married, Cathy gave in to the pressure around her and began writing an account not only of her ordeal, but also of the man to whom she owed—oh, how she hated to admit it!—*her happiness.*

Yes, despite everything that had happened, for the first time in her life Cathy Markham felt truly happy—

which had nothing to do with the six-figure, multi-book deal her agent had just brokered; had nothing to do with the rights to the movie for her yet unreleased follow-up to *Slumbering in the Stone,* or that she and her new husband would never have to work again. No, all Cathy Markham was thankful for was Sam. She tried never to think about the irony of how they came together, or what she would tell their children when they asked how she and Daddy met.

There'll be time to sort it out later.

A cool breeze blew off the river, ruffling the pages of the high school reading list in her husband's hand as he settled in beside her. She would never have thought to ask him, but was nonetheless thrilled when Sam told her on their honeymoon that he was leaving the FBI. She had actually cried when he surprised her later that spring with his new teaching job: English, at a private high school in Connecticut, starting in the fall.

Yes, Cathy knew all about Michelle, and she understood that this was just part of her husband's way of *sorting it all out.* And Cathy loved him for it, for Cathy also understood that he was sorting it out *for her.*

Cathy's cell phone rang—Beethoven, *Für Elise.* She looked at the number then muted it.

"Not going to answer it?"

"Private number."

"Let me see."

"Please, Sam, it's Sunday."

Markham snatched the phone and pretended he was about to open it. Cathy sighed—knew that he was baiting her—but did not bite. And just as she expected, her husband let the phone ring into voice mail. He cast it aside on the wicker sofa and snuggled closer to her. Yes, just like her, Sam Markham preferred simply to sit next to his spouse in the cool quiet oblivion of the river breeze.

Yes, Cathy thought. *There'll be time to sort it out later.*

Miles away, Special Agent in Charge Bill Burrell closed his cell phone. He did not care to leave a message on the pretty art history professor's voice mail.

She's been through so much, Burrell thought. *I just hope I can get hold of them before the fucking vultures get here.*

Bulldog took a long, deep drag from his Marlboro as Special Agent Rachel Sullivan came up beside him.

"Any luck, Chief?"

"No answer on either of their cells. Get a car sent out ASAP—somewhere in Mystic I think they're living. Address is in the database."

"Right."

As Special Agent Sullivan disappeared up the steps behind him, Burrell gazed out across the courtyard past the sea of blue FBI jackets to the marble white figure at the opposite end. The SAC did not need his team to tell him who it was—would have recognized the statue of the naked, muscular man with the curly hair even if he had never heard of The Michelangelo Killer.

Just what has this son of a bitch started?

Bulldog heeled his cigarette into the steps and opened his cell phone. It was going to be a long day. He would have to telephone the wife to say he wasn't coming home tonight.

No. After twenty years with the Bureau it just never gets any fucking easier.

ACKNOWLEDGMENTS

The Sculptor would not have been possible without the faith of two men: my agent, William Reiss, at John Hawkins & Associates; and my editor, John Scognamiglio, at Kensington Publishing Corp. For their excitement, insight, and guidance throughout this project I am eternally grateful. In between its first draft and publication, there were many in my family who offered to read *The Sculptor,* and thus helped me iron out a lot of the wrinkles: my loving wife, Angela, who has always been my biggest fan and my harshest critic; my father, Anthony, and my brother, Michael; my mother, Linda Ise; my uncle, Raymond Funaro, and my aunt, Marilyn DiStefano. To all of them I owe much love and gratitude. Further appreciation goes out to my coterie of readers here at East Carolina University: my colleagues John Shearin, Jill Matarelli-Carlson, Jeffery Phipps, Robert Caprio, and Patch Clark. And last but not least, I would like to thank my student Michael Combs for giving me the opportunity to learn from him.

More Books From Your Favorite Thriller Authors